EL OMBÚ

DAVID MILLER was born in Melbourne, Australia, in 1950, and has lived in London since 1972. His more recent publications include *The Dorothy and Benno Stories* (2005), *Black, Grey and White: A Book of Visual Sonnets* (2011), *Spiritual Letters (Series 1-5)* (2011) and *Reassembling Still: Collected Poems* (2014). He has compiled *British Poetry Magazines 1914-2000: A History and Bibliography of 'Little Magazines'* (with Richard Price, 2006) and edited *The Lariat and Other Writings* by Jaime de Angulo (2009) and *The Alchemist's Mind: a book of narrative prose by poets* (2012). He wrote his PhD thesis on W H Hudson, and published a book based on the thesis, *W H Hudson and the Elusive Paradise*, in 1990.

EL OMBÚ

W H Hudson

RESCRIPT BOOKS

ReScript Books is an imprint of
Reality Street
63 All Saints Street, Hastings TN34 3BN
www.realitystreet.co.uk/rescript-books.php

First published 1902
First ReScript Books edition, 2015

A catalogue record for this book is available from
the British Library

ISBN: 978-1-874400-69-1

CONTENTS

To My Friend
R B CUNNINGHAME GRAHAM
(*"Singularisimo escritor ingles"*)

Who has lived with and knows (even to
the marrow as they themselves would
say) the horsemen of the Pampas, and
who alone of European writers has
rendered something of the vanishing
colour of that remote life.

(W H Hudson)

Introduction

EL OMBÚ is one of W H Hudson's greatest artistic achievements; in fact, only the novel *Green Mansions* is of the same imaginative order as the two main stories in this volume, "El Ombú" and "Marta Riquelme". Ruth Tomalin says outright that "El Ombú" "is a masterpiece"; while John T Frederick remarks of the story: "Few works of fiction of comparable length, in English or any other literature, equal it in essential power or in completeness of achievement."[1] The power and the tragic intensity of the story are only equalled in Hudson's own work by "Marta Riquelme" and by the last part of *Green Mansions*.

"The Story of a Piebald Horse" and "Niño Diablo" can be dealt with first, however, because they can be assumed to be chronologically prior to the other stories, and more importantly because they are much slighter pieces which I will therefore treat very summarily.[2] "The Story of a Piebald Horse" and "Niño Diablo" are brief sketches, picturesque, anecdotal, and concerned with exotic local detail, and here a comparison with R B Cunninghame Graham's sketches would be apt, except that Hudson's writing is somewhat more skilful than Cunninghame Graham's.[3]

My interest in "The Story of a Piebald Horse" is with its projection of the notion of fate or destiny – a notion central to *El Ombú* as a whole. The narrator of the story says: "I can laugh, too, knowing that all things are ordered by destiny; otherwise I might sit down and cry."[4] The chain of occurrences, and what happens to a person through that chain or sequence, is what I understand by the term "fate" – the process by which one thing comes to pass rather than another. In "The Story of a Piebald Horse", we can see this chain as being forged partly

through chance, and partly through a nexus of personal qualities and actions – including Torcuato's arrogance, and the
perverse spirit of Chapaco, the man who helps bring about his
death while they are marking cattle. The chain will dictate the
strange way that Torcuato's (unrelated) foster-brother and
foster-sister, Anacleta and Elaria, are freed to marry each
other. The piebald horse is a small thing in this narrative of
fate, but a decisive one; it is while riding the piebald that Torcuato comes to his death, and it is through recognising the
piebald that Anacleto discovers what has happened to Torcuato. The owner of the estancia where Torcuato has met his
death, a man named Sotelo, leaves the piebald horse outside a
pulpería, hoping that someone will recognise it and let the
deceased man's relatives know of his death. Elaria has been
charged by her foster-father at his death to marry Torcuato,
although she loves Anacleto; hence, she and Anacleto have
waited to find out the missing Torcuato's fate before they can
marry: the piebald, and the story which Soleto has to tell in
regard to it, bring their waiting to an end.

In "Niño Diablo" it is the person of Niño that is of particular
interest. Niño is marked out by the singularity of his personal
being. He has a nearness to the realm of nature, with his
sharp senses and his receptiveness and knowledge of the
sounds and signs of wild life. His moral character is uncon-
ventional, but he is in no way amoral; he is a horse-thief, but
steals only from the Indians (who killed his relations when
Niño was a child, and are regarded by the other characters in
the story as the "infidel") or from those who offend him; and
when asked by a stranger to rescue his captive wife from the
Indians, Niño complies selflessly – without hesitation, and
without regard for reward.

He appears mysteriously – materialises as if out of thin air – in the household of Gregory Gorostiaga, and the mystery and the stealth are equally of the essence of the enigmatic Niño:

"*Madre del Cielo*, how you frightened me!" screamed one of the twins, giving a great start.

The cause of this sudden outcry was discovered in the presence of a young man quietly seated on the bench at the girl's side. He had not been there a minute before, and no person had seen him enter the room – what wonder that the girl was startled! He was slender in form and had small hands and feet, and oval, olive face, smooth as a girl's except for the incipient moustache on his lip. In the place of a hat he wore only a scarlet ribbon bound about his head, to keep back the glossy black hair that fell to his shoulders; and he was wrapped in a white woollen Indian poncho, while his lower limbs were cased in white colt-skin coverings, shaped like stockings to his feet, with the red tassels of his embroidered garters falling to the ankles.[5]

The singularity of Niño is set in relief by the ordinariness of most of the characters – though Hudson manages to give their bustling small world a picturesque, lively aspect – and by the evil-minded, blustering character of Polycarp (whom Niño tricks by stealing his horses); the latter acts as a foil to Niño through his incarnation of a type – a stupid, arrogant buffoon – while Niño both eludes the typical, and stands as Polycarp's contrast in his quickness of mind, his quiet personal impressiveness, and the absence in him of Polycarp's vain boastfulness. Gregory remarks of Niño:

"When he comes the dogs bark not – who knows why? His tread

is softer than the cat's; the untamed horse is tamed for him. Always in the midst of dangers, yet no harm, no scratch. Why? Because he stoops like the falcon, makes his stroke and is gone – Heaven knows where!"[6]

Perhaps more tellingly, he also says, earlier in the story: "...the Niño... is freer than the wild things which Heaven has made."[7] While it is certainly rudimentary, we can glimpse here the projection of an essentially enigmatic dimension to the person of Niño. The categories of psychological analysis can easily provide a causal relationship between Niño's captivity as a child with the Indians and their murder of his relations, and his predilection for stealing horses from them. Yet apart from this, he remains elusive. Given the slightness of the story itself and the small space we are allowed for an unfolding of Niño's personhood, it would be wrong to make *too* much of this; but it is possible to say that in his elusiveness and in his closeness to nature Niño prefigures something of the personal dimensions to be found in the figure of Rima in *Green Mansions*.

"El Ombú" is a story of fierce gravity; "a succession of disasters", as Ruth Tomalin says, "yet so skilfully told that it has the pathos and dignity of Greek tragedy."[8] Told by Nicandro, an old man who has witnessed the "succession of disasters", the tale is established from the first sentence as one of ruin and desolation: the estate called El Ombú – after the huge ombú tree "standing solitary, where there is [now] no house" – is "ownerless and ruined."[9] There is immediately projected a sense of inevitability: "...into every door sorrow must enter – sorrow and death that comes to all men; and every house must fall at last."[10]

Edward Garnett said that in "El Ombú" "we feel that character and destiny are one."[11] At certain points in the narrative, this is true; but we have to go beyond this formulation to understand the story more fully.

An equivalence or correlation between character and fate could be posited in relation to the way Hudson presents the fate of one of the characters at least: Don Santos Ugarte. The owner of El Ombú, Ugarte's character is deftly and concretely established:

> In all houses, for many leagues around, the children were taught to reverence him, calling him "uncle", and when he appeared they would run and, dropping to their knees before him, cry out "*Benedición mi tío*". He would give them his blessing; then, after tweaking a nose and pinching an ear or two, he would flourish his whip over their heads to signify that he had done with them, and that they must quickly get out of his way.[12]

The imperiousness and self-importance of the man are further illustrated as the story proceeds; and they are turned towards very considerable cruelty in the treatment of his third wife, who is reduced to a desperately unhappy and frightened creature by Ugarte because of her childlessness. Nicandro indeed speaks of "his indomitable temper and his violence."[13] But he also characterises him as "so strong, so brave, so noble"; and recounts his generosity to both the poor and to the religious orders.[14] The tragic quality of Ugarte's story resides in this division of his nature: he is a man who is capable of much good; but he is also a man flawed by arrogance and cruelty, and in this resides the cause of his downfall. This comes about through his anger over a young slave, Meliton, whom Ugarte has favoured over all his other slaves. Meliton buys his freedom, in accordance with law, while wishing to remain in Ugarte's service – without payment, but not as a slave. Ugarte's inflated self-regard causes him to see this as "ingratitude", and he throws the money into Meliton's face, with such force that Meliton is cut and bruised, and then orders him off the estate. Two years later Meliton returns, hoping for forgiveness; Ugarte shoots him dead, and then has to flee first to Buenos Aires, and from there to Montevideo, where he remains while trying to arrange for a pardon. The pardon, however, never comes. The Advocate and the Judge assigned to the case quarrel about how Ugarte's bribe is to be shared out, or so it is assumed, and Ugarte becomes forgotten, eventually slipping into insanity and dying without ever seeing El Ombú again. The estate has in the meanwhile fallen into ruins – before eventually becoming the home of the unfortunate Valerio de la Cueva.

Valerio's fate is also worth recounting in some detail, because whereas we can see Ugarte's downfall in correlation with his flawed character, Valerio's story eludes this correlation – at any rate, in such a straightforward and unambiguous way.

Valerio is a poor man who is able to reside at El Ombú because no one else will live there – the reason being that it is supposedly inhabited by ghosts. Nicandro describes Valerio in a more "high-flown" manner than is customary with him, as if endeavouring to do full justice to his friend: "Perhaps in rising and going out, on some clear morning in summer, he looked at the sun when it rose, and perceived an angel sitting in it, and as he gazed, something from that being fell upon and passed into and remained with him. Such a man was Valerio."[15] He also characterises him as: "He who was so brave, so generous, even in his poverty, of so noble a spirit, yet so gentle; whose words were sweeter than honey to me!"[16] Nicandro and Valerio are inducted into the army, under a brutal commander named Colonel Barboza; after an arduous, gruelling campaign, the men are paid off so miserably that they ask Valerio to act as their spokesman in complaining to Barboza; the Colonel responds by having Valerio given two hundred lashes of the whip after which he is thrown into the road. Nicandro discovers him, being cared for by a compassionate storekeeper; and Nicandro and Valerio set off back to El Ombú. Valerio dies just in front of the house, before his wife and child can reach him.

Unlike Ugarte, Valerio is not undone by a flaw of character. One might want to claim that his virtue – in his generous and brave willingness to bear the complaints of the soldiers to Barboza, despite the latter's brutal, ruthless nature – is itself the means of his downfall, and that we have again some sort of correlation between character and fate. Hudson's narrative, however, incorporates a different view. Nicandro says, speaking of Valerio's destiny: "...when misfortune has singled out a man for its prey, it will follow him to the end, and he shall not escape from it though he mount up to the clouds like the falcon, or thrust himself deep down into the earth like the armadillo."[17] This might be taken as merely the view of Hudson's character Nicandro, and not that of Hudson himself. But the last tragic event of "El Ombú" – the lapse into insanity of Monica, the girl who had been adopted by Valerio's widow, Donata – is so clearly an example of the sheer force of tragic occurrence crushing some vital part of an innocent human life (in this case, the reason), that the chain or build-up of occurrence – the fate or destiny – is thrown into relief, demanding consideration independently of any simple correlation with character. It is impossible in terms of what we know, to say why these things should so happen that as a consequence Monica should lose her reason, and if we concede this, I think it can be said that the same is true of Valerio. (This is not to say that there may not be some further – complex, subtle – correlation that can be drawn between character and fate; but it would be one that goes beyond the "facts" or events of the story, and, I should say, beyond the facts that we generally have at our disposal in everyday life.) That this is not the same thing as an *actively employed* power called "misfortune" – as Nicandro means to posit – I would grant; I believe it is necessary to read between the lines, as it were, of Nicandro's narration in order to attend to what the narrative is disclosing. The gratuitously tragic build-up of events disclosed in "El Ombú" can be seen as the very inversion of that purposiveness which Hudson, elsewhere, wanted to see at work in the universe; and in "Marta Riquelme" the "negativity" of this build-up attains an obdurate and terrible "darkness" comparable to that dealt with in the later works of Herman Melville.[18]

There is also a different way of suggesting a space between character and destiny, and this can be instanced in the way that Valerio's personal qualities transcend the vicissitudes of his fate. Donata says of him: "No misfortune and no injustice could change that heart, or turn that sweetness sour."[19] His complete lack of bitterness at the treatment he has received at Barboza's hands – despite the great pain this has left him in – carries conviction that Donata's view of him is thoroughly accurate.[20] The good of certain characters, like Valerio, acts as a contrast to the "negativity" or "darkness" in Hudson's writings; in this, it assumes the same function as the epiphanic beauty of nature, or the sublimity of Rima in *Green Mansions*.

Before turning to "Marta Riquelme" I want to say a little

about the specifically artistic qualities of "El Ombú". Hudson's "ordered telling of life as it must have happened", as Ezra Pound called it, has in its measured, even sentences a finely-wrought simplicity, which can rise to imagistic lyricism, as in the following passage about the ombú tree.[21]

> ...there are other things [besides memories] that come back to us from the past; I mean ghosts. Sometimes, at midnight, the whole tree, from its great roots to its topmost leaves, is seen from a distance shining like white fire. What is that fire, seen of so many, which does not scorch the leaves?[22]

The image is given, not for decorativeness, but to disclose and bear in upon the mind the sense of tragedy that lies at the heart of "El Ombú": only the ghostly white fire and the sounds of ghostly people and animals are left to inhabit the estate. Similarly, Hudson's prose narrates events of terrible violence and madness in the same even, quiet register. This simple presentation which, as it were, lets events speak out for themselves, gathers to itself a considerable power. That this power can be more affective, more haunting and moving, than the use of a more rhetorical mode, may be seen in the account of Barboza's death. Barboza – now a General – is attacked by an assassin, who turns out to be Valerio's son, Bruno; Barboza kills him, and drinks the blood from his death-wound. Afterwards, he falls prey to a strange malady, which someone advises him is due to "a failure of a natural heat of the blood, and only by means of animal heat, not by drugs, could health be recovered."[23] The body of a live bull is cut open, and General Barboza consents to being placed naked inside the body. This is Hudson's description of the result of this "treatment":

Then very suddenly [the old soldier recounted], almost before the bellowing had ceased, shrieks were heard from the enclosure, and in a moment, while we [that is, the General's men] all stood staring and wondering, out rushed the General stark naked, reddened with that bath of warm blood he had been in, a sword which he had hastily snatched up in his hand. Leaping over the barrier, he stood still for an instant, then catching sight of the great mass of men before him he flew at them, yelling and whirling his sword so that it looked like a shining wheel in the sun. The men seeing that he was raving mad fled before him, and for a space of a hundred yards or more he pursued them; then the superhuman energy was ended; the sword flew from his hand, he staggered, and fell prostrate on the earth.[24]

The remarkable restraint of this passage, in which the murderous Barboza enters the bull like entering his own element – the element of blood – only to reap the rewards of insanity and death, makes possible the quick transition from this moment of horror to an ending of moving tragedy. Monica falls to the ground senseless when she finds out that Barboza's assailant was Bruno, whom she loved; and she is insane from that time on. This, of course, repeats – but in a reversal – Barboza's end; whereas he went insane and fell to the ground never to rise again, Monica falls to the ground and then rises, insane. The lyrical image with which "El Ombú" ends brings home the tragedy of Monica, but also quietly insists upon the difference between her end and those of Ugarte, Valerio, Bruno and the other unhappy characters of the story. Monica spends her time watching flamingos; and in her simple joy in watching them, there is a picture of pathetic redemption from the overwhelmingly tragic nexus of events and lives: "...every time she catches sight of a flock moving like a red line across the lake she cries out with delight. That is her one happiness – her life. And she is the last of all those who have lived in my time at El Ombú."[25]

"Marta Riquelme" takes place in a desolate, isolated region which is not merely a geographical region, but a region of the human spirit. The ruin of the estate in "El Ombú" mirrors and symbolises the human ruin within the story; but it is also causally related to the downfall of the first of the story's principal characters, Ugarte. Although the state of mind of the narrator (Brother Sepulvida, the Jesuit priest) in "Marta Riquelme" is, conversely, causally related, at least in part, to the geographical desolation and remoteness, at another level it is related to the human and spiritual (or, from another perspective, contra- or anti-spiritual) qualities he finds in the place. However, what relation there is between spiritual fate and the qualities of the region (at whatever level), cannot be posited in terms of a rigid determinism in "Marta Riquelme" – nor, for that matter, in any of Hudson's other work.[26] Marta's fate reflects or rather brings to a singularly intense focus the spiritual (or anti-spiritual) "darkness" of the region; which in turn corresponds to the geographical aspects.

The priest describes the Andean province of Jujuy as:

The remotest of our provinces, and divided from the countries of the Pacific by the great range of the Cordillera; a region of mountains and forest, torrid heats and great storms; and although in itself a country half as large as the Spanish peninsula, it possesses as its only means of communication with the outside world, a few insignificant roads; which are scarcely more than mule-paths.[27]

The priest is attached to a settlement in Jujuy called Yala, which appears to him as "a rude, desolate chaos of rocks and gigantic mountains."[28] He further characterises Jujuy as a whole as a place in which the Christian gospel has been accepted only at a superficial level; where his efforts as a priest have no effect on his parishioners; where the Devil wages "an equal war amongst [Christ's] followers".[29] He also discovers problematic aspects to his own character – which are drawn forth by the place and the people. He gives way to feelings of passion, which, as a priest, he feels as a temptation and a torment. When the priest first meets Marta, she is a girl of fifteen, pure Spanish as distinct from the Indians of Jujuy. The "Christian affection" that he originally feels for her "insensibly [degenerates] into a mundane passion" of great intensity.[30] Because of this he feels it necessary to stop visiting the house of Marta and her mother – the one house in Yala where he had found pleasurable company.

He also gives way to angry and violent emotions at being unable to dissuade a peasant from what the priest considers "superstition". The "superstition" is that of the Kakué, so that the priest's discovery of one failing – his inability to hold back a violent temper – is strangely linked to his other failing (or what he considers to be such), his passion for Marta; for Marta is destined to become a Kakué, "a fowl frequenting the most gloomy and sequestered forests and known to everyone for its terrible voice" – a voice which the priest describes in the following way: "In sound it was a human cry, yet expressing a degree of agony and despair surpassing the power of any human soul to feel."[31] The natives believe that the Kakué "is a metamorphosed human being, that women and sometimes men, whose lives have been darkened with great suffering and calamities, are changed by compassionate spirits into the lugubrious birds."[32] The metamorphosis is linked to the idea of an exceeding of what a human being could feel, as if in going beyond some limit one becomes something-else-than-human. Unlike Rosaura in Hudson's story "Pelino Viera's Confession", who becomes a bird-woman through applying a magical ointment to her body, the Kakué-figure is neither demonic nor morally evil as such; rather, it symbolises all that is "darkest" or most terrible in the human soul in the way of despair and agony – sufficiently, excessively "dark" as to be unrecognisable as "human".[33]

The narration of "Marta Riquelme" is in part a narration of fault – that is, where it is not a witnessing of misfortune. The priest states that "the secret enemy of my soul had revealed itself to me" in those "sudden violent outbursts of passion" to which he is prone.[34] His passion for Marta, which of course he also feels to be a sin, leads to another fault; this is in relation to Marta's marriage, when, because of his own feelings for the girl, he refuses to assist Marta's mother in dissuading her from the union.

The misfortunes that overtake the blameless Marta need only be briefly outlined here. She makes an unwise marriage with a man named Cosme Luna, a gambler and idler – according to the priest – "possessing a hundred vices under a pleasant exterior and not one redeeming virtue".[35] Luna is inducted into the army while away on one of his periodic absences, and when Marta, with their small child, goes in search of him she is captured by a band of Indians, forced into marriage, and very brutally treated – remaining in captivity for five years, during which time she bears the Indian three children. She escapes with another captive, aided by the latter's Indian husband, taking only her youngest child with her – and the Indian, presumably considering it a burden, secretly drops the child into a deep stream. To the years of brutality and enforced marriage, has to be added, then, the separation from her children and the murder of the youngest of them. It can scarcely be wondered that when Marta makes her way back to Yala, the priest finds her greatly changed:

> Was this woman indeed Marta, once the pride of Yala! It was hard to believe it, so darkened with the burning suns and winds of years was her face, once so fair; so wasted and furrowed with grief and the many hardships she had undergone! Her figure, worn almost to a skeleton, was clothed with ragged garments, while her head, bowed down with sorrow and despair, was divested of that golden crown which had been her chief ornament.[36]

However, her misfortune has not come to an end with her return; she recovers somewhat, but does so while putting her hopes for the future on the return of her husband, Cosme, and that is the cause of her ruin; for when Cosme does return, he refuses to recognise Marta as the woman he married, claiming to know that Marta is dead. This is an excuse for abandoning her; and Marta's desolation is mixed with shame at her treatment. From this point on, Marta seeks solitude – the solitude of the woods near Yala – in which she gives vent to her anguish, and to accusations against God: "...casting herself on the earth, [she would] break forth into the most heart-rending cries and lamentations, loudly exclaiming that God had unjustly punished her, that He was a being filled with malevolence, and speaking many things against Him very dreadful to hear."[37]

The scene of Marta's metamorphosis is one of the most powerful passages in Hudson's writing. "Marta Riquelme" shares with "El Ombú" that restraint or reserve with which events of tragic and sometimes violent character are narrated, with intense, grave and moving effect. The scene takes place on a day when "even the elements were charged with unusual gloom": "...the trees, in that still, thick atmosphere, were like figures of trees hewn out of solid inky-black rock and set up in some shadowy subterranean region to mock its inhabitants with an imitation of the upper world."[38] This extraordinary description sets the key for Marta's metamorphosis by placing it, figuratively, in a "shadowy subterranean region". The description of what the priest sees when he finds Marta is worth quoting at some length. Marta is discovered sitting

> on the trunk of a fallen tree, which was sodden with the rain and half buried under great creepers and masses of dead and rotting foliage. She was in a crouching position, her feet gathered under her garments, which were now torn to rags and fouled with clay; her elbows were planted on her drawn-up knees, and her long bony fingers thrust into her hair, which fell in tangled disorder over her face. To this pitiable condition had she been brought by great and unmerited sufferings.
>
> Seeing her, a cry of compassion escaped my lips, and casting myself off my mule I advanced towards her. As I approached, she raised her eyes to mine, and then I stood still, transfixed with amazement and horror at what I saw; for they were no longer those soft violet orbs which had retained until recently their sweet pathetic expression; now they were round and wild-looking, open to thrice their ordinary size, and filled with a lurid yellow fire, giving them a resemblance to the eyes of some hunted wild animal.[39]

He sees that she has lost her reason, and holds up his crucifix before her:

> This movement seemed to infuriate her; the insane, desolate eyes, from which all human expression had vanished, became like two burning balls, which seemed to shoot out sparks of fire; her short hair rose up until it stood like an immense crest on her head; and suddenly bringing down her skeleton-like hands she thrust the crucifix violently from her, uttering at the same time a succession of moans and cries that pierced my heart with pain to hear. And presently flinging up her arms, she burst forth into shrieks so terrible in the depth of agony they expressed that overcome by the sound I sank upon the earth and hid my face.[40]

At this moment, she changes – in the belief of the priest, and those who are with him – into a Kakué. For when the priest looks again, Marta is not there: "In another form – that strange form of the Kakué – she had fled out of our sight for ever to hide in those gloomy woods which were henceforth to be her dwelling place."[41] As indicated earlier, Marta's transformation involves a movement of the soul, that is, the immaterial part of her being, and also provides a picture of metamorphosis as tragic occurrence. We have in Marta's fate a symbol of the power of "darkness", where the person is plunged beyond the limits of what we recognise as "human" – plunged into a domain of insanity and abysmal anguish, a domain that is linked to the supernatural in terms of the narrative, at least.[42] This is, with *Green Mansions*, the furthest point of W H Hudson's exploration of "darkness", for here he inverts the traditional symbolism of metamorphosis, in its main thrust – a symbolism of continuity between separate life-forms and beyond the apparent discontinuity of life and death – to give this largely "positive" power a "negative" form. In "Marta Riquelme" it is "darkness" that has the power of effecting continuity, where by dint of the utter extremity of her desolation Marta exceeds the limits of the "human" but continues life in another form. Marta's transformation is also one of the most harrowing examples in Hudson's writing of what I would refer to as "negative epiphany", wherein we are given a glimpse into a terrible emptiness, or a situation or moment of dread or horror – involving an illumination of (one mode or aspect of) the ground of our being.[43]

David Miller

Note:
This Introduction is adapted from: David Miller, W H Hudson and the Elusive Paradise, *1990, Macmillan, reproduced with permission of Palgrave Macmillan.*

1 Tomalin, "Introduction" to W H Hudson, *South American Romances*, p xiii; Frederick, *William Henry Hudson*, p 48. (*South American Romances* collects three of Hudson's books of fiction – *The Purple Land, El Ombú* and *Green Mansions* – into one volume.)

2 As to the dates of these pieces, "The Story of a Piebald Horse" was originally part of his early novel *The Purple Land that England Lost*, published in 1885; while "Niño Diablo" was first published in 1890 in *Macmillan's Magazine*. I have not discovered any clear indication of when "Marta Riquelme" and "El Ombú" were completed, although Ruth Tomalin states that "El Ombú" – while based on a much earlier notebook – was begun in 1890 (see *W H Hudson: A Biography*, London: Faber, 1982, p 193). The greater maturity of the writing in these two stories – both in the skill which is displayed in the handling of language and of the themes that are developed, as

well as in the "deepened" vision involved – suggests some gap in time between the completion of these and the shorter pieces in the volume.

3 The book is indeed dedicated to Cunninghame Graham. Hudson's dedication appropriately fastens upon the knowledge and the rendering of local detail in Cunninghame Graham's work; it is the gravity and imaginative vision of "El Ombú" and "Marta Riquelme" – going beyond these qualities – which sets them apart from both "Niño Diablo" and "The Story of a Piebald Horse" and from Cunninghame Graham's writing.

4 p 77.

5 p 100.

6 p 103.

7 p 97.

8 Tomalin, "Introduction" to *South American Romances*, op cit.

9 p 29.

10 p 30.

11 Garnett, "A Note on Hudson's Romances", in *Green Mansions*, London: Duckworth, 1923, p vi. (*Green Mansions* was originally published in 1904.) Garnett's remark recalls Heraclitus' Fragment DK B119. (In Guy Davenport's paraphrase, this reads: "Action is character, and character fate." *The Geography of the Imagination: Forty Essays*, SF: North Point Press, 1981, p 264.)

12 p 31.

13 p 40.

14 p 40.

15 p 45.

16 p 53.

17 p 46.

18 With regard to the role of purposiveness in Hudson's views, see Chapter 8 of my book *W H Hudson and the Elusive Paradise*. For a discussion of Melville and Hudson, see pp 89-92 of the same book.

19 p 63

20 pp 51-2.

21 Pound, *Selected Prose 1909-1965*, ed William Cookson, London: Faber, 1973, p 402.

22 p 30.

23 p 71.

24 p 71-2.

25 p 74. Nicandro says, regarding Monica: "Some have died of pure grief... but the crazed may live many years. We sometimes think it would be better if they were dead; but not in all cases – not, señor, in this." (p 73.)

26 By contra- or anti-spiritual, I refer to what may be seen as that which deforms, crushes or negates spiritual life.

27 p 119.

28 p 121.

29 p 119.

30 p 128.

31 p 122.

32 p 123.

33 Rosaura, Viera's wife, turns herself into a bird-woman in order to participate in a witches' Sabbath. Viera describes her transformation in the following passage:

> Suddenly I heard a rushing noise like the sound of great wings above me; then it seemed to me as if beings of some kind had alighted on the roof; the walls shook, and I heard voices calling , "Sister! sister!" Rosaura rose and threw off her night-dress, then, taking ointment from the pot and rubbing it on the palms of her hands, she passed it rapidly over her whole body, arms and legs, only leaving her face untouched. Instantly she became covered with a plumage of a slaty-blue colour; only on her face were no feathers. At the same from her shoulders sprang wings which were incessantly agitated. She hurried forth, closing the door after her; once more the walls trembled or seemed to tremble; a sound of rushing wings was heard, and, mingling with it, shrill peals of laughter; then all was still.

(Hudson, *Tales of the Pampas*, NY: Knopf, 1939, pp 116-7. *Tales of the Pampas* is an American edition of El Ombú, augmented by the additional pieces "Pelino Viera's Confession" and "Tecla and the Little Men".) Metamorphosis is used here to symbolise the more-than-natural – in its demonic form.

34 p 125.

35 p 129.

36 p 134. Marta's hair had been cut off by her Indian husband.

37 p 139.

38 139, 140.

39 p 140-1.

40 p 141.

41 pp 141-2.

42 I want to emphasise that in Marta's case this does not involve moral fault on her part. As to the supernatural aspects here, we are of course being told the story from the perspective of the priest, and the priest has reluctantly become convinced of the existence of a creature called the Kakué, which owes its form to a supernatural transformation.

43 Epiphanic vision is basic in Hudson; and we must speak of two main kinds of epiphany: the "affirmative" epiphany which affirms the earthly by intuiting the divine through or within it; and "negative" epiphany which negates the earthly by opening up a yawning, dizzying chasm beneath us, an abyss of affliction, evil or oblivion.

EL OMBÚ

*This history of a house that had been was told in the shade,
one summer's day, by Nicandro, that old man to whom we
all loved to listen, since he could remember and properly
narrate the life of every person he had known in his native
place, near to the lake of Chascomus, on the southern pampas of Buenos Ayres.*

I

IN ALL THIS DISTRICT, though you should go twenty leagues to
this way and that, you will not find a tree as big as this ombú,
standing solitary, where there is no house; therefore it is
known to all as "the ombú," as if but one existed; and the
name of all this estate, which is now ownerless and ruined, is
El Ombú. From one of the higher branches, if you can climb,
you will see the lake of Chascomus, two thirds of a league
away, from shore to shore, and the village on its banks. Even
smaller things will you see on a clear day; perhaps a red line
moving across the water—a flock of flamingos flying in their
usual way. A great tree standing alone, with no house near it;
only the old brick foundations of a house, so overgrown with
grass and weeds that you have to look closely to find them.
When I am out with my flock in the summer time, I often
come here to sit in the shade. It is near the main road; travellers, droves of cattle, the diligence, and bullock-carts pass
in sight. Sometimes, at noon, I find a traveller resting in the
shade, and if he is not sleeping we talk and he tells me the
news of that great world my eyes have never seen. They say
that sorrow and at last ruin comes upon the house on whose
roof the shadow of the ombú tree falls; and on that house
which now is not, the shadow of this tree came every summer
day when the sun was low. They say, too, that those who sit

much in the ombú shade become crazed. Perhaps, sir, the bone of my skull is thicker than in most men, since I have been accustomed to sit here all my life, and though now an old man I have not yet lost my reason. It is true that evil fortune came to the old house in the end; but into every door sorrow must enter—sorrow and death that comes to all men; and every house must fall at last.

Do you hear the *mangangá*, the carpenter bee, in the foliage over our heads? Look at him, like a ball of shining gold among the green leaves, suspended in one place, humming loudly! Ah, señor, the years that are gone, the people that have lived and died, speak to me thus audibly when I am sitting here by myself. These are memories; but there are other things that come back to us from the past; I mean ghosts. Sometimes, at midnight, the whole tree, from its great roots to its topmost leaves, is seen from a distance shining like white fire. What is that fire, seen of so many, which does not scorch the leaves? And, sometimes, when a traveller lies down here to sleep the siesta, he hears sounds of footsteps coming and going, and noises of dogs and fowls, and of children shouting and laughing, and voices of people talking; but when he starts up and listens, the sounds grow faint, and seem at last to pass away into the tree with a low murmur as of wind among the leaves.

As a small boy, from the time when I was able, at the age of about six years, to climb on to a pony and ride, I knew this tree. It was then what it is now; five men with their arms stretched to their utmost length could hardly encircle it. And the house stood there, where you see a bed of nettles—a long, low house, built of bricks, when there were few brick houses in this district, with a thatched roof.

The last owner was just touching on old age. Not that he

looked aged; on the contrary, he looked what he was, a man among men, a head taller than most, with the strength of an ox; but the wind had blown a little sprinkling of white ashes into his great beard and his hair, which grew to his shoulders like the mane of a black horse. That was Don Santos Ugarte, known to all men in this district as the White Horse, on account of the whiteness of his skin where most men look dark; also because of that proud temper and air of authority which he had. And for still another reason—the number of children in this neighbourhood of which he was said to be the father. In all houses, for many leagues around, the children were taught to reverence him, calling him "uncle," and when he appeared they would run and, dropping on their knees before him, cry out "*Bendición mi tío.*" He would give them his blessing; then, after tweaking a nose and pinching an ear or two, he would flourish his whip over their heads to signify that he had done with them, and that they must quickly get out of his way.

These were children of the wind, as the saying is, and the desire of his heart was for a legitimate son, an Ugarte by name, who would come after him at El Ombú, as he had come after his father. But though he had married thrice, there was no son born, and no child. Some thought it a mystery that one with so many sons should yet be without a son. The mystery, friend, was only for those who fail to remember that such things are not determined by ourselves. We often say, that He who is above us is too great to concern Himself with our small affairs. There are so many of us; and how shall He, seated on his throne at so great a distance, know all that passes in his dominions! But Santos was no ordinary person, and He who was greater than Santos had doubtless had his attention drawn to this man; and had considered the matter, and had said, "You shall not have your desire; for though you are a devout man, one who gives freely of his goods to the church and my poor, I am not wholly satisfied with you." And so it came to pass that he had no son and heir.

His first two wives had died, so it was said, because of his bitterness against them. I only knew the third—Doña Mericie, a silent, sad woman, who was of less account than any servant, or any slave in the house. And I, a simple boy, what could I know of the secrets of her heart? Nothing! I only saw her pale and silent and miserable, and because her eyes followed me, I feared her, and tried always to keep out of her way. But one morning, when I came to El Ombú and went into the kitchen, I found her there alone, and before I could escape she caught me in her arms, and lifting me off my feet strained me against her breast, crying, *hijo de mi alma*, and I knew not what beside; and calling God's blessing on me, she covered my face with kisses. Then all at once, hearing Santos' voice without, she dropped me and remained like a woman of stone, staring at the door with scared eyes.

She, too, died in a little while, and her disappearance made no difference in the house, and if Santos wore a black band on his arm, it was because custom demanded it and not because he mourned for her in his heart.

II

THAT SILENT GHOST of a woman being gone, no one could say of him that he was hard; nor could anything be said against him except that he was not a saint, in spite of his name. But, sir, we do not look for saints among strong men, who live in the saddle, and are at the head of big establishments. If there was one who was a father to the poor it was Santos; therefore he was loved by many, and only those who had done him an injury or had crossed him in any way had reason to fear and hate him. But let me now relate what I, a boy of ten, witnessed one day in the year 1808. This will show you what the man's temper was; and his courage, and the strength of his wrists.

It was his custom to pay a visit every two or three months to a monastery at a distance of half-a-day's journey from El Ombú.

He was greatly esteemed by the friars, and whenever he went to see them he had a led horse to carry his presents to the Brothers;—a side of fat beef, a sucking-pig or two, a couple of lambs, when they were in season, a few fat turkeys and ducks, a bunch of big partridges, a brace or two of armadillos, the breast and wings of a fat ostrich; and in summer, a dozen ostriches' eggs, and I know not what besides.

One evening I was at El Ombú, and was just starting for home, when Santos saw me, and cried out, "Get off and let your horse go, Nicandro. I am going to the monastery to-morrow, and you shall ride the laden horse, and save me the trouble of leading it. You will be like a little bird perched on his back and he will not feel your few ounces' weight. You can sleep on a sheepskin in the kitchen, and get up an hour before daybreak."

The stars were still shining when we set out on our journey the next morning, in the month of June, and when we crossed the river Sanborombón at sunrise the earth was all white with hoar frost. At noon, we arrived at our destination, and were received by the friars, who embraced and kissed Santos on both cheeks, and took charge of our horses. After breakfast in the kitchen, the day being now warm and pleasant, we went and sat out of doors to sip maté and smoke, and for an hour or longer, the conversation between Santos and the Brothers had been going on when, all at once, a youth appeared coming at a fast gallop towards the gate, shouting as he came, "*Los Ingleses! Los Ingleses!*" We all jumped up and ran to the gate, and climbing up by the posts and bars, saw at a distance of less than half-a-league to the east, a great army of men marching in the direction of Buenos Ayres. We could see that the foremost part of the army had come to a halt on the banks of a stream which flows past the monastery and empties itself into the Plata, two leagues further east. The army was all composed of infantry, but a great many persons on horseback could be seen following it, and these, the young man said, were neighbours who had come out to look at the English invaders; and he also said that the soldiers, on arriving at the stream, had begun to throw away their blankets, and that the people were picking them up. Santos, hearing this, said he would go and join the crowd, and mounting his horse and followed by me, and by two of the Brothers, who said they wished to get a few blankets for the monastery, we set out at a gallop for the stream.

Arrived at the spot, we found that the English, not satisfied with the ford, which had a very muddy bottom, had made a new crossing-place for themselves by cutting down the bank on both sides, and that numbers of blankets had been folded and laid in the bed of the stream where it was about twenty-five yards wide. Hundreds of blankets were also being thrown away, and the people were picking them up and loading their horses with them. Santos at once threw himself into the crowd and gathered about a dozen blankets, the best he could find, for the friars; then he gathered a few for himself and ordered me to fasten them on the back of my horse.

The soldiers, seeing us scrambling for the blankets, were much amused; but when one man among us cried out, "These people must be mad to throw their blankets away in cold weather— perhaps their red jackets will keep them warm when they lie down to-night"—there was one soldier who understood, and could speak Spanish, and he replied, "No, sirs, we have no further need of blankets. When we next sleep it will be in the best beds in the capital." Then Santos shouted back, "That, sirs, will perhaps be a sleep from which some of you will never awake." That speech attracted their attention to Santos, and the soldier who had spoken before returned, "There are not many men like you in these parts, therefore what you say does not alarm us." Then they looked at the friars fastening the blankets Santos had given them on to their horses, and seeing that they wore heavy iron spurs strapped on their bare feet, they shouted with laughter, and the one who talked with us cried out, "We are sorry, good Brothers, that we have not boots as well as blankets to give you."

But our business was now done, and bidding good-bye to the friars, we set out on our return journey, Santos saying that we should be at home before midnight.

It was past the middle of the afternoon, we having ridden about six leagues, when we spied at a distance ahead a great number of mounted men scattered about over the plain, some standing still, others galloping this way or that.

"El pato! el pato!" cried Santos with excitement, "Come, boy, let us go and watch the battle while it is near, and when it is passed on we will go our way." Urging his horse to a gallop, I following, we came to where the men were struggling for the ball, and stood for a while looking on. But it was not in him to remain a mere spectator for long; never did he see a cattlemarketing, or parting, or races, or a dance, or any game, and above all games, el Pato, but he must have a part in it. Very soon he dismounted to throw off some of the heaviest parts of his horse-gear, and ordering me to take them up on my horse and follow him, he rode in among the players.

About forty or fifty men had gathered at that spot, and were sitting quietly on their horses in a wide circle, waiting to see the result of a struggle for the Pato between three men who had hold of the ball. They were strong men, well mounted, each resolved to carry off the prize from the others. Sir, when I think of that sight, and remember that the game is no longer played because of the Tyrant who forbade it, I am ready to cry out that there are no longer men on these plains where I first saw the light! How they tugged and strained and sweated, almost dragging each other out of the saddle, their trained horses leaning away, digging their hoofs into the turf, as when they resist the shock of a lassoed animal, when the lasso stiffens and the pull comes! One of the men was a big, powerful mulatto, and the by-standers thinking the victory would be his, were only waiting to see him wrest the ball from the others to rush upon and try to deprive him of it before he could escape from the crowd.

Santos refused to stand inactive, for was there not a fourth handle to the ball to be grasped by another fighter? Spurring his horse into the group, he very soon succeeded in getting hold of the disengaged handle. A cry of resentment at

this action on the part of a stranger went up from some of
those who were looking on, mixed with applause at the daring from others, while the three men who had been fighting
against each other, each one for himself, now perceived that
they had a common enemy. Excited as they were by the
struggle, they could not but be startled at the stranger's
appearance—that huge man on a big horse, so white-skinned
and long-haired, with a black beard, that came down over his
breast, and who showed them, when he threw back his poncho, the knife that was like a sword and the big brass-barrelled pistol worn at his waist. Very soon after he joined in
the fray all four men came to the earth. But they did not fall
together, and the last to go down was Santos, who would not
be dragged off his horse, and in the end horse and man came
down on the top of the others. In coming down, two of the
men had lost their hold of the ball; last of all, the big mulatto,
to save himself from being crushed under the falling horse,
was forced to let go, and in his rage at being beaten, he
whipped out his long knife against the stranger. Santos, too
quick for him, dealt him a blow on the forehead with the
heavy silver handle of his whip, dropping him stunned to the
ground. Of the four, Santos alone had so far escaped injury,
and rising and remounting, the ball still in his hand, he rode
out from among them, the crowd opening on each side to
make room for him.

Now in the crowd there was one tall, imposing-looking
man, wearing a white poncho, many silver ornaments, and a
long knife in an embossed silver sheath; his horse, too, which
was white as milk, was covered with silver trappings. This
man alone raised his voice; "Friends and comrades," he
cried, "is this to be the finish? If this stranger is permitted to
carry the Pato away, it will not be because of his stronger

wrist and better horse, but because he carries firearms. Comrades, what do you say?"

But there was no answer. They had seen the power and resolution of the man, and though they were many they preferred to let him go in peace. Then the man on a white horse, with a scowl of anger and contempt, turned from them and began following us at a distance of about fifty yards. Whenever Santos turned back to come to close quarters with him, he retired, only to turn and follow us again as soon as Santos resumed his course. In this way we rode till sunset. Santos was grave, but calm; I, being so young, was in constant terror. "Oh, uncle," I whispered, "for the love of God fire your pistol at this man and kill him, so that he may not kill us!"

Santos laughed. "Fool of a boy," he replied, "do you not know that he wants me to fire at him! He knows that I could not hit him at this distance, and that after discharging my pistol we should be equal, man to man, and knife to knife; and who knows then which would kill the other? God knows best, since He knows everything, and He has put it into my heart not to fire."

When it grew dark we rode slower, and the man then lessened the distance between us. We could hear the chink-chink of his silver trappings, and when I looked back I could see a white misty form following us like a ghost. Then, all at once, there came a noise of hoofs and a whistling sound of something thrown, and Santos' horse plunged and reared and kicked, then stood still trembling with terror. His hind legs were entangled in the bolas which had been thrown. With a curse Santos threw himself off, and, drawng his knife, cut the thong which bound the animal's legs, and remounting we went on as before, the white figure still following us.

At length, about midnight, the Sanborombón was

reached, at the ford where we had crossed in the morning, where it was about forty yards wide, and the water only high as the surcingle in the deepest parts.

"Let your heart be glad, Nicandro!" said Santos, as we went down into the water; "for our time is come now, and be careful to do as I bid you."

We crossed slowly, and coming out on the south side, Santos quietly dropped off his horse, and, speaking in a low voice, ordered me to ride slowly on with the two horses and wait for him in the road. He said that the man who followed would not see him crouching under the bank, and thinking it safe would cross over, only to receive the charge fired at a few yards' distance.

That was an anxious interval that followed, I waiting alone, scarcely daring to breathe, staring into the darkness in fear of that white figure that was like a ghost, listening for the pistol shot. My prayer to heaven was to direct the bullet in its course, so that it might go to that terrible man's heart, and we be delivered from him. But there was no shot, and no sound except a faint chink of silver and sound of hoof-beats that came to my ears after a time, and soon ceased to be heard. The man, perhaps, had some suspicion of the other's plan and had given up the chase and gone away.

Nothing more do I remember of that journey which ended at El Ombú at cock-crow, except that at one spot Santos fastened a thong round my waist and bound me before and behind to the saddle to prevent my falling from my horse every time I went to sleep.

III

REMEMBER, señor, that I have spoken of things that passed when I was small. The memories of that time are few and scattered, like the fragments of tiles and bricks and rusty iron which one may find half-buried among the weeds, where the house once stood. Fragments that once formed part of the building. Certain events, some faces, and some voices, I remember, but I cannot say the year. Nor can I say how many years had gone by after Doña Mericie's death, and after my journey to the monastery. Perhaps they were few, perhaps many. Invasions had come, wars with a foreigner and with the savage, and Independence, and many things had happened at a distance. He, Santos Ugarte, was older, I know, greyer, when that great misfortune and calamity came to one whom God had created so strong, so brave, so noble. And all on account of a slave, a youth born at El Ombú, who had been preferred above the others by his master. For, as it is said, we breed crows to pick our eyes out. But I will say nothing against that poor youth, who was the cause of the disaster, for it was not wholly his fault. Part of the fault was in Santos—his indomitable temper and his violence. And perhaps, too, the time was come when He who rules over all men had said, "You have raised your voice and have ridden over others long enough. Look, Santos! I shall set my foot upon you, and under it you shall be like a wild pumpkin at the end of summer, when it is dryer and more brittle than an empty eggshell."

Remember that there were slaves in those days, also that there was a law fixing every man's price, old or young, so that if any slave went, money in hand, to his master and offered him the price of his liberty, from that moment he became a free man. It mattered not that his master wished not to sell him. So just was the law.

Of his slaves Santos was accustomed to say, "These are my children, and serve because they love me, not because they are slaves; and if I were to offer his freedom to any one among them, he would refuse to take it." He saw their faces, not their hearts.

His favourite was Meliton, black but well favoured, and though but a youth, he had authority over the others, and dressed well, and rode his master's best horses, and had horses of his own. But it was never said of him that he gained that eminence by means of flattery and a tongue cunning to frame lies. On the contrary, he was loved by all, even by those he was set above, because of his goodness of heart and a sweet and gay disposition. He was one of those who can do almost anything better than others; whatever his master wanted done, whether it was to ride a race, or break a horse, or throw a lasso, or make a bridle, or whip, or surcingle, or play on a guitar, or sing, or dance, it was Meliton, Meliton. There was no one like him.

Now this youth cherished a secret ambition in his heart, and saved, and saved his money; and at length one day he came with a handful of silver and gold to Santos, and said, "Master, here is the price of my freedom, take it and count it, and see that it is right, and let me remain at El Ombú to serve you henceforth without payment. But I shall no longer be a slave."

Santos took the money into his hand, and spoke, "It was for this then that you saved, even the money I gave you to spend and to run with, and the money you made by selling the animals I gave you—you saved it for this! Ingrate, with a heart blacker than your skin! Take back the money, and go from my presence, and never cross my path again if you wish for a long life." And with that he hurled the handful of silver and gold into the young man's face with such force, that he was cut and bruised with the coins and well nigh stunned. He went back staggering to his horse, and mounting, rode away, sobbing like a child, the blood running down from his face.

He soon left this neighbourhood and went to live at Las Vivoras, on the Vecino river, south of Dolores, and there made good use of his freedom, buying fat animals for the market; and for a space of two years he prospered, and every man, rich or poor, was his friend. Nevertheless, he was not happy, for his heart was loyal and he loved his old master, who had been a father to him, and desired above all things to be forgiven. And, at length, hoping that Santos had outlived his resentment and would be pleased to see him again, he one day came to El Ombú and asked to see the master.

The old man came out of the house and greeted him jovially. "Ha, Meliton," he cried with a laugh, "you have returned in spite of my warning. Come down from your horse and let me take your hand once more."

The other, glad to think he was forgiven, alighted, and advancing, put out his hand. Santos took it in his, only to crush it with so powerful a grip, that the young man cried out aloud, and blinded with tears of pain, he did not see that his master had the big brass pistol in his left hand, and did not know that his last moment had come. He fell with a bullet in his heart.

Look, señor, where I am pointing, twenty yards or so from the edge of the shadow of the ombú, do you see a dark green weed with a yellow flower on a tall stem growing on the short, dry grass? It was just there, on the very spot where the yellow flower is, that poor Meliton fell, and was left lying, covered with blood, until noon the next day. For no person dared take up the corpse until the Alcalde had been informed of the matter and had come to inquire into it.

Santos had mounted his horse and gone away without a word, taking the road to Buenos Ayres. He had done that for which he would have to pay dearly; for a life is a life, whether the skin be black or white, and no man can slay another deliberately, in cold blood, and escape the penalty. The law is no respecter of persons, and when he who commits such a deed is a man of substance, he must expect that Advocates and Judges, with all those who take up his cause, will bleed him well before they procure him a pardon.

Ugarte cared nothing for that, he had been as good as his word, and the devil in his heart was satisfied. Only he would not wait at his estancia to be taken, nor would he go and give himself up to the authorities, who would then have to place him in confinement, and it would be many months before his liberation. That would be like suffocation to him; to such a man a prison is like a tomb. No, he would go to Buenos Ayres and embark for Montevideo, and from that place he would put the matter in motion, and wait there until it was all settled and he was free to return to El Ombú.

Dead Meliton was taken away and buried in consecrated ground at Chascomus. Rain fell, and washed away the red stains on the ground. In the spring, the swallows returned and built their nests under the eaves; but Ugarte came not back, nor did any certain tidings of him reach us. It was said, I know not whether truly or not, that the Advocate who defended him, and the Judge of First Instance, who had the case before him, had quarrelled about the division of the reward, and both being rich, proud persons, they had allowed themselves to forget the old man waiting there month after month for his pardon, which never came to him.

Better for him if he never heard of the ruin which had fallen on El Ombú during his long exile. There was no one in authority: the slaves, left to themselves, went away; and there was no person to restrain them. As for the cattle and horses, they were blown away like thistle-down, and every-one was free to pasture his herds and flocks on the land.

The house for a time was in charge of some person placed there by the authorities, but little by little it was emptied of its contents; and at last it was abandoned, and for a long time no one could be found to live in it on account of the ghosts.

IV

THERE WAS living at that time, a few leagues from El Ombú, one Valerio de la Cueva, a poor man, whose all consisted of a small flock of three or four hundred sheep and a few horses. He had been allowed to make a small rancho, a mere hut, to shelter himself and his wife Donata and their one child, a boy named Bruno; and to pay for the grass his few sheep consumed he assisted in the work at the estancia house. This poor man, hearing of El Ombú, where he could have house and ground for nothing, offered himself as occupant, and in time came with wife and child and his small flock, and all the furniture he possessed—a bed, two or three chairs, a pot and kettle, and perhaps a few other things. Such poverty El Ombú had not known, but all others had feared to inhabit such a place on account of its evil name, so that it was left for Valerio, who was a stranger in the district.

Tell me, señor, have you ever in your life met with a man, who was perhaps poor, or even clothed in rags, and who yet when you had looked at and conversed with him, has caused you to say: Here is one who is like no other man in the world? Perhaps on rising and going out, on some clear morning in summer, he looked at the sun when it rose, and perceived an angel sitting in it, and as he gazed, something from that being fell upon and passed into and remained in him. Such a man was Valerio. I have known no other like him.

"Come, friend Nicandro," he would say, "let us sit down in the shade and smoke our cigarettes, and talk of our animals. Here are no politics under this old Ombú, no ambitions and intrigues and animosities—no bitterness except in these green leaves. They are our laurels—the leaves of the ombú.

Happy Nicandro, who never knew the life of cities! I wish that I, too, had seen the light on these quiet plains, under a thatched roof. Once I wore fine clothes and gold ornaments, and lived in a great house where there were many servants to wait on me. But happy I have never been. Every flower I plucked changed into a nettle to sting my hand. Perhaps that maleficent one, who has pursued me all my days, seeing me now so humbled and one with the poor, has left me and gone away. Yes, I am poor, and this frayed garment that covers mc will I press to my lips because it does not shine with silk and gold embroidery. And this poverty which I have found will I cherish, and bequeath it as a precious thing to my child when I die. For with it is peace."

The peace did not last long; for when misfortune has singled out a man for its prey, it will follow him to the end, and he shall not escape from it though he mount up to the clouds like the falcon, or thrust himself deep down into the earth like the armadillo.

Valerio had been two years at El Ombú when there came an Indian invasion on the southern frontier. There was no force to oppose it; the two hundred men stationed at the Guardia del Azul had been besieged by a part of the invaders in the fort, while the larger number of the savages were sweeping away the cattle and horses from the country all round. An urgent order came to the commander at Chascomus to send a contingent of forty men from the department; and I, then a young man of twenty, who had seen no service, was cited to appear at the Commandancia, in readiness to march. There I found that Valerio had also been cited, and from that moment we were together. Two days later we were at the Azul, the Indians having retired with their booty; and when all the contingents from the various departments had come in, the commander, one Colonel Barboza, set out with about six hundred men in pursuit.

It was known that in their retreat the Indians had broken up their force into several parties, and that these had taken different directions, and it was thought that these bodies would reunite after a time, and that the larger number would return to their territory by way of Trinqué Lauquén, about seventy-five leagues west of Azul. Our Colonel's plan was to go quickly to this point and wait the arrival of the Indians. It was impossible that they, burdened with the thousands of cattle they had collected, could move fast, while we were burdened with nothing, the only animals we drove before us being our horses. These numbered about five thousand, but many were unbroken mares, to be used as food. Nothing but mare's flesh did we have to eat.

It was the depth of winter, and worse weather I have never known. In this desert I first beheld that whiteness called snow, when the rain flies like cotton-down before the wind, filling the air and whitening the whole earth. All day and every day our clothes were wet, and there was no shelter from the wind and rain at night, nor could we make fires with the soaked grass and reeds, and wood there was none, so that we were compelled to eat our mare's flesh uncooked.

Three weeks were passed in this misery, waiting for the Indians and seeking for them, with the hills of Gaumini now before us in the south, and now on our left hand; and still no sight and no sign of the enemy. It seemed as if the earth had opened and swallowed him up. Our Colonel was in despair, and we now began to hope that he would lead us back to the Azul.

In these circumstances one of the men, who was thinly clad and had been suffering from a cough, dropped from his horse, and it was then seen that he was likely to die, and that in any case he would have to be left behind. Finding that there was no hope for him, he begged that those who were with him would remember, when they were at home again, that he had perished in the desert and that his soul was suffering in purgatory, and that they would give something to the priests to procure him ease. When asked by his officer to say who his relations were and where they lived, he replied that he had no one belonging to him. He said that he had spent many years in captivity among the Indians at the Salinas Grandes, and that on his return he had failed to find any one of his relations living in the district where he had been born. In answer to further questions, he said that he had been carried away when a small boy, that the Indians on that occasion had invaded the Christian country in the depth of winter, and on their retreat, instead of returning to their own homes, they had gone east, toward the sea coast, and had encamped on a plain by a small stream called Curumamuel, at Los Tres Arroyos, where there was firewood and sweet water, and good grass for the cattle, and where they found many Indians, mostly women and children, who had gone thither to await their coming; and at that spot they had remained until the spring.

The poor man died that night, and we gathered stones and piled them on his body so that the foxes and caranchos should not devour him.

At break of day next morning we were on horseback marching at a gallop toward sunrise, for our Colonel had determined to look for the Indians at that distant spot near the sea where they had hidden themselves from their pursuers so many years before. The distance was about seventy leagues, and the journey took us about nine days. And at last, in a deep valley near the sea, the enemy was discovered by our scouts, and we marched by night until we were within less than a league of their encampment, and could see their fires. We rested there for four hours, eating raw flesh and sleeping. Then every man was ordered to mount his best horse, and we were disposed in a half-moon, so that the free horses could easily be driven before us. The Colonel, sitting on his horse, addressed us. "Boys," he said, "you have suffered much, but now the victory is in our hands, and you shall not lose the reward. All the captives you take, and all the thousands of horses and cattle we succeed in recovering, shall be sold by public auction on our return, and the proceeds divided among you."

He then gave the order, and we moved quietly on for a space of half a league, and coming to the edge of the valley saw it all black with cattle before us, and the Indians sleeping in their camp; and just when the sun rose from the sea and God's light came over the earth, with a great shout we charged upon them. In a moment the multitude of cattle, struck with panic, began rushing away, bellowing in all directions, shaking the earth beneath their hoofs. Our troop of horses, urged on by our yells, were soon in the encampment, and the savages, rushing hither and thither, trying to save themselves, were shot and speared and cut down by swords. One desire was in all our hearts, one cry on all lips—kill! kill! kill! Such a slaughter had not been known for a long time, and birds and foxes and armadillos must have grown fat on the flesh of the heathen we left for them. But we killed only the men, and few escaped; the women and children we made captive.

Two days we spent in collecting the scattered cattle and horses, numbering about ten thousand; then with our spoil we set out on our return and arrived at the Azul at the end of

August. On the following day, the force was broken up into the separate contingents of which it was composed, and each in its turn was sent to the Colonel's house to be paid. The Chascomus contingent was the last to go up, and on presenting ourselves, each man received two months' soldiers' pay, after which Colonel Barboza came out and thanked us for our services, and ordered us to give up our arms at the fort and go back to our district, every man to his own house.

"We have spent some cold nights in the deserts together, neighbour Nicandro," said Valerio, laughing, "but we have fared well—on raw horse flesh; and now to make it better we have received money. Why, look, with all this money I shall be able to buy a pair of new shoes for Bruno. Brave little man! I can see him toddling about among the cardoon thistles, searching for hens' eggs for his mother, and getting his poor little feet full of thorns. If there should be any change left he shall certainly have some sugarplums."

But the others on coming to the fort began to complain loudly of the treatment they had received, whereupon Valerio, rebuking them, told them to act like men and tell the Colonel that they were not satisfied, or else hold their peace.

"Will you, Valerio, be our spokesman?" they cried, and, he consenting, they all took up their arms again and followed him back to the Colonel's house.

Barboza listened attentively to what was said and replied that our demands were just. The captives and cattle, he said, had been placed in charge of an officer appointed by the authorities and would be sold publicly in a few days. Let them now return to the fort and give up their arms, and leave Valerio with him to assist in drawing up a formal demand for their share of the spoil.

We then retired once more, giving *vivas* to our Colonel.

But no sooner had we given up our arms at the fort than we were sharply ordered to saddle our horses and take our departure. I rode out with the others, but seeing that Valerio did not overtake us I went back to look for him.

This was what had happened. Left alone in his enemy's hands, Barboza had his arms taken from him, then ordered his men to carry him out to the patio and flay him alive. The men hesitated to obey so cruel a command, and this gave Valerio time to speak; "My Colonel," he said, "you put a hard task on these poor men, and my hide when taken will be of no value to you or to them. Bid them lance me or draw a knife across my throat, and I will laud your clemency."

"You shall not lose your hide nor die," returned the Colonel, "for I admire your courage. Take him, boys, and stake him out, and give him two hundred lashes; then throw him into the road so that it may be known that his rebellious conduct has been punished."

This order was obeyed, and out upon the road he was thrown. A compassionate storekeeper belonging to the place saw him lying there insensible, the carrion-hawks attracted by his naked bleeding body hovering about him; and this good man took him and was ministering to him when I found him. He was lying, face down, on a pile of rugs, racked with pains, and all night long his sufferings were terrible; nevertheless, when morning came, he insisted on setting out at once on our journey to Chascomus. When his pain was greatest and caused him to cry out, the cry, when he saw my face, would turn to a laugh. "You are too tender hearted for this world we live in," he would say. "Think nothing of this, Nicandro. I have tasted man's justice and mercy before now. Let us talk of pleasanter things. Do you know that it is the first of September to-day? Spring has come back, though we hardly notice it yet in this cold southern country. It has been winter, winter with us, and no warmth of sun or fire, and no flowers and no birds' song. But our faces are towards the north now; in a few days we shall sit again in the shade of the old ombú, all our toil and suffering over, to listen to the *mangangá* humming among the leaves and to the call of the yellow *bienteveo*. And better than all, little Bruno will come to us with his hands full of scarlet verbenas. Perhaps in a few years' time you, too, will be a father, Nicandro, and will know what it is to hear a child's prattle. Come, we have rested long enough, and have many leagues to ride!"

The leagues were sixty by the road, but something was gained by leaving it, and it was easier for Valerio when the horses trod on the turf. To gallop or to trot was impossible, and even walking I had to keep at his side to support him with my arm; for his back was all one ever-bleeding wound, and his hands were powerless, and all his joints swollen and inflamed as a result of his having been stretched out on the stakes. Five days we travelled, and day by day and night by night he grew feebler, but he would not rest; so long as the light lasted he would be on the road; and as we slowly pressed on, I supporting him, he would groan with pain and then laugh and begin to talk of the journey's end and of the joy of seeing wife and child again.

It was afternoon on the fifth day when we arrived. The sight of the ombú which we had had for hours before us, strongly excited him; he begged me, almost with tears, to urge the horses to a gallop, but it would have killed him, and I would not do it.

No person saw our approach, but the door stood open, and when we had walked our horses to within about twenty yards we heard Bruno's voice prattling to his mother. Then suddenly Valerio slipped from the saddle before I could jump down to assist him, and staggered on for a few paces towards the door. Running to his side I heard his cry—"Donata! Bruno! let my eyes see you! one kiss!" Only then his wife heard, and running out to us, saw him sink, and with one last gasp expire in my arms.

Strange and terrible scenes have I witnessed, but never a sadder one than this! Tell me, señor, are these things told in books,—does the world know them?

Valerio was dead. He who was so brave, so generous even in his poverty, of so noble a spirit, yet so gentle; whose words were sweeter than honey to me! Of what his loss was to others—to that poor woman who was the mother of his one child, his little Bruno—I speak not. There are things about which we must be silent, or say only, turning our eyes up, Has He forgotten us! Does He know? But to me the loss was greater than all losses: for he was my friend, the man I loved above all men, who was more to me than any other, even than Santos Ugarte, whose face I should see no more.

For he, too, was dead.

And now I have once more mentioned the name of that man, who was once so great in this district, let me, before proceeding with the history of El Ombú, tell you his end. I heard of it by chance long after he had been placed under the ground.

It was the old man's custom in that house, on the other side of the Rio de la Plata where he was obliged to live, to go down every day to the waterside. Long hours would he spend there, sitting on the rocks, always with his face towards Buenos Ayres. He was waiting, waiting for the pardon which would, perhaps, in God's good time, come to him from that forgetful place. He was thinking of El Ombú; for what was life to him away from it, in that strange country? And that unsatisfied desire, and perhaps remorse, had, they say, made his face terrible to look at, for it was like the face of a dead man who had died with wide-open eyes.

One day some boatmen on the beach noticed that he was seated on the rocks far out and that when the tide rose he made no movement to escape from the water. They saw him sitting waist-deep in the sea, and when they rescued him from his perilous position and brought him to the shore, he stared at them like a great white owl and talked in a strange way.

"It is very cold and very dark," he said, "and I cannot see your faces, but perhaps you know me. I am Santos Ugarte, of El Ombú. I have had a great misfortune, friends. To-day in my anger I killed a poor youth whom I loved like a son—my poor boy Meliton! Why did he despise my warning and put himself in my way! But I will say no more about that. After killing him I rode away with the intention of going to Buenos Ayres, but on the road I repented of my deed and turned back. I said that with my own hands I would take him up and carry him in, and call my neighbours together to watch with me by his poor body. But, sirs, the night overtook me and the Sanborombón is swollen with rains, as you no doubt know, and in swimming it I lost my horse. I do not know if he was drowned. Let me have a fresh horse, friends, and show me the way to El Ombú, and God will reward you."

In that delusion he remained till the end, a few days later, when he died. May his soul rest in peace!

V

SEÑOR, when I am here and remember these things, I sometimes say to myself: Why, old man, do you come to this tree to sit for an hour in the shade, since there is not on all these plains a sadder or more bitter place? My answer is, To one who has lived long, there is no house and no spot of ground, overgrown with grass and weeds, where a house once stood and where men have lived, that is not equally sad. For this sadness is in us, in a memory of other days which follows us into all places. But for the child there is no past: he is born into the world light hearted like a bird; for him gladness is everywhere.

That is how it was with little Bruno, too young to feel the loss of a father or to remember him long. It was her great love of this child which enabled Donata to live through so terrible a calamity. She never quitted El Ombú. An embargo had been placed on the estancia so that it could not be sold, and she was not disturbed in her possession of the house. She now shared it with an old married couple, who, being poor and having a few animals, were glad of a place to live in rent free. The man, whose name was Pascual, took care of Donata's flock and the few cows and horses she owned along with his own. He was a simple, good-tempered old man, whose only fault was indolence, and a love of the bottle, and of play. But that mattered little, for when he gambled he invariably lost through not being sober, so that when he had any money it was quickly gone.

Old Pascual first put Bruno on a horse and taught him to ride after the flock, and to do a hundred things. The boy was like his father, of a beautiful countenance, with black curling hair, and eyes as lively as a bird's. It was not strange that Donata loved him as no mother ever loved a son, but as he grew up a perpetual anxiety was in her heart lest he should hear the story of his father's death and the cause of it. For she was wise in this; she knew that the most dangerous of all passions is that of revenge, since when it enters into the heart all others, good or bad, are driven out, and all ties and interests and all the words that can be uttered are powerless to restrain a man; and the end is ruin. Many times she spoke of this to me, begging me with tears never to speak of my dead friend to Bruno, lest he should discover the truth, and that fatal rage should enter into his heart.

It had been Donata's custom, every day since Valerio's death, to take a pitcher of water, fresh from the well, and pour it out on the ground, on the spot where he had sunk down and expired, without that sight of wife and child, that one kiss, for which he had cried. Who can say what caused her to do such a thing? A great grief is like a delirium, and sometimes gives us strange thoughts, and makes us act like demented persons. It may have been because of the appearance of the dead face as she first saw it, dry and white as ashes, the baked black lips, the look of thirst that would give everything for a drink of cold water; and that which she had done in the days of anguish, of delirium, she had continued to do.

The spot where the water was poured each day being but a few yards from the door of the house was of a dryness and hardness of firebaked bricks, trodden hard by the feet of I know not how many generations of men, and by hoofs of horses ridden every day to the door. But after a long time of watering a little green began to appear in the one spot; and the green was of a creeping plant with small round malva-like leaves, and little white flowers like porcelain shirt buttons. It spread and thickened, and was like a soft green carpet about two yards long placed on that dry ground, and it was of an emerald greenness all the year round, even in the hot weather when the grass was dead and dry and the plains were in colour like a faded yellow rag.

When Bruno was a boy of fourteen I went one day to help him in making a sheepfold, and when our work was finished in the afternoon we went to the house to sip maté. Before going in, on coming to that green patch, Bruno cried out, "Have you ever seen so verdant a spot as this, Nicandro, so soft and cool a spot to lie down on when one is hot and tired?" He then threw himself down full length upon it, and, lying at ease on his back, he looked up at Donata, who came out to us, and spoke laughingly, "Ah, little mother of my soul! A thousand times have I asked you why you poured water every day on this spot and you would not tell me. Now I have found out. It was all to make me a soft cool spot to lie on when I come back tired and hot from work. Look! is it not like a soft bed with a green and white velvet coverlid; bring water now, mother mine, and pour it on my hot, dusty face."

She laughed, too, poor woman, but I could see the tears in her eyes—the tears which she was always so careful to hide from him.

All this I remember as if it had happened yesterday; I can see and hear it all—Donata's laugh and the tears in her eyes which Bruno could not see. I remember it so well because this was almost the last time I saw her before I was compelled to go away, for my absence was long. But before I speak of that change let me tell you of something that happened about two years before at El Ombú, which brought a new happiness into that poor widow's life.

It happened that among those that had no right to be on

the land, but came and settled there because there was no one to forbid them, there was a man named Sanchez, who had built himself a small rancho about half a league from the old house, and kept a flock of sheep. He was a widower with one child, a little girl named Monica. This Sanchez, although poor, was not a good man, and had no tenderness in his heart. He was a gambler, always away from his rancho, leaving the flock to be taken care of by poor little Monica. In winter it was cruel, for then the sheep travel most, and most of all on cold, rough days; and she without a dog to help her, barefooted on the thistle-grown land, often in terror at the sight of cattle, would be compelled to spend the whole day out of doors. More than once on a winter evening in bad weather I have found her trying to drive the sheep home in the face of the rain, crying with misery. It hurt me all the more because she had a pretty face: no person could fail to see its beauty, though she was in rags and her black hair in a tangle, like the mane of a horse that has been feeding among the burrs. At such times I have taken her up on my saddle and driven her flock home for her, and have said to myself: "Poor lamb without a mother, if you were mine I would seat you on the horns of the moon; but, unhappy one! he whom you call father is without compassion."

At length, Sanchez, finding himself without money, just when strangers from all places were coming to Chascomus to witness a great race, and anxious not to lose this chance of large winnings, sold his sheep, having nothing of more value to dispose of. But instead of winning he lost, and then leaving Monica in a neighbour's house he went away, promising to return for her in a few days. But he did not return, and it was believed by everybody that he had abandoned the child.

It was then that Donata offered to take her and be a

mother to the orphan, and I can say, señor, that the poor child's own mother, who was dead, could not have treated her more tenderly or loved her more. And the pretty one had now been Donata's little daughter and Bruno's playmate two years when I was called away, and I saw them not again and heard no tidings of them for a space of five years—the five longest years of my life.

VI

I WENT AWAY because men were wanted for the army, and I was taken. I was away, I have said, five years, and the five would have been ten, and the ten twenty, supposing that life had lasted, but for a lance wound in my thigh, which made me a lame man for the rest of my life. That was the reason of my discharge and happy escape from that purgatory. Once back in these plains where I first saw heaven's light, I said in my heart: I can no longer spring light as a bird on to the back of an unbroken animal and laugh at his efforts to shake me off; nor can I throw a lasso on a running horse or bull and digging my heel in the ground, pit my strength against his; nor can I ever be what I have been in any work or game on horseback or on foot; nevertheless, this lameness, and all I have lost through it, is a small price to pay for my deliverance.

But this is not the history of my life; let me remember that I speak only of those who have lived at El Ombú in my time, in the old house which no longer exists.

There had been no changes when I returned, except that those five years had made Bruno almost a man, and more than ever like his father, except that he never had that I-know-not-what something to love in the eyes which made Valerio different from all men. Donata was the same, but older. Grey hair had come to her in her affliction; now her hair which should have been black was all white—but she was more at peace, for Bruno was good to her, and as a widow's only son, was exempt from military service. There was something else to make her happy. Those two, who were everything to her, could not grow up under one roof and not love; now she could look with confidence to a union between them, and there would be no separation. But even so, that old fear she had so often spoken of to me in former days was never absent from her heart.

Bruno was now away most of the time, working as a cattle drover, his ambition being, Donata informed me, to make money so as to buy everything needed for the house.

I had been back, living in that poor rancho, half a league from El Ombú, where I first saw the light, for the best part of a year, when Bruno, who had been away with his employer buying cattle in the south, one day appeared at my place. He had not been to El Ombú, and was silent and strange in his manner, and when we were alone together I said to him: "What has happened to you, Bruno, that you have the face of a stranger and speak in an unaccustomed tone to your friend?"

He answered: "Because you, Nicandro, have treated me like a child, concealing from me that which you ought to have told me long ago, instead of leaving me to learn it by accident from a stranger."

"It has come," I said to myself, for I knew what he meant: then I spoke of his mother.

"Ah, yes," he said with bitterness, "I know now why she pours water fresh from the well every day on that spot of ground near the door. Do you, Nicandro, think that water will ever wash away that old stain and memory? A man who is a man, must in such a thing obey, not a mother's wish, nor any woman, but that something which speaks in his heart."

"Let no such thought dwell in you to make you mad," I replied. "Look, Bruno, my friend's son and my friend, leave it to God who is above us, and who considers and remembers all evil deeds that men do, and desires not that anyone should take the sword out of his hand."

"Who is he—this God you talk of?" he answered. "Have you seen or spoken with him that you tell me what his mind is in this matter? I have only this voice to tell me how a man should act in such a case," and he smote his breast; then overcome with a passion of grief he covered his face with his hands and wept.

Vainly I begged him not to lose himself, telling him what the effect of his attempt, whether he succeeded or failed, would be on Donata and on Monica—it would break those poor women's hearts. I spoke, too, of things I had witnessed in my five years' service; the cruel sentences from which there was no appeal, the torments, the horrible deaths so often inflicted. For these evils there was no remedy on earth: and he, a poor, ignorant boy, what would he do but dash himself to pieces against that tower of brass!

He replied that within that brazen tower there was a heart full of blood; and with that he went away, only asking me as a favour not to tell his mother of this visit to me.

Some ten days later she had a message from him, brought from the capital by a traveller going to the south. Bruno sent word that he was going to Las Mulitas, a place fifty leagues west of Buenos Ayres, to work on an estancia there, and would be absent some months.

Why had he gone thither? Because he had heard that General Barboza—for that man was now a General—owned a tract of land at that place, which the Government had given him as a reward for his services on the southern frontier; and that he had recently returned from the northem provinces to Buenos Ayres and was now staying at this estancia at Las Mulitas.

Donata knew nothing of his secret motives, but his absence filled her with anxiety; and when at length she fell ill

I resolved to go in search of the poor youth and try to persuade him to return to El Ombú. But at Las Mulitas I heard that he was no longer there. All strangers had been taken for the army in the frontier department, and Bruno, in spite of his passport, had been forced to go.

When I returned to El Ombú with this sad news Donata resolved at once to go to the capital and try to obtain his release. She was ill, and it was a long journey for her to perform on horseback, but she had friends to go with and take care of her. In the end she succeeded in seeing the President, and throwing herself on her knees before him, and with tears in her eyes, implored him to let her have her son back.

He listened to her, and gave her a paper to take to the War Office. There it was found that Bruno had been sent to El Rosario, and an order was despatched for his immediate release. But when the order reached its destination the unhappy boy had deserted.

That was the last that Donata ever heard of her son. She guessed why he had gone, and knew as well as if I had told her that he had found out the secret so long hidden from him. Still, being his mother, she would not abandon hope; she struggled to live. Never did I come into her presence but I saw in her face a question which she dared not put in words. If, it said, you have heard, if you know, when and how his life ended, tell me now before I go. But it also said, If you know, do not tell me so that I and Monica may go on hoping together to the end.

"I know, Nicandro," she would say, "that if Bruno returns he will not be the same—the son I have lost. For in that one thing he is not like his father. Could another be like Valerio? No misfortune and no injustice could change that heart, or turn his sweetness sour. In that freshness and gaiety of temper he was like a child, and Bruno as a child was like him. My son! my son! where are you? God of my soul, grant that he may yet come to me, though his life be now darkened with some terrible passion—though his poor hands be stained with blood, so that my eyes may see him again before I go!"

But he came not, and she died without seeing him.

VII

IF MONICA, left alone in the house with old Pascual and his wife, had been disposed to listen to those who were attracted by her face she might have found a protector worthy of her. There were men of substance among those who came for her. But it mattered nothing to her whether they had land and cattle or not, or what their appearance was, and how they were dressed. Hers was a faithful heart. And she looked for Bruno's return, not with that poor half-despairing hope which had been Donata's and had failed to keep her alive, but with a hope that sustained and made her able to support the months and years of waiting. She looked for his coming as the night-watcher for the dawn. On summer afternoons, when the heat of the day was over, she would take her sewing outside the gate and sit there by the hour, where her sight commanded the road to the north. From that side he would certainly come. On dark, rainy nights a lantern would be hung on the wall lest he, coming at a late hour, should miss the house in the dark. Glad, she was not, nor lively; she was pale and thin, and those dark eyes that looked too large because of her thinness were the eyes of one who had beheld grief. But with it all, there was a serenity, an air of one whose tears, held back, would all be shed at the proper time, when he returned. And he would, perhaps, come to-day, or, if not to-day, then to-morrow, or perhaps the day after, as God willed.

Nearly three years had passed by since Donata's death when, one afternoon, I rode to El Ombú, and on approaching the house spied a saddled horse, which had got loose, going away at a trot. I went after, and caught, and led it back, and then saw that its owner was a traveller, an old soldier, who with or without the permission of the people of the house, was lying down and asleep in the shade of the ombú.

There had lately been a battle in the northern part of the province, and the defeated force had broken up, and the men carrying their arms had scattered themselves all over the country. This veteran was one of them.

He did not wake when I led the horse up and shouted to him. He was a man about fifty to sixty years old, grey-haired, with many scars of sword and lance wounds on his sun-blackened face and hands. His carbine was leaning against the tree a yard or two away, but he had not unbuckled his sword and what now attracted my attention as I sat on my horse regarding him, was the way in which he clutched the hilt and shook the weapon until it rattled in its scabbard. His was an agitated sleep; the sweat stood in big drops on his face, he ground his teeth and moaned, and muttered words which I could not catch.

At length, dismounting, I called to him again, then shouted in his ear, and finally shook him by the shoulder. Then he woke with a start, and struggling up to a sitting position, and staring at me like one demented, he exclaimed, "What has happened?"

When I told him about his horse he was silent, and sitting there with eyes cast down, passed his hand repeatedly across his forehead. Never in any man's face had I seen misery compared to his. "Pardon me, friend," he spoke at last. "My ears were so full of sounds you do not hear that I paid little attention to what you were saying."

"Perhaps the great heat of the day has overcome you," I said; "or maybe you are suffering from some malady caused by an old wound received in fight."

"Yes, an incurable malady," he returned, gloomily. "Have you, friend, been in the army?"

"Five years had I served when a wound which made me lame for life delivered me from that hell."

"I have served thirty," he returned, "perhaps more. I know that I was very young when I was taken, and I remember that a woman I called mother wept to see me go. That any eyes should have shed tears for me! Shall I now in that place in the South where I was born find one who remembers my name? I look not for it! I have no one but this"—and here he touched his sword.

After an interval, he continued, "We say, friend, that in the army we can do no wrong, since all responsibility rests with those who are over us; that our most cruel and sanguinary deeds are no more a sin or crime than is the shedding of the blood of cattle, or of Indians who are not Christians, and are therefore of no more account than cattle in God's sight. We say, too, that once we have become accustomed to kill, not men only, but even those who are powerless to defend themselves—the weak and the innocent—we think nothing of it, and have no compunction nor remorse. If this be so, why does He, the One who is above, torment me before my time? Is it just? Listen: no sooner do I close my eyes than sleep brings to me that most terrible experience a man can have—to be in the midst of a conflict and powerless. The bugles call: there is a movement everywhere of masses of men, foot and horse, and every face has on it the look of one who is doomed. There is a murmur of talking all round me, the officers are shouting and waving their swords; I strive in vain to catch the word of command; I do not know what is happening; it is all confusion, a gloom of smoke and dust, a roar of guns, a great noise and shouting of the enemy charging through us. And I am helpless. I awake, and slowly the noise and terrible scene fade from my mind, only to return when sleep again overcomes me. What repose, what refreshment can I know! Sleep, they say, is a friend to everyone, and makes all equal, the rich and the poor, the guilty and the innocent; they say, too, that this forgetfulness is like a draught of cold water to the thirsty man. But what shall I say of sleep? Often with this blade would I have delivered myself from its torture but for the fear that there may be after death something even worse than this dream."

After an interval of silence, seeing that he had recovered from his agitation, I invited him to go with me to the house. "I see smoke issuing from the kitchen," I said, "let us go in so that you may refresh yourself with maté before resuming your journey."

We went in and found the old people boiling the kettle; and in a little while Monica came in and sat with us. Never did she greet me without that light which was like sunshine in her dark eyes; words were not needed to tell me of the gratitude and friendliness she felt toward me, for she was not one to forget the past. I remember that she looked well that day in her white dress with a red flower. Had not Bruno said that he liked to see her in white, and that a flower on her bosom or in her hair was an ornament that gave her most grace? And Bruno might arrive at any moment. But the sight of that grey-haired veteran in his soiled and frayed uniform, and with his clanking sword and his dark scarred face, greatly disturbed her. I noticed that she grew paler and could scarcely keep her eyes off his face while he talked.

When sipping his maté he told us of fights he had been in, of long marches and sufferings in desert places, and of some of the former men he had served under. Among them he, by chance, named General Barboza.

Monica, I knew, had never heard of that man, and on this

account I feared not to speak of him. It had, I said, been reported, I knew not whether truthfully or not, that Barboza was dead.

"On that point I can satisfy you," he returned, "since I was serving with him, when his life came to an end in the province of San Luis about two years ago. He was at the head of nineteen hundred men when it happened, and the whole force was filled with amazement at the event. Not that they regretted his loss; on the contrary, his own followers feared, and were glad to be delivered from him. He exceeded most commanders in ferocity, and was accustomed to say scoffingly to his prisoners that he would not have gunpowder wasted on them. That was not a thing to complain of, but he was capable of treating his own men as he treated a spy or a prisoner of war. Many a one have I seen put to death with a blunted knife, he, Barboza, looking on, smoking a cigarette. It was the manner of his death that startled us, for never had man been seen to perish in such a way.

"It happened on this march, about a month before the end, that a soldier named Bracamonte went one day at noon to deliver a letter from his captain to the General. Barboza was sitting in his shirt sleeves in his tent when the letter was handed to him, but just when he put out his hand to take it the man made an attempt to stab him. The General throwing himself back escaped the blow, then instantly sprang like a tiger upon his assailant, and seizing him by the wrist, wrenched the weapon out of his hand only to strike it quick as lightning into the poor fool's throat. No sooner was he down than the General bending over him, before drawing out the weapon, called to those who had run to his assistance to get him a tumbler. When, tumbler in hand, he lifted himself up and looked upon them, they say that his face was of the whiteness of iron made white in the furnace, and that his eyes were like two flames. He was mad with rage, and cried out with a loud voice, "Thus, in the presence of the army do I serve the wretch who thought to shed my blood!" Then with a furious gesture he threw down and shattered the reddened glass, and bade them take the dead man outside the camp and leave him stripped to the vultures.

"This ended the episode, but from that day it was noticed by those about him that a change had come over the General. If, friend, you have served with, or have even seen him, you know the man he was—tall and well-formed, blue eyed and fair, like an Englishman, endowed with a strength, endurance and resolution that was a wonder to every one: he was like an eagle among birds,—that great bird that has no weakness and no mercy, whose cry fills all creatures with dismay, whose pleasure it is to tear his victim's flesh with his crooked talons. But now some secret malady had fallen on him which took away all his mighty strength; the colour of his face changed to sickly paleness, and he bent forward and swayed this way and that in the saddle as he rode like a drunken man, and this strange weakness increased day by day. It was said in the army that the blood of the man he had killed had poisoned him. The doctors who accompanied us in this march could not cure him, and their failure so angered him against them that they began to fear for their own safety. They now said that he could not be properly treated in camp, but must withdraw to some town where a different system could be followed; but this he refused to do.

"Now it happened that we had an old soldier with us who was a curandero. He was a native of Santa Fé, and was famed for his cures in his own department; but having had the misfortune to kill a man, he was arrested and condemned to serve ten years in the army. This person now informed some of the officers that he would undertake to cure the General, and Barboza, hearing of it, sent for and questioned him. The curandero informed him that his malady was one which the doctors could not cure. It was a failure of a natural heat of the blood, and only by means of animal heat, not by drugs, could health be recovered. In such a grave case the usual remedy of putting the feet and legs in the body of some living animal opened for the purpose would not be sufficient. Some very large beast should be procured and the patient placed bodily in it.

"The General agreed to submit himself to this treatment; the doctors dared not interfere, and men were sent out in quest of a large animal. We were then encamped on a wide sandy plain in San Luis, and as we were without tents we were suffering much from the great heat and the dustladen winds. But at this spot the General had grown worse, so that he could no longer sit on his horse, and here we had to wait for his improvement.

"In due time a very big bull was brought in and fastened to a stake in the middle of the camp. A space, fifty or sixty yards round, was marked out and roped round, and ponchos hung on the rope to form a curtain so that what was being done should not be witnessed by the army. But a great curiosity and anxiety took possession of the entire force, and when the bull was thrown down and his agonizing bellowings were heard, from all sides officers and men began to move toward that fatal spot. It had been noised about that the cure would be almost instantaneous, and many were prepared to greet the reappearance of the General with a loud cheer.

"Then very suddenly, almost before the bellowings had ceased, shrieks were heard from the enclosure, and in a moment, while we all stood staring and wondering, out rushed the General, stark naked, reddened with that bath of warm blood he had been in, a sword which he had hastily snatched up in his hand. Leaping over the barrier, he stood still for an instant, then catching sight of the great mass of men before him he flew at them, yelling and whirling his sword round so that it looked like a shining wheel in the sun. The men seeing that he was raving mad fled before him, and for a space of a hundred yards or more he pursued them; then that superhuman energy was ended; the sword flew from his hand, he staggered, and fell prostrate on the earth. For some minutes no one ventured to approach him, but he never stirred, and at length, when examined, was found to be dead."

The soldier had finished his story, and though I had many questions to ask I asked none, for I saw Monica's distress, and that she had gone white even to the lips at the terrible things the man had related. But now he had ended, and would soon depart, for the sun was getting low.

He rolled up and lighted a cigarette, and was about to rise from the bench, when he said, "One thing I forgot to mention about the soldier Bracamonte, who attempted to assassinate the General. After he had been carried out and stripped for the vultures, a paper was found sewn up in the lining of his tunic, which proved to be his passport, for it contained his right description. It said that he was a native of this department of Chascomus, so that you may have heard of him. His name was Bruno de la Cueva."

Would that he had not spoken those last words! Never, though I live to be a hundred, shall I forget that terrible scream that came from Monica's lips before she fell senseless to the floor!

As I raised her in my arms, the soldier turned and said, "She is subject to fits?"

"No," I replied, "that Bruno, of whose death we have now heard for the first time, was of this house."

"It was destiny that led me to this place," he said, "or perhaps that God who is ever against me; but you, friend, are my witness that I crossed not this threshold with a drawn weapon in my hand." And with these words he took his departure, and from that day to this I have never again beheld his face.

She opened her eyes at last, but the wings of my heart drooped when I saw them, since it was easy to see that she had lost her reason; but whether that calamity or the grief she would have known is greatest who can say? Some have died of pure grief—did it not kill Donata in the end? —but the crazed may live many years. We sometimes think it would be better if they were dead; but not in all cases—not, señor, in this.

She lived on here with the old people, for from the first she was quiet and docile as a child. Finally an order came from a person in authority at Chascomus for those who were in the house to quit it. It was going to be pulled down for the sake of the material which was required for a building in the village. Pascual died about that time, and the widow, now old and infirm, went to live with some poor relations at Chascomus and took Monica with her. When the old woman died Monica remained with these people: she lives with them to this day. But she is free to come and go at will, and is known to all in the village as *la loca del Ombú*. They are kind to her, for her story is known to them, and God has put compassion in their hearts.

To see her you would hardly believe that she is the Monica I have told you of, whom I knew as a little one, running bare-footed after her father's flock. For she has grey hairs and wrinkles now. As you ride to Chascomus from this point you will see, on approaching the lake, a very high bank on your left hand, covered with a growth of tall fennel, hoarhound, and cardoon thistle. There on most days you will find her, sitting on the bank in the shade of the tall fennel bushes, looking across the water. She watches for the flamingos. There are many of those great birds on the lake, and they go in flocks, and when they rise and travel across the water, flying low, their scarlet wings may be seen at a great distance. And every time she catches sight of a flock moving like a red line across the lake she cries out with delight. That is her one happiness—her life. And she is the last of all those who have lived in my time at El Ombú.

STORY OF A PIEBALD HORSE

THIS IS all about a piebald. People there are, like birds, that come down in flocks, hop about chattering, gobble up their seed, then fly away, forgetting what they have swallowed. I love not to scatter grain for such as these. With you, friend, it is different. Others may laugh if they like at the old man of many stories, who puts all things into his copper memory. I can laugh, too, knowing that all things are ordered by destiny; otherwise I might sit down and cry.

The things I have seen! There was the piebald that died long ago; I could take you to the very spot where his bones used to lie bleaching in the sun. There is a nettle growing on the spot. I saw it yesterday. What important things are these to remember and talk about! Bones of a dead horse and a nettle; a young bird that falls from its nest in the night and is found dead in the morning; puff-balls blown about by the wind; a little lamb left behind by the flock bleating at night amongst the thorns and thistles, where only the fox or wild dog can hear it! Small matters are these, and our lives, what are they? And the people we have known, the men and women who have spoken to us and touched us with warm hands—the bright eyes and red lips! Can we cast these things like dead leaves on the fire? Can we lie down full of heaviness because of them, and sleep and rise in the morning without them? Ah, friend!

Let us to the story of the piebald. There was a cattle-marking at neighbour Sotelo's estancia, and out of a herd of three thousand head we had to part all the yearlings to be branded. After that, dinner and a dance. At sunrise we gathered, about thirty of us; all friends and neighbours, to do the work. Only with us came one person nobody knew. He joined us when we were on our way to the cattle; a young man, slender, well-formed, of pleasing countenance and dressed as few could dress in those days. His horse also shone with silver trappings. And what an animal! Many horses have I seen in this life, but never one with such a presence as this young stranger's piebald.

Arrived at the herd, we began to separate the young animals, the men riding in couples through the cattle, so that each calf when singled out could be driven by two horsemen, one on each side, to prevent it from doubling back. I happened to be mounted on a demon with a fiery mouth—there was no making him work, so I had to leave the parters and stand with little to do, watching the yearlings already parted, to keep them from returning to the herd.

Presently neighbour Chapaco rode up to me. He was a good-hearted man, well-spoken, half Indian and half Christian; but he also had another half, and that was devil.

"What! neighbour Lucero, are you riding on a donkey or a goat, that you remain here doing boy's work?"

I began telling him about my horse, but he did not listen; he was looking at the parters.

"Who is that young stranger?" he asked.

"I see him to-day," I replied, "and if I see him again to-morrow then I shall have seen him twice."

"And in what country of which I have never heard did he learn cattle-parting?" said he.

"He rides," I answered, "like one presuming on a good horse. But he is safe, his fellow-worker has all the danger."

"I believe you," said Chapaco. "He charges furiously and hurls the heifer before his comrade, who has all the work to keep it from doubling, and all the danger, for at any moment his horse may go over it and fall. This our young stranger does knowingly, thinking that no one here will resent it. No, Lucero, he is presuming more on his long knife than on his good horse."

Even while we spoke, the two we were watching rode up to us. Chapaco saluted the young man, taking off his hat, and said—"Will you take me for a partner, friend?"

"Yes; why not, friend? " returned the other; and together the two rode back to the herd.

Now I shall watch them, said I to myself, to see what this Indian devil intends doing. Soon they came out of the herd driving a very small animal. Then I knew what was coming. "May your guardian angel be with you to avert a calamity, young stranger!" I exclaimed. Whip and spur those two came towards me like men riding a race and not parting cattle. Chapaco kept close to the calf, so that he had the advantage, for his horse was well trained. At length he got a little ahead, then, quick as lightning, he forced the calf round square before the other. The piebald struck it full in the middle, and fell because it had to fall. But, Saints in Heaven! why did not the rider save himself? Those who were watching saw him throw up his feet to tread his horse's neck and leap away; nevertheless man, horse, and calf came down together. They ploughed the ground for some distance, so great had been their speed, and the man was under. When we picked him up he was senseless, the blood flowing from his mouth. Next morning, when the sun rose and God's light fell on the earth, he expired.

Of course there was no dancing that night. Some of the people, after eating, went away; others remained sitting about all night, talking in low tones, waiting for the end. A few of us were at his bedside watching his white face and closed eyes. He breathed, and that was all. When the sunlight came over the world he opened his eyes, and Sotelo asked him how he did. He took no notice, but presently his lips began to move, though they seemed to utter no sound. Sotelo bent his ear down to listen. "Where does she live?" he asked. He could not answer—he was dead.

"He seemed to be saying many things," Sotelo told us, "but I understood only this— 'Tell her to forgive me . . . I was wrong. She loved him from the first. . . . I was jealous and hated him. . . . Tell Elaria not to grieve—Anacleto will be good to her.' Alas! my friends, where shall I find his relations to deliver this dying message to them?"

The Alcalde came that day and made a list of the dead man's possessions, and bade Sotelo take charge of them till the relations could be found. Then, calling all the people together, he bade each person cut on his whip-handle and on the sheath of his knife the mark branded on the flank of the piebald, which was in shape like a horse-shoe with a cross inside, so that it might be shown to all strangers, and made known through the country until the dead man's relations should hear of it.

When a year had gone by, the Alcalde told Sotelo that, all inquiries having failed, he could now take the piebald and the silver trappings for himself. Sotelo would not listen to this, for he was a devout man and coveted no person's property, dead or alive. The horse and things, however, still remained in his charge.

Three years later I was one afternoon sitting with Sotelo, taking maté, when his herd of dun mares were driven up. They came galloping and neighing to the corral and ahead of them, looking like a wild horse, was the piebald, for no person ever mounted him.

"Never do I look on that horse," I remarked, "without remembering the fatal marking, when its master met his death."

"Now you speak of it," said he, "let me inform you that I am about to try a new plan. That noble piebald and all those silver trappings hanging in my room are always reproaching my conscience. Let us not forget the young stranger we put under ground. I have had many masses said for his soul's repose, but that does not quite satisfy me. Somewhere there is a place where he is not forgotten. Hands there are, perhaps, that gather wild flowers to place them with lighted candles before the image of the Blessed Virgin; eyes there are that weep and watch for his coming. You know how many travellers and cattle-drovers going to Buenos Ayres from the south call for refreshment at the *pulpería*. I intend taking the piebald and tying him every day at the gate there. No person calling will fail to notice the horse, and some day perhaps some traveller will recognise the brand on its flank and will be able to tell us what department and what estancia it comes from."

I did not believe anything would result from this, but said nothing, not wishing to discourage him.

Next morning the piebald was tied up at the gate of the *pulpería*, at the roadside, only to be released again when night came, and this was repeated every day for a long time. So fine an animal did not fail to attract the attention of all strangers passing that way, still several weeks went by and nothing was discovered. At length, one evening, just when the sun was setting, there appeared a troop of cattle driven by eight men. It had come a great distance, for the troop was a large one—about nine hundred head—and they moved slowly, like cattle that had been many days on the road. Some of the men came in for refreshments; then the storekeeper noticed that one remained outside leaning on the gate.

"What is the capatas doing that he remains outside?" said one of the men.

"Evidently he has fallen in love with that piebald," said another, "for he cannot take his eyes off it."

At length the capatas, a young man of good presence, came in and sat down on a bench. The others were talking and laughing about the strange things they had all been doing the day before; for they had been many days and nights on the road, only nodding a little in their saddles, and at length becoming delirious from want of sleep, they had begun to act like men that are half-crazed.

"Enough of the delusions of yesterday," said the capatas, who had been silently listening to them, "but tell me, boys, am I in the same condition to-day?"

"Surely not!" they replied. "Thanks to those horned devils being so tired and footsore, we all had some sleep last night."

"Very well then," said he, "now you have finished eating and drinking, go back to the troop, but before you leave look well at that piebald tied at the gate. He that is not a cattle-drover may ask, 'How can my eyes deceive me?' but I know that a crazy brain makes us see many strange things when the drowsy eyes can only be held open with the fingers."

The men did as they were told, and when they had looked well at the piebald, they all shouted out, "He has the brand of the estancia de Silva on his flank, and no counter-brand—claim the horse, capatas, for he is yours." And after that they rode away to the herd.

"My friend," said the capatas to the storekeeper, "will you explain how you came possessed of this piebald horse?"

Then the other told him everything, even the dying words of the young stranger, for he knew all.

The capatas bent down his head, and covering his face

shed tears. Then he said, "And you died thus, Torcuato, amongst strangers! From my heart I have forgiven you the wrong you did me. Heaven rest your soul, Torcuato; I cannot forget that we were once brothers. I, friend, am that Anacleto of whom he spoke with his last breath."

Sotelo was then sent for, and when he arrived and the *pulpería* was closed for the night, the capatas told his story, which I will give you in his own words, for I was also present to hear him. This is what he told us:

I was born on the southern frontier. My parents died when I was very small, but Heaven had compassion on me and raised up one to shelter me in my orphanhood. Don Loreto Silva took me to his estancia on the Sarandi, a stream half a day's journey from Tandil, towards the setting sun. He treated me like one of his own children, and I took the name of Silva. He had two other children, Torcuato, who was about the same age as myself, and his daughter, Elaria, who was younger. He was a widower when he took charge of me, and died when I was still a youth. After his death we moved to Tandil, where we had a house close to the little town; for we were all minors, and the property had been left to be equally divided between us when we should be of age. For four years we lived happily together; then when we were of age we preferred to keep the property undivided. I proposed that we should go and live on the estancia, but Torcuato would not consent, liking the place where we were living best. Finally, not being able to persuade him, I resolved to go and attend to the estancia myself. He said that I could please myself and that he should stay where he was with Elaria. It was only when I told Elaria of these things that I knew how much I loved her. She wept and implored me not to leave her.

"Why do you shed tears, Elaria?" I said; "is it because you

love me? Know, then, that I also love you with all my heart, and if you will be mine, nothing can ever make us unhappy. Do not think that my absence at the estancia will deprive me of this feeling which has ever been growing up in me."

"I do love you, Anacleto," she replied, "and I have also known of your love for a long time. But there is something in my heart which I cannot impart to you; only I ask you, for the love you bear me, do not leave me, and do not ask me why I say this to you."

After this appeal I could not leave her, nor did I ask her to tell me her secret. Torcuato and I were friendly, but not as we had been before this difference. I had no evil thoughts of him; I loved him and was with him continually; but from the moment I announced to him that I had changed my mind about going to the estancia, and was silent when he demanded the reason, there was a something in him which made it different between us. I could not open my heart to him about Elaria, and sometimes I thought that he also had a secret which he had no intention of sharing with me. This coldness did not, however, distress me very much, so great was the happiness I now experienced, knowing that I possessed Elaria's love. He was much away from the house, being fond of amusements, and he had also begun to gamble. About three months passed in this way, when one morning Torcuato, who was saddling his horse to go out, said, "Will you come with me, to-day, Anacleto?"

"I do not care to go," I answered.

"Look, Anacleto," said he; "once you were always ready to accompany me to a race or dance or cattle-marking. Why have you ceased to care for these things? Are you growing devout before your time, or does my company no longer please you?"

"It is best to tell him everything and have done with secrets," said I to myself, and so replied—

"Since you ask me, Torcuato, I will answer you frankly. It is true that I now take less pleasure than formerly in these pastimes; but you have not guessed the reason rightly."

"What then is this reason of which you speak?"

"Since you cannot guess it," I replied, "know that it is love."

"Love for whom? " he asked quickly, and turning very pale.

"Do you need ask? Elaria," I replied.

I had scarcely uttered the name before he turned on me full of rage.

"Elaria!" he exclaimed. "Do you dare tell me of love for Elaria! But you are only a blind fool, and do not know that I am going to marry her myself."

"Are you mad, Torcuato, to talk of marrying your sister?

"She is no more my sister than you are my brother," he returned. "I," he continued, striking his breast passionately, "am the only child of my father, Loreto Silva. Elaria, whose mother died in giving her birth, was adopted by my parents. And because she is going to be my wife, I am willing that she should have a share of the property; but you, a miserable foundling, why were you lifted up so high? Was it not enough that you were clothed and fed till you came to man's estate? Not a hand's-breadth of the estancia land should be yours by right, and now you presume to speak of love for Elaria."

My blood was on fire with so many insults, but I remembered all the benefits I had received from his father, and did not raise my hand against him. Without more words he left me. I then hastened to Elaria and told her what had passed.

"This," I said, "is the secret you would not impart to me.

Why, when you knew these things, was I kept in ignorance?"

"Have pity on me, Anacleto," she replied, crying. "Did I not see that you two were no longer friends and brothers, and this without knowing of each other's love? I dared not open my lips to you or to him. It is always a woman's part to suffer in silence. God intended us to be poor, Anacleto, for we were both born of poor parents, and had this property never come to us, how happy we might have been!"

"Why do you say such things, Elaria? Since we love each other, we cannot be unhappy, rich or poor."

"Is it a little matter," she replied, "that Torcuato must be our bitter enemy? But you do not know everything. Before Torcuato's father died, he said he wished his son to marry me when we came of age. When he spoke about it we were sitting together by his bed."

"And what did you say, Elaria?" I asked, full of concern.

"Torcuato promised to marry me. I only covered my face, and was silent, for I loved you best even then, though I was almost a child, and my heart was filled with grief at his words. After we came here, Torcuato reminded me of his father's words. I answered that I did not wish to marry him, that he was only a brother to me. Then he said that we were young and he could wait until I was of another mind. This is all I have to say; but how shall we three live together any longer? I cannot bear to part from you, and every moment I tremble to think what may happen when you two are together."

"Fear nothing," I said. "To-morrow morning you can go to spend a week at some friend's house in the town; then I will speak to Torcuato, and tell him that since we cannot live in peace together we must separate. Even if he answers with insults I shall do nothing to grieve you, and if he refuses to listen to me, I shall send some person we both respect to arrange all things between us."

This satisfied her, but as evening approached she grew paler, and I knew she feared Torcuato's return. He did not, however, come back that night. Early next morning she was ready to leave. It was an easy walk to the town, but the dew was heavy on the grass, and I saddled a horse for her to ride. I had just lifted her to the saddle when Torcuato appeared. He came at great speed, and throwing himself off his horse, advanced to us. Elaria trembled and seemed ready to sink upon the earth to hide herself like a partridge that has seen the hawk. I prepared myself for insults and perhaps violence. He never looked at me; he only spoke to her.

"Elaria," he said, "something has happened—something that obliges me to leave this house and neighbourhood at once. Remember when I am away that my father, who cherished you and enriched you with his bounty, and who also cherished and enriched this ingrate, spoke to us from his dying bed and made me promise to marry you. Think what his love was; do not forget that his last wish is sacred, and that Anacleto has acted a base, treacherous part in trying to steal you from me. He was lifted out of the mire to be my brother and equal in everything except this. He has got a third part of my inheritance—let that satisfy him; your own heart, Elaria, will tell you that a marriage with him would be a crime before God and man. Look not for my return tomorrow nor for many days. But if you two begin to laugh at my father's dying wishes, look for me, for then I shall not delay to come back to you, Elaria, and to you, Anacleto. I have spoken."

He then mounted his horse and rode away. Very soon we learned the cause of his sudden departure. He had quarrelled over his cards and in a struggle that followed had stabbed his adversary to the heart. He had fled to escape the penalty. We did not believe that he would remain long absent; for Torcuato was very young, well off, and much liked, and this was, moreover, his first offence against the law. But time went on and he did not return, nor did any message from him reach us, and we at last concluded that he had left the country. Only now after four years have I accidentally discovered his fate through seeing his piebald horse.

After he had been absent over a year, I asked Elaria to become my wife. "We cannot marry till Torcuato returns," she said. "For if we take the property that ought to have been all his, and at the same time disobey his father's dying wish, we shall be doing an evil thing. Let us take care of the property till he returns to receive it all back from us; then, Anacleto, we shall be free to marry."

I consented, for she was more to me than lands and cattle. I put the estancia in order and leaving a trustworthy person in charge of everything I invested my money in fat bullocks to resell in Buenos Ayres, and in this business I have been employed ever since. From the estancia I have taken nothing, and now it must all come back to us—his inheritance and ours. This is a bitter thing and will give Elaria great grief.

Thus ended Anacleto's story, and when he had finished speaking and still seemed greatly troubled in his mind, Sotelo said to him, " Friend, let me advise you what to do. You will now shortly be married to the woman you love and probably some day a son will be born to you. Let him be named Torcuato, and let Torcuato's inheritance be kept for him. And if God gives you no son, remember what was done for you and for the girl you are going to marry, when you were orphans and friendless, and look out for some unhappy child in the same condition, to protect and enrich him as you were enriched."

"You have spoken well", said Anacleto. "I will report your words to Elaria, and whatever she wishes done that will I do."

So ends my story, friend. The cattle-drover left us that night and we saw no more of him. Only before going he gave the piebald and the silver trappings to Sotelo. Six months after his visit, Sotelo also received a letter from him to say that his marriage with Elaria had taken place; and the letter was accompanied with a present of seven cream-coloured horses with black manes and hoofs.

NIÑO DIABLO

THE WIDE pampa rough with long grass; a vast level disc now growing dark, the horizon encircling it with a ring as faultless as that made by a pebble dropped into smooth water; above it the clear sky of June, wintry and pale, still showing in the west the saffron hues of the afterglow tinged with vapoury violet and grey. In the centre of the disc a large low rancho thatched with yellow rushes, a few stunted trees and cattle enclosures grouped about it; and dimly seen in the shadows, cattle and sheep reposing. At the gate stands Gregory Gorostiaga, lord of house, lands and ruminating herds, leisurely unsaddling his horse; for whatsoever Gregory does is done leisurely. Although no person is within earshot he talks much over his task, now rebuking his restive animal, and now cursing his benumbed fingers and the hard knots in his gear. A curse falls readily and not without a certain natural grace from Gregory's lips; it is the oiled feather with which he touches every difficult knot encountered in life. From time to time he glances towards the open kitchen door, from which issue the far-flaring light of the fire and familiar voices, with savoury smells of cookery that come to his nostrils like pleasant messengers.

The unsaddling over at last the freed horse gallops away, neighing joyfully, to seek his fellows; but Gregory is not a four-footed thing to hurry himself; and so, stepping slowly and pausing frequently to look about him as if reluctant to quit the cold night air, he turns towards the house.

The spacious kitchen was lighted by two or three wicks in cups of melted fat, and by a great fire in the middle of the clay floor that cast crowds of dancing shadows on the walls and filled the whole room with grateful warmth. On the walls were fastened many deer's heads, and on their convenient prongs were hung bridles and lassos, ropes of onions and garlics, bunches of dried herbs, and various other objects. At the fire a piece of beef was roasting on a spit; and in a large pot suspended by hook and chain from the smoke-blackened central beam, boiled and bubbled an ocean of mutton broth, puffing out white clouds of steam redolent of herbs and cumin-seed. Close to the fire, skimmer in hand, sat Magdalen, Gregory's fat and florid wife, engaged in frying pies in a second smaller pot. There also, on a high, straight-backed chair, sat Ascension, her sister-in-law, a wrinkled spinster; also, in a low rush-bottomed seat, her mother-inlaw, an ancient white-headed dame, staring vacantly into the flames. On the other side of the fire were Gregory's two eldest daughters, occupied just now in serving maté to their elders—that harmless bitter decoction the sipping of which fills up all vacant moments from dawn to bedtime—pretty dove-eyed girls of sixteen, both also named Magdalen, but not after their mother nor because confusion was loved by the family for its own sake; they were twins, and born on the day sacred to Santa Magdalena. Slumbering dogs and cats were disposed about the floor, also four children. The eldest, a boy, sitting with legs outstretched before him, was cutting threads from a slip of colt's hide looped over his great toe. The two next, boy and girl, were playing a simple game called nines, once known to English children as nine men's morrice; the lines were rudely scratched on the clay floor, and the men they played with were bits of hardened clay, nine red and as many white. The youngest, a girl of five, sat on the floor nursing a kitten that purred contentedly on her lap and drowsily winked its blue eyes at the fire; and as she swayed

herself from side to side she lisped out the old lullaby in her
baby voice:—

> *A-ro-ró mi niño*
> *A-ro-ró mi sol,*
> *A-ro-ró pedazos*
> *De mi corazon.*

Gregory stood on the threshold surveying this domestic
scene with manifest pleasure.

"Papa mine, what have you brought me?" cried the child
with the kitten.

"Brought you, interested? Stiff whiskers and cold hands to
pinch your dirty little cheeks. How is your cold to-night,
mother?"

"Yes, son, it is very cold to-night; we knew that before you
came in," replied the old dame testily as she drew her chair a
little closer to the fire.

"It is useless speaking to her," remarked Ascension. "With
her to be out of temper is to be deaf."

"What has happened to put her out?" he asked.

"I can tell you, papa," cried one of the twins. "She wouldn't let
me make your cigars today, and sat down out of doors to make
them herself. It was after breakfast when the sun was warm."

"And of course she fell asleep," chimed in Ascension.

"Let me tell it, auntie!" exclaimed the other. "And she fell
asleep, and in a moment Rosita's lamb came and ate up the
whole of the tobacco-leaf in her lap."

"It didn't!" cried Rosita, looking up from her game. "I
opened its mouth and looked with all my eyes, and there was
no tobacco-leaf in it."

"That lamb! that lamb!" said Gregory slily. "Is it to be

wondered at that we are turning grey before our time—all except Rosita! Remind me to-morrow, wife, to take it to the flock; or if it has grown fat on all the tobacco-leaf, aprons and old shoes it has eaten—"

"Oh no, no, no!" screamed Rosita, starting up and throwing the game into confusion, just when her little brother had made a row and was in the act of seizing on one of her pieces in triumph.

"Hush, silly child, he will not harm your lamb," said the mother, pausing from her task and raising eyes that were tearful with the smoke of the fire and of the cigarette she held between her good-humoured lips. "And now, if these children have finished speaking of their important affairs, tell me, Gregory, what news do you bring?"

"They say," he returned, sitting down and taking the maté-cup from his daughter's hand, "that the invading Indians bring seven hundred lances, and that those that first opposed them were all slain. Some say they are now retreating with the cattle they have taken; while others maintain that they are waiting to fight our men."

"Oh, my sons, my sons, what will happen to them!" cried Magdalen, bursting into tears.

"Why do you cry, wife, before God gives you cause?" returned her husband. "Are not all men born to fight the infidel? Our boys are not alone—all their friends and neighbours are with them."

"Say not this to me, Gregory, for I am not a fool nor blind. All their friends indeed! And this very day I have seen the Niño Diablo; he galloped past the house, whistling like a partridge that knows no care. Why must my two sons be called away, while he, a youth without occupation and with no mother to cry for him, remains behind?"

"You talk folly, Magdalen," replied her lord. "Complain that the ostrich and puma are more favoured than your sons, since no man calls on them to serve the state; but mention not the Niño, for he is freer than the wild things which Heaven has made, and fights not on this side nor on that."

"Coward! Miserable!" murmured the incensed mother.

Whereupon one of the twins flushed scarlet and retorted, "He is not a coward, mother!"

"And if not a coward why does he sit on the hearth among women and old men in times like these? Grieved am I to hear a daughter of mine speak in defence of one who is a vagabond and a stealer of other men's horses!"

The girl's eyes flashed angrily, but she answered not a word.

"Hold your tongue, woman, and accuse no man of crimes," spoke Gregory. "Let every Christian take proper care of his animals; and as for the infidel's horses, he is a virtuous man that steals them. The girl speaks truth; the Niño is no coward, but he fights not with our weapons. The web of the spider is coarse and ill-made compared with the snare he spreads to entangle his prey." Thus fixing his eyes on the face of the girl who had spoken, he added: "Therefore be warned in season, my daughter, and fall not into the snare of the Niño Diablo."

Again the girl blushed and hung her head.

At this moment a clatter of hoofs, the jangling of a bell, and shouts of a traveller to the horses driven before him, came in at the open door. The dogs roused themselves, almost overturning the children in their hurry to rush out; and up rose Gregory to find out who was approaching with so much noise.

"I know, *papita*," cried one of the children. "It is Uncle Polycarp."

"You are right, child," said her father. "Cousin Polycarp always arrives at night, shouting to his animals like a troop of Indians." And with that he went out to welcome his boisterous relative.

The traveller soon arrived, spurring his horse, scared at the light and snorting loudly, to within two yards of the door. In a few minutes the saddle was thrown off, the fore feet of the bell-mare fettered, and the horses allowed to wander away in quest of pasturage; then the two men turned into the kitchen.

A short, burly man aged about fifty, wearing a soft hat thrust far back on his head, with truculent greenish eyes beneath arched bushy eyebrows, and a thick shapeless nose surmounting a bristly moustache—such was Cousin Polycarp. From neck to feet he was covered with a blue cloth poncho, and on his heels he wore enormous silver spurs that clanked and jangled over the floor like the fetters of a convict. After greeting the women and bestowing the avuncular blessing on the children, who had clamoured for it as for some inestimable boon—he sat down, and flinging back his poncho displayed at his waist a huge silver-hilted knife and a heavy brass-barrelled horse-pistol.

"Heaven be praised for its goodness, Cousin Magdalen," he said. "What with pies and spices your kitchen is more fragrant than a garden of flowers. That's as it should be, for nothing but rum have I tasted this bleak day. And the boys are away fighting, Gregory tells me. Good! When the eaglets have found out their wings let them try their talons. What, Cousin Magdalen, crying for the boys! Would you have had them girls?"

"Yes, a thousand times," she replied, drying her wet eyes on her apron.

"Ah, Magdalen, daughters can't be always young and sweet-tempered, like your brace of pretty partridges yonder. They grow old, Cousin Magdalen—old and ugly and spiteful; and are more bitter and worthless than the wild pumpkin. But I speak not of those who are present, for I would say nothing to offend my respected cousin Ascension, whom may God preserve, though she never married."

"Listen to me, Cousin Polycarp," returned the insulted dame so pointedly alluded to. "Say nothing to me nor of me, and I will also hold my peace concerning you; for you know very well that if I were disposed to open my lips I could say a thousand things."

"Enough, enough, you have already said them a thousand times," he interrupted. "I know all that, cousin; let us say no more."

"That is only what I ask," she retorted, "for I have never loved to bandy words with you; and you know already, therefore I need not recall it to your mind, that if I am single it is not because some men whose names I could mention if I felt disposed—and they are the names not of dead but of living men—would not have been glad to marry me; but because I preferred my liberty and the goods I inherited from my father; and I see not what advantage there is in being the wife of one who is a brawler and a drunkard and spender of other people's money, and I know not what besides."

"There it is!" said Polycarp, appealing to the fire. "I knew that I had thrust my foot into a red ant's nest—careless that I am! But in truth, Ascension, it was fortunate for you in those distant days you mention that you hardened your heart against all lovers. For wives, like cattle that must be branded with their owner's mark, are first of all taught submission to their husbands; and consider, cousin, what tears! what sufferings!" And having ended thus abruptly, he planted his elbows on his knees and busied himself with the cigarette he had been trying to roll up with his cold drunken fingers for the last five minutes.

Ascension gave a nervous twitch at the red cotton kerchief on her head, and cleared her throat with a sound "sharp and short like the shrill swallow's cry," when—

"*Madre del Cielo*, how you frightened me!" screamed one of the twins, giving a great start.

The cause of this sudden outcry was discovered in the presence of a young man quietly seated on the bench at the girl's side. He had not been there a minute before, and no person had seen him enter the room—what wonder that the girl was startled! He was slender in form, and had small hands and feet, and oval olive face, smooth as a girl's except for the incipient moustache on his lip. In place of a hat he wore only a scarlet ribbon bound about his head, to keep back the glossy black hair that fell to his shoulders; and he was wrapped in a white woollen Indian poncho, while his lower limbs were cased in white colt-skin coverings, shaped like stockings to his feet, with the red tassels of his embroidered garters falling to the ankles.

"The Niño Diablo!" all cried in a breath, the children manifesting the greatest joy at his appearance. But old Gregory spoke with affected anger. "Why do you always drop on us in this treacherous way, like rain through a leaky thatch?" he exclaimed. "Keep these strange arts for your visits in the infidel country; here we are all Christians, and praise God on the threshold when we visit a neighbour's house. And now, Niño Diablo, what news of the Indians?"

"Nothing do I know and little do I concern myself about specks on the horizon," returned the visitor with a light laugh. And at once all the children gathered round him, for the Niño they considered to belong to them when he came, and not to their elders with their solemn talk about Indian warfare and lost horses. And now, now he would finish that wonderful story, long in the telling, of the little girl alone and lost in the great desert, and surrounded by all the wild animals met to discuss what they should do with her. It was a grand story, even mother Magdalen listened, though she pretended all the time to be thinking only of her pies—and the teller, like the grand old historians of other days, put most eloquent speeches, all made out of his own head, into the lips (and beaks) of the various actors—puma, ostrich, deer, cavy, and the rest.

In the midst of this performance supper was announced, and all gathered willingly round a dish of Magdalen's pies, filled with minced meat, hard-boiled eggs chopped small, raisins, and plenty of spice. After the pies came roast beef; and, finally, great basins of mutton broth fragrant with herbs and cumin-seed. The rage of hunger satisfied, each one said a prayer, the elders murmuring with bowed heads, the children on their knees uplifting shrill voices. Then followed the concluding semi-religious ceremony of the day, when each child in its turn asked a blessing of father, mother, grandmother, uncle, aunt, and not omitting the stranger within the gates, even the Niño Diablo of evil-sounding name.

The men drew forth their pouches, and began making their cigarettes, when once more the children gathered round the story-teller, their faces glowing with expectation.

"No, no," cried their mother. "No more stories to-night—to bed, to bed!"

"Oh, mother, mother!" cried Rosita pleadingly, and struggling to free herself; for the good woman had dashed in among them to enforce obedience. "Oh, let me stay till the story ends! The reed-cat has said such things! Oh, what will they do with the poor little girl?"

"And oh, mother mine!" drowsily sobbed her little sister; "the armadillo that said—that said nothing because it had nothing to say, and the partridge that whistled and said—" and here she broke into a prolonged wail. The boys also added their voices until the hubbub was no longer to be borne, and Gregory rose up in his wrath and called on some one to lend him a big whip; only then they yielded, and still sobbing and casting many a lingering look behind, were led from the kitchen.

During this scene the Niño had been carrying on a whispered conversation with the pretty Magdalen of his choice, heedless of the uproar of which he had been the indirect cause; deaf also to the bitter remarks of Ascension concerning some people who, having no homes of their own, were fond of coming uninvited into other people's houses, only to repay the hospitality extended to them by stealing their silly daughters' affections, and teaching their children to rebel against their authority.

But the noise and confusion had served to arouse Polycarp from a drowsy fit; for like a boa constrictor, he had dined largely after his long fast, and dinner had made him dull; bending towards his cousin he whispered earnestly: "Who is this young stranger, Gregory?"

"In what corner of the earth have you been hiding to ask who the Niño Diablo is?" returned the other.

"Must I know the history of every cat and dog?"

"The Niño is not cat nor dog, cousin, but a man among men, like a falcon among birds. When a child of six the Indians killed all his relations and carried him into captivity.

After five years he escaped out of their hands, and, guided by sun and stars and signs on the earth, he found his way back to the Christian's country, bringing many beautiful horses stolen from his captors; also the name of Niño Diablo first given to him by the infidel. We know him by no other."

"This is a good story; in truth I like it well—it pleases me mightily," said Polycarp. "And what more, Cousin Gregory?"

"More than I can tell, cousin. When he comes the dogs bark not—who knows why? his tread is softer than the cat's; the untamed horse is tame for him. Always in the midst of dangers, yet no harm, no scratch. Why? Because he stoops like the falcon, makes his stroke and is gone—Heaven knows where!"

"What strange things are you telling me? Wonderful! And what more, Cousin Gregory?"

"He often goes into the Indian country, and lives freely with the infidel, disguised, for they do not know him who was once their captive. They speak of the Niño Diablo to him, saying that when they catch that thief they will flay him alive. He listens to their strange stories, then leaves them, taking their finest ponchos and silver ornaments, and the flower of their horses."

"A brave youth, one after my own heart, Cousin Gregory. Heaven defend and prosper him in all his journeys into the Indian territory! Before we part I shall embrace him and offer him my friendship, which is worth something. More, tell me more, Cousin Gregory?"

"These things I tell you to put you on your guard; look well to your horses, cousin,"

"What!" shouted the other, lifting himself up from his stooping posture, and staring at his relation with astonishment and kindling anger in his countenance.

The conversation had been carried on in a low tone, and the sudden loud exclamation startled them all—all except the Niño, who continued smoking and chatting pleasantly to the twins.

"Lightning and pestilence, what is this you say to me, Gregory Gorostiaga!" continued Polycarp, violently slapping his thigh and thrusting his hat farther back on his head.

"Prudence!" whispered Gregory. "Say nothing to offend the Niño, he never forgives an enemy—with horses."

"Talk not to me of prudence!" bawled the other. "You hit me on the apple of the eye and counsel me not to cry out. What! have not I, whom men call Polycarp of the South, wrestled with tigers in the desert, and must I hold my peace because of a boy—even a boy devil? Talk of what you like, cousin, and I am a meek man—meek as a sucking babe; but touch not on my horses, for then I am a whirlwind, a conflagration, a river flooded in winter, and all wrath and destruction like an invasion of Indians! Who can stand before me? Ribs of steel are no protection! Look at my knife; do you ask why there are stains on the blade? Listen; because it has gone straight to the robber's heart!" And with that he drew out his great knife and flourished it wildly, and made stabs and slashes at an imaginary foe suspended above the fire.

The pretty girls grew silent and pale and trembled like poplar leaves; the old grandmother rose up, and clutching at her shawl toddled hurriedly away, while Ascension uttered a snort of disdain. But the Niño still talked and smiled, blowing thin smoke-clouds from his lips, careless of that tempest of wrath gathering before him; till, seeing the other so calm, the man of war returned his weapon to its sheath, and glancing round and lowering his voice to a conversational tone, informed his hearers that his name was Polycarp, one known and feared by all men,—especially in the south; that he was disposed to live in peace and amity with the entire human race, and he therefore considered it unreasonable of some men to follow him about the world asking him to kill them. "Perhaps," he concluded, with a touch of irony, "they think I gain something by putting them to death. A mistake, good friends; I gain nothing by it! I am not a vulture, and their dead bodies can be of no use to me."

Just after this sanguinary protest and disclaimer the Niño all at once made a gesture as if to impose silence, and turned his face towards the door, his nostrils dilating, and his eyes appearing to grow large and luminous like those of a cat.

"What do you hear, Niño?" asked Gregory.

"I hear lapwings screaming," he replied.

"Only at a fox perhaps," said the other. "But go to the door, Niño, and listen,"

"No need," he returned, dropping his hand, the light of a sudden excitement passing from his face. "'Tis only a single horseman riding this way at a fast gallop,"

Polycarp got up and went to the door, saying that when a man was among robbers it behoved him to look well after his cattle. Then he came back and sat down again. "Perhaps," he remarked, with a side glance at the Niño, "a better plan would be to watch the thief. A lie, Cousin Gregory; no lapwings are screaming; no single horseman approaching at a fast gallop. The night is serene, and earth as silent as the sepulchre."

"Prudence!" whispered Gregory again. "Ah, cousin, always playful like a kitten; when will you grow old and wise? Can you not see a sleeping snake without turning aside to stir it up with your naked foot?"

Strange to say, Polycarp made no reply. A long experience

in getting up quarrels had taught him that these impassive men were, in truth, often enough like venomous snakes, quick and deadly when roused. He became secret and watchful in his manner.

All now were intently listening. Then said Gregory, "Tell us, Niño, what voices, fine as the trumpet of the smallest fly, do you hear coming from that great silence? Has the mother skunk put her little ones to sleep in their kennel and gone out to seek for the pipit's nest? Have fox and armadillo met to challenge each other to fresh trials of strength and cunning? What is the owl saying this moment to his mistress in praise of her big, green eyes?"

The young man smiled slightly but answered not; and for full five minutes more all listened, then sounds of approaching hoofs became audible. Dogs began to bark, horses to snort in alarm, and Gregory rose and went forth to receive the late night-wanderer. Soon he appeared, beating the angry barking dogs off with his whip, a white-faced, wild-haired man, furiously spurring his horse like a person demented or flying from robbers.

"*Ave María!*" he shouted aloud; and when the answer was given in suitable pious words, the scared-looking stranger drew near, and bending down said, "Tell me, good friend, is one whom men call Niño Diablo with you; for to this house I have been directed in my search for him?"

"He is within, friend," answered Gregory. "Follow me and you shall see him with your own eyes. Only first unsaddle, so that your horse may roll before the sweat dries on him."

"How many horses have I ridden their last journey on this quest!" said the stranger, hurriedly pulling off the saddle and rugs. "But tell me one thing more: is he well—no indisposition? Has he met with no accident—a broken bone, a sprained ankle?"

"Friend," said Gregory, "I have heard that once in past times the moon met with an accident, but of the Niño no such thing has been reported to me."

With this assurance the stranger followed his host into the kitchen, made his salutation, and sat down by the fire. He was about thirty years old, a good-looking man, but his face was haggard, his eyes bloodshot, his manner restless, and he appeared like one half-crazed by some great calamity. The hospitable Magdalen placed food before him and pressed him to eat. He complied, although reluctantly, despatched his supper in a few moments, and murmured a prayer; then, glancing curiously at the two men seated near him, he addressed himself to the burly, well-armed, and dangerous-looking Polycarp. "Friend," he said, his agitation increasing as he spoke, "four days have I been seeking you, taking neither food nor rest, so great was my need of your assistance. You alone, after God, can help me. Help me in this strait, and half of all I possess in land and cattle and gold shall be freely given to you, and the angels above will applaud your deed!"

"Drunk or mad?" was the only reply vouchsafed to this appeal.

"Sir," said the stranger with dignity, "I have not tasted wine these many days, nor has my great grief crazed me."

"Then what ails the man?" said Polycarp. "Fear perhaps, for he is white in the face like one who has seen the Indians."

"In truth I have seen them. I was one of those unfortunates who first opposed them, and most of the friends who were with me are now food for wild dogs. Where our houses stood there are only ashes and a stain of blood on the ground. Oh, friend, can you not guess why you alone were in my thoughts when this trouble came to me—why I have ridden day and night to find you?"

"Demons!" exclaimed Polycarp, "into what quagmires would this man lead me? Once for all I understand you not! Leave me in peace, strange man, or we shall quarrel." And here he tapped his weapon significantly.

At this juncture, Gregory, who took his time about everything, thought proper to interpose. "You are mistaken, friend," said he. "The young man sitting on your right is the Niño Diablo, for whom you inquired a little while ago."

A look of astonishment, followed by one of intense relief, came over the stranger's face. Turning to the young man he said, "My friend, forgive me this mistake. Grief has perhaps dimmed my sight; but sometimes the iron blade and the blade of finest temper are not easily distinguished by the eye. When we try them we know which is the brute metal, and cast it aside to take up the other, and trust our life to it. The words I have spoken were meant for you, and you have heard them."

"What can I do for you, friend?" said the Niño.

"Oh, sir, the greatest service! You can restore my lost wife to me. The savages have taken her away into captivity. What can I do to save her—I who cannot make myself invisible, and fly like the wind, and compass all things!" And here he bowed his head, and covering his face gave way to over-mastering grief.

"Be comforted, friend," said the other, touching him lightly on the arm. "I will restore her to you."

"Oh, friend, how shall I thank you for these words!" cried the unhappy man, seizing and pressing the Niño's hand.

"Tell me her name—describe her to me."

"Torcuata is her name—Torcuata de la Rosa. She is one finger's width taller than this young woman," indicating one of the twins who was standing. "But not dark; her cheeks are rosy—no, no, I forget, they will be pale now, whiter than the grass plumes, with stains of dark colour under the eyes. Brown hair and blue eyes, but very deep blue. Look well, friend, lest you think them black and leave her to perish."

"Never!" remarked Gregory, shaking his head.

"Enough—you have told me enough, friend," said the Niño, rolling up a cigarette.

"Enough!" repeated the other, surprised. "But you do not know; she is my life; my life is in your hands. How can I persuade you to be with me? Cattle I have. I had gone to pay the herdsmen their wages when the Indians came unexpectedly; and my house at La Chilca, on the banks of the Langueyú, was burnt, and my wife taken away during my absence. Eight hundred head of cattle have escaped the savages, and half of them shall be yours; and half of all I possess in money and land."

"Cattle!" returned the Niño, smiling, and holding a lighted stick to his cigarette. "I have enough to eat without molesting myself with the care of cattle."

"But I told you that I had other things," said the stranger, full of distress.

The young man laughed, and rose from his seat.

"Listen to me," he said. "I go now to follow the Indians—to mix with them, perhaps. They are retreating slowly, burdened with much spoil. In fifteen days go to the little town of Tandil, and wait for me there. As for land, if God has given so much of it to the ostrich it is not a thing for a man to set a great value on." Then he bent down to whisper a few words in the ear of the girl at his side; and immediately afterwards, with a simple "good-night" to the others, stepped lightly from the kitchen. By another door the girl also hurriedly left the room, to hide her tears from the watchful censuring eyes of mother and aunt.

Then the stranger, recovering from his astonishment at the abrupt ending of the conversation, started up, and crying aloud, "Stay! stay one moment—one word more!" rushed out after the young man. At some distance from the house he caught sight of the Niño, sitting motionless on his horse, as if waiting to speak to him.

"This is what I have to say to you," spoke the Niño, bending down to the other. "Go back to Langueyú, and rebuild your house, and expect me there with your wife in about thirty days. When I bade you go to the Tandil in fifteen days, I spoke only to mislead that man Polycarp, who has an evil mind. Can I ride a hundred leagues and back in fifteen days? Say no word of this to any man. And fear not. If I fail to return with your wife at the appointed time take some of that money you have offered me, and bid a priest say a mass for my soul's repose; for eye of man shall never see me again, and the brown hawks will be complaining that there is no more flesh to be picked from my bones."

During this brief colloquy, and afterwards, when Gregory and his women-folk went off to bed, leaving the stranger to sleep in his rugs beside the kitchen fire, Polycarp, who had sworn a mighty oath not to close his eyes that night, busied himself making his horses secure. Driving them home, he tied them to the posts of the gate within twenty-five yards of the kitchen door. Then he sat down by the fire and smoked and dozed, and cursed his dry mouth and drowsy eyes that were so hard to keep open. At intervals of about fifteen minutes he would get up and go out to satisfy himself that his precious horses were still safe. At length in rising, some time after midnight, his foot kicked against some loud-sounding metal object lying beside him on the floor, which, on examination, proved to be a copper bell of a peculiar shape, and curiously like the one fastened to the neck of his bell-mare. Bell in hand, he stepped to the door and put out his head, and lo! his horses were no longer at the gate! Eight horses: seven iron-grey geldings, every one of them swift and sure-footed, sound as the bell in his hand, and as like each other as seven claret-coloured eggs in the tinamou's nest; and the eighth the gentle piebald mare—the *madrina* his horses loved and would follow to the world's end, now, alas! with a thief on her back! Gone—gone!

He rushed out, uttering a succession of frantic howls and imprecations; and finally, to wind up the performance, dashed the now useless bell with all his energy against the gate, shattering it into a hundred pieces. Oh, that bell, how often and how often in how many a wayside public-house had he boasted, in his cups and when sober, of its mellow, far-reaching tone,—the sweet sound that assured him in the silent watches of the night that his beloved steeds were safe! Now he danced on the broken fragments, digging them into the earth with his heel; now in his frenzy, he could have dug them up again to grind them to powder with his teeth!

The children turned restlessly in bed, dreaming of the lost little girl in the desert; and the stranger half awoke, muttering, "Courage, O Torcuata—let not your heart break . . . Soul of my life, he gives you back to me—on my bosom, *rosa fresca, rosa fresca!*" Then the hands unclenched themselves again, and the muttering died away. But Gregory woke fully, and instantly divined the cause of the clamour. "Magdalen! Wife!" he cried. "Listen to Polycarp; the Niño has paid him out for his insolence! Oh, fool, I warned him, and he would not listen!" But Magdalen refused to wake; and so, hiding his head under the coverlet, he made the bed shake with suppressed laughter, so pleased was he at the clever trick played on his blustering cousin. All at once his laughter ceased, and out popped his head again, showing in the dim light a somewhat long and solemn face. For he had suddenly thought of his pretty daughter asleep in the adjoining room. Asleep! Wide awake, more likely, thinking of her sweet lover, brushing the dews from the hoary pampas grass in his southward flight, speeding away into the heart of the vast mysterious wilderness. Listening also to her uncle, the desperado, apostrophizing the midnight stars; while with his knife he excavates two deep trenches, three yards long and intersecting each other at right angles—a sacred symbol on which he intends, when finished, to swear a most horrible vengeance. "Perhaps," muttered Gregory, "the Niño has still other pranks to play in this house."

When the stranger heard next morning what had happened, he was better able to understand the Niño's motive in giving him that caution overnight; nor was he greatly put out, but thought it better that an evil-minded man should lose his horses than that the Niño should set out badly mounted on such an adventure.

"Let me not forget," said the robbed man, as he rode away on a horse borrowed from his cousin, "to be at the Tandil this day fortnight, with a sharp knife and a blunderbuss charged with a handful of powder and not fewer than twenty-three slugs."

Terribly in earnest was Polycarp of the South! He was there at the appointed time, slugs and all; but the smooth-checked, mysterious, child-devil came not; nor, stranger still, did the scared-looking de la Rosa come clattering in to look for his lost Torcuata. At the end of the fifteenth day de la Rosa was at Langueyú, seventy-five miles from the Tandil, alone in his new rancho, which had just been rebuilt with the aid of a few neighbours. Through all that night he sat alone by the fire, pondering many things. If he could only recover his lost wife, then he would bid a long farewell to that wild frontier and take her across the great sea, and to that old tree-shaded stone farm-house in Andalusia, which he had left a boy, and where his aged parents still lived, thinking no more to see their wandering son. His resolution was taken; he would sell all he possessed, all except a portion of land in the Langueyú with the house he had just rebuilt; and to the Niño Diablo, the deliverer, he would say, "Friend, though you despise the things that others value, take this land and poor house for the sake of the girl Magdalen you love; for then perhaps her parents will no longer deny her to you."

He was still thinking of these things, when a dozen or twenty military starlings—that cheerful scarlet-breasted song-ster of the lonely pampas—alighted on the thatch outside, and warbling their gay, careless winter-music told him that it was day. And all day long, on foot and on horseback, his thoughts were of his lost Torcuata; and when evening once more drew near his heart was sick with suspense and longing; and climb-ing the ladder placed against the gable of his rancho he stood on the roof gazing westwards into the blue distance. The sun, crimson and large, sunk into the great green sea of grass, and from all the plain rose the tender fluting notes of the tinamou-partridges, bird answering bird. "Oh, that I could pierce the haze with my vision," he murmured, " that I could see across a hundred leagues of level plain, and look this moment on your sweet face, Torcuata!"

And Torcuata was in truth a hundred leagues distant from him at that moment; and if the miraculous sight he wished for had been given, this was what he would have seen: A wide barren plain scantily clothed with yellow tufts of grass and thorny shrubs, and at its southern extremity, shutting out the view on that side, a low range of dune-like hills. Over this level ground, towards the range, moves a vast herd of cattle and horses—fifteen or twenty thousand head—followed by a scattered horde of savages armed with their long lances. In a small compact body in the centre ride the captives, women and children. Just as the red orb touches the horizon the hills are passed, and lo! a wide grassy valley beyond, with flocks and herds pasturing, and scattered trees, and the blue gleam of water from a chain of small lakes! There full in sight is the Indian settlement, the smoke rising peacefully up from the clustered huts. At the sight of home the savages burst into loud cries of joy and triumph, answered, as they drew near, with piercing screams of welcome from the village population, chiefly composed of women, children and old men.

It is past midnight; the young moon has set; the last fires are dying down; the shouts and loud noise of excited talk and laughter have ceased, and the weary warriors, after feasting on sweet mare's flesh to repletion, have fallen asleep in their huts, or lying out of doors on the ground. Only the dogs are excited still and keep up an incessant barking. Even the captive women, huddled together in one hut in the middle of the settlement, fatigued with their long rough journey, have cried themselves to sleep at last.

At length one of the sad sleepers wakes, or half wakes, dreaming that some one has called her name. How could such a thing be? Yet her own name still seems ringing in her brain, and at length, fully awake, she finds herself intently listening. Again it sounded—"Torcuata"—a voice fine as the pipe of a mosquito, yet so sharp and distinct that it tingled in her ear. She sat up and listened again, and once more it sounded "Torcuata!" "Who speaks?" she returned in a fearful whisper. The voice, still fine and small, replied, "Come out from among the others until you touch the wall." Trembling she obeyed, creeping out from among the sleepers until she came into contact with the side of the hut. Then the voice sounded again, "Creep round the wall until you come to a small crack of light on the other side." Again she obeyed, and when she reached the line of faint light it widened quickly to an aperture, through which a shadowy arm was passed round her waist; and in a moment she was lifted up, and saw the stars above her, and at her feet dark forms of men wrapped in their ponchos lying asleep. But no one woke, no alarm was given; and in a very few minutes she was mounted, man-fashion, on a bare-backed horse, speeding swiftly over the dim plains, with a shadowy form of her mysterious deliverer some yards in advance, driving before him a score or so of horses. He had only spoken half-a-dozen words to her since their escape from the hut, but she knew by those words that he was taking her to Langueyú.

El OMBÚ

MARTA RIQUELME

(From the Sepulvida MSS.)

I

Far away from the paths of those who wander to and fro on the earth, sleeps Jujuy in the heart of this continent. It is the remotest of our provinces, and divided from the countries of the Pacific by the giant range of the Cordillera; a region of mountains and forests, torrid heats and great storms; and although in itself a country half as large as the Spanish peninsula, it possesses, as its only means of communication with the outside world, a few insignificant roads which are scarcely more than mule-paths.

The people of this region have few wants; they aspire not after progress, and have never changed their ancient manner of life. The Spanish were long in conquering them: and now, after three centuries of Christian dominion, they still speak the Quichua, and subsist in a great measure on patay, a sweet paste made from the pod of the wild algarroba tree; while they still retain as a beast of burden the llama, a gift of their old masters the Peruvian Incas.

This much is common knowledge, but of the peculiar character of the country or of the nature of the things which happen within its borders, nothing is known to those without; Jujuy being to them only a country lying over against the Andes, far removed from and unaffected by the progress of the world. It has pleased Providence to give me a more intimate knowledge, and this has been a sore affliction and great burden now for many years. But I have not taken up my pen to complain that all the years of my life are consumed in a region where the great spiritual enemy of mankind is still permitted to challenge the supremacy of our Master, waging an equal war against his followers: my sole object is to warn, perhaps also to comfort, others who will be my successors in this place, and who will come to the church of Yala ignorant of the means which will be used for the destruction of their souls. And if I set down anything in this narrative which might be injurious to our holy religion, owing to the darkness of our understandings and the little faith that is in us, I pray that the sin I now ignorantly commit may be forgiven me, and that this manuscript may perish miraculously, unread by any person.

I was educated for the priesthood, in the city of Cordova, that famous seminary of learning and religion; and in 1838, being then in my twenty-seventh year, I was appointed priest to a small settlement in the distant province of which I have spoken. The habit of obedience, early instilled in me by my Jesuit masters, enabled me to accept this command unmurmuringly, and even with an outward show of cheerfulness. Nevertheless it filled me with grief, although I might have suspected that some such hard fate had been designed for me, since I had been made to study the Quichua language, which is now only spoken in the Andean provinces. With secret bitter repinings I tore myself from all that made life pleasant and desirable—the society of innumerable friends, the libraries, the beautiful church where I had worshipped, and that renowned University which has shed on the troubled annals of our unhappy country whatever lustre of learning and poetry they possess.

My first impressions of Jujuy did not serve to raise my spirits. After a trying journey of four weeks' duration—the roads being difficult and the country greatly disturbed at the time—I reached the capital of the province, also called Jujuy, a town of about two thousand inhabitants. Thence I journeyed to my destination, a settlement called Yala, situated on the northwestern border of the province, where the river Yala takes its rise, at the foot of that range of mountains which, branching eastwards from the Andes, divides Jujuy from Bolivia. I was wholly unprepared for the character of the place I had come to live in. Yala was a scattered village of about ninety souls—ignorant, apathetic people, chiefly Indians. To my unaccustomed sight the country appeared a rude, desolate chaos of rocks and gigantic mountains, compared with which the famous sierras of Cordova sunk into mere hillocks, and of vast gloomy forests, whose death-like stillness was broken only by the savage screams of some strange fowl, or by the hoarse thunders of a distant waterfall.

As soon as I had made myself known to the people of the village, I set myself to acquire a knowledge of the surrounding country; but before long I began to despair of ever finding the limits of my parish in any direction. The country was wild, being only tenanted by a few widely separated families, and like all deserts it was distasteful to me in an eminent degree; but as I would frequently be called upon to perform long journeys, I resolved to learn as much as possible of its geography. Always striving to overcome my own inclinations, which made a studious, sedentary life most congenial, I aimed at being very active; and having procured a good mule I began taking long rides every day, without a guide and with only a pocket compass to prevent me from losing myself. I could never altogether overcome my natural aversion to silent deserts, and in my long rides I avoided the thick forest and deep valleys, keeping as much as possible to the open plain.

One day having ridden about twelve or fourteen miles from Yala, I discovered a tree of noble proportions growing by itself in the open, and feeling much oppressed by the heat I alighted from my mule and stretched myself on the ground under the grateful shade. There was a continuous murmur of lecheguanas—a small honey wasp —in the foliage above me, for the tree was in flower, and this soothing sound soon brought that restful feeling to my mind which insensibly leads to slumber. I was, however, still far from sleep, but reclining with eyes half closed, thinking of nothing, when suddenly, from the depths of the dense leafage above me, rang forth a shriek, the most terrible it has ever fallen to the lot of any human being to hear. In sound it was a human cry, yet expressing a degree of agony and despair surpassing the power of any human soul to feel, and my impression was that it could only have been uttered by some tortured spirit allowed to wander for a season on the earth. Shriek after shriek, each more powerful and terrible to hear than the last, succeeded, and I sprang to my feet, the hair standing erect on my head, a profuse sweat of terror breaking out all over me. The cause of all these maddening sounds remained invisible to my eyes; and finally running to my mule I climbed hastily on to its back and never ceased flogging the poor beast all the way back to Yala.

On reaching my house I sent for one Osuna, a man of substance, able to converse in Spanish, and much respected in the village. In the evening he came to see me, and I then gave an account of the extraordinary experience I had encountered that day.

"Do not distress yourself, Father—you have only heard the Kakué," he replied. I then learnt from him that the Kakué is a fowl frequenting the most gloomy and sequestered forests and known to every one in the country for its terrible voice. Kakué, he also informed me, was the ancient name of the country, but the word was misspelt Jujuy by the early explorers, and this corrupted name was eventually retained. All this, which I now heard for the first time, is historical; but when he proceeded to inform me that the Kakué is a metamorphosed human being, that women and sometimes men, whose lives have been darkened with great suffering and calamities, are changed by compassionate spirits into these lugubrious birds, I asked him somewhat contemptuously whether he, an enlightened man, believed a thing so absurd.

"There is not in all Jujuy," he replied, "a person who disbelieves it."

"That is a mere assertion," cried I, "but it shows which way your mind inclines. No doubt the superstition concerning the Kakué is very ancient, and has come down to us together with the Quichua language from the aborigines. Transformations of men into animals are common in all the primitive religions of South America. Thus, the Guaranies relate that flying from a conflagration caused by the descent of the sun to the earth many people cast themselves into the river Paraguay, and were incontinently changed into capybaras and caymans; while others who took refuge in trees were blackened and scorched by the heat and became monkeys. But to go no further than the traditions of the Incas who once ruled over this region, it is related that after the first creation the entire human family, inhabiting the slopes of the Andes, were changed into crickets by a demon at enmity with man's first creator. Throughout the continent these ancient beliefs are at present either dead or dying out; and if the Kakué legend still maintains its hold on the vulgar here it is owing to the isolated position of the country, hemmed in by vast mountains and having no intercourse with neighbouring states."

Perceiving that my arguments had entirely failed to produce any effect I began to lose my temper, and demanded whether he, a Christian, dared to profess belief in a fable born of the corrupt imagination of the heathen?

He shrugged his shoulders and replied, "I have only stated what we, in Jujuy, know to be a fact. What is, is; and if you talk until tomorrow you cannot make it different, although you may prove yourself a very learned person."

His answer produced a strange effect on me. For the first time in my life I experienced the sensation of anger in all its power. Rising to my feet I paced the floor excitedly, and using many gestures, smiting the table with my hands and shaking my clenched fist close to his face in a threatening manner, and with a violence of language unbecoming in a follower of Christ, I denounced the degrading ignorance and heathenish condition of mind of the people I had come to live with; and more particularly of the person before me, who had some pretensions to education and should have been free from the gross delusions of the vulgar. While addressing him in this tone he sat smoking a cigarette, blowing rings from his lips and placidly watching them rise towards the ceiling, and with his studied supercilious indifference aggravated my rage to such a degree that I could scarcely restrain myself from flying at his throat or striking him to the earth with one of the cane-bottomed chairs in the room.

As soon as he left me, however, I was overwhelmed with remorse at having behaved in a manner so unseemly. I spent the night in penitent tears and prayers, and resolved in future to keep a strict watch over myself, now that the secret enemy of my soul had revealed itself to me. Nor did I make this resolution a moment too soon. I had hitherto regarded myself as a person of a somewhat mild and placid disposition; the sudden change to new influences, and, perhaps also, the secret disgust I felt at my lot, had quickly developed my true character, which now became impatient to a degree and prone to sudden violent outbursts of passion during which I had little control over my tongue. The perpetual watch over myself and struggle against my evil nature which had now become necessary was the cause of but half my trouble. I discovered that my parishioners, with scarcely an exception, possessed that dull apathetic temper of mind concerning spiritual things, which had so greatly exasperated me in the man Osuna, and which obstructed all my efforts to benefit them. These people, or rather their ancestors centuries ago, had accepted Christianity, but it had never properly filtered down into their hearts. It was on the surface still; and if their half-heathen minds were deeply stirred it was not by the story of the Passion of our Lord, but by some superstitious belief inherited from their progenitors. During all the years I have spent in Yala I never said a Mass, never preached a sermon, never attempted to speak of the consolations of faith, without having the thought thrust on to me that my words were useless, that I was watering the rock where no seed could germinate, and wasting my life in vain efforts to impart religion to souls that were proof against it. Often have I been reminded of our holy and learned Father Guevara's words, when he complains of the difficulties encountered by the earlier Jesuit missionaries. He relates how he endeavoured to impress the Chiriguanos with the danger they incurred by refusing baptism, picturing to them their future condition when they would be condemned to everlasting fire. To which they only replied that they were not disturbed by what he told them, but were, on the contrary, greatly pleased to hear that the flames of the future would be unquenchable, for that would save them infinite trouble, and if they found the fire too hot they would remove themselves to a proper distance from it. So hard it was for their heathen intellects to comprehend the solemn doctrines of our faith!

II

MY KNOWLEDGE of the Quichua language acquired solely by the study of the vocabularies, was at first of little advantage to me. I found myself unable to converse on familiar topics with the people of Yala; and this was a great difficulty in my way, and a cause of distress for more reasons than one. I was unprovided with books, or other means of profit and recreation, and therefore eagerly sought out the few people in the place able to converse in Spanish, for I have always been fond of social intercourse. There were only four: one very old man, who died shortly after my arrival; another was Osuna, a man for whom I had conceived an unconquerable aversion; the other two were women, the widow Riquelme and her daughter. About this girl I must speak at some length, since it is with her fortunes that this narrative is chiefly concerned. The widow Riquelme was poor, having only a house in Yala, but with a garden sufficiently large to grow a plentiful provision of fruit and vegetables, and to feed a few goats, so that these women had enough to live on, without ostentation, from their plot of ground. They were of pure Spanish blood; the mother was prematurely old and faded; Marta, who was a little over fifteen when I arrived at Yala, was the loveliest being I had ever beheld; though in this matter my opinion may be biased, for I only saw her side by side with the dark-skinned coarse-haired Indian women, and compared with their faces of ignoble type Marta's was like that of an angel. Her features were regular; her skin white, but with that pale darkness in it seen in some whose families have lived for generations in tropical countries. Her eyes, shaded by long lashes, were of that violet tint seen sometimes in people of

Spanish blood—eyes which appear black until looked at closely. Her hair was, however, the crown of her beauty and chief glory, for it was of great length and a dark shining gold colour—a thing wonderful to see!

The society of these two women, who were full of sympathy and sweetness, promised to be a great boon to me, and I was often with them; but very soon I discovered that, on the contrary, it was only about to add a fresh bitterness to my existence. The Christian affection I felt for this beautiful child insensibly degenerated into a mundane passion of such over-mastering strength that all my efforts to pluck it out of my heart proved ineffectual. I cannot describe my unhappy condition during the long months when I vainly wrestled with this sinful emotion, and when I often thought in the bitterness of my heart that my God had forsaken me. The fear that the time would come when my feelings would betray themselves increased on me until at length, to avoid so great an evil, I was compelled to cease visiting the only house in Yala where it was a pleasure for me to enter. What had I done to be thus cruelly persecuted by Satan? was the constant cry of my soul. Now I know that this temptation was only a part of that long and desperate struggle in which the servants of the prince of the power of the air had engaged to overthrow me.

Not for five years did this conflict with myself cease to be a constant danger—a period which seemed to my mind not less than half a century. Nevertheless, knowing that idleness is the parent of evil, I was incessantly occupied; for when there was nothing to call me abroad, I Iaboured with my pen at home, filling in this way four volumes, which in the end may serve to throw some light on the great historical question of the Incas' Cis-Andean dominion, and its effect on the conquered nations.

When Marta was twenty years old it became known in Yala that she had promised her hand in marriage to one Cosme Luna, and of this person a few words must be said. Like many young men, possessing no property or occupation, and having no disposition to work, he was a confirmed gambler, spending all his time going about from town to town to attend horse-races and cock-fights. I had for a long time regarded him as an abominable pest in Yala, a wretch possessing a hundred vices under a pleasing exterior, and not one redeeming virtue, and it was therefore with the deepest pain that I heard of his success with Marta. The widow, who was naturally disappointed at her daughter's choice, came to me with tears and complaints, begging me to assist her in persuading her beloved child to break off an engagement which promised only to make her unhappy for life. But with that secret feeling in my heart, ever-striving to drag me down to my ruin, I dared not help her, albeit I would gladly have given my right hand to save Marta from the calamity of marrying such a man.

The tempest which these tidings had raised in my heart never abated while the preparations for the marriage were going on. I was forced now to abandon my work, for I was incapable of thought; nor did all my religious exercises avail to banish for one moment the strange, sullen rage which had taken complete possession of me. Night after night I would rise from my bed and pace the floor of my room for hours, vainly trying to shut out the promptings of some fiend perpetually urging me to take some desperate course against this young man. A thousand schemes for his destruction suggested themselves to my mind, and when I had resolutely dismissed them all and prayed that my sinful temper might be forgiven, I would rise from my knees still cursing him a thousand times more than ever.

In the meantime, Marta herself saw nothing wrong in Cosme, for love had blinded her. He was young, good looking, could play on the guitar and sing, and was master of that easy, playful tone in conversation which is always pleasing to women. Moreover, he dressed well and was generous with his money, with which he was apparently well provided.

In due time they were married, and Cosme, having no house of his own, came to live with his mother-in-law in Yala. Then, at length, what I had foreseen also happened. He ran out of money, and his new relations had nothing he could lay his hands on to sell. He was too proud to gamble for coppers, and the poor people of Yala had no silver to risk; he could not or would not work, and the vacant life he was living began to grow wearisome. Once more he took to his old courses, and it soon grew to be a common thing for him to be absent from home for a month or six weeks at a time. Marta looked unhappy, but would not complain or listen to a word against Cosme; for whenever he returned to Yala then his wife's great beauty was like a new thing to him, bringing him to her feet, and making him again for a brief season her devoted lover and slave.

She at length became a mother. For her sake I was glad; for now with her infant boy to occupy her mind Cosme's neglect would seem more endurable. He was away when the child was born; he had gone, it was reported, into Catamarca, and for three months nothing was heard of him. This was a season of political troubles, and men being required to recruit the forces, all persons found wandering about the country not engaged in any lawful occupation, were taken for military service. And this had happened to Cosme. A letter from him reached Marta at last, informing her that he had been carried away to San Luis, and asking her to send him two hundred pesos, as with that amount he would be able to purchase his release. But it was impossible for her to raise the money; nor could she leave Yala to go to him, for her mother's strength was now rapidly failing, and Marta could not abandon her to the care of strangers. All this she was obliged to tell Cosme in the letter she wrote to him, and which perhaps never reached his hands, for no reply to it ever came.

At length, the widow Riquelme died; then Marta sold the house and garden and all she possessed, and taking her child with her, went out to seek her husband. Travelling first to the town of Jujuy, she there, with other women, attached herself to a convoy about to start on a journey to the southern provinces. Several months went by, and then came the disastrous tidings to Yala that the convoy had been surprised by Indians in a lonely place and all the people slain.

I will not here dwell on the anguish of mind I endured on learning Marta's sad end: for I tried hard to believe that her troubled life was indeed over, although I was often assured by my neighbours that the Indians invariably spare the women and children.

Every blow dealt by a cruel destiny against this most unhappy woman had pierced my heart; and during the years that followed, and when the villagers had long ceased to speak of her, often in the dead of the night I rose and sought the house where she had lived, and walking under the trees in that garden where I had so often held intercourse with her, indulged a grief which time seemed powerless to mitigate.

III

MARTA WAS NOT DEAD; but what happened to her after her departure from Yala was this. When the convoy with which she journeyed was attacked the men only were slain, while the women and children were carried away into captivity. When the victors divided the spoil among themselves, the child, which even in that long painful journey into the desert, with the prospect of a life of cruel slavery before her, had been a comfort to Marta, was taken forcibly from her arms to be conveyed to some distant place, and from that moment she utterly lost sight of it. She herself was bought by an Indian able to pay for a pretty white captive, and who presently made her his wife. She, a Christian, the wife of a man loved only too well, could not endure this horrible fate which had overtaken her. She was also mad with grief at the loss of her child, and stealing out one dark stormy night she fled from the Indian settlement. For several days and nights she wandered about the desert, suffering every hardship and in constant fear of jaguars, and was at length found by the savages in a half-starved condition and unable longer to fly from them. Her owner, when she was restored to him, had no mercy on her: he bound her to a tree growing beside his hovel, and there every day he cruelly scourged her naked flesh to satisfy his barbarous resentment, until she was ready to perish with excessive suffering. He also cut off her hair, and braiding it into a belt wore it always round his waist,—a golden trophy which doubtless won him great honour and distinction amongst his fellow savages. When he had by these means utterly broken her spirit and reduced her to the last condition of weakness, he released her from the tree, but at the same time fastened a log of wood to her ankle, so that only with great labour, and drawing herself along with the aid of her hands, could she perform the daily tasks her master imposed on her. Only after a whole year of captivity, and when she had given birth to a child, was the punishment over and her foot released from the log. The natural affection which she felt for this child of a father so cruel was now poor Marta's only comfort. In this hard servitude five years of her miserable existence were consumed; and only those who know the stern, sullen, pitiless character of the Indian can imagine what this period was for Marta, without sympathy from her fellow-creatures, with no hope and no pleasure beyond the pleasure of loving and caressing her own infant savages. Of these she was now the mother of three.

When her youngest was not many months old Marta had one day wandered some distance in search of sticks for fire-wood, when a woman, one of her fellow-captives from Jujuy, came running to her, for she had been watching for an opportunity of speaking with Marta. It happened that this woman had succeeded in persuading her Indian husband to take her back to her home in the Christian country, and she had at the same time won his consent to take Marta with them, having conceived a great affection for her. The prospect of escape filled poor Marta's heart with joy, but when she was told that her children could on no account be taken, then a cruel struggle commenced in her breast. Bit-terly she pleaded for permission to take her babes, and at last, overcome by her importunity, her fellow-captive con-sented to her taking the youngest of the three; though this concession was made very reluctantly.

In a short time the day appointed for the flight arrived, and Marta carrying her infant met her friends in the wood.

They were quickly mounted, and the journey began which was to last for many days, and during which they were to suffer much from hunger, thirst and fatigue. One dark night as they journeyed through a hilly and wooded country, Marta being overcome with fatigue so that she could scarcely keep her seat, the Indian with affected kindness relieved her of the child she always carried in her arms. An hour passed, and then pressing forward to his side and asking for her child she was told that it had been dropped into a deep, swift stream over which they had swum their horses some time before. Of what happened after that she was unable to give any very clear account. She only dimly remembered that through many days of scorching heat and many nights of weary travel she was always piteously pleading for her lost child—always seeming to hear it crying to her to save it from destruction. The long journey ended at last. She was left by the others at the first Christian settlement they reached, after which, travelling slowly from village to village, she made her way to Yala. Her old neighbours and friends did not know her at first, but when they were at length convinced that it was indeed Marta Riquelme that stood before them she was welcomed like one returned from the grave. I heard of her arrival, and hastening forth to greet her found her seated before a neighbour's house already surrounded by half the people of the village.

Was this woman indeed Marta, once the pride of Yala! It was hard to believe it, so darkened with the burning suns and winds of years was her face, once so fair; so wasted and furrowed with grief and the many hardships she had undergone! Her figure, worn almost to a skeleton, was clothed with ragged garments, while her head, bowed down with sorrow and despair, was divested of that golden crown which had been her chief ornament. Seeing me arrive she cast herself on her knees before me and taking my hand in hers covered it with tears and kisses. The grief I felt at the sight of her forlorn condition mingled with joy for her deliverance from death and captivity overcame me; I was shaken like a reed in the wind, and covering my face with my robe I sobbed aloud in the presence of all the people.

IV

EVERYTHING that charity could dictate was done to alleviate her misery. A merciful woman of Yala received her into her house and provided her with decent garments. But for a time nothing served to raise her desponding spirits; she still grieved for her lost babe, and seemed ever in fancy listening to its piteous cries for help. When assured that Cosme would return in due time that alone gave her comfort. She believed what they told her, for it agreed with her wish, and by degrees the effects of her terrible experience began to wear off, giving place to a feeling of feverish impatience with which she looked forward to her husband's return. With this feeling, which I did all I could to encourage, perceiving it to be the only remedy against despair, came also a new anxiety about her personal appearance. She grew careful in her dress, and made the most of her short, and sunburnt hair. Beauty she could never recover; but she possessed good features which could not be altered; her eyes also retained their violet colour, and hope brought back to her something of the vanished expression of other years.

At length, when she had been with us over a year, one day there came a report that Cosme had arrived, that he had been seen in Yala, and had alighted at Andrada's door—the store in the main road. She heard it and rose up with a great cry of joy. He had come to her at last—he would comfort her! She could not wait for his arrival: what wonder! Hurrying forth she flew like the wind through the village, and in a few moments stood on Andrada's threshold, panting from her race, her cheeks glowing, all the hope and life and fire of her girlhood rushing back to her heart. There she beheld Cosme, changed but little, surrounded by his old companions, listening in silence and with a dismayed countenance to the story of Marta's sufferings in the great desert, of her escape and return to Yala, where she had been received like one come back from the sepulchre. Presently they caught sight of her standing there. "Here is Marta herself arrived in good time," they cried. "Behold your wife!"

He shook himself from them with a strange laugh. "What, that woman my wife—Marta Riquelme!" he replied. "No, no, my friends, be not deceived; Marta perished long ago in the desert, where I have been to seek for her. Of her death I have no doubt; let me pass."

He pushed by her, left her standing there motionless as a statue, unable to utter a word, and was quickly on his horse riding away from Yala.

Then suddenly she recovered possession of her faculties, and with a cry of anguish hurried after him, imploring him to return to her; but finding that he would not listen to her she was overcome with despair and fell upon the earth insensible. She was taken up by the people who had followed her out and carried back into the house. Unhappily she was not dead, and when she recovered consciousness it was pitiful to hear the excuses she invented for the remorseless wretch who had abandoned her. She was altered, she said, greatly altered—it was not strange that Cosme had refused to believe that she could be the Marta of six years ago! In her heart she knew that nobody was deceived: to all Yala it was patent that she had been deserted. She could not endure it, and when she met people in the street she lowered her eyes and passed on, pretending not to see them. Most of her time was spent indoors, and there she would sit for hours without speaking or stirring, her cheeks resting on her hands, her eyes fixed on vacancy. My heart bled for her; morning and evening I remembered her in my prayers; by every argument I sought to cheer her drooping spirit, even telling her that the beauty and freshness of her youth would return to her in time, and that her husband would repent and come back to her.

These efforts were fruitless. Before many days she disappeared from Yala, and though diligent search was made in the adjacent mountains she could not be found. Knowing how empty and desolate her life had been, deprived of every object of affection, I formed the opinion that she had gone back to the desert to seek the tribe where she had been a captive in the hope of once more seeing her lost children. At length, when all expectation of ever seeing her again had been abandoned, a person named Montero came to me with tidings of her. He was a poor man, a charcoal-burner, and lived with his wife and children in the forest about two hours' journey from Yala, at a distance from any other habitation. Finding Marta wandering lost in the woods he had taken her to his rancho, and she had been pleased to find this shelter, away from the people of Yala who knew her history; and it was at Marta's own request that this good man had ridden to the village to inform me of her safety. I was greatly relieved to hear all this, and thought that Marta had acted wisely in escaping from the villagers, who were always pointing her out and repeating her wonderful history. In that sequestered spot where she had taken refuge, removed from sad associations and gossiping tongues, the wounds in her heart would perhaps gradually heal and peace return to her perturbed spirit.

Before many weeks had elapsed, however, Montero's wife came to me with a very sad account of Marta. She had grown day by day more silent and solitary in her habits, spending most of her time in some secluded spot among the trees, where she would sit motionless, brooding over her memories for hours at a time. Nor was this the worst. Occasionally she would make an effort to assist in the household work, preparing the patay or maize for the supper, or going out with Montero's wife to gather firewood in the forest. But suddenly, in the middle of her task, she would drop her bundle of sticks and, casting herself on the earth, break forth into the most heart-rending cries and lamentations, loudly exclaiming that God had unjustly persecuted her, that He was a being filled with malevolence, and speaking many things against Him very dreadful to hear. Deeply distressed at these tidings I called for my mule and accompanied the poor woman back to her own house; but when we arrived there Marta could nowhere be found.

Most willingly would I have remained to see her, and try once more to win her back from these desponding moods, but I was compelled to return to Yala. For it happened that a fever epidemic had recently broken out and spread over the country, so that hardly a day passed without its long journey to perform and death-bed to attend. Often during those days, worn out with fatigue and want of sleep, I would dismount from my mule and rest for a season against a rock or tree, wishing for death to come and release me from so sad an existence.

When I left Montero's house I charged him to send me news of Marta as soon as they should find her; but for several days I heard nothing. At length word came that they had discovered her hiding-place in the forest, but could not induce her to leave it, or even to speak to them; and they implored me to go to them, for they were greatly troubled at her state, and knew not what to do.

Once more I went out to seek her; and this was the saddest journey of all, for even the elements were charged with unusual gloom, as if to prepare my mind for some unimaginable calamity. Rain, accompanied by terrific thunder and lightning, had been falling in torrents for several days, so that the country was all but impassable: the swollen streams roared between the hills, dragging down rocks and trees, and threatening, whenever we were compelled to ford them, to carry us away to destruction. The rain had ceased, but the whole sky was covered by a dark motionless cloud, unpierced by a single ray of sunshine. The mountains, wrapped in blue vapours, loomed before us, vast and desolate; and the trees, in that still, thick atmosphere, were like figures of trees hewn out of solid ink-black rock and set up in some shadowy subterranean region to mock its inhabitants with an imitation of the upper world.

At length we reached Montero's hut, and, followed by all the family, went to look for Marta. The place where she had concealed herself was in a dense wood half a league from the house, and the ascent to it being steep and difficult, Montero was compelled to walk before, leading my mule by the bridle. At length we came to the spot where they had discovered her, and there, in the shadow of the woods, we found Marta still in the same place, seated on the trunk of a fallen tree, which was sodden with the rain and half buried under great creepers and masses of dead and rotting foliage. She was in a crouching attitude, her feet gathered under her garments, which were now torn to rags and fouled with clay; her elbows were planted on her drawn-up knees, and her long bony fingers thrust into her hair, which fell in tangled disorder over her face. To this pitiable condition had she been brought by great and unmerited sufferings.

Seeing her, a cry of compassion escaped my lips, and casting myself off my mule I advanced towards her. As I approached she raised her eyes to mine, and then I stood still, transfixed with amazement and horror at what I saw; for they were no longer those soft violet orbs which had retained until recently their sweet pathetic expression; now they were round and wild-looking, opened to thrice their ordinary size, and filled with a lurid yellow fire, giving them a resemblance to the eyes of some hunted savage animal.

"Great God, she has lost her reason!" I cried; then falling on my knees I disengaged the crucifix from my neck with trembling hands, and endeavoured to hold it up before her sight. This movement appeared to infuriate her; the insane, desolate eyes, from which all human expression had vanished, became like two burning balls, which seemed to shoot out sparks of fire; her short hair rose up until it stood like an immense crest on her head; and suddenly bringing down her skeleton-like hands she thrust the crucifix violently from her, uttering at the same time a succession of moans and cries that pierced my heart with pain to hear. And presently flinging up her arms, she burst forth into shrieks so terrible in the depth of agony they expressed that overcome by the sound I sank upon the earth and hid my face. The others, who were close behind me, did likewise, for no human soul could endure those cries, the remembrance of which, even now after many years, causes the blood to run cold in my veins.

"The Kakué! The Kakué!" exclaimed Montero, who was close behind me.

Recalled to myself by these words I raised my eyes only to discover that Marta was no longer before me. For even in that moment, when those terrible cries were ringing through my heart, waking the echoes of the mountain solitudes, the awful change had come, and she had looked her last with human eyes on earth and on man! In another form—that strange form of the Kakué—she had fled out of our sight for ever to hide in those gloomy woods which were henceforth to be her dwelling place. And I—most miserable of men, what had I done that all my prayers and strivings had been thus frustrated, that out of my very hands the spirit of the power of darkness had thus been permitted to wrest this unhappy soul from me!

I rose up trembling from the earth, the tears pouring unchecked down my cheeks, while the members of Montero's family gathered round me and clung to my garments. Night closed on us, black as despair and death, and with the greatest difficulty we made our way back through the woods. But I would not remain at the rancho; at the risk of my life I returned to Yala, and all through that dark solitary ride I was incessantly crying out to God to have mercy on me. Towards midnight I reached the village in safety, but the horror with which that unheard-of tragedy infected me, the fears and the doubts which dared not yet shape themselves into words, remained in my breast to torture me. For days I could neither eat nor sleep. I was reduced to a skeleton and my hair began to turn white before its time. Being now incapable of performing my duties, and believing that death was approaching I yearned once more for the city of my birth. I escaped at length from Yala, and with great difficulty reached the town of Jujuy, and from thence by slow stages I journeyed back to Cordova.

V

"ONCE MORE do I behold thee, O Cordova, beautiful to my eyes as the new Jerusalem coming down from Heaven to those who have witnessed the resurrection! Here, where my life began, may I now be allowed to lie down in peace, like a tired child that falls asleep on its mother's breast."

Thus did I apostrophize my natal city, when, looking from the height above, I at last saw it before me, girdled with purple hills and bright with the sunshine, the white towers of the many churches springing out of the green mist of groves and gardens.

Nevertheless Providence ordained that in Cordova I was to find life and not death. Surrounded by old beloved friends, worshipping in the old church I knew so well, health returned to me, and I was like one who rises after a night of evil dreams and goes forth to feel the sunshine and fresh wind on his face. I told the strange story of Marta to one person only; this was Father Irala, a learned and discreet man of great piety, and one high in authority in the church at Cordova. I was astonished that he was able to listen calmly to the things I related; he spoke some consoling words, but made no attempt then or afterwards to throw any light on the mystery. In Cordova a great cloud seemed to be lifted from my mind which left my faith unimpaired; I was once more cheerful and happy—happier than I had ever been since leaving it. Three months went by; then Irala told me one day that it was time for me to return to Yala, for my health being restored there was nothing to keep me longer from my flock.

O that flock, that flock, in which for me there had been only one precious lamb!

I was greatly disquieted; all those nameless doubts and

fears which had left me now seemed returning; I begged him to spare me, to send some younger man, ignorant of the matters I had imparted to him, to take my place. He replied that for the very reason that I was acquainted with those matters I was the only fit person to go to Yala. Then in my agitation I unburdened my heart to him. I spoke of that heathenish apathy of the people I had struggled in vain to overcome, of the temptations I had encountered—the passion of anger and earthly love, the impulse to commit some terrible crime. Then had come the tragedy of Marta Riquelme, and the spiritual world had seemed to resolve itself into a chaos where Christ was powerless to save; in my misery and despair my reason had almost forsaken me and I had fled from the country. In Cordova hope had revived, my prayers had brought an immediate response, and the Author of salvation seemed to be near to me. Here in Cordova, I said in conclusion, was life, but in the soul-destroying atmosphere of Yala death eternal.

"Brother Sepulvida," he answered, "we know all your sufferings and suffer with you; nevertheless you must return to Yala. Though there in the enemy's country, in the midst of the fight, when hard pressed and wounded, you have perhaps doubted God's omnipotence, He calls you to the front again, where He will be with you and fight at your side. It is for you, not for us, to find the solution of those mysteries which have troubled you; and that you have already come near to the solution your own words seem to show. Remember that we are here not for our own pleasure, but to do our Master's work; that the highest reward will not be for those who sit in the cool shade, book in hand, but for the toilers in the field who are suffering the burden and heat of the day. Return to Yala and be of good heart, and in due time all things will be made clear to your understanding."

These words gave me some comfort, and meditating much on them I took my departure from Cordova, and in due time arrived at my destination.

I had, on quitting Yala, forbidden Montero and his wife to speak of the manner of Marta's disappearance, believing that it would be better for my people to remain in ignorance of such a matter; but now, when going about in the village on my return I found that it was known to every one. That "Marta had become a Kakué," was mentioned on all sides; yet it did not affect them with astonishment and dismay that this should be so, it was merely an event for idle women to chatter about, like Quiteria's elopement or Maxima's quarrel with her mother-in-law.

It was now the hottest season of the year, when it was impossible to be very active, or much out of doors. During those days the feeling of despondence began again to weigh heavily on my heart. I pondered on Irala's words, and prayed continually, but the illumination he had prophesied came not. When I preached, my voice was like the buzzing of summer flies to the people: they came and sat or knelt on the floor of the church, and heard me with stolid unmoved countenances, then went forth again unchanged in heart. After the morning Mass I would return to my house, and, sitting alone in my room, pass the sultry hours, immersed in melancholy thoughts, having no inclination to work. At such times the image of Marta, in all the beauty of her girlhood, crowned with her shining golden hair, would rise before me, until the tears gathering in my eyes would trickle through my fingers. Then too I often recalled that terrible scene in the wood—the crouching figure in its sordid rags, the glaring furious eyes,—again those piercing shrieks seemed to ring through me, and fill the dark mountain's forest with echoes, and I would start up half maddened with the sensations of horror renewed within me.

And one day, while sitting in my room, with these memories for only company, all at once a voice in my soul told me that the end was approaching, that the crisis was come, and that to whichever side I fell, there I should remain through all eternity. I rose up from my seat staring straight before me, like one who sees an assassin enter his apartment dagger in hand and who nerves himself for the coming struggle. Instantly all my doubts, my fears, my unshapen thoughts found expression, and with a million tongues shrieked out in my soul against my Redeemer. I called aloud on Him to save me, but He came not; and the spirits of darkness, enraged at my long resistance, had violently seized on my soul, and were dragging it down to perdition. I reached forth my hands and took hold of the crucifix standing near me, and clung to it as a drowning mariner does to a floating spar. "Cast it down!" cried out a hundred devils in my ear. "Trample under foot this symbol of a slavery which has darkened your life and made earth a hell! He that died on the cross is powerless now; miserably do they perish who put their trust in Him! Remember Marta Riquelme, and save yourself from her fate while there is time."

My hands relaxed their hold on the cross, and falling on the stones, I cried aloud to the Lord to slay me and take my soul, for by death only could I escape from that great crime my enemies were urging me to commit.

Scarcely had I pronounced these words before I felt that the fiends had left me, like ravening wolves scared from their quarry. I rose up and washed the blood from my bruised forehead, and praised God; for now there was a great calm in my heart, and I knew that He who died to save the world was with me, and that His grace had enabled me to conquer and deliver my own soul from perdition.

From that time I began to see the meaning of Irala's words, that it was for me and not for him to find the solution of the mysteries which had troubled me, and that I had already come near to finding it. I also saw the reason of that sullen resistance to religion in the minds of the people of Yala; of the temptations which had assailed me—the strange tempests of anger and the carnal passions, never experienced elsewhere, and which had blown upon my heart like hot blighting winds; and even of all the events of Marta Riquelme's tragic life; for all these things had been ordered with devilish cunning to drive my soul into rebellion. I no longer dwelt persistently on that isolated event of her transformation, for now the whole action of that tremendous warfare in which the powers of darkness are arrayed against the messengers of the Gospel began to unfold itself before me.

In thought I went back to the time, centuries ago, when as yet not one ray of heavenly light had fallen upon this continent; when men bowed down in worship to gods, which they called in their several languages Pachacamac, Viracocho, and many others; names which being translated mean, The All-powerful, Ruler of Men, The Strong Comer, Lord of the Dead, The Avenger. These were not mythical beings; they were mighty spiritual entities, differing from each other in character, some taking delight in wars and destruction, while others regarded their human worshippers with tolerant and even kindly feelings. And because of this belief in powerful benevolent beings some learned Christian writers have held that the aborigines possessed a knowledge of the true God, albeit obscured by many false notions. This is a manifest error; for if in the material world light and darkness cannot mingle, much less can the Supreme Ruler stoop to share His sovereignty with Belial and Moloch, or in this continent, with Soychii, Tupa, and Viracocho: but all these demons, great and small, known by various names, were angels of darkness who had divided amongst themselves this new world and the nations dwelling in it. Nor need we be astonished at finding here resemblance to the true religion—majestic and graceful touches suggesting the Divine Artist; for Satan himself is clothed as an angel of light, and scruples not to borrow the things invented by the Divine Intelligence. These spirits possessed unlimited power and authority; their service was the one great business of all men's lives; individual character and natural feelings were crushed out by an implacable despotism, and no person dreamed of disobedience to their decrees, interpreted by their high priests; but all men were engaged in raising colossal temples, enriched with gold and precious stones, to their honour, and priests and virgins in tens of thousands conducted their worship with a pomp and magnificence surpassing those of ancient Egypt or Babylon. Nor can we doubt that these beings often made use of their power to suspend the order of nature, transforming men into birds and beasts, causing the trembling of the earth which ruins whole cities, and performing many other stupendous miracles to demonstrate their authority or satisfy their malignant natures. The time came when it pleased the Ruler of the world to overthrow this evil empire, using for that end the ancient, feeble instruments despised of men, the missionary priests, and chiefly those of the often persecuted Brotherhood founded by Loyola, whose zeal and holiness have always been an offence to the proud and carnal-minded. Country after country, tribe after tribe, the old gods were deprived of their kingdom, fighting always with all their weapons to keep back the tide of conquest. And at length, defeated at all points, and like an army fighting in defence of its territory, and gradually retiring before the invader to concentrate itself in some apparently inaccessible region and there stubbornly resist to the end; so have all the old gods and demons retired into this secluded country, where, if they cannot keep out the seeds of truth they have at least succeeded in rendering the soil it falls upon barren as stone. Nor does it seem altogether strange that these once potent beings should be satisfied to remain in comparative obscurity and inaction when the entire globe is open to them, offering fields worthy of their evil ambition. For great as their power and intelligence must be they are, nevertheless, finite beings, possessing, like man, individual characteristics, capabilities and limitations; and after reigning where they have lost a continent, they may possibly be unfit or unwilling to serve elsewhere. For we know that even in the strong places of Christianity there are spirits enough for the evil work of leading men astray; whole nations are given up to damnable heresies, and all religion is trodden under foot by many whose portion will be where the worm dieth not and the fire is not quenched.

From the moment of my last struggle, when this revelation began to dawn upon my mind, I have been safe from their persecutions. No angry passions, no sinful motions, no doubts and despondence disturb the peace of my soul. I was filled with fresh zeal, and in the pulpit felt that it was not my voice, but the voice of some mighty spirit speaking with my lips and preaching to the people with an eloquence of which I was not capable. So far, however, it has been powerless to win their souls. The old gods, although no longer worshipped openly, are their gods still, and could a new Tupac Amaru

arise to pluck down the symbols of Christianity, and pro-
claim once more the Empire of the Sun, men would everywhere bow down to worship his rising beams and joyfully
rebuild temples to the Lightning and the Rainbow.

Although the lost spirits cannot harm they are always
near me, watching all my movements, ever striving to frus-
trate my designs. Nor am I unmindful of their presence.
Even here, sitting in my study and looking out on the mountains, rising like stupendous stairs towards heaven and losing their summits in the gathering clouds, I seem to discern
the awful shadowy form of Pachacamac, supreme among the
old gods. Though his temples are in ruins, where the
Pharaohs of the Andes and their millions of slaves worshipped him for a thousand years, he is awful still in his
majesty and wrath that plays like lightning on his furrowed
brows, kindling his stern countenance, and the beard which
rolls downward like an immense white cloud to his knees.
Around him gather other tremendous forms in their cloudy
vestments—the Strongcomer, the Lord of the Dead, the
Avenger, the Ruler of men, and many others whose names
were once mighty throughout the continent. They have met
to take counsel together; I hear their voices in the thunder
hoarsely rolling from the hills, and in the wind stirring the
forest before the coming tempest. Their faces are towards
me, they are pointing to me with their cloudy hands, they are
speaking of me—even of me, an old, feeble, worn-out man!
But I do not quail before them; my soul is firm though my
flesh is weak; though my knees tremble while I gaze, I dare
look forward even to win another victory over them before I
depart.

Day and night I pray for that soul still wandering lost in
the great wilderness; and no voice rebukes my hope or tells

me that my prayer is unlawful. I strain my eyes gazing out towards the forest; but I know not whether Marta Riquelme will return to me with the tidings of her salvation in a dream of the night, or clothed in the garments of the flesh, in the full light of day. For her salvation I wait, and when I have seen it I shall be ready to depart; for as the traveller, whose lips are baked with hot winds, and who thirsts for a cooling draught and swallows sand, strains his eyeballs to see the end of his journey in some great desert, so do I look forward to the goal of this life, when I shall go to Thee, O my Master, and be at rest!

El OMBÚ

APPENDIX TO *EL OMBÚ*

The English Invasion and the Game of El Pato

I MUST SAY at once that *El Ombú* is mostly a true story, although the events did not occur exactly in the order given. The incidents relating to the English invasion of June and July, 1807, is told pretty much as I had it from the old gaucho called Nicandro in the narrative. That was in the sixties. The undated notes which I made of my talks with the old man, containing numerous anecdotes of Santos Ugarte and the whole history of El Ombú, were written, I think, in 1868—the year of the great dust storm. These ancient notes are now before me, and look very strange, both as to the writing and the quality of the paper; also as to the dirtiness of the same, which makes me think that the old manuscript must have been out in that memorable storm, which, I remember, ended with rain—the rain coming down as liquid mud.

There were other old men living in that part of the country who, as boys, had witnessed the march of an English army on Buenos Ayres, and one of these confirmed the story of the blankets thrown away by the army, and of the chaff between some of the British soldiers and the natives.

I confess I had some doubts as to the truth of this blanket story when I came to read over my old notes; but in referring to the proceedings of the court-martial on Lieutenant-General Whitelocke, published in London in 1808, I find that the incident is referred to. On page 57 of the first volume occurs the following statement, made by General Gower in his evidence. "The men, particularly of Brigadier-General Lumley's brigade, were very much exhausted, and Lieutenant-General White-locke, to give them a chance of getting on with tolerable rapidity, ordered all the blankets of the army to be thrown down."

There is nothing, however, in the evidence about the blankets having been used to make a firmer bottom for the army to cross a river, nor is the name of the river mentioned.

Another point in the old gaucho's story may strike the English reader as very strange and almost incredible; this is, that within a very few miles of the army of the hated foreign invader, during its march on the capital, where the greatest excitement prevailed and every preparation for defence was being made, a large number of men were amusing themselves at the game of El Pato. To those who are acquainted with the character of the gaucho there is nothing incredible in such a fact; for the gaucho is, or was, absolutely devoid of the sentiment of patriotism, and regarded all rulers, all in authority from the highest to the lowest, as his chief enemies, and the worst kind of robbers, since they robbed him not only of his goods but of his liberty.

It mattered not to him whether his country paid tribute to Spain or to England, whether a man appointed by some one at a distance as Governor or Viceroy had black or blue eyes. It was seen that when the Spanish dominion came to an end his hatred was transferred to the ruling cliques of a so-called Republic. When the gauchos attached themselves to Rosas, and assisted him to climb into power, they were under the delusion that he was one of themselves, and would give them that perfect liberty to live their own lives in their own way, which is their only desire. They found out their mistake when it was too late.

It was Rosas who abolished the game of El Pato, but before saying more on that point it would be best to describe the game. I have never seen an account of it in print, but for a very long period, and down to probably about 1840, it was the most popular outdoor game on the Argentine pampas.

Doubtless it originated there; it was certainly admirably suited to the habits and disposition of the horsemen of the plains; and unlike most outdoor games it retained its original simple, rude character to the end.

Pato means duck; and to play the game a duck or fowl, or, as was usually the case, some larger domestic bird—turkey, gosling, or muscovy duck—was killed and sewn up in a piece of stout raw hide, forming a somewhat shapeless ball, twice as big as a football, and provided with four loops or handles of strong twisted raw hide made of a convenient size to be grasped by a man's hand. A great point was to have the ball and handles so strongly made that three or four powerful men could take hold and tug until they dragged each other to the ground without anything giving way.

Whenever it was resolved at any place to have a game, and someone had offered to provide the bird, and the meeting place had been settled, notice would be sent round among the neighbours; and at the appointed time all the men and youths within a circle of several leagues would appear on the spot, mounted on their best horses. On the appearance of the man on the ground carrying the duck the others would give chase; and by-and-by he would be overtaken, and the ball wrested from his hand; the victor in his turn would be pursued, and when overtaken there would perhaps be a scuffle or scrimmage, as in football, only the strugglers would be first on horseback before dragging each other to the earth. Occasionally when this happened a couple of hot-headed players, angry at being hurt or worsted, would draw their weapons against each other in order to find who was in the right, or to prove which was the better man. But fight or no fight, some one would get the duck and carry it away to be chased again. Leagues of ground would be gone over by the players in this way, and at last some one, luckier or better mounted than his fellows, would get the duck and successfully run the gauntlet of the people scattered about on the plain, and make good his escape. He was the victor, and it was his right to carry the bird home and have it for his dinner. This was, however, a mere fiction; the man who carried off the duck made for the nearest house, followed by all the others, and there not only the duck was cooked, but a vast amount of meat to feed the whole of the players. While the dinner was in preparation, messengers would be despatched to neighbouring houses to invite the women; and on their arrival dancing would be started and kept up all night.

To the gauchos of the great plains, who took to the back of a horse from childhood, almost as spontaneously as a parasite to the animal on which it feeds, the Pato was the game of games, and in their country as much as cricket and football and golf together to the inhabitants of this island. Nor could there have been any better game for men whose existence, or whose success in life, depended so much on their horsemanship; and whose chief glory it was to be able to stick on under difficulties, and, when sticking on was impossible, to fall off gracefully and, like a cat, on their feet. To this game the people of the pampas were devoted up to a time when it came into the head of a President of the Republic to have no more of it, and with a stroke of the pen it was abolished for ever.

It would take a strong man in this country to put down any outdoor game to which the people are attached; and he was assuredly a very strong man who did away with El Pato in that land. If any other man who has occupied the position of head of the State at any time during the last ninety years had attempted such a thing, a universal shout of derision would have been the result, and wherever such an absurd decree had appeared pasted up on the walls and doors of churches, shops, and other public places, the gauchos would have been seen filling their mouths with water to squirt it over the despised paper. But this man was more than a president; he was that Rosas, called by his enemies the "Nero of America." Though by birth a member of a distinguished family, he was by predilection a gaucho, and early in life took to the semi-barbarous life of the plains. Among his fellows Rosas distinguished himself as a dare-devil, one who was not afraid to throw himself from the back of his own horse on to that of a wild horse in the midst of a flying herd into which he had charged. He had all the gaucho's native ferocity, his fierce hates and prejudices; and it was in fact his intimate knowledge of the people he lived with, his oneness in mind with them, that gave him his wonderful influence over them, and enabled him to carry out his ambitious schemes. But why, when he had succeeded in making himself all-powerful by means of their help, when he owed them so much, and the ties uniting him to them were so close, did he deprive them of their beloved pastime? The reason, which will sound almost ridiculous after what I have said of the man's character, was that he considered the game too rough. It is true that it had (for him) its advantages, since it made the men of the plains hardy, daring, resourceful fighters on horseback —the kind of men he most needed for his wars; on the other hand, it caused so much injury to the players, and resulted in so many bloody fights and fierce feuds between neighbours that he considered he lost more than he gained by it.

There were not men enough in the country for his wants; even boys of twelve and fourteen were sometimes torn from the arms of their weeping mothers to be made soldiers of; he could not afford to have full-grown strong men injuring and killing each other for their own amusement. They must, like good citizens, sacrifice their pleasure for their country's sake. And at length, when his twenty years' reign was over, when people were again free to follow their own inclinations without fear of bullet and cold steel—it was generally cold steel in those days—those who had previously played the game had had roughness enough in their lives, and now only wanted rest and ease; while the young men and youths who had not taken part in El Pato nor seen it played, had never come under its fascination, and had no wish to see it revived.

BIBLIOGRAPHY:
Books about W H Hudson

Arocena, Felipe. *William Henry Hudson: Life, Literature and Science*, tr Richard Manning. Jefferson, NC: McFarland, 2003.

Frederick, John T. *William Henry Hudson*. NY: Twayne, 1972.

Goddard, Harold. *W H Hudson: Bird-man*. NY: Dutton, 1928.

Hamilton, Robert. *W H Hudson: The Vision of Earth*. London: Dent, 1946.

Haymaker, Richard E. *From Pampas to Hedgerows and Downs: A Study of W H Hudson*. NY: Bookman Associates, 1954.

Looker, Samuel J (ed). *William Henry Hudson: A Tribute by Various Writers*. Worthing: Aldridge Brothers, 1947.

Miller, David. *W H Hudson and the Elusive Paradise*. Basingstoke and London: Macmillan, 1990.

Payne, John R. *W H Hudson: A Bibliography*. Folkestone: Dawson Brothers, 1977.

Roberts, Morley. *W H Hudson: A Portrait*. London: Eveleigh Nash, 1924.

Ronner, Amy D. *W H Hudson: The Man, the Novelist, the Naturalist*. NY: AMS Press, 1986.

Shrubsall, Denis. *W H Hudson: Writer and Naturalist*. Tisbury, Wiltshire: Compton Press, 1978.

Tomalin, Ruth. *W H Hudson*. London: H F & G Witherby, 1954.

Tomalin, Ruth. *W H Hudson: A Biography*. London: Faber, 1982.

Wilson, G F. *A Bibliography of the Writings of W H Hudson*. London: The Bookman's Journal, 1922.

Wilson, Jason. *W H Hudson: The Colonial's Revenge*. London: University of London, Institute of Latin American Studies, 1981.

Also published by ReScript Books...

The Nature of a Crime

Joseph Conrad & Ford Madox Ford

THE NATURE OF A CRIME, the third of three collaborations between Joseph Conrad and Ford Madox Ford, was originally written when the two men were living in Winchelsea, Sussex, in 1906, but not published in book form until 1924, shortly after Conrad's death.

The story takes the form of a series of love letters written by the unnamed narrator to a married woman, who is visiting Rome. In them, he states his intention to commit suicide as he anticipates being found out in a financial scandal.

This new edition includes both writers' prefaces, and Ford's description of his first collaboration with Conrad (on the novel *Romance*) as an appendix. Edited by Robert Hampson, it also includes an informative Afterword and is fully annotated.

ReScript Books, 2012, ISBN 978-1-874400-60-8, UK price £9.00

for peace, fighting for truth, fighting for our rights, and WE were vilified for it. Our governments took control of us right in front of our faces and lied every step of the way.

It got to the point where they even acknowledged what was happening because they couldn't avoid it anymore. This is when they started implementing a digital ID system that could trace every post on social media, every text message, every phone call, our locations, our jobs, our salaries, and even our bank accounts, under the guise of battling illegal immigration.

They tracked everything that opposed their agenda, and the moment they collected every piece of "incriminating evidence", they'd show up at our front door, walk in without a warrant, and give us an option. Give them our phones and accompany them to the police station, or they'd take them and us by force. The results were the same, and we'd be locked up in a prison cell for years for things they wouldn't even consider a crime ten years ago.

The Left called the Right authoritarians and dictators, yet they were the ones issuing bills that allowed courts to function without a jury, allowed criminals to decide the fates of innocent people, because they didn't align with their agenda. They used the civil liberties that we believed in and manipulated them for their benefit. They weaponised our identities, our guilt, and used them against us. Because they didn't want to give up their power, they brought in foreign invaders to steal votes to keep it.

Just like the Roman Empire. Because of greed and a lust for power, they brought in immigrants to do the work that apparently, nobody else wanted to do or weren't qualified for, pushing their citizens aside. This brought in a cycle of inflation and a lack of resources and boosted the cost of living, resulting in people like us losing everything. A managed decline. Only this time, it was disastrously different. This time, we have religious fanatics hellbent on ensuring one religion ruled this earth and were willing to do anything to achieve it.

They couldn't defeat us with a full frontal assault. Guns, bombs, missiles and terror. Doing so would most assuredly turn the world against them, and they would undoubtedly fail in their mission. This time, they invaded us under the guise of immigration and asylum, and with the help of our short-sighted governments, they became a step closer each day to total domination.

They waited until they became an overwhelming force, outnumbering anyone who could fight back.

Third-world militant warriors asserted themselves inside Western lands, strategically placing themselves inside key cities, into towns intersecting main roads, nearby police stations, military bases, hospitals, schools, and even mayoral positions and arming themselves to the teeth with guns and ammunition, makeshift explosives, and recruiting the very same people they would later eliminate once they achieved their one unified goal. Total domination.

They were patient, charming, cunning, and worst of all, they were ghosts living amongst us. They started converting easy targets, collaborators, virtue signalling inclusion and reciprocity. Then they started converting the LGBTQ+ community, defending them as if they were family. Then they started acting as if they were the heroes we were all waiting for. People we could look towards for safety, because they preached that they would fight for us against our governments. They won the people's favour slowly but surely, but those who weren't fooled knew that it was just a façade. It was all just a part of their plan.

Those with eyes that could still see saw how the invaders ran rampant in the United Kingdom. Fires were burning every night… another car bomb, another church burnt down, more innocent lives taken or imprisoned, people leaving in flocks, invaders cheering for victory. They were pushing it. They were seeing how far they could go until even the government said "enough." That was the signal. All it took was seven hours for the entire United Kingdom to fall.

It began at the stroke of midnight. It all started in the migrant hotels; they all stormed out of their rooms like an angry horde of zombies fiending for flesh. With their bare hands, they murdered every hotel employee. Blood poured throughout the hotel floors, blood spattered on the walls, and screams of despair could be heard throughout the hotel.

They didn't cheer; they stayed silent, rummaging through the kitchens and offices, grabbing all sorts of knives to cut through new victims, taking fire extinguishers to hide their cover, creating makeshift Molotov cocktails for their next assault, patiently waiting for their next move.

Every migrant hotel was strategically placed between the closest police stations, and so they all gathered nearby and prepared for a coordinated attack. Once the fire was lit, they stormed the police stations so fast that it caught many of the police officers off guard. A few shots were fired, but it didn't faze the invaders at all, because to them, death meant paradise. They quickly overwhelmed the officers before they could get the call out to the military for support. The police takeover was quick; the invaders had people on the inside to assist.

They tortured the remaining police officers in honour of their God, then they raided their armoury, taking control over every weapon they had in stock. Handguns, rifles, shotguns, sniper rifles, stun and smoke grenades, even fucking RPGs. And again, they waited until everyone was ready.

From Penzance to Kirkwall, and from Belfast to Dunquin, blood poured into the streets near every police station, and by 2 AM, a force of eight hundred thousand unarmed men turned into a force of eight hundred thousand armed combatants.

Into trucks, and whatever vehicle they could bust into, they travelled to every military base on the mainland, and stalked the perimeter outside the defensive walls, like wolves waiting to attack their next meal. But like the Trojan horse, they had people inside those bases too. The government had planned to house these invaders inside the very bases used to defend our lands, and these invaders did not waste this opportunity.

A handful of men snuck into the control rooms and eliminated the guards posted inside. Now they had access to every gate, every door, every surveillance camera, and anything that could communicate to the outside world. The wolves didn't rush in. They didn't want to risk annihilation. They waited for the ghosts inside to eliminate the threats that could oppose them, and when the gates opened, the snipers took out the guards in the watchtowers before they could sound the alarm. They crept in like shadows.

Inside every accommodation block, they stood at the doors, waiting for their troops to stand in position, and in one fell swoop, rained fire on every sleeping troop, killing them as they slept. The women who survived that ordeal weren't so lucky. Even with bullets inside their bodies, they were given no mercy. You can only imagine what they did. Hour by hour, dozens of bases fell, thousands of military personnel died. They won. They cheered. They glorified their God for their victory. Unless you were nearby, you would have been completely unaware.

Everybody woke up that morning not knowing they had been conquered. Even the monarchy wasn't safe. The invaders didn't believe in Kings. Only God. The Prince woke up to alarm bells, and as a father, he thought not of himself, but of his family. The invaders had already breached the palace walls, so he didn't have much time.

With a trusted few, he ordered that his children be taken down to a secret exit to ensure their safety. He bought them a little time to get them out, but not long enough for his children to hear his bludgeoned screams of death. The fate of the Princess is unknown.

For everyone else, it wasn't until the Prime Minister had a press conference that morning that they realised what he had done. Every politician who supported these invaders was rounded up that morning after the attack, all standing before him with guns to their heads.

The politicians who infiltrated the government, the ones he thought were his friends, turned against him as they always planned to do. Without a single word, every politician was forced to their knees, and each met with a bullet to the back of their head, ending their lives. The bullets sprayed the blood so far that it struck the Prime Minister's face, with utter shock in his eyes and urine pouring down his pants. He stood there in utter disbelief.

With the cameras still rolling, broadcasting live to every citizen in the United Kingdom, the media were forced to run the live feed. Every scream, every gunshot, and every person who dropped dead was heard and seen by anyone who was tuned in.

"This is the revolution", they said.

"We have conquered your lands. Submit to our God... or die".

By midday, the Prime Minister was naked and humiliated, paraded through the streets like a whimpering dog. Covered in trash, faeces, and whatever they could throw at him, his eyes scampered towards anyone who he thought could help him. Then the thought dawned on him. Hundreds, if not thousands, of innocent women and children were harmed or lost their lives to these invaders, and he and his administration did nothing.

He understood nobody would come to his aid. He inflicted so much fear on his people that none of them would even dare defend themselves, let alone someone else. But now, there would be no arrests. Only bullets. They knew that. The invaders knew that. He knew that.

By that afternoon, it became global news. His face and the faces of the tormented dead were plastered on the screens of every television and every cell phone in the world. World leaders are panicking, and invaders in other nations are celebrating their success. And us? Standing in fear as if the world stood still. You can't help but think how beautifully they planned it, how patient they were. But then you realised how openly they talked about their plans, almost to the point you thought,

"Yeah, as if they could do all that."

But we chose to be blind to it. And guess what? You asked for it. Even worse… we asked for it, and they happily obliged.

The rest of the world understood the severity of the situation and what was considered an inconceivable nightmare, became reality. The United States fought heavily to prevent Iran from obtaining nuclear capabilities, but they hadn't considered that the true enemy was hidden right in the midst of their former allies.

Now the invaders have their hands on two hundred and twenty-five nuclear warheads. One step in the wrong direction could mean the end of civilisation as we know it. The President had to be careful.

Deep down, the President suspected this would happen; he saw weak and corrupt leaders all around him, and what began as a plank walk turned into a tightrope. He was used to working with people who thought of themselves as master deceivers but were, in fact, open books in cheap suits. Still, he now had to deal with an unpredictable militant force emboldened by the idea that they had conquered a great nation in a single night. His enemies were within his borders and inside his own government.

There weren't many directions to go but forward. Any attempt at contacting these invaders was met with silence, but across the pond, collaborators were eliminated first as they'd served their purpose, then the LGBTQ+ community were next to go because their Allah did not allow their kind to exist, then infidels were forced to convert, and death was meted out to those who refused. The women were forced into slavery or taken as wives to the victors. It truly had become Satan's paradise.

We thought we knew oppression. We were just finding out the extent of what these invaders were truly capable of. There were fifty-seven nations where these invaders originated, and only three of these nations condemned this invasion. We could only assume the rest celebrated in secret.

CHAPTER TWO

Across The Seas

Anyone who they thought was a Christian or Jew was murdered. My mother's devastated. Her husband was beheaded right in front of her. Her daughter was brutalised, mutilated and murdered. Everything she's ever known is gone, and now all she has left is an empty shell of what was once her eldest child. Anyone who was able escaped by boat. The seas were rough on the way to France, and the cold winter weather didn't help either. We couldn't help but bundle up with strangers just to keep warm from the cold winds and sea. People you'd never expect to be sitting next to each other were trauma-bonding, sharing stories of the people they've lost.

"Hey, you," a fellow refugee said. "You're the one from that court case… your sister, right?"

As if I didn't need to be reminded. "Yeah, that's me," I said.

Everyone around me apologised for my sister's death, and I wanted to return my sympathies, but I was frozen. I looked at my mother, and all I saw was an empty look on her face with tears dripping from her eyes.

I heard somebody say, "I can't believe they would do something like this, after everything we did for them." I thought to myself, "I recognise that voice."

I looked up, and there she was.

"You," I said. "You were at that rally; you threw coffee at us if I remember correctly. You called us fascists."

You could almost see her spine crawl up her back as everyone stared at her. Before she could speak, one by one, everybody had something to say to her.

"Traitor! Why are you on this boat with us?! You wanted them! You should be with them! You're here to rat on us, aren't you?!"

She stammered, she explained herself and told us her husband was murdered by them, they took her daughter, and they were going to take her too. She almost couldn't admit to it, but she left her daughter behind.

"I didn't want to die!" she said.

It enraged the company around her. Before I knew it, the other women started attacking her.

"You're a disgrace to Britain!" they said.

One woman slapped her so hard, you could hear the impact echoing away from the boat. Then the men started to jump in.

"You think you can get away? What do you think they're doing to your daughter right now?" they asked.

She couldn't say anything.

Stricken with grief, she stood up and apologised, and before we knew it, a man kicked her overboard. Many of us were so mad at her that we didn't bother saving her. We watched as the tides drifted her away from us. She begged us to save her up to the point the waves dragged her beneath the surface.

"What do we do now?" Someone asked.

They were met with silence, assuming everyone was thinking the same thing. Were we that spiteful that we let someone die because of a difference of opinion? Or did we all turn into savages that very moment?

When Cherbourg Port was in our sights, we were so relieved to see land, but the feeling was short-lived.

Upon France hearing the news of what had happened with their neighbours across the sea, riots began to ensue, and it was clear that the French had had enough. They weren't about to let what happened in the UK happen in their motherland, too. French natives fought against anyone who looked Muslim, and the Muslims reciprocated their actions tenfold.

The French fought with fear that they would be next, after all, the French President did the same thing as our Prime Minister. Before we reached the port, we could already see people fighting against each other. One man against three others, carrying knives, bats, or a metal pipe. In the distance, a car is running over innocent civilians. You could even hear the screams from where we were. We were in disbelief.

I thought I was going crazy, but I heard chanting coming from around the corner. Muslims in force, attacking anyone they could see. Most of them had wooden planks as weapons, and some had machetes, leading the way.

"Allahu Akbar!" They yelled.

Then screams of pain began to follow. There were Frenchmen on rooftops dropping Molotov Cocktails on the lot of them, and the invaders began to scatter, scurrying to take their clothes off to put the fire out. Some dropped to the ground after a few moments, presumably to their deaths. Others began to climb the buildings like rabid apes, but they were all getting shot down. Anyone who wasn't harmed retreated elsewhere, causing the Frenchmen to celebrate.

When we stepped off the boat, we all ran in different directions. Some wanted to fend for themselves, and others preferred to stay together. My mother and I, and a few other people, decided to stick together for the time being. We ran as fast as we could, jumping over dead bodies towards anywhere that gave a semblance of safety. There was a café nearby. It looked like somebody had just closed up, so we went around the back and broke through the door. We barred it on the inside to make sure nobody else could get in. We were hungry, so the café seemed like the best bet.

The adrenaline in our bodies began to spike. My hands couldn't stop shaking. A teenager who accompanied us turned the TV on. We couldn't speak French, but it wasn't that hard to understand that France was in utter chaos.

In Paris, journalists captured bodies all over the main streets, and texts on the walls saying "les arabes rentrent chez eux".

Then it switched to an earlier recording about the French President urging his citizens to stay calm before glass bottles were thrown at him, and then, in the blink of an eye, he was shot right through the neck. Screams began to follow, and panic began to ensue. If you had a bird's point of view, it would be like ants blitzing off into different directions.

A news reporter then came onto the screen and said, "Restez chez vous, ne sortez pas, verrouillez vos portes et soyez prêts à vous défendre si necessaire," before cutting off.

We switch to other channels to find the same things happening all across Europe. German police were overwhelmed, the daughters of the Royal Family of Spain were missing, the King of Denmark was murdered, and the fates of the rest of Europe's royal families were unknown. We had every reason to be terrified. Europe was the last place you ever wanted to be, but even with all the destruction happening all around us, there was still a little hope because at least Europe was forewarned.

The invaders couldn't enact the same plan because this time, Europe was on high alert. They had no choice but to change tactics.

I started to get to know my new companions as the hours went by. Elia, seventeen, is only alive today because her brother lost his life rescuing her. Something I couldn't do for my own sister. She likes caramel slices and Pokémon plushies.

Jacob, thirty-two, woke up to his roommates screaming for help. He jumped out of his window, and he didn't turn back. He seems pretty introverted.

Adam, twenty-six, was beaten half to death until a group of Englishmen came to his rescue. They brought him to safety and haven't seen them since.

Annabeth, nineteen. She was raped and left for dead. She was already on that boat when we got there.

Sophia, twenty-nine, watched her whole family get slaughtered. She may have implied killing those involved, but she didn't really get into it.

Before I could say anything, we heard noises from outside the café. Voices. I think they heard us, and we had no idea if they were friendlies. We went into the kitchen to grab some knives, and as we came back, they had barged through the door. We all stood there like a deer in headlights. Should we attack? Should we wait? Sophia didn't hesitate. She charged right at them with a battle cry for the ages.

One of the men stepped up and drove a machete right through her stomach. The rest of the men charged at us before Sophia fell to the ground. They grabbed the nearby chairs and threw them at us. One of those seats struck me in the face. Fucking hurt.

Before I could react, a knife was embedded in my arm. I used whatever strength I had and jammed my knife into his neck. The utter shock he had on his face when I actually got him back. I struggled to pull the knife out of my arm, but I got there eventually.

Elia was throwing plates at them like frisbees, but most of them missed. My mother was using herself as a shield to protect Annabeth. She even took a stab at the leg for it. Jacob and Adam did most of the fighting and were able to kill two of them and fend off the rest before they fled.

We didn't bother sticking around; we couldn't risk them coming back in larger numbers. We felt guilty but had to leave Sophia's body behind. What could we have done with her?

It was pitch black, and we had no idea where we were going. We could hear a lot of angry voices in the distance, thus creating distance between them was our best option. We used the cover of night to get away. Maybe an hour had gone by, and we avoided streetlights as best we could to stay hidden.
"You think we're far enough?" Elia asked.

"I think so… what do we do now?" Annabeth replied.

I told them we had two options: find a place to sleep or find a car so we could get out of here. Adam suggested we get back on that boat and sail for the States. We all chuckled. Jacob said we should find a car and then head for the airport. I said that even if we make it to the airport, we don't have our passports, and we don't have money to pay for flights.

"You don't need passports, remember?" Jacob said. "We have digital ID, should be enough."

"What about the money?" I asked?

Jacob suggested we just steal it. The place had gone to shit anyway. It didn't matter at that point. Some of us were apprehensive about the idea of stealing, but considering the things we had done today, Jacob was right. It didn't really matter anymore.

"Does anyone know how to hotwire a car?" I asked the group.

My mother raised her hand, and I looked at her like I didn't know her. My mother? A criminal? We scoured the streets looking for a car that could fit all of us, and we found an SUV with shattered windows. It was an easy win for us. It didn't have much fuel, we didn't know where we were going, and our phones were dead, so we were driving aimlessly, looking for a petrol station, avoiding groups of people that could be deemed threats along the way.

It took a while, and thankfully, Elia had a good eye and spotted a petrol station far off in the distance. The only problem was that we had to drive past a lot of people on the way there. We didn't have much of a window if they decided to go after us.

"We're going to have to be quick," Adam said. "While the cars getting fuelled up, some of you head into the station and grab some supplies. Food, water, portable chargers. If they head after us, we have to be quick. There are too many of them."

The girls, along with Jacob, ran into the store and grabbed what they could, and the rest of us kept watch. Jacob jumped over the counter and broke open the cash register. It wasn't a lot, just a couple of hundred dollars, enough for us to get by. Annabeth heard a noise coming from the bathroom, suspecting somebody was inside. A Muslim woman was hiding in there with her baby. She stood in fear. Annabeth was conflicted.

The woman seemed harmless, but in Annabeth's eyes, they were all the same, her body cloaked in a dark garment, everything but her eyes covered. Annabeth did the unthinkable. She grabbed an empty canister from the shelf, stepped outside and filled it with gasoline. She walked back in, took a lighter from the counter, and walked back to the bathroom and doused the woman and her baby in gasoline. Elia yelled at her to stop.

To think Annabeth would commit such an act, she slammed the door closed and barred it from the outside and set them aflame from the other side. She didn't have to see the consequence of her actions, but to hear it was enough.

She was emotionless as the panicked screams got louder. That woman was banging on the door with all her strength. That baby's screams were hard to process.

"What have you done?" Elia asked with shock and concern.

"They all need to pay," she replied.

Annabeth's rants could be heard from outside, "They asked for this. How many of us do you think they've killed? I'm simply returning the favour."

I could hear the woman's screams from the outside, but I didn't have time to process what was happening. Elia stared at me blankly, and Jacob stared blankly at Annabeth.

"We have to go," I said. "They're coming."

Annabeth stared right through me as she went back to the car. As we drove off, I could see the smoke rising from the station. Elia told me what happened, while Annabeth stared off into the distance with anger building up inside of her. I didn't know what to feel. Would I have done the same? Not all of them were evil. Oh God... that poor baby.

The ride was silent from then on. As much as I hated them, I couldn't comprehend the idea of violence other than to defend myself, and she just did it without a second's thought. We found ourselves in Caen, where my mother pulled off on the side of the road. Jacob pulled out some cigarettes he had taken from the station. I hadn't smoked a cigarette in years, but given the circumstances, it was well deserved. Adam pulled his phone out and checked the maps, while Elia was looking for any news happening around France.

Adam said there was an airport nearby that we could go to, but I said that we may have to wait because I doubt there were any flights going out at this time of night. We were all tired, so we decided to take this time to rest and head to the airport at first light. Elia started crying because the stress got to her, and besides Annabeth, the rest of us huddled up around her to comfort her as best we could. We were all feeling the same, and I was just trying my best to keep it all together.

As everyone was heading back inside the car to keep warm, Annabeth stayed outside. She sat on the hood of the car.

'Do you want to talk about it? I asked.

She looked at me so empty,

"Did I do the right thing?" she asked me.

I didn't know what to tell her. I understood her anger. They forced me to watch what they did to my sister. Annabeth experienced it first-hand. Maybe I shouldn't have said it. I didn't want to encourage her.

"Maybe you did," I said.

Part of me thought she was brave because she stepped into the fight. I respected her for the fact that she wasn't afraid to act. But I was also disgusted by the fact that it was an innocent woman and an innocent baby whose life she took. Maybe that woman wasn't innocent, but that baby certainly *was*.

I said to her, "Just because the world's slowly gone to shit, doesn't mean we should stoop down to the same level as them. We don't know how things will end. For all we know, this could just be a dark chapter, and maybe everything will be as it was."

She went back inside the car after that. I stayed outside to keep watch.

I woke up to the morning light hitting my face. It was so quiet. Almost eerie. I banged on the hood of the car to wake everyone up. It was like waking up on a new planet. The vibe was different, like the air had changed. The boys went to relieve themselves, then we headed straight for the airport. It was surprising to see that it was packed when we got there. Cars were lined up, and guards were posted at the entrance.

Before any vehicle passed through, the guards would check for any weapons or explosives. We were nervous. Were they looking for us? It was just our anxiety talking, but once we passed through, it was just pure chaos. People would just leave their cars unattended and run straight into the airport.

Did they know something we were unaware of? There was an alert on the monitors that said they were evacuating people out of Europe. Turns out that the invaders followed through on their plans after all. They couldn't take out all the military bases, but they took enough to put up a good fight. Hundreds of people were running out to the tarmac, getting on any flight out of the country.

For us, there was a plane heading for New York. The President of the United States sent out an announcement that any refugees affected by the attacks in Europe were welcome to enter the United States. We rushed onto that plane battered and bruised. Through all that chaos, we found ourselves a moment of peace.

With a French accent, the pilot announces, "Good morning, ladies and gentlemen. As your captain, I hope you are all well, and I express my deepest sympathies for what you all are going through. Today's destination will be New York. The flight will be approximately nine hours. When we arrive, American border control will be waiting for us for security purposes. Please sit back, relax and enjoy the flight as best you can. We will be taking off shortly."

In a whirling sound of an engine roaring, the plane began to move, positioning itself at the start of the runway, ready to take off. To us, it felt like a literal warzone. Updates were broadcasting themselves on screens in front of us.

Journalists had captured men with machetes chanting in the streets, holding up decapitated heads in their hands, women gangraped in the background and children looking for their parents, a parent's face popping up on their child's phone, bottles and such thrown all over the street, bins on fire, people running scared. How the fuck did it get so bad so quickly? It had only been a few days, and yet it somehow felt like Europe was overrun with terrorists who enjoyed every moment of it. They didn't do it for their God; they did it because their holy book taught them to do so.

We considered ourselves lucky. We looked at each other with the thought that we'd made it, but now that I was given a real moment to breathe, panic began to ensue. I began hyperventilating. I felt like I was losing my mind.

It took a while, but a flight attendant crouched down beside me and took my hand.

"Just breathe," she said. "Deep breaths. That's it... There you go. I'll get you some water, okay?"

She came back with that water and some anti-anxiety meds from her bag.

"This'll help," she said.

Understandably, I gobbled those up like tictacs… could've sworn I was high. I thanked the stewardess and clocked right out. I dreamt about the old days before everything flipped upside down. Before I graduated from high school, immigration wasn't so bad, coming from an immigrant family myself. Immigrants back then entered the country the right way, with papers, clearance checks and a little patience, and if they were lucky, a job offer.

My parents moved to England for a better life. My father worked a corporate job, and my mother was a nurse. Both of them worked overtime for my sister and me to ensure we had everything we needed. We were happy.

Shortly after I graduated, the EU passed a bill for open borders, hoping that experienced people would enter the country to boost the economy. It worked for a little while until the EU was flooded with people from Africa, Pakistan and the Middle East. They obeyed the laws like every other civilised person in the country, but when they started pushing for their own laws, they began to alienate themselves, calling "Islamophobia" whenever they didn't get their way. It got worse when they started inserting themselves into government.

They prioritised their own people over the rest of the country, villainising the rest of us. Then it started with a couple of hundred people marching through the streets.

"Allahu Akbar! We await orders!"

Then it turned into thousands. They became emboldened with their numbers, and because their own people were in government, with a few collaborators, they began to commit crimes. It started with battery and assault, then breaking into homes, armed robbery, and then they started committing jihad. They started grooming children, drugging and then raping women, and then killing them if they had the chance. The UK left the EU shortly after that, but by then, it was already too late, and this is when they started coming in by boat.

Because our corrupt government wanted the votes to stay in power, they were willing to destabilise the nation to get what they wanted. Germany had the worst of it earlier on, with the number of asylum seekers entering their borders, and terrorist attacks began to skyrocket as a result. It was hard to comprehend that there were natives who were supportive of these people's actions. We called them "Antifa."

They were paid to bring chaos by wealthy billionaires, and they were protected by two-tier policing despite the violence they brought upon the innocent civilians around them. I wondered at the time if what they were doing was right. Why cover their faces? They targeted anyone who was against them, particularly those they labelled as "far right". Antifa was all over the globe. From the United States all the way down to Australia. They were a public nuisance, blocking traffic, vandalising buildings, destroying property, all for money.

In Australia, the Victorian Premier Alayna Jacqueline, the second greatest traitor Australia has ever known, second to the Prime Minister, has led her political campaign with gaslighting, virtue signalling and sociocultural suicidal empathy by allowing years of Free Palestine protests that encourage violence, hate speech, bigotry and radicalism against the right-wing and conservative people, but when the Hamas terrorist group they supported began executing Palestinian separatists on the side of peace, they fell silent.

The Left's spread of violence under the guise of transgenderism, inclusivity, and race has been greatly encouraged without the fear of persecution; however, the Right's non-violent responses were met with extreme persecution, facing jail time simply for asking, "Why do they still get to walk free even after brutally assaulting a bystander at a remigration rally?"

Because of her one-sided policies, these terror attacks happen daily, making their way from Melbourne to Sydney. Their government and their media have begun downplaying these events in hopes of de-escalating the situation; however, all it's done is keep us ill-informed.

Only after receiving an update days later would outrage amongst the people begin to ensue. Maybe forty years ago, people would have believed the government's gaslighting, but with a new generation with access to information all over the globe, lies begin to sound less believable when they can find the truth themselves. Their lies have only spread the division between the people and governments who swore to protect them.

There was a time when the invaders were marching through the streets, and an Antifa member said that they were on the same side, and you know what they said?

"No, we're not!"

That should've been enough to understand the mistake they made, but they were so short-sighted, they brought about the destruction of their homes, their culture and their way of life.

It sickened me every time I heard on the news that another child was harmed because of these people. It set me off when I found out about the grooming gangs that were running rampant all around the UK, and our own government was covering it up. And it may not be a big deal to some people, but when they started jumping Christian preachers out on the streets, and then the police arrested those Christian preachers because *they* were making Muslims uncomfortable, it made my skin crawl. These Muslims would be a nuisance to those around them by preaching about their God and praying on the streets in large numbers.

Why weren't they arrested? Why were they left alone? Why were they the ones protected? When a white man spoke about these atrocities, they'd be arrested, but a Muslim who preaches violence against their neighbours, nothing would be done about it? We used to be able to walk the streets, and we'd be safe, but now, we have to worry about people following us home. There are so many people I know who were struck because they rejected a sexual advance from these people. Why wasn't anything done about that? Why are we persecuted for speaking out?

Eight billion people are living in this world, and every single one of us has become so used to living in a world full of lies that the truth has become offensive and something to be feared. Is it so wrong to live truthfully? Even if it hurts? Or are we so comfortable living in a lie just to avoid the truth? If we had stood up together and used our voices before it was too late, maybe none of this would have happened. All this political correctness, this virtue signalling, this white guilt, this inclusivity.

It became the downfall for all of us. If we had done all of this for the right reasons, and not for power and control, maybe we'd be living in a better world.

CHAPTER THREE

Seek Refuge For Vengeance

As we were a few hours away from New York, I woke up to people yelling. Our plane had been infiltrated, assuming that they snuck on board using the chaos as cover. Was this thing going to be another 9/11? Fuck. These terrorists had knives, and they began stabbing people who were too frantic. Thankfully, they didn't have control of the plane just yet. They were still trying to pry the door open to the cockpit. We were sitting at the back of the plane, so we had a good view of everything. A terrorist was standing right beside us with a knife in his hand.

"Don't get any ideas," I said to Jacob.

Without hesitating, Jacob quietly unbuckled his seatbelt. When the terrorist was looking away, Jacob grappled him to the ground and took the knife out of his hand. One of the passengers was startled, and her scream alerted the rest on board. I could've sworn that Jacob was about to slap the shit out of her. Instead, he took that knife and pierced it right through the terrorist's skull. One of the terrorists witnessed his comrades' death.

He grabbed one of the women beside him and said, "Put the knife down, or I will kill this woman."

Coldly, Jacob replied, "It's better you kill a handful of us than kill all of us."

The terrorist hesitated, and then Jacob said to the rest of the passengers on board,

"You can all continue to sit there in fear like a bunch of pussies, or you can fight these bastards. They can't take on all of us."

Jacob jumped to the other side of the aisle and charged at the terrorist, and one of the other passengers grabbed his arm to prevent him from slashing the woman's throat. He yelled to alert the others before Jacob rammed his knife right into his open mouth. One by one, passenger by passenger, stood up and rallied behind Jacob.

Those at the head of the plane heard the commotion and used that distraction to charge at the terrorists. If they were going to die, at least they went down fighting. One by one, a terrorist fell, but not without the loss of a few passengers.

One of them pulled a gun from the back of his pants and pointed it at us. "Back up or I'll shoot!" he said.

Jacob was at peace, "Go ahead, you rag-headed bastard. You don't have enough bullets for all of us," he said and charged at him. Jacob tanked a few bullets before collapsing, but it gave some of the other passengers time to apprehend the terrorist.

I saw Jacob's body laying there, eyes still wide open, his blood leaking from his body. I suspect his irrational behaviour was because of the guilt he carried for leaving his roommates to die, and I figured this was his way to repent for his cowardice. He died a hero. The last terrorist had their arms bound by other passengers, with their gun laid right in front of them. I picked up that gun and crouched in front of him. He spat in my face.

"Go ahead", he said. "Paradise is waiting for me on the other side."

I wiped his filth off my face, and I said to him,

"You think your Allah is waiting for you? You were commanded by the devil."

I pulled the magazine out of the gun and counted the bullets inside. Four bullets, one in the chamber.

I fired one into one of his kneecaps.

"Are you afraid?" I asked him.

He screamed in agony.

"What? You thought you could just terrorise us and you wouldn't face the consequences?" I said.

He began to swear at me. He tried standing up, but I put another into his other knee. I pistol-whipped him and tore the flesh over his eyebrow. I pulled his pants off, which revealed a monstrosity. I raised his gun and pointed it at his most prized possession. He begged me not to do it. I chuckled at him before I pulled the trigger. The passengers watched in horror, just like the day these savages murdered my sister. It felt good to enact a little vengeance; no wonder Annabeth popped off. The man screamed in so much pain, I almost felt bad for him. Almost.

"Please stop," he said. "I'm sorry!"

I never felt so disgusted in that moment.

"You killed my friend, and now you're saying sorry?"

I hadn't realised, but the bullet had ruptured both his testicles. It was like a half-mutilated chicken egg that wasn't fully developed. The man was moving erratically before I put another one into his stomach.

"Please stop," he pleaded.

I looked at him, dead in the eyes and said, "I don't want to kill you just yet. I want you to suffer. It's only fair that, since you believe paradise is waiting for you on the other side, a little pain is well deserved."

I used the heel of my boot and crushed what remained of his mutilated jewels. The more I stomped on it, the louder his agonising screams became. I stopped when his dick was torn off and flattened like a wet waffle.

The passengers around me urged me to stop. They said I was going too far.

I asked them,

"What do you think was going to happen if they took control of this plane? I guarantee you, we'd all be dead."

Even as he was suffering, he laughed at what I said. It only angered me. So out of anger, I stomped on all the places where I shot him. I kept going until his blood was spattered all around him. I thought about putting a bullet into his skull, but that would have been too easy. Instead, I turned him around, forced the gun up his asshole, and gave him the last bullet.

His body stiffened up like a Christmas tree, but somehow, the guy was still alive. I took the knife from Jacobs' corpse, used it to carve the terrorists' eyes out, and left him for dead. After that, I walked up to the cockpit and told them that everything was fine. Turns out, they were watching the whole thing go down from the cabin.

While everyone else was still processing what was happening, I caught Annabeth staring at me with an almost look of gratitude, making her actions justified for what *she* had done. I calmly returned to my seat, blood still covering my hands. I stared blankly at the monitor ahead of me. I could hear the faint whispers of people talking about what I had done. I wanted to feel guilty, but I was so angry.

Images of my sister kept coming back to me in those moments. My fists clenched, fighting the tears from coming out. My mother sat beside me and pulled me close. I mirrored the moment I shared with Annabeth.

"Did I do the right thing?" I asked with the tears forcing themselves out.

"No, Sweetheart. You went too far. But you were right, they were going to kill us and probably use this plane to crash into another building, but you didn't need to kill him like that."

Accepting what I had done, my mother forced me to see the monster I was turning myself into. All I could do was apologise.

Just as we landed, armed forces stormed the plane.

"Everyone, stay seated!" They instructed.

They checked the bodies of the dead before escorting everyone off the plane. As I was exiting, I slowly walked towards Jacob. There, I said goodbye to him one last time. One of the officers spoke to the captain, assuming to debrief on what had happened. I figured they'd say something about what I did to that terrorist, but they didn't. One of the other passengers did. Rat bastard.

One of the officers then pulled me aside for questioning. "Did you do that to that man?" They asked.

"Yeah, they were planning on killing us anyway," I said sternly.

He looked at me in disbelief that someone like me could do something like that to a person.

"I have it in my right mind to arrest you for doing something like that," he said.

In my head, I was thinking to myself that this was it. I am going to spend the rest of my life in a federal prison while the rest of the world goes to shit.

"But I won't," he said. "Between you and me, you gave him what he deserved. Maybe a bit too much, but still. He deserved it."

His saying that gave me some relief.

After he let me go, Elia came running to me. "Look at this," she said.

What was happening in Europe was happening globally, especially right here in the States, where I thought we were going to be safe. The threat was greatly more evident because they had access to firearms, but hope was just as strong because *we* did, too. In Australia, Melbourne and Sydney had been battling the influx of invaders. Terrorist flags were raised around the main landmarks.

The Harbour Bridge, the Opera House, the Melbourne Skydeck, Flinders Street, The State Library, Saint Patrick's Cathedral, and the Shrine of Remembrance. Fortunately, they were still fighting strongly across the rest of Australia. Here in the States, Michigan fell, along with New York, the financial capital of the world. It was a gruesome scene; Muslims charging in numbers, more innocent people dying. Canada was on the verge of collapse, but who'd be surprised?

"We have to do something," Elia said to me.

"What the fuck are we supposed to do?" I asked her. We barely made it out of Europe alive.

"She's right," Annabeth said. "We can join a resistance group or the military. We can hunt them down and kill them all. They want a fight. Let's give them what they want. "

It was completely illegal, but we joined a militia a few days after they relocated us to a refugee centre in Fairfield, New York. We trained for weeks, learnt how to use weapons, and learnt how to fight. We learnt everything that basic trainees would learn in the military, particularly reconnaissance and guerrilla warfare, minus the discipline. Excluding my mother, we all succumbed to the violence. My mother had nursing experience, so she stayed back to tend to the wounded.

Our objective was simple, but we didn't know who we were targeting. If they looked Muslim, we'd gun them down. We'd find any Mosque and burn it to the ground along with anyone in it. Any tactic they used on us, we used on them. Blood for blood, that's how life became now, and we were okay with it because, for *our* freedom, we were willing to do anything.

There was something about embracing the darker side of human nature. I mean, before all of this, I'd run from any confrontation, but now, I'm taking lives like it's a sport. The actual police and military were already spread thin fighting against all the terrorist attacks around the country. Muslims would "peacefully" protest, chanting "Islamophobia" because they felt that they were being targeted, and not even a day after that, they'd go and drop pipe bombs at a festival. They knew how to play the victim card so well after 9/11 that they used it to their advantage.

It was such a perfect cover for them. Before all this, we were afraid to speak out against them. I was only two years old when those planes flew into those buildings, but as I grew up, the fear they instilled in all of us was enough for me to be apprehensive about all of them. They can be so kind and so charming; it was so easy to believe that they really could be the good guys, and that maybe *we* were the ones living amongst the wolves. My father told me never to trust a charming man because charming men hide the most secrets.

December celebrations were almost underway, and as we all know, these guys despised anything that wasn't Muslim. It wasn't hard to conclude that every Christian nation was on high alert. Our governments knew something that we didn't, as they urged all families to stay home at this time. As a group, we became like family, so we decided to celebrate as a family. We wanted to see the big Christmas tree they propped up at the Rockefeller Center each year, you know? Just to experience something good out of a terrible year. It was clear that a lot of people had the same idea when we arrived. I guess people wanted to believe that there was still some semblance of good left.

"It's a lot bigger than I had expected," Annabeth said as her eyes were fixed on the Christmas tree.

Adam smirked, "That's what she said," he replied.

We all couldn't help but laugh. Our joy was cut short because there were preachers nearby where we were.

"Islam is here to stay! We will not surrender!"

He was getting more aggressive by the second. His voice could be heard through all the singing and white noise from the crowd. Hundreds of people were surrounding him. I was so disgusted by the fact that some were agreeing with him. I wasn't the only one. Voices were heard opposing him.

"Fuck you and go back to your country! Terrorist scum! Raghead! Muslim dog!"

People were piling on and on, but it didn't deter him. There was something in the air. I could feel the vibes flip.

As more gathered, I figured he was going to get jumped.

"Allahu Akbar!" He yelled.

Followed by more voices chanting the same phrase. Another man yelled the same thing about twenty feet away from us, and before you knew it, explosions followed shortly after. They were suicide bombers. The explosions blew us right off our feet. Everything seemed to have slowed down, and that ringing in my ear was unbearable. As I was looking around, people were fleeing the scene, and just by the road, a man was standing there, almost as if he was admiring the scene before he walked off.

When I had the strength to stand on my feet, I went to check on everyone. Elia and Annabeth were passed out. My mother was a little concussed, but nothing she couldn't recover from. Adam was closest to the blast. Half of his face was torn off in the explosion. His eye was popping out like a bubble ready to burst.

Flashing lights of red and blue began to circle our location, and police officers quickly jumped out of their vehicles, immediately checking on the victims. Next thing I knew, gunfire and flashes of light began to pierce through in the distance. A few cops went down before the other officers retaliated. A few civilians got caught in the crossfire, too. It was another massacre.

An idea that we thought was so blatantly obvious that we refused to believe would happen. How fucking stupid were we? We ran for cover, hiding behind some cars that were nearby. More cops began to flood the area during the shootout, and then boom. When they started to circle the gunman, more terrorists showed up out of nowhere and started circling them.

Some women in burqas with suicide vests ran towards the cops. They amped themselves up with their war cries, and then they blew themselves to pieces. The National Guard started arriving from the east in their Hum-Vs and let their cannons loose. 50-cals, echoing through the streets, blowing holes right through terrorists' chests.

"We have to get out of here," I said.

There was nothing we could do here. The stench of blood was all around us; it almost made me throw up.

We ran over to St. Patrick's Cathedral, where we thought it was going to be safe, only to find it set on fire. The sound of sirens could be heard in every direction we turned.

"Grand Central Station is a few blocks down," Elia said to us, so we ran in that direction as fast as we could.

Another coordinated attack. We should have known. Gunfire, explosions, people screaming. It was all around us. We had no weapons. We were helpless.

"Run as fast as you can!" I said.

I reverted to the coward that I once was. People were being attacked all around us.

"We have to help them!" Annabeth yelled.

She ran to aid a mother who was shielding her child from an attacker. She came up from behind him and threw him over her shoulder, snapping his neck in the process.

"Find somewhere to hide," she said to the mother.

"We can't help everyone here," I said. "We need to get out of here right now."

We headed straight for the station, but not without Annabeth looking at me with disapproval. The station was flooded with people by the time we got there. Perfect for another attack. We waited for the next train, "4 minutes until arrival." It felt like hours. Every second,

I thought, "Another attack is coming, another attack is coming, another attack is coming."

When that train arrived, each carriage was packed with civilians, and again I thought to myself,

"Another attack is coming."

I was ready for it. Expect the worst, and nothing could surprise you. Thousands died that night.

We made it back home safe, if not a little rattled. Elia entered into a rant. "Why do people like this even exist? What? Their Allah permits them to murder, to steal, to rape, to marry children, to keep people as slaves, to lie for the sake of spreading the influence of Islam, but eating pork is off limits? Why the fuck are they claiming to be the religion of peace, just to stab us in the back and terrorise us?

If we had better leaders and if they had learned from our history, they would have wiped every Muslim off the map. In fourteen hundred years, their agenda hasn't changed. You'd think we'd be over this by now, but we aren't. Either every Muslim is being lied to, they're forced to be Muslim, or they're Muslim because they get to spread violence. To top it off, every voice that speaks up about this is just another excuse to add more laws to protect these bastards."

I interjected, "Not all of them are bad."

"Then why aren't they speaking up?" Elia asked.

"Because they're afraid. Muslim women are tortured simply for asking for better laws that could protect them. They've also been killed for less. One man speaks up, and their whole family dies with them", I said to her.

"Then let them die!" Elia says.

The morning after, there was an announcement on the news about the incident. This initiated a domino effect that prompted the United States, Canada and Mexico to declare war on the Muslim Brotherhood, announcing that those involved in terror attacks, or planning terror attacks, would be shot on sight. Given the severity of the terror attacks that have occurred in the past few weeks, they authorised all citizens to kill or be killed as the number of law enforcement officers had dwindled out of fear or death.

Across the continent, cities erupted in chaos. Some had embraced this new law as a way to reclaim their victory, while those who had no violent bone in their body had questioned the morality of such a law being granted to the public. This law allowed terrorists to maximise the damage they could cause. Neighbourhood watches were formed, primarily from whiter neighbourhoods, but they took advantage of this new law, not just targeting Muslims, but all races.

In the midst of this newfound lawlessness, a journalist named Mya stood at the heart of this storm. Despite being targeted and shot at, she still advocated for peace amongst the people, but her voice, even though powerful, had been drowned out by the noise of war. She ventured deep into the war-torn streets, where she began to realise that the very fabric of society had unravelled to the point of no return.

People whom she once knew as friends had begun to look at her with suspicion. Every step became a potential threat to her life. The line between right and wrong was no longer clear. As she stood on a street corner, watching a group of armed civilians gunning down an innocent family, she had to decide – fight for survival? Or stand against this violence that could one day take her life?

You think we'd had enough by then? Did we need more death to wake up?

CHAPTER FOUR

The Broken Path Forward

When we got to 2025, cities were returning to how they used to be, but to a different kind of normal. The world had shattered. Armed forces that were stationed outside of their countries were sent back home to fight the war within. Though if we had to pick a winner? They won. Unless you converted to Islam, it wasn't all that bad. So long as you followed their laws, you wouldn't be dismembered or killed. A lot of converters opted out of having kids, though, because the girls were often married off to Muslim authorities if they were deemed desirable, and the parents didn't have much choice in the matter.

Unless you were born Muslim, the ones who converted were still treated as second-rate citizens. The Christians who refused to convert but were willing to submit paid their new masters taxes for "protection", but those who refused to pay taxes altogether were mocked and crucified for everyone to see. It only drove more people away from Christianity.

Another attack happened as I slept. This one was all across the other side of the globe. Sydney, Australia. Three Muslim men gunned down a crowd of one thousand on the first day of the celebration of Hanukkah. Children died that day. What monster would line their sights up at a child and pull the trigger?

The media's footage of these savages was crystal clear. The hate in their eyes is unmistakable. There were Muslim bystanders around, yes. The gunmen didn't even bother looking at them. They attacked everyone *but* them.

Their Prime Minister, gaslighting as always, claimed that he was prioritising the safety and well-being of Australian citizens and Australian Jews, and yet let one million unvetted immigrants from the Middle East, who very well could be terrorists, into the country. Funnily enough, the ASIO had the terrorists on a watch list for 6 months. They knew the attack was coming, and now, they're deflecting blame to anyone else but themselves.

Had Australia's government not banned the right to firearms, this would not have happened. Banning firearms does not take away the evil. It only ensures compliance. Had they not banned firearms, brave Australians would have taken the fight to them and ended it, instead of relying on police officers who have forgotten the meaning of "protect and serve" and chose to hide and take cover instead of protecting those they were meant to protect. Instead, they let those terrorists rain fire on innocent civilians for twenty minutes, allowing them to suffer pain that did not belong to them.

Instead of enforcing laws that are already in place, their government are now planning on creating more laws that force compliance instead of safety. To top it off? That Under-16s social media ban they have? There were kids under 16 there. They didn't get the memo that there was a terrorist attack. There was an immediate alert a few minutes in. An alert that reached adults. Those kids were completely oblivious.

They didn't realise until the bullets flew past their heads. Banning them for safety, yeah? Didn't age well. Children got hurt, Prime Minister. What have you got to say about your policies now?

If there was a time for humanity to stand together, it would have been for this moment. Many were outraged by the terrorist attack, but more so by the government, which did nothing. Thoughts and prayers aren't enough this time, unfortunately. Now is the time for action. These terrorists don't hide their plans. They aren't smart enough to be deceitful. That's our politicians' jobs.

They are, however, smart enough to tell us the truth right to our faces, so much so that we refuse to believe it. Australia really should allow its citizens to carry firearms if they're to stand a chance. It just makes it easier for a takeover if all they have to defend themselves are cowardly police officers and military personnel who have not seen war.

My life began to spiral by the day, and my faith began to dwindle. I stopped speaking to him for help because I felt as though he wasn't responding to me. I figured, when they took my sister, I'd rebuke his name, say the holy spirit wasn't real, but in my heart, I couldn't deny his power, but when we began to live as if we were just spare mouths to feed, I asked myself if this was all that he could give us. Why not just end our suffering? Take our will to fight and be done with it?

That was the part I couldn't understand. My soul shattered like glass, only to be repaired, then destroyed once more. An excruciating cycle I prayed would end.

The Nice Attack, Muslim. The Paris Attacks, Muslim. The Shoe Bomber, Muslim. The Orlando Attack, Muslim. The Beltway Attack, Muslim. The Fort Hood Attack, Muslim. The Underwear Bomber, Muslim. The Westminster Attack, Muslim. The 2005 Bali Bombings,

Muslim. The U.S.S. Cole Bombers, Muslim. The London Bridge Attack, Muslim. The Madrid Train Bombers, Muslim. The Charlie Hebdo Attack, Muslim. The San Bernardino Attack, Muslim. The Surabaya Bombings, Muslim. The Minnesota Mall Stabbings, Muslim. The 7/7 Bombers, Muslim. The Moscow Theatre Attackers, Muslim. The Boston Marathon Bombers, Muslim. The Ankara Airport Attack, Muslim. The Manchester Arena Bombing, Muslim. The Pan-Am #103 Bombers, Muslim. The Iranian Embassy Takeover, Muslim. The Air France Hijackers, Muslim. The 2002 Bali Nightclub Attack, Muslim. The Batta Meena Attack, Muslim. The Beirut Embassy Bombers, Muslim. The Libyan U.S. Embassy Attack, Muslim. The Yazidi Massacre of 2014, Muslim. The Beheading of a French Priest, Muslim. The Buenos Aires Bombers, Muslim. The Khobar Tower Bombers, Muslim. The Beirut Marine Bombers, Muslim. The Besian School Attackers, Muslim. The First WTC Bombers, Muslim. The Beheading of Daniel Pearl, Muslim. The Achille Lauro Hijackers, Muslim. The Bombay Attackers, Muslim. The 9/11 Hijackers, Muslim. The Bondi Hanukkah Attack, Muslim. They cannot preach the religion of peace if this is what they're responsible for. If there are any good Muslims. I sincerely urge them to speak up against this violence. Otherwise, there *are* no good Muslims.

The sun didn't rise for us anymore. We lived in an eternal darkness with but a single star above our heads. Heaven, a divine place where no essence of sadness existed, had borne sorrow as it witnessed the corruption of the Lord's creation. The angels had wept for us so much that it filled the Earth with endless rain for months. God became so angered that his children were dying that the evil that plagued the Earth was plagued with their own sickness. A sickness only the Holy Spirit could extinguish. Devout Christians believed that this was all part of the Lord's plan.

For whosoever would save their life shall lose it, and whosoever will lose their life for My sake shall find it,

As the Lord says. It *was* a test. Create a force to sow fear, to take the lives of the faithful and bring them home, and to root out the pretenders and the disbelievers. I understood that God sent the Muslims to test us, and the lives they took would be saved. I think if the Muslims understood this, that they were just pawns in our true God's will, they would be offended, and maybe they'd stop.

Each day, innocent people like us were walking a thin line between speaking dangerous truths or allowing our governments' lies to rain down on us like hellfire. You. Are you one of the few brave enough to speak out? To tell the truth, others are afraid to speak? To tell the truth, others are afraid to hear? Or are you part of the problem? Hellbent on destroying your home because you've been all alone and forgotten your whole life? What difference are you here to make? To leave the world in a better place? Or to destroy it because of your petty little grievances?

Terrorism was a way to ensure compliance amongst the people. It took over twenty years, but they finally got it done. Fear was embedded in the people so deeply that it became a driving force in each of their lives. Terrorism, corruption, false flag attacks, they're all the same. The same people playing the same cards for the same agenda, without care for the consequences.

Money makes the Devils' grin grow wilder, and weaker the bones of the malnourished become. The truth is that life isn't so deceitful once you know from where these lies are born, and in a world of 8.3 billion people, only a few seem to understand. Those same few have the power to rewrite the world's destiny. They can, if they choose, lead the world in the right direction or remain silent while the world crumbles around them.

In Nepal, traditional politicians and corrupt politicians had ignored the youth for too long. Gen Z had enough of them and decided to take matters into their own hands. They attacked those politicians and made them pay for their crimes. They drove them out of their offices and out of their homes and toppled the government from within. When they were finished, they appointed new leaders who could better serve them on Discord. In Bulgaria, its citizens had accused their government of corruption for years, and through weeks of protests led by Gen Z, forced the Prime Minister and his goons to resign ahead of the government's no-confidence vote.

The citizens of Bulgaria stood together in a way most governments would fear. The greatest act of non-compliance by millions of Bulgarians. It showed us what it would look like to fight against corruption without losing a sense of humanity. Nepal showed us what it would look like once we've had enough.

It's only a matter of time; my story of what used to be a localised event is happening all around the world. Three asylum seekers broke into a young, newly engaged couple's car in Italy. They smashed through the window, pulled the young man out of the car and beat him senseless. While one man held him down, they did the same to his eighteen-year-old fiancée and raped her in turns in front of him, making him watch. Imagine yourself in his position. No matter how strong you think you are, you can feel absolutely helpless knowing there is nothing you can do to save the one you love. Now imagine being forced to feel someone else's warmth inside of you, knowing the one you love is being forced to watch and can do nothing to stop them. Now imagine many bystanders watching in horror, knowing that they can do something but choose not to out of fear, and instead wait for someone to make the first move to help you before gaining the courage to help you too. But they won't. That's compliance.

We were watching from the other side of the globe. A press conference was underway following the Bondi Beach attack.

The Prime Minister said in his speech before the questions came flooding in. "We do not believe that the perpetrators were radicalised, but we accept that this *was* a terrorist attack. The perpetrators had been on a watchlist for the past six months, but we did not have actionable intel. To prevent this from happening again, we must enforce stricter gun laws."

His words were met with swift silence followed by muttered whispers. A young, brave reporter speaks up, angry, visibly upset.

He raised his hand and asked, "Prime Minister... Why?"

"Why, what?" the Prime Minister replied.

The brave reporter took a deep breath, knowing he could be arrested for it, and said,

"For twenty-odd years, we have sent our soldiers off to terrorist born countries all over the Middle East, fighting against the ideologies that mean to destroy us, particularly those in the West. For twenty-odd years, our soldiers have died protecting the freedoms that we have now. Why, Prime Minister, why are you letting these same people that we fought into our lands unvetted? Why are you letting the same people who raise terrorist flags raise those same flags in our country, free to roam near our landmarks? Why are you letting them march united in the streets, chanting for our destruction? Why are you letting ISIS brides into our country? Why do you hate us so much that you were willing to destroy Australian values for the sake of your petty grievances? Why are you taking after

China and the UK with these harsh social media policies, targeting only what you call the far-right?"

Before the Prime Minister could reply, the young reporter said,

"Don't give me some political bullshit answer, Bono. Tell us the truth".

The Prime Minister smirked and said, "I don't know where you're getting this information from, but none of that has happened. You can't just make up some overblown scenario because of something that happened at Bondi-".

The reporter jolted out of his stance, cutting the Prime Minister off, "Something that happened?! FIFTEEN PEOPLE AND RISING ARE DEAD BECAUSE YOU SYMPATHISED WITH TERRORISTS FOR VOTES! You recognised a Palestinian state in which there wasn't one to begin with, and in doing so, you emboldened terrorist agendas within our borders. This attack happened because of you. You are the one to blame as much as those terrorists! I can bet you won't even charge the gunman who survived. You'll probably let him off with an insanity plea and sentence him to community service. You're a traitor, Bono, and you deserve to be hanged."

The reporter was dragged out of the press room as he yelled profanities at the Prime Minister, and if you watched him closely, you could see the mask slip off his face as plain as day. All of a sudden, in the following days, there was an inrush of military and police raids against potential terrorist cells that they had been monitoring. It showed the people that they could have acted far sooner, but they chose not to.

They let those innocent people die, and they let hundreds be injured. Since the day the Prime Minister was called out for his bullshit, he has been inactive on social media and avoided all appearances. In his absence, there was a petition that had over one hundred thousand signatures and climbing, calling for his resignation following the attack. I doubt he'll listen. If he did, it would be the only good thing he'd have done in his term.

Back here in the States, the Bondi Attack was the only thing people could talk about. Compared to the rest of the world, the number of people who died didn't even come close to the same numbers, but because this was the greatest tragedy that happened in Australia, it practically trumped the rest of the world's problems.

Bono was the second biggest talk of the town. The rest of the world despised him more than the Australians did. They even despised him more than the UK Prime Minister. I wonder where he's at now. The world shamed Bono like a rotten pig. Some even threatened to kill him on behalf of all Australians. No wonder why he went into hiding.

Did you know that this man spent $750,000 taxpayer dollars on a vacation while preaching about the need to lower carbon emissions, while flying on a private jet that emits two tonnes of CO2 per hour? China emits 32% of the world's CO2. Australia's about 1.3%. The hypocrisy. Did you know that this man is also solely responsible for approving visas for one million new immigrants within a single year from terrorist born nations, completely unvetted? That's a threat to national security if ever I saw one. Man, they really hate him.

Upon hearing the news about Bono, the President himself called him out for treason and said he should be held accountable for betraying his country. He even went as far as to say that if the situation in Australia escalated to the point where they couldn't manage the problem themselves, the United States would go to war with the newly grown cancerous cells in Australia itself. This would mean turning Australia into the United States newest colony.

Aussies, despite having so much love for their country, begged the President to do it. They saw him as their last hope. They weren't as brave as the Nepalese, and they weren't as united as the Bulgarians to take the country back themselves. That was the problem with Australia. They lacked decisiveness during times when it was needed most, and their government used that weakness against them.

They were conditioned to be fearful and complacent. You know, Australia has this policy: should an individual be naturalised and given citizenship, their rights to that citizenship can be revoked if said individual was a danger to society. Terrorism, treason, espionage, foreign interference. Yet, they had not considered revoking this terrorist's right to citizenship and sending him back to the dump he came from, because it was against their leftist beliefs.

Instead, they protect his rights to privacy and arrest those for simply wanting the truth. Australia was simply too slow to accept that its government were not nor ever working for the nation's best interest, instead, was only interested in lining their own pockets with cash and vacations. Fabian elitists, all of them.

Kings used to be in the front lines, rallying their knights to battle. They would kill alongside them, get injured alongside them, win alongside them or die alongside them. Instead, leaders send the people they don't care about to fight the wars they started, at the expense of their limbs or their lives, and when you're no longer of any use to them, they'll discard you for the next piece of meat they throw into the grinder.

Pushing through orders in the safest place they can be, they don't have to worry about loss of life, approval ratings or any of that, because no matter who succeeds them, the agenda is always the same. Give the people what they think they want, but then introduce the real policies that force compliance right under their noses. Maybe skim a little taxpayer dosh off the top.

I doubt we'll ever understand why our leaders do the things they do. Both Russia and China are communist nations, and their leaders are worth billions, while their people struggle to make do. The West have a proper democracy, but the corruption that our people face daily trumps communism by far. Yes, communism shares everything amongst the people equally, but the majority of the wealth and resources go to the top.

Capitalism means you get to keep your own private wealth. That's also where things get sticky. Communist leaders aren't hiding the fact that they're absorbing their nation's wealth for themselves, but capitalist leaders are hiding it in policies, government aids and non-profit organisations, skimming the cash off the top, making sure nobody notices, racking up millions of dollars a year. The worst of it? It's all taxpayer dollars. I believe the West want the same thing Russia and China have, but has no clue how to achieve it without heavy pushback.

Where was I? Oh yeah. With Adam, Jacob and Sophia gone, it was just me, Elia, Annabeth and my mother. The journey to "safety" wasn't without its moments. In an age of lawlessness, we still took lives when we had to, and only with reason. If a particular group were harassing bystanders, we'd shoot them down, and there'd be a gunfight, but nothing we couldn't handle.

When we saw people preaching hate online and sermons about taking over the West, we'd find them and burn them alive. When we heard news of women or children being raped and the perpetrators' faces were plastered all over the news, we'd find them and make them hurt. We could see why they saw the appeal. The look on their faces when we gave back what they gave to us.

I think Elia changed the most during this time. Annabeth was doing it out of righteous anger, and I was doing it purely out of vengeful rage. Elia? She enjoyed that shit. It was as if her hunger for blood couldn't ever be sated. The look on her face when she carved them up was complete euphoria to her, like she could almost taste the death on her tongue. The last guy we chased after, he was in the process of raping a woman off a side road. We were in our truck and flashed the high beams at him. He stopped what he was doing, pulled his pants up and ran off. I decided to run him over and left the weight of the truck on his legs while we tended to the woman. That bastard was screaming for help of all things.

We offered to take the woman to the hospital, but she refused.

"They aren't going to do anything about it, anyway", she said.

She fixed herself up and walked away into the distance. We went back to our truck, and we were watching the man struggling to break free. Annabeth grabbed a shovel from the truck bed and struck him with it. With zip ties and tape, we bound the man's limbs together and then hogtied him with some rope. We took him to the farm we live in now. The government provided it for us on the condition that we continued the upkeep, providing for the animals there and tending to the crops. Under the barn, there was a bunker of sorts, two levels down. We played with him down there.

We removed his clothes and put his limbs in chains, elevating him just a foot off the ground. With his arms hanging above his head, legs free to dangle and dried blood on the side of his face from where he was struck, he woke up startled with no recollection of where he was. His first sight was us staring back at him.

"That's a small penis", I said to him.

"Fuck you! Let me go! I have people, they'll come looking for me," he replied.

Annabeth laughed, "They'll find pieces of you, but they won't find you."

Elia followed up with a question, "So you raped that woman?"

The man laughed. "Any white woman is ripe for the taking! It is Allah's will! All infidels must suffer", he replied.

I rolled my eyes and picked up a machine that was beside me and placed it on the table in front of him.

"You know what this is?" I asked him. "This is a table-top sex machine. Attach anything you want that connects to the mount and go crazy."

I smiled. I looked him dead in the eyes and asked him, "Have you ever taken it up the ass?"

The man shook his chains and said, "You aren't doing shit to me!"

"Poor choice of words," I chuckled.

I put some gloves on and grabbed a dirty dildo about 13 inches long and 4 inches in diameter.

With an uncontrollable grin on my face, I attached it to the sex machine.

"I'll lube it up for ya… I'm not *that* mean," I said.

The girls grabbed some large hooks and put them around his ankles, then attached the chain to the nearby wall, giving the impression he was hanging at a 135-degree angle.

He struggled, wriggled around, but he wasn't going anywhere. He screamed for help, but nobody was going to hear him. I put a stool behind him and placed the sex machine on top to get it ready. I tried putting it in him, but it was too big. Clearly, it was his first time. I grabbed an anal spreader that was covered in old shit, roughly the same size as the dildo, but thin at the top for easier insertion, which grew wider the deeper you inserted it. I stuck the tip inside of him, and once the first part was stuck, I struck a hard hook punch into it, forcing the spreader inside him. The pain in his screams made us laugh.

"Now you know how it feels," I said.

It was barely half the dildo's length, but it was enough to cause him pain. When I pulled it out of him, blood started to leak out of the tears from his anus. I didn't care. I slid the dildo inside him and set the machine on max setting. The guy sounded like a baby walrus being run over. Despite the pain, I'm pretty sure he orgasmed. His eyes were rolling to the back of his head.

In full speed and full thrust, the guy's head was following the wave of the machine's movements, whimpering the whole way round.

"Would you like to do the honours?" I asked Elia.

She smiled and said, "I'd love to."

She grabbed a serrated knife and put it behind her back before walking towards the man. She looked him in the eyes before licking her hand and grabbing his cock. She jerked him off without breaking eye contact. Elia's extremely attractive. She could catch anyone's attention. When the man got hard, he tried to kiss her.

Why the fuck would he do that?

The sensual, erotic look Elia had on her face was wiped clean off and turned into the living embodiment of death. She took the knife she had behind her back and cut his cock off. She smiled. He was confused for a bit before the pain started to kick in. You could see the dildo pummelling him from behind so hard that you could see it bulging from his stomach. The blood from his cock was spurting out like a sprinkler, and the guy was screaming in agony, shaking around like a fish out of water. Elia's laugh was fucking menacing, man.

When the man passed out from the pain, Annabeth put the man's fingers in between some hedge shears, cutting four of his fingers off, waking him up in an instant. She did the same with his toes, one by one, until he had none left. He begged us to stop. He wanted us to let him go.

"Where did all that bravado go?" I asked.

He tried to catch his breath, but then Annabeth cut his ear off like Vincent Van Gogh. This guy was a mutilated mess, but we weren't done. I flayed him alive from the ankles up to his neck. If you do too much, they'll die from shock, you see. He was a live human anatomy doll with his muscles all out on display. Imagine it, all his skin peeled off, penetrated by a monster cock behind him, begging for us to stop.

"You're all the same," Elia said.

She grabbed a blowtorch, set it ablaze and directed the flames onto her knife until it turned red. She plunged that knife right at the centre of the man's solar plexus. The smell of his flesh burning overpowered the blood that was all over the floor. In searing pain, he yells out in agony as the red blade burns him from within.

"You all deserve the same," Elia said, before dragging the knife down to his pelvic bone.

His blood gushed all over Elia's arm. His guts fell all the way down to the floor. All he could do was stare at Elia before the life faded from his eyes. Elia took a deep breath as if inhaling the last remnants of his soul. We chopped him up into tiny little pieces and fed him to the pigs when we were done with him. Darkness took control of her eyes.

"Let's find another," Elia said.

We were anti-heroes. The terrorists called *us* terrorists. They didn't like that we were going after their own, but they were happy enough to take the blood of the innocents. We made it clear that we were never going to stop, not until they all leave or die.

CHAPTER FIVE

Let Them All Hang

We cleansed ourselves from the blood of our enemy. My mother knew what we were doing, but she said she wanted nothing to do with it, claiming that we had gone too far. I simply reminded her of how her daughter, my sister, died, that if she had it in her, she'd be doing the same thing. I didn't care that she disapproved. A lot can change in a few years.

"Feel like driving to Michigan?" Annabeth asked.

Michigan was overrun with Muslims. Their council office started naming streets after known terrorists, and when people complained, they were driven out of the state.

"What do you have in mind?" I asked.

There are about 140 mosques in Michigan alone, and Dearborn has the highest percentage of Muslims than anywhere else in the United States, other than New York.

"I'm not entirely sure, but I think they're using Dearborn as a central hub for their terrorism ops." Said Annabeth.

Sensing there was a plan, I asked her, "Where are you going with this?"

Annabeth had suggested that we scope around the mosques and see which ones were preaching hateful rhetoric against other religions and people in the West, and if they did, capture their imam and hang them from the top of the mosque in the middle of the night so they could gaze upon them in the morning.

"You're insane… Let's do it," Elia said.

We packed our bags and left the next day. The drive towards Michigan was as peaceful as you could get in this day and age. Of course, you could still hear gunshots in the distance, and Jihadi flags hung down atop bridges and main roads, but I was really hoping to see terrorists hang off them instead. We used their arrogance to our advantage when we arrived. A lot of these mosques weren't too worried about outsiders hearing about their violent escapades and jihadi schemes; they wouldn't expect us dressed in niqabs. There was one particular imam who preached,

"There is no better way to honour Allah than by killing an infidel. You can ask them to convert nicely, and if not, that's okay, you can just shoot them! Allah will permit it."

Children hear that bullshit early. No wonder.

We stuck close to that imam all the way to his home. He had a beautiful family. Three wives, seven children. We waited til nightfall. Assuming they were all asleep, we snuck in through the back. We checked every room and found the kids' bedrooms first. We slit their throats… we didn't want interruptions. We found two of the imam's wives, so we gagged them and bound their limbs together just like we did with that other guy. Then we found the imam's bedroom, sharing the bed with what I assumed was his first wife. She was a screamer that one. Annabeth shut her up real quick by swinging a mallet across her face, dropping her cold.

"What are you doing?! Who are you?!" The imam asked us.

I walked up beside him and said, "Who we are is none of your concern. I just hope you understand that it was your kind who started this war. We're just returning the favour, you see."

He tried to strike me, but I dodged it, so I pistol-whipped him, resulting in his eyebrow ripping open. He grunted in pain, but he didn't want to give up. We both struggled, but Annabeth struck him from behind before he could land a blow, knocking him out.

"Thanks," I said.

"Don't mention it," Annabeth replied.

We dumped them in the back of our truck along with their dead children. Elia went down to the basement to check for any valuables. She looks around, and the area is unfinished, with the walls not even boarded up yet. She finds a locked door right at the end and tries to pick the lock open, but she fails. She finds wood carving tools and a hammer nearby, so she uses them to pry the door open. She turns the light on, but freezes. She scatters upstairs to come get us.

"Guys!" She said.

"What is it?" I asked her.

She leads us downstairs, "Holy shit," said Annabeth.

There were twins, no older than twenty were in that room, along with another girl about seventeen. They all looked malnourished, chained to separate walls with a few blankets used as bedding and for warmth. They looked terrified. It fucking smelt like shit in there. I could only assume they were used as sex slaves for the family.

"Don't be scared, we're gonna get you all out of here, okay? We just need to take care of something first." I said.

"Please take us with you!" said the seventeen-year-old.

"We can't. There's something we need to do first, and it's better if you all aren't there to see it. We'll come back, I promise." I said to her.

"Trust us," said Elia.

We said our goodbyes and took the imam and his wives back to the mosque. We kept them all bound and tied a rope around their necks.

"Please, you don't have to do this," said the imam.

I repeated back to him what he said earlier that day,

"There is no better way to honour Allah than by killing an infidel. You can ask them to convert nicely, and if not, that's okay, you can just shoot them! Allah will permit it. That's what you said, wasn't it? You were even brandishing a handgun."

The imam had a look of defeat on his face when he concluded that there was nothing he could do. His wives even begged us to spare them.

"No witnesses," I said.

We ripped their clothes off, leaving them bare naked. We hung them up one by one on each of the flag poles stuck on the walls. It was funny watching them wriggle around like that. We dumped their children beneath them and waited until they were all dead. Just in case, Elia stabbed them all in the heart for good measure. Afterwards, we drove back to their home to free the girls they had locked up. When we got there, I told everyone to look around for the imam's keys; Elia found em by his bedside drawer. I was already with the girls when Elia ran back down.

"What are your names?" I asked them.

"Nasreen"

"Catherine"

"Isabelle"

"Well, it's nice to meet you all even under these circumstances. This is Annabeth, the girl who's out of breath, is Elia, and I'm-".

Isabelle cuts me off, "I know who you are. Your court case was all over the internet."

"Yeah, okay, well there you go. Look, Elia's got the keys to get you all out of here. Do you all have family you can go home to? Did you have a number you can call?"

Ever since Michigan turned to shit, teenagers and young girls were torn from their families. These girls were no different. Isabelle only had her father, and when she was taken in broad daylight, her father tried to fight off her abductors but was shot in the chest and left for dead. Nasreen and Catherine were from a slave trade led by Muslim women. They had nobody.

"Maybe we should just take them with us," Elia suggested.

"If that's something you want?" I asked them.

They all nodded in agreement. I suggested to Isabelle that if she wanted to, we could take her home to grab some of her things, documents and whatnot, just to make life easier for her in the future. We took her home to a small two-bedroom house. When we got the door open, we were met with a stench of a decaying dog in the bathroom. It was her pet, Siggy. I didn't bother asking, but I figured Isabelle was held captive for a while. I instructed the girls to take a shower and for Isabelle to grab her things.

"Looks like we aren't staying here. We can't keep doing this if we have to watch over them." I said.

"Yeah, you're right," said Annabeth.

"They can do what we do," Elia suggested.

"Let's just get to know them first. They've been through enough as it is. We'll take 'em back home, and we'll go from there." I said.

"Fine," Elia replied.

After a little while, the girls started to come out. Nasreen and Catherine came out covered in towels.

"Do you have clean clothes?" Catherine asked.

Isabelle comes from out of the corner, hair wet, but really wavy, dressed up in sweatpants and a sweater. "Here," she said.

She handed the girls some of her old clothes, and they separated into different rooms to get changed.

"What do we do now?" Isabelle asked.

I told Isabelle that we were living in New York, and that we were here for… work. I caught her up on how we all met each other and how we came to the United States. I also told her that there were more of us, but they died along the way.

"Are you fighting them?" Isabelle asked.

"Yes," We replied.

"I want in."

Elia looked at me as if she were saying, "I told you so."

Isabelle's story sounded like a nightmare. She was raped orally, vaginally, and anally, not just by the imam, but his sons as well, for well over a year. Out of jealousy, the imam's wives withheld food and sanitary products from her, forcing her to use the blankets she slept on for her menstrual cycles. The imam said she would have better living conditions if she just converted to Islam and married him, but she refused, only angering the imam. Isabelle was a Christian, and she understood the meaning of Islam. She would never submit.

The twins came a few months into Isabelle's captivity. The imam wouldn't touch them, but his sons were allowed full access. I guess he liked the younger one. They were grooming those girls to do as they wished. They were forced to perform oral and vaginal sex together and were rewarded with full meals by the imam's wives, but the wives ensured to stay in the room until the twins finished all their food to make sure they wouldn't share any with Isabelle.

To bathe the girls, the imam's wives would wash them with buckets. One bucket filled with soap, and another with plain water. They'd come back in intervals, throwing it at them, soaking the walls and floor around them. They often got sick because of it, because they'd never dry them off. They didn't bother washing Isabelle, so she'd wait until they left, and she'd use the water on the floor to wipe herself down and drink from.

Isabelle tried to escape a few times, but she'd always be beaten half to death for it, then she'd be gangraped by all the men. Worst of all, the twins had to watch it all unfold. No matter how hurt she'd get, she would always find the strength to comfort the girls. She'd just about had it when we came along.

Even though the girls were stripped of their identity, they couldn't be more grateful that we found them. It made me wonder if God sent us to them. Yes, we did horrible things, but we were always fighting for our God and his children as much as they were fighting for theirs.

As we were ready to leave, I told the girls that we'd be driving home. I said we'd drop them off at home and have them get situated. Isabelle then asked us if we were driving back to Michigan afterwards, but we weren't entirely sure. It might get a little too hot, considering what we left behind.

We stopped a little over halfway at a roadside diner. I figured they were hungry, so I told them to order whatever they wanted. Isabelle ordered two large burritos with pulled pork, a side of fries and a large drink. The twins ordered two heavy-loaded cheeseburger meals. Annabeth and Elia ordered turkey club sandwiches, and I ordered myself a smoothie. The girls were crying as they ate. They tasted freedom with each bite.

"How much longer do we have to be on the road?" Isabelle asked.

"Just a couple more hours," I replied.

She asked if we could just hang out around the diner for a bit. None of us had any objections. Given her circumstances, she probably never got to stare at the moon for over a year, let alone smell the fresh air. But yeah, the lady at the diner gave us the meal free of charge, which was quite nice of her. The group hung around outside while I went to the convenience store next door. I bought myself a pack of cigarettes and a couple of sodas for the girlies. I came back outside, and Isabelle was lying on the hood of the truck just staring at the moon.

I passed the sodas around, and Annabeth went atop the hood of the truck to join Isabelle. I couldn't hear what they were talking about, but I can assume they were venting their feelings, while the twins slept in the car. I headed towards the main road.
Elia decided to join me.

We sat down on the side of the road, watching the few cars go by. I ripped off the plastic from the cigarette pack and tore off the paper that was inside. I flipped the pack around and tapped it against my palm, and when I opened the pack again, I took out a cigarette and flipped it around. I took another out and gave it to Elia, and then I took one out for myself. Then I lit our cigarettes with the Zippo I had in my pocket.

"Why do you do all that?" Elia asked curiously.

"Do what?" I replied.

"You know, the whole tappy flippy cigarette thing," Elia replied with one too many hand gestures.

I chuckled, "Oh! It's like a ritual. Turn the pack around and pack the tobacco in, grab a ciggy and flip it around as the last drag. The last cigarette is supposed to be good luck." I said.

"You believe in luck?" Elia asked.

"No, not really. I believe everything happens for a reason, and that good things take time. This whole ritual thing is just something I used to do." I said nostalgically.

Elia rested her head on my shoulder and told me she was reminiscent of the old days, before things started to change. As was I. There was something in that moment with her that felt so calming. As if the world was burning all around us, and we'd just accepted that we were good as long as we had each other. I don't know what this is, but I definitely didn't want to lose it.

"You think we'll win?" Elia asked.

I said to her, "There are two billion Muslims around the world, and five million of them live here in the States, but for some reason, they're dominating us right now. I think we *can* win, but not if it's just a handful of groups like us fighting back. We have to rally the people, but a lot of them are leftists, and they'd rather watch this country burn."

"They're *that* retarded, aren't they?" Elia asked.

Both of us laughed at the world's stupidity, wondering how they could let something like this get so far. I criticised the world leaders and said the world would be a better place if we had younger leaders who understood the world's capacity for change, and if we had leaders who were willing to make the hard decisions, then I'd be almost certain that none of this would have happened. Out of all the Muslim nations, none have any Christian churches built, or have had them burned down. But here, and the rest of the world, they're free to build mosques all over the place, playing a call to prayer five times a day without the consent of the city councils.

Elia said that world governments had no compunctions or regard for any of their citizens, which reminded me of something. I once heard someone say something interesting. I told her;

"As long as the government survives, humanity survives."

This implied that our lives were inconsequential to them. It didn't matter to them that we could lose our lives because of the mess they made, because out of eight billion, we're just one life … we could easily be replaced. These people always talk about fixing a problem, but to them, it's just a matter of optics. Make it look like something that needs attention, then do a bait-and-switch. Say what you need to say to win, then do the complete opposite once you have what you wanted. Tell everyone they're safe while a neighbour is being slaughtered. Just lie. Never admit you're wrong. Lie for the performance. Hide from the results.

Our world had stepped into a dystopian reality. Countries all over the world had announced cancellations of Christmas celebrations for "security concerns," but avoided addressing the security concerns directly. This is what I mean when they use a Band-Aid for a bullet wound or electrical tape for a pipe leak; temporary solutions don't fix the underlying issue. It only builds up like a pressure cooker until something drastic happens and pops the lid. People die.

What terrifies me the absolute most is a dream that comes to fruition. I have these déjà vu dreams that come true when I least expect them. I used to shrug it off when I was a kid, but when I started seeing parts of a new chapter in my life, I started to keep track of them. There was one dream where it looked like I was in the Holocaust, but Muslims holding machetes and AK47s, standing on or around pick-up trucks, were the ones in charge, and it wasn't just Jews that were rounded up, but Germans, and French, people with crucifixes around their necks, and those who did not look like one of them. A boy ran away from the crowd, and he was shot down, picked up and then thrown into the nearest garbage can like litter on the street.

The crowd screamed, but one Muslim let his rifle loose and told them, "Shut the fuck up, or you're next!"

Women were holding back tears, children were hiding behind anyone they could, and men were containing their anger. One man couldn't stop staring at the Muslim who shot that boy down, so that Muslim walked up to him and killed him too at point-blank range. I was just floating, watching all of it unfold.

I had no idea what it meant at the time, but dreams are magical things. Sometimes they can show us the future or tell us an answer to a question you were searching for from the past. Then it hit me when they started marching in the streets of Britain. When they started killing people on live television, when they started raping women and children in the middle of the street. It was horrible.

What gave me hope was the dreams that came after. I was living in a place I didn't recognise, and I was heading to church. The drive there felt peaceful, despite the skeletons all over the side of the road. Parking my car, I greet some other churchgoers and a few friends. They're all covered in blood, but they were happy. In fact, they've never been happier to be where they are right now.

As I walked closer to the building, I could see my reflection. I'm wearing mostly white, but my skin and parts of my clothes were stained with blood. I give a close friend of mine a big hug, and we walk inside the church together. As we sit down, the roof above us disappears, and sunlight falls on us. I look at my best friend, and they're crying tears of joy. Then they faded away, along with everyone else in that church. Then I faded away. Next thing I knew, everything around me was white with tints of blue. I don't know what that meant, but I don't think I'll be around long if that dream comes to pass.

I never wanted to hate them, these Muslims. Hate is too strong a word… But I do. I hate them… Or at least my mind does. My heart feels otherwise. It's just… they kept hurting us, and we didn't do anything to deserve it. Only that we believed in different Gods, or maybe we believed in the same God, but their prophet twisted his beliefs and made a new God that was pure evil to hide his sin and make them holy. I know my God isn't evil. But I also hope they aren't the same. Their prophet disgusts me. Marries a 9-year-old, has multiple wives, owned sex slaves, tortured and robbed his enemies, initiated eighty wars in his lifetime, marked his actions as guided by divine law, and his believers claimed he was the perfect model of ideal conduct.

In Pakistan, girls like Isabelle, Nasreen and Catherine are abducted, either because they refused to convert to Islam, they were bought and paid for by those in power, or they were desired and sought out for marriage. Islam rules the system in places like Pakistan, whether it was the streets, the schools, the courts or even the police, but most definitely the military. What Islamic Pakistanis do to Muslim girls is beyond horrific. They're abducted in the name of Islam, forced to convert, forced into marriages with their abductors, or terrorised into silence by Islamist mobs.

To the rest of the world, it's considered corruption, but under Islam, this is what it looks like, functioning exactly as designed in an Islamic state. This is a recognisable pattern that has been documented for decades, and nobody did anything to prevent it from spreading. Girls are kidnapped, raped, converted and married off, and the perpetrators, more often than not, Muslim men, are protected by their system. That is what Pakistan represents, and it's happening all over the globe now. The left treats it as honour, but from what we've seen, and what those girls went through, it's hell on earth, and nothing more.

"How do you know so much of this?" Elia asked me.

"Because after what they did to my sister, I refused to be blind to it," I said.

Annabeth walked up to us and suggested that we get going. Elia stopped me in my tracks and said,

"I know I haven't said this to you yet, but I'm sorry about what happened to your sister," and she hugged me.

It was at that point that I began to see Elia in a different kind of light.

CHAPTER SIX

New Blood

We made it back home around midday, and *I* am exhausted. The farm was quieter than usual. I walked into the house to greet my mother, but my greetings were met with silence. I searched all over the house to find it empty, but Annabeth found a note from my mother in the kitchen.

"It's from your mother," Annabeth said as she handed me the letter.

"Sweetheart, I want you to know that I love you so much, but the road you're taking, and the person you're becoming, isn't the child I want to remember. Amara wouldn't want to see you like this, and you know it. I know you want to fight them, and I completely understand your reasons why, but to torture them is where I assume you'd draw the line. You and the girls have tortured dozens, Sweetheart, but you've killed hundreds. I have watched you turn into the same monsters who brutalised and murdered your sister, and I cannot and will not watch you take another step from where you cannot return. I'll be taking time for myself, and I don't know when I'll be coming back, if I even choose to return. I don't want you looking for me. Take care of the girls. Take care of yourself. Take your vengeance, but don't lose yourself in the process.

I love you, Sweetheart. — Mom."

"Well, that's unfortunate. My mother left," I said to everyone.

"Are you okay?" Elia asked.

"Yeah," I replied.

Before I could say anything else, Isabelle turned the TV on, and what was broadcast was the bodies we left outside the mosque. Isabelle looked right at us and pointed at the TV.

"This you?" she asked.

I raised my hands, shrugged my shoulders and said, "Who knows. Could've been anyone."

One of the mosque goers said that this attack was unwarranted and that they did nothing wrong. That this attack was purely driven by Islamophobia, blah blah blah. Isabelle scoffed at the Muslim and cursed at the TV. Then the next scene depicted a large crowd of Muslims chanting for vengeance, calling for the killers' heads; *our* heads. Annabeth laughed and suggested that we go back to Michigan just to fuck with them.

Surprisingly, Elia was the cautious one, warning us not to push our luck. I told 'em to think on it for a few days before making any quick decisions. In the meantime, I showed our new arrivals to their rooms and gave them a tour of the place. After which, I had them assist me in tending to the farm animals and crops.

"So, the government just gave you this place?" Isabelle asked.

"Yeah, as long as we took care of the place, the animals and the crops," I replied.
"Do you have to give them the produce?" She asked.

"No, as long as we took care of the place and the animals, we were free to live here. They gave us this home to live in, since we came here as refugees, but with those caveats. We sell the produce to pay for the bills, but that's about it. Since we're technically farmers now, we help feed our community with the other farmers." I replied.

"Sounds like a good deal," She said.

It *was* a good deal. Not only did we have a place to stay with our own produce, but it also saved us a lot of money. Not to mention how secluded this place is, with no other farm for miles. Isabelle was helping me shovel up the pig shit. She noticed a bit of flesh that hadn't properly been digested, and she froze.

"You guys kill people, don't you?" She asked.

I hesitated… I wasn't sure whether or not to confirm her suspicions. She'd only speculated thus far, but it hadn't yet been confirmed. "Would it make you uncomfortable if I said yes?" I replied.

"Just Muslims?" she asked.

"If they've been bad. Yes," I replied hesitantly.

"Their kind abused me for more than a year. I figured y'all were just exacting the same pain they give to others, but I didn't think you'd be killing any of them… But you swear you're only targeting Muslims, right?" She replied.

I said to her, "They're either a Muslim who refrains from violence but supports other Muslims enacting it, or they're a Muslim because they love spreading violence under the guise of religion. Their goal will always be to spread Islam, either by ballot or by bullet, and that will never change because they radicalise their children with these violent ideologies, so we must kill them all to prevent them from spreading. They're like a cancer. You can't just cut a piece out and hope the rest will disappear on its own. You must cut it all out to stop its spread completely."

She slowly nodded her head, contemplating my answer.

"Ok, well, like I said earlier. I want in," she said.

"When an opportunity presents itself, you may join us. Just don't force yourself if you don't have the stomach for it," I replied.

Hmm… something's off with this one. This one's a different kind of broken. She seemed uncomfortable when she knew we were killing people, but then she says she wants to be a part of it? Looks like I've got to test where her allegiances lie.

Elia's gotten a bit restless since coming home, as her bloodlust hadn't been properly sated. Of course, we were meant to be in Michigan for at least a few days and didn't get the kill count we wanted. She checked the internet for new terror attacks in the area but became frustrated when she came up short. On a whim, she decided to go for a drive to cool off to Syracuse. The cravings Elia felt for wanting to take a Muslims life were the same craving a person has when they want a cigarette. She just couldn't help herself.

You're probably wondering how someone like her switched up like this so quickly in just a few years. Remember when I told you earlier that she was only alive because her brother lost his life saving her? Well, her parents died when she was 13, and her brothers been taking care of her ever since. When the Muslims started attacking everybody after their takeover, Elia and her brother were at the farmers' market shopping for produce.

She said she could hear a stampede coming from the west, then screaming started following shortly after. Her brother grabbed her arm and took her back to the car, but it was in the direction of the horde. When they could glimpse the corner, people were getting stabbed and bottled and impaled right in their line of sight.

Elia had never felt more terrified than in that moment, you see. Her brother had to yank her arm to keep moving. Anyways, she was so fixed on her brother leading her that she hadn't realised someone was trailing right behind them. She was struck in the back with a machete, slicing open a large portion.

When she dropped to the ground, her brother saw the blood dripping from her back, locked eyes with the bastard and went to work. He was able to land a few blows before being struck in the leg with that same machete. Her brother snatched it from the bastard and used it to lunge it into his stomach. The realisation of killing a man hit him instantly. Courage turned to panic; he picked Elia up and carried her out of there.

They weren't able to get so far because the wound in his leg was making it difficult for him to move. A group of Muslims spotted them struggling to get away and went after them immediately. They both made it so close to their car before they were caught again.

"Can you move?" Elia's brother asked.

"Yeah, but my back," Elia replied.

"I know. Here, take the keys, lock yourself in the car. If I don't come back to you, just drive, okay? Elia's brother said.

"What? You're insane, I'm not leaving you." Elia replied.

"For once, just do what I tell you to do. Mum and Dad will kill me if I let something happen to you. Love ya, kiddo." He said.

Elia's brother had just enough time to get her in the driver's seat and lock the doors before he was thrown onto the ground. They started kicking him first, stomping on his ribs and his skull, while other Muslims tried to pry the car door open. Then they started using weapons, striking Elia's brother over and over again.

"GO!" He kept saying.

Elia kept screaming at them to stop, but they just kept laughing at her. It wasn't until one of them broke through the passenger side window that she decided to take off. In her rear-view mirror, she could see her brother being stabbed to death. She screamed, and out of rage, she turned that car around and began running them over, with blood splattered all over the car, and the dents their bodies left behind from the impact.

By the time she got out and checked on her brother, he was already lifeless, lying in a pool of his own blood.

With all her might, she carried him onto the rear seat and took them both to the hospital. The doctors stitched her up, but there was nothing that could be done about her brother. She checked herself out, and then we met on that boat.

As we all got to know each other, I realised with all the missions and everything, that she always felt like she wasn't doing enough. During our learning phase, she always needed a little more help than the others, but things happen, you know? We're a team, and that's what we do, but I think she was living with a survivor's guilt that she was finding trouble getting over, so she's using this violence to get over it, because every time she felt helpless, we were just reminding her of what happened that day, so now she's overcompensating for it.

Now she's one of those crazy psycho girls you see on those Korean dramas.

While in Syracuse, Elia parked the truck by Onondaga Lake and sat by the pier like a siren. She'd talk to anyone who walked by. Just an innocent little girl enjoying the lake by herself; of course, it would make her a target. Lo and behold, Abdul walks by and says hello, and Elia's happy, cause she's about to get what she's been looking for.

"Hey Mr – pretty view isn't it?" She asks.

"It is a lovely view. What are you doing here all by yourself, little one? You know it's not safe in such a time as this." He replied.

"Oh, I can take care of myself, Mr – unless you want to take care of me?" she asks.

This Abdul sits down next to her and puts his arm around her, resting his hand on her waist and says, "I can take care of you. Come closer, darling, let me keep you warm." Then he starts getting handsy with Elia, but she isn't stopping him. If anything, she's encouraging it.

"Getting a little handsy there, don't you think?" She asks.

"Not at all. I think it's warming you up, don't you think?" He asks.

Elia chuckles at him, and she says, "Hmm, do you want to hang out at my place? It's not too far from here."

Of course, Abdul agrees. They both stand up and head back to the truck, and Abdul's got his arm around her, sniffing her hair like a fucking creep. When they get in the truck, Abdul buckles himself in.

"How long is the drive?" He asked.

"About 30 minutes, maybe? Is that okay?" Elia replied.

"Yeah. That's okay," He said.

As they get going, Abdul's inching closer to Elia, tracing his hand closer and closer to her pussy. He touches it lightly, getting a feel for how far he can go. You'd think Elia would stop him, but no, she encourages it some more and spreads her legs.

"Is that it?" She asks.

Abdul smiles and unbuttons her shorts and pulls the zipper down, revealing a hint of Elia's laced panties. He slips his hand down and starts rubbing it, and Elia's getting into it. She wants him to believe she's enjoying it. Besides, she'll only have to endure for a little while, and she's gonna take her time with him, and the thought of *that* turns her on. When he pulls his hand out, he tastes his fingers.

"mmm you taste good, little one." He says.

"You like it, Daddy?" She replies cheekily.

Abdul chuckles, "Yes, Daddy likes it very much."

Abdul lubricates his middle and ring fingers with his saliva and puts them back down her shorts, slipping between her panties and finally feeling the soft flesh beneath. She's a little wet, and he likes that. When he slips his fingers inside of her, she moans a little bit, gasping the pleasurable air.

"How old are you, little one?" He asked?

With a sound of enjoyment, grinding against his fingers, lies about her age, "I'm 16," she replied.

"I like them young." He said.

"Why else would you be here if you didn't?" Elia replied.

When Abdul pushed his fingers in deeper, Elia groaned a little bit. It was at this point that he took his hand out again and pulled *his* pants down, pulling out a thick little stubby. Elia tried not to laugh, reached for his cock, and began to stroke it lightly.

"How bad do you want to put it inside me?" She asked.

"Pull over right now, and I'll show you." He replied.

"We're almost home. You can fuck me as hard as you want when we get there, I promise. In the meantime, tell me about yourself. I don't want you to cum just yet." She said.

Abdul shared a little about himself, while Elia asked probing questions. She wanted to make sure that she had the right target. She asked if he was Muslim, since he said he was from Turkey, and he asked if it was a problem.

"Not at all, I think this whole war is pointless. Might as well have fun, no?" She said.

The two went back and forth, feeling each other up. It got to the point where Elia was dripping in her own nectar. When they got back home, Elia parked near the barn and walked towards the entry to the levels beneath.

"You trust me?" She asks while she strokes his cock.

Abdul nods his head, and Elia removes her shirt, revealing her half-naked body. Nipples hard, Abdul leans over to taste them. Elia pushes him away lightly and ties her shirt around his head, covering his eyes.

"Come with me," she says.

Getting downstairs, Elia pushes Abdul against the wall and starts kissing him. Distracted long enough, and she manages to bind his hand with some cuffs. This startles Abdul, prompting him to take Elia's shirt off his face, but she stops him.

"Don't you trust me? It's my turn," as she drops down to suck his cock, prompting Abdul to lower his arm, giving Elia the chance to bind that hand too.

Now, Abdul's stuck right where she wants him.

"You're fucking disgusting, you know that? Filthy," Elia said.

Abdul was confused as he should be. The cuffs Abdul was bound to were connected to a pulley system that would raise whoever was connected above the ground.

"This is gonna hurt a little bit," Elia said before activating the pulley system, raising him from the ground about two feet, just about levelling his cock with her face.

"I have some bad news for you… You're not here to fuck me. You're here to die."

"Why are you doing this?" He asks.

"Because I want to." She replied.

Elia excuses herself from him and calls us to come down. What a beautiful sight it was to see a Muslim paedophile chained up in our little torture grounds.

"He must be scared out of his mind," I said.

"Go get Isabelle, would you? Elia suggested.

Elia and Annabeth were taking swings at him as I was going back upstairs. I went into the house and grabbed Isabelle. The twins wanted to come too. I hadn't realised, but they had a greater propensity for violence than any of us.

"You wanted in? That's what you said, right? What you're about to see is beyond illegal, and there's no turning back once you head downstairs. You can kiss the idea of human rights goodbye." I said to her.

Once I opened the entrance downstairs, you could hear Abduls groans echoing through the halls. Isabelle looked at me like "you're kidding". Honestly, I didn't want to tell her, but if she changed her mind, she was a dead woman. I wasn't about to let her ruin a good thing just because she backed out. Isabelle walked in first and saw the girls letting him have it. They were swinging crowbars against his legs as hard as they could. The lower they got towards his shins, the sharper his screams became.

When Annabeth spotted Isabelle, she gave her the crowbar. "Go ahead," she said.

"Who is he?" Isabelle asked.

"A Muslim who wanted to fuck a 16-year-old. This guy looks like he's around 40." Elia replied.

"Elia?" I asked.

"Yeah?" she replied.

"I should have asked this earlier, but why are you half naked?" I asked hesitantly.

"Oh, right… Sorry," she said before putting her shirt back on. "You just gonna stand there? Or you gonna do something with that?" Elia asked Isabelle.

She hesitated because she's never hurt anyone before. I grabbed both her hands, and I told her to hold on tight to it and swing.

"You can't take your revenge on the people who hurt you because they're dead, but there are people out there just like them, like this one right here," I said.

She thought about it. She really had to dig up the pain she buried to feel the rage again. Images of the imam and his sons began to flash inside her mind. She could feel their warmth again, and when she popped her top, she let out a roar, swinging the crowbar towards Abdul's rib, slicing it open with the sharp tip.

The twins and I sat back for the beginning; We just wanted to watch. I watched Annbeth burn the soles of Abdul's feet, and when he kicked her in the face, she punched him in the balls so hard that he pissed himself. I watched Elia pull the fingernails off Abdul's fingers with some pliers, and I saw his blood dripping off his fingers like melted ice cream. I watched Isabelle batter the limbs of Abdul so hard I could hear his bones crack under the impact.

"You wanna give him the best seller?" Elia asked me.

"That's it? Are you done with him? I asked.

"I'm tired," Elia replied.

As I was carving him up, over the top of Abdul's screams, I told Isabelle,

"This is our secret, and you're a part of it now. Everyone has suffered some kind of pain because of these Muslim ideologies. We all lost someone; they've all done things to us. They believe that the more terror they spread, the more people they force into submission, the more they'll be rewarded in their heaven. And if they die a martyr, then they will be rewarded greatly. So, this is us making sure they receive

every single blessing they can get before they ascend, because God only knows how much pain *they* have caused in honour of their God."
Annabeth added on,

"It is their mission to spread Islam to every corner of the globe. We want to give them a reason not to. We want to disrupt their plans so much that they'll give up. We want them to be afraid of us. If they want to live like savages, then they can do so in their own lands, not here. We want them to experience Vlad the Impaler, part two."

Elia added on,

"I just wanna kill 'em all."

We all looked at Elia, "Yeah, that too." I said.

"Then who's killing this one?" Isabelle asked.

"You," I said.

Annabeth gave Isabelle a knife. She slowly walks towards Abdul, "Please don't," he pleads. They stare directly into each other's eyes. Fear in Abduls', hesitation in Isabelle's.

"I don't think I can do this," she says.

"Then don't," Elia says before snatching the knife from Isabelle's hand and slashing Abdul's throat, spraying his blood all over Isabelle's face. Before Isabelle could speak, Elia sternly reminded Isabelle that she *did* beat Abdul senseless with a crowbar.

"You know, Elia, she's never actually killed anyone before," I said to her.

Isabelle kept her eyes locked on Abdul's face as the life slipped away from him, body twitching as if he believed he could still escape. The blood dripped down his body like a streaming river, covering the hairs on his body like a flood.

She stood like a statue in a state of shock. "Isabelle," I said.

She looked towards me with fear in her eyes. "Breathe," I said.

She began to hyperventilate at the smell of blood that she was drenched with, "Maybe she's not cut out for this," Annabeth said.

I told everybody that it was fine, that she would come around. Of course, if she hadn't, we'd have had to get rid of her, but to save you the guessing, she's still around, though we had to… find a way to force the killer out of her. She suffered for more than a year because of her captors, but we had to show her that they were all the same. She had to experience it again, firsthand from someone else.

Elia, Isabelle and I took a trip to the city a couple of days later to buy some clothes and whatnot for the girls, while Annabeth stayed with the twins at home. We purposely walked through Brooklyn, around Flatbush and Midwood, which is predominantly a Muslim-majority area.

We received a lot of stares, as was expected. Before their "revolution," they wouldn't attack so boldly, but now that the truth was out, they had no reason to hide it anymore. A couple of guys followed us around for a while until they had us cornered, and when they surrounded us, they took us to some "Peace Community Centre." Elia and I were pretty calm, but Isabelle was freaking out.

They pushed us inside, locked the doors and took us to a backroom. Elia and I feigned weakness so that they'd pin us down first. I assumed they'd go after Isabelle first since she was the youngest. They had me in a headlock while Elia was pinned to the ground.

Elia and I agreed that if we were to be taken by somebody, then we should let them do whatever they wanted to Isabelle. At least long enough for her to put up a fight and then realise it was pointless. Only then would we intervene. We let them rip her clothes, we let them caress our bodies, we let them rape her. Isabelle fought for a few minutes after that, then she went limp like the weight of the world was crushing down on her.

That's when I pulled the push dagger that I had hidden out of my back pocket and plunged it through the groin of the man holding me down. When he let go of me, I quickly spun around and slit his throat. Then I killed the man pinning Elia down. When Elia stood up, she pulled a hairpin knife from the bun of her hair and lunged at the man holding down Isabelle's legs, puncturing his eye. I stabbed the man holding one of Isabelle's arms down through the neck, bleeding out instantly. Elia killed the other man, holding down Isabelle's other arm, leaving alive the man who was still inside of her. I kicked him in the face, knocking him out of her.

He tried escaping, but I tripped him over before he could run out the door. I plunged my push dagger through the base of his spine, paralysing him instantly.

Isabelle rushed to put her clothes back on, eyes still red from the tears, and hair messed up all over, "You… you raped me," Isabelle said to him.

Elia said bluntly. "Not gonna lie, I'm kinda glad they only got to one of us."

I replied plainly. "Dude."

With her adrenaline spiking, Isabelle pulls Elia's knife out of her hand and stabs her rapist all over his body with tears flowing out of her eyes as she does so. She yells at him as she takes his life. Her hands, her face, parts of her body covered in blood.

I gently put my hand on her shoulder, and she turns to attack me. I catch her hand and snap her out of the red, "He's dead," I said to her.

She breaks down and drops her hands to the floor. I looked at Elia, thinking we had broken Isabelle. It's a secret that we'll take to our graves. We took her into the facility's bathroom, cleaned her up and put her into some new clothes.

"They're all the same, we can't keep pretending that they're not," I said.

Elia asked how we get out of here. I told her we'd go out the back, "wipe down everything you touched, and when you're done, we'll jump out the back. I'll check if there's CCTV here."

I wiped the footage of us entering and took the drives. As we were exiting through the back, I could hear Isabelle mutter to herself, "Kill them all, kill them all." I felt bad for her, but it's not like we all haven't had to go through it at some point, and now she knows that it wasn't just a localised event of pain coming from one family, but a whole community. At least now, she won't forget it.

When we got home, it was hard watching Isabelle retreat into herself like that. I almost felt bad for making her live through it. She was living in a horrible state of mind. She barely ate, barely drank any water.

Even the twins couldn't cheer her up. Annabeth thought we'd gone mad for letting her go through that. She knew damn well that we could have prevented it. But what would you have done? Stop them before they could have done anything to her, and hope she got the message? Or let her have it so she can really understand what they're truly like? I'd rather go for absolutes than an almost. Now, whenever she looks at them, she'll start to think, "They're gonna attack me. It's going to happen again," and you know what? It could.

CHAPTER SEVEN

When Darkness Meets The Light

I've never met anyone who regretted leaving Islam. I've heard about plenty of them hearing the voice of Jesus Christ or seeing Him in their dreams, and then converting the moment they wake. I've also heard stories about Muslims stopped in their tracks by a force they cannot explain when they tried murdering an innocent Christian and then converting because of that power.

I've read about thousands of Muslim women escaping their families or countries to pursue advanced education, freeing themselves from Islam, never to return to their old lives ever again. I've heard about Muslim parents honour killing their children because *they* believed their children were destined for eternal damnation for converting to Christianity.

I have experienced firsthand beautiful signs of his existence when I speak to Him and ask Him questions. Sometimes I may recognise a thought that does not belong to me or see a post that aligns directly with a question I asked earlier. There are even times when I'll just feel this calming presence flow right through me, and it brings me an unexplainable sense of joy.

I'm not going to tell you that I've read the Bible or the Quran cover to cover, but by what I've read, I can tell that a lot of passages in the Quran have been stolen, rephrased, rewritten, added onto, but at the end of the day, taken from the Bible.

For example, the Bible tells us He created Light and Dark on the first day, calling it Day and Night. On the second day, He created the vault between the Water and the Sky. On the third day, He creates the separation between the Land and the Sea and the Plants and the Trees. On the fourth day, He creates the Lights that mark the Sacred Times, and the Days and the Years, and the Moon for the Darkness and the Stars for the Guides. On the fifth day, He created living Creatures for the Sky, the Land and the Seas, and on the sixth day, He created Man.

It also implied that He rested on the Seventh Day, not for Himself, but for Man. However, the Quran simply states that their Allah created the Heavens and the Earth in six days, and on the seventh day, established Himself on the Throne, which implies that He did *not* need to rest. The difference in that alone says, "My God is far superior to yours," but completely disregarded the fact that the rest wasn't for Him, but for us. It was Him leading by example.

This alone separates the fundamental differences between Christianity and Islam. Christianity tells you, "Yes, worship me, do great things in my name, be there for your neighbours, but don't forget about yourself too." Islam is about, "Worship me and only me, you are irrelevant, I am the only thing that matters. Kill those who don't worship me or refuse to worship me, and you will be rewarded." Another thing is Heaven. In my Lord's Heaven, we are with family and friends if they've accepted Jesus Christ as their Saviour. There is no sorrow, no anger, no regrets. Just happiness and peace and our animals.

In Islam, their Heaven for men is 72 virgins that never lose their virginity, and boundless alcohol, which is full of lust and sin. A woman's Heaven is having ONE sex slave for eternity that YOU can choose to marry or keep as a slave, and they are loyal only to you. To top it off, their Allah isn't even with them. He's somewhere else entirely, whereas my Lord is with us, _always_. In Heaven or on Earth, He is with us.

Most Muslims don't even know if they're going to make it to Heaven because their own prophet didn't even know himself. He expressed his uncertainty about his final destination, stating that he did not know what his Allah would do with him. Don't all prophets make it to Heaven? Muhammad even had to assure his followers that his Divine teachings weren't given by the Devil, but by Gabriel the Archangel, even after saying that his Allah was the greatest of deceivers.

I can also understand why women are the larger demographic in Muslim communities converting to Christianity, simply because of how they are treated. Under Islam, you can be beaten, flogged, stoned, raped or killed simply because you refused to dress modestly by covering your hair or your entire body with a niqab. You can be beaten for disrespecting your husband or for refusing to obey him. Under Christianity, a woman's sanctity is protected no matter what they choose to wear, and abuse against them is completely shunned. Life was created by God, and by God's will, continued by women; so why abuse them because they denied you? Muslims worship an abuser, but we Christians? We Christians worship a protector.

I hate how they put limitations on God's power. They say that he cannot have a Son, because he physically cannot produce one. He's the Creator. Whatever He wills, will be done so. The Father cannot be the Son, and it cannot be the Holy Spirit. The Son cannot be the Father, and it cannot be the Holy Spirit. The Holy Spirit cannot be the Father, and it cannot be the Son, but the Father, the Son, and the Holy Spirit <u>came</u> from God; God <u>can</u> be all three, hence the Trinity. They say their Allah is the Creator of all things, and whatever He wills, will be so, but then they'll limit their own Allah's power when you suggest that their Allah is with them because he is not a physical being. Make it make sense.

The rise of Islam was a cancer. We hadn't realised that was an issue until it was too late. They used to be so kind when I was a kid. They were the kind of people that you could rely on, but now, they demand Sharia Law, spread violence and cry Islamophobia when people call them out for it.

As much as it pains me, I can never understand their devotion to a prophet who preaches violence and then claims that he was the final and most divine. But you know what? Maybe he was. Maybe he tried to live like Christ, but created his own version of what he believed Christ to be. Maybe he idolised Christ so much that he wanted to be the Messiah just like him. Maybe he made every disgusting sin he did divine law because he wasn't capable of being sinless like Christ. Maybe he got so angry that God wasn't speaking to him as Jesus spoke to his disciples that he created a version of his own God and forced people to believe in it or die. Maybe that's why all his believers now are so violent and hateful.

Maybe that's why there are so many Muslims. They're afraid that if they convert to Christianity, they'll be killed for it. Maybe there are Christians in Islam, but they're hiding. Maybe that's why they aren't as violent as their brethren. It's quite unfortunate, really, because it's us they turned into monsters.

I remember I had a friend in high school named Maximus, and he was Muslim. The kindest guy you could ever meet, you couldn't smell the radical Muslim off him at all. I moved school, and it wasn't til I started university that I saw him again. We didn't talk; we just connected eyes, gave each other a head nod, and that was that, but there was so much anger in his eyes. Like the good was taken away from him. I think the more they learn about Islam, the more the Holy Spirit departs from them, because why else would they look at someone who wasn't Muslim with so much hate?

The Holy Spirit guides us throughout our entire lives to live like Christ. The Holy Spirit is the reason why we feel love towards our neighbours, our family, and our friends. It is the reason why we long for peace above violence. It is the reason for our strengths in times of the hardest tests, like the one we're going through now. I think the Holy Spirit left them, and that's why they are the way they are. I think the Holy Spirit is working overtime for these Muslims who are not too far gone, but if there is a chance to save any of them from eternal damnation, all I can do is hope that they listen.

The Bible and His disciples tell you themselves that Jesus was Sinless. Even the Quran tells you that Jesus was Pure, and though they reject his crucifixion, they still say that He rose to Heaven alive by God's will and will return to earth before Judgement Day. Yet they hunt Christians down and force them to submit to their Allah. Just something to think about.

The President ran into a problem. New York. Before the war began, he thought he had a very productive relationship with the new mayor of New York. The first-ever Muslim mayor for a state that was attacked by Muslims. The President wasn't well-informed about Islam. Just surface-level stuff. What he didn't know was that the Mayor was practising a jihad called Taqiyya, which means lying to non-Muslims to advance Islam by any means necessary.

Jihad can be practised in many forms; Politics, Teaching, Law, Medicine, War, Deception and so on.

It's simple, infiltrate the keyways of the non-Muslim way of life, and assert Islamic dominance hidden in 200-300 page policies, demand new laws that benefit only Muslims or by taking it by force as they did in the UK. In the time that the new mayor had come into office, he's so far only hired Muslims, and more particularly, a Muslim who has a record for committing armed robbery and assault.

This new mayor has become a blueprint for Jihadi success here in the United States, because now, the corrupt government in the UK are now in league with the New York mayor. This is why crime has surged to record highs, and why Muslim patrols are enforcing laws that aren't even part of the constitution. A lot of liberal women have been targets of these patrols, which have led to verbal and even sexual assaults. They've even started to blame the Republican party for what THEY voted for. When the mayor said he'd make housing and groceries cheaper for his community, he really meant *his* community, prioritising the Muslim population for cheaper housing and marking lower prices for them at government-owned grocery stores, leaving others struggling behind.

Because of the President's indecision to terminate the new mayor's position and appoint someone more trustworthy, the financial capital of the world had been overrun by third-world terrorists, who don't even understand the damage that could be caused by incestual inbreeding. Now he's stuck with a mayor who is most likely receiving funds from terrorist organisations to fund terrorist cells within the United States, which is also probably the reason why the President is having trouble removing this cancer from the nation.

If the presidency had been won by that laughingstock of an alcoholic, we'd be fighting the Russians, Chinese and North Koreans instead of the Muslims, and there probably wouldn't even be a world left to live in.

If liberals win the next election, we can expect this shitshow to dial up to 100, and you can assume the First and Second Amendments be removed and be just like the UK and Australia. This would mean absolute government control and complete government overreach. We're talking Digital ID, social credit systems like China, unlawful arrests and unlawful detainment.

Who knows, they might even remove jury trials for most crimes to silence the opposition. Canada has even begun the process of implementing their own Digital

ID system, stricter hate speech laws, and easier avenues to persecute all religions, regardless of their ideologies. Unfortunately, when it comes to violent rhetoric by Muslim preachers, law enforcement still doesn't have the balls to put an end to it.

I know what you're thinking: I'm a far-right fascist who's so hellbent on sowing division and hate towards the minority. Well, this minority makes up 26% of the entire world's population. Two billion of them. If you said only 2% of them were radicals, it is still forty million people hellbent on destroying you. Now it's safe to say that 30% of them are willing to do anything to spread Islam across every corner of the globe. That 30% is about six hundred million radical Muslims hellbent on killing you. I guess I'm only far right because I woke up, and you're still sleeping. Don't let blind ignorance be your downfall.

If you bothered to use your own brain and do some research instead of believing the lies your politicians tell you about the non-existent threat of Islam, you'll come to realise that the threat is real and it is has come. Take it from me. I was just like you, believing every word of the government's lies because they fought for things we thought we wanted, and then the next thing we knew, we lost the United Kingdom. I get it. You're lonely, and you want to belong to something, to be part of something. You want to be part of the movement that changes the world. I see you. I see the quiet kid who used to be bullied. I see the outcast that nobody cared for. I see the child who just wanted love but never got it. I see the person who was uncomfortable in their own skin.

You can change your hair, you can believe you can change your gender, you can scream, "Down with the constitution!" all you want, and you can even side with people who want the same things as you until they get what they want. Just understand, the people they'll go after first when they've won is you.

Back home in the UK, they've created a new Islamic Caliphate, housed in the former Royal Family home, Buckingham Palace. A rotten corpse down to the bone is hanging off the Queen Victoria Memorial, and one can assume it was the Prince who refused to convert to Islam. Resources have been hoarded by the Muslim communities and only given out to the native Brits if they swore their allegiance and beliefs to Islam, but even then, they didn't receive much.

Many were kicked out of their homes and forced to sleep on the streets, while new Muslim families took over their residences. At the beginning of their revolution, popular names who opposed the spread of Islam were captured, paraded, and then killed. Many Brits were forced to line up single file and forced to convert to Islam, and those who refused were executed in front of the lot of 'em. They also executed a lot of the men who could fight back. They left the boys alive, though, either to be sodomised or made to convert.

Many women were captured, detained and sold to the highest bidder. Many were sold as slaves, and others for marriage. Some were bought just to be tortured and killed. The news that was broadcast in the UK was mainly about the island's surrender to the "Superior Muslim Brotherhood", and the glory thanks to their Allah. Every few days, they'd have public executions just to remind the people what would happen if they stepped out of line, and even if they did, they'd have nothing to fight with.

The police turned into Muslim Patrol, mostly youths and some adults, to lead the way with their own arms and ammunition. The military turned from a strong sixty thousand Brits to over five hundred thousand Jihadi terrorists. Former military leaders were replaced with the new Caliphate, and former military personnel were executed. The former Prime Minister? Yeah, they beheaded the guy, put his head on a spike and left it in a glass box in Trafalgar Square.

The United Kingdom was entirely lost to the mob. Spain had a history with these Muslims, and while they were overrun for a time, they slowly recaptured their lands and drove most of them out. The rest were captured and detained. Spain was dealing with a lot of Muslims who came from Africa, many of whom assaulted a lot of the older generation. While we assumed that the daughters of the Spanish king were missing, they were instead taken to Palma, Mallorca, to hide.

It was unfortunate to hear that the King was murdered, but the Queen did survive, however, not without some trauma that left her mute. The eldest daughter assumed the throne, not just for the country, but for vengeance. Her first ruling was dissolving parliament and redirecting full control back to the Monarchy.

The new queen then announced a shoot-to-kill order for every Muslim and any individual committing any illegal activity. Hate preachers would be executed, Muslim preachers would be executed, illegal immigrants would be executed, and rapists would be castrated without anaesthesia and then executed. She was out for blood, you see, and while a lot of the older generation didn't agree with her methods, her generation took the reins and led the way to a new era.

When the Muslims were driven out of Spain and retreated to Portugal, the new queen contacted the Portuguese Prime Minister and gave him an option: that Portugal could follow in the steps of Spain and drive the Muslims out, or Spain would invade and do it themselves. The queen did not want to risk another silent invasion during her rule.

Portugal did not have the will nor the resources to fight the horde of Muslims escaping through its borders, so the Prime Minister allowed the Spanish military to execute "The Sweep," which meant bolstering the Spanish military's numbers from 147,000 to 1,300,000 active personnel to sweep the east of Portugal right to the beaches in the west, killing any Muslim in their path. Many sandy beaches in Portugal turned red from the blood of the dead. The blood could be seen by satellite as it washed into the sea. The rest of the Muslims surrendered, but the Queen did not want any of them alive and had them executed. It was temporary, but the Queen assumed control of Portugal until the dust settled, temporarily uniting both sovereign states into one.

France was divided, from La Rochelle to Lyon; anywhere south belonged to the Muslims, but they were struggling to hold on to the territory. They couldn't take the capital, though; they did come close. After the President's death, the military took control and assumed martial law. The French military was just as savage as the Queen of Spain.

Illegal immigrants were shot on sight and left to rot, and were only moved after the fighting died down. They weren't bothered to bury them, so the bodies were dumped in the catacombs stretching for miles. Even now, they haven't completely gotten rid of the smell. Most Frenchmen started wearing masks again.

They'd get terrorist attacks now and then, but since the military allowed born Frenchmen and women to carry firearms, the attacks against French natives were reduced greatly. This sowed fear into Muslim terrorists, mainly armed with melee weapons and the occasional IED. The north of France is still fighting the south, but they're getting restless. They even suggested that Southern France evacuate to the North to allow bombs to drop, killing any Muslims in the area. Of course, if Muslims tried to flee to the North as refugees, they'd be executed.

Belgium and the Netherlands met the same fate as the UK. Most of its citizens were too liberal and kind of just… rolled over their bellies and took it. Maybe a couple thousand died? But most of them converted without a fight. The daughters of the Dutch royal family were still alive but weren't particularly well. The would-be Queen was chained up along with her siblings in their own home. Of course, they're now slaves to the Caliphate leaders. Videos of them were circulating all over the internet.

Their captors showed them no mercy. Germany was a bit of an outlier. They were getting overwhelmed in the beginning, but once the Chancellor forfeited his power to the military, the entire nation went blitzkrieg 2.0. Its citizens were marking locations and addresses of known Muslims, particularly where the undocumented went to gather. Muslims and collaborators were executed, many of whom were burned alive because the citizens mainly had melee weapons and makeshift Molotov cocktails. They took Germany back in just a few days.

In Italy, its citizens were hunted for sport. They were the ones most opposed to a Muslim takeover, so the fake asylum seekers thought it fitting to have them suffer the most. A lot of the women who were captured, particularly around Naples and Rome, were stripped, chained and bound inside city squares where foot traffic is most dense. They were as young as seven and as old as fifty. With a Muslim majority, these women and young girls were used as toys right in the public eye, guarded by Antifa and Al-Shabaab militant groups to prevent their rescue. Anyone who attempted to rescue them would be killed.

They didn't murder anyone who refused to convert; instead decided to humiliate them and make them take their own lives by threatening to kill their family members if they refused. I doubt Italy can find their way back to normal because while the UK had an influx of illegal immigrants, Italy had the highest number of illegals entering the country. If you were white and walking around Italy, I would feel bad for you.

Russia, of all places, came to the rescue for the rest of Europe, but some still speculated that they were in it for their own agenda. Russia, a predominantly Christian land, did not face any of the Muslim assaults because they only made up 15% of the Russian population… and well, you don't really fuck with the Russians and their faith. Corruption was in the nation's roots, but the Russian President would rather die than see his Mother Russia fall to foreign invaders.

The nation ran a tight ship when it came to immigration; they would immediately deport anyone they deemed a threat or posed a security risk. Cut off from the rest of the world like a forgotten city, they ran the nation independently, taking whatever measures necessary to ensure the nation's safety. When they heard the news in the UK and the growing attacks by the Muslim population in the rest of Europe, the President labelled the Muslim population in Russia a threat to national security.

The President showed mercy, though I guess he had more morals than the rest of the world. He gave the Muslim population an option,

"I'm sure you are all aware of the atrocities that have occurred in the United Kingdom and the growing assaults in Western Europe. I will do whatever is necessary to defend Mother Russia from potential terrorist attacks. The Muslim population have a choice. It is plain and simple. Leave… or die. You have three days," he says.

Honestly, from where I'm standing, what he did back then was probably the best decision he ever made. The rest of the world waited for the Muslims to fuck things up, but the Russian President stepped in before they even got started. Many Muslims believed he was bluffing, while a few hundred thousand packed what they could and left for Belarus or Kazakhstan, and others tried entering China through Mongolia.

Those who stayed were dragged from their homes and shot dead in their driveway, recorded and broadcast for the rest of Russia to see as a warning for the rest of the Muslim population who decided to stay. The Muslims expected the Russian population to revolt with them, but they were met with the same silence you'd hear at 3am. They were shot down at their protests, shot down in their cars, shot down in the train stations, and shot down all the way to the borders.

If you stood up on a hill and looked down to the Russian border, I bet you could see bodies sprawled all over the place. It was funny, though, because the rest of the world condemned their actions, knowing damn well they were doing the same thing too. The only difference was that Russia wasn't hiding it.

When they were done, they offered their assistance to their neighbours who were overwhelmed. Some took their help, and some refused, as they believed it was just a part of their plan to sneak their forces in and take the land once they had secured all defensive positions.

China was so ruthless that it made me want to be Chinese. Islam was a recognised religion in China; however, the CCP cared less for their beliefs and ensured their religion was sinicised and aligned with the ideologies of the CCP. This meant that all 25 million Muslims had to be registered and run by state-sanctioned patriotic associations, in which they were required to spread Chinese culture rather than Islamic culture.

Those who practised Islam illegally were detained in internment camps where they were forced to denounce their faith and pledge their allegiance to the CCP. These Muslims were then surveilled, ensuring they didn't store halal foods, which was construed as a sign of extremism, and even demolished a lot of their mosques for not adhering to the ideologies of the CCP. They even criminalised many common practices of Islam, such as fasting during Ramadan, forcing those such as civil servants, teachers and students to record themselves eating during Ramadan to prove that they were eating, and also banned long beards and face coverings and forced those in detention centres to eat pork.

None of those Muslims could fight back, you see, because of China's advanced surveillance systems. You commit a crime? Sure, you can get away, but they'll meet you at your house before you get there. Those who tried to enter from Russia were turned away, leaving many of them displaced. The Russian President forewarned the Chinese President of an influx of Muslims seeking asylum, and those who forced their way in despite being turned away were shot down. China saw the looming threat of Islam and prepared years before anyone else did, and because of this preparation, have prevented the rapid spread of Islam.

CHAPTER EIGHT

The Quiet Uncertainty

Despite all the dangers around the world, it didn't feel dangerous anymore. There was just this quiet uncertainty that loomed over us, but it felt right. Religion had gotten so efficient that it had become a driving force between Christianity and Islam, and minor religious beliefs began to choose sides. Whatever churches that were still standing began giving shorter sermons with security posted outside, security detail, once a novelty, were now as common, their presence a stark reminder of the fragility of peace. The shorter sermons, once a pragmatic response to immediate threats, had become the norm, a silent acknowledgement of the ever-present danger.

A sermon too long, and it was like Jihadis were drawn to them like a magnet. In some mosques, imams spoke about love while endorsing laws that erased entire groups of people. In churches, pastors preached discipline while ignoring the bruises carried home by those who obeyed too well. The bruises, both visible and invisible, carried by those who adhered too strictly to these teachings, were a testament to a different kind of violence, one sanctioned by faith and ignored by its leaders. Belief was loud, it was confident, it was everywhere, but to those in power, it was dangerous.

In the mosques, the imams' words of love felt hollow, a thin veil over the harsh realities of the laws they championed. These laws, often cloaked with religious righteousness, systematically dismantled the rights and existence of minority groups, their voices silenced, their histories erased. The irony was a bitter pill. Love preached, while hatred legislated. Similarly, in the churches, the sermons on discipline, on obedience to a higher power, resonated with a chilling undertone. The line between devotion and subjugation had blurred, and many found themselves trapped in its oppressive embrace.

Major cable networks began sharing Bible verses during news broadcasts and advertisements to show solidarity amongst the Christian faith. Even known celebrities who were known to be atheists established their faith in Christianity for the world to hear. Faith no longer demanded transformation, and it was no longer something that was felt amongst these groups, but instead, it's become, "Yes, I'm Christian, you're Christian too, so protect me."

People prayed with phones in their hands and violence in their assumptions. I can assume I wasn't the only one who recognised the pattern long before anyone else cared to name it, long before anyone else bothered to do something about it, long before anyone else found the strength to say, "I was wrong." The Christians, devout in their faith, began to lose it by the day as more of their brethren fell, but the more certain Muslims became about their Allah, the less human they became. We stopped calling them "Man" and started calling them "They". I've even begun to call *myself* a monster.

The war between Christians and Muslims began to escalate again. Many had even considered reviving the Crusade. There was a level of dissatisfaction amongst the Western people, regarding the ache of the fight that had been waging for so long, which they believed had not gone anywhere in their favour. The air was thick with a tension that hummed beneath the surface of our everyday life. It wasn't the usual overt, explosive violence that dominated new cycles in other parts of the world; they began to silence it. To shrug it under the rug to be forgotten. It was a creeping, insidious pressure that reshaped society from within.

The dissatisfaction in the West wasn't just about the endless wars in distant lands; it was a deeper, more existential weariness. The promise of progress, of a world united by shared values, had evaporated, replaced by a sense of stagnation and a gnawing fear that their own societies were fracturing from within. The ache of the fight was not just the physical toll of conflict, but the moral and spiritual exhaustion of a generation that had seen little but division and strife.

The idea of a new crusade, once a fringe notion, began to gain traction in certain circles, fuelled by a desperate desire for a clear enemy, a definitive battle to end the perceived endlessness of the conflict. It was a dangerous fantasy, born from frustration and a profound misunderstanding of history, yet it resonated with a populace yearning for resolution, however violent.

The world had become a mosaic of fortified communities, each clinging to its own truth, its own interpretation of the divine. Borders, once lines on a map, were now psychological barriers, reinforced by suspicion and fear. The global village had fractured into countless warring tribes, each convinced of its own righteousness, each prepared to defend it with unwavering conviction. The quiet uncertainty that had once felt right had morphed into a pervasive dread, a silent scream echoing across a world where belief, once a source of comfort, had become the most potent weapon of all.

Despite all the darkness that enveloped my life, despite all the violence I inflicted, I still believed that my faith mattered, especially in times when I *could* find restraint, where I could prevent myself from using violence, where I could prevent myself from enjoying it. In the times when I failed, it was like there was a fog that drifted over me. Like it blinded me from my own actions, as if revealing my own truth would destroy me. It was like faith had stopped asking me questions, like it had gone to sleep with its eyes open.

I hadn't realised that my actions against these Muslims were made in vain. Why would I, a Christian, stoop so low to their level that I would inflict the same pain they gave to us? Why would I use vengeance to justify taking lives? I know they didn't take my sister, I know they didn't. For all I know, those men who *did* are still walking free, doing it to more innocent girls out there. Why take it out on those who weren't involved… no. They're all involved. They're all the same. They *all* took my sister. *They* made me this way.

In the shadows of my life, a constant battle raged between my hatred of the Muslims and the light of faith. I often found myself standing at the precipice, teetering between the desire for peace and the instinct for retribution. It was a conflict that felt as old as time, echoing in the stories of countless other souls that have walked this earth on the same path. Yet, for me, it was more than just a tale. It was my reality, a gnawing struggle that intertwined itself with my very existence.

Faith, once a guiding light, began to fade into a distant memory. In its place, I felt the heavy weight of vengeance settle upon my shoulders. Each act of violence I committed was a step further away from the person I once aspired to be. The person, for a time, was what my mother saw in me. The fog that enveloped my thoughts blinded me from recognising the futility of my actions. I believed that by inflicting pain, I could somehow reclaim the power that had been stripped from me. But with each blow, I lost a piece of myself, drowning in a sea of anger and despair.

As I reflect on my journey, I realise that my faith mattered most in the moments I chose restraint. It was then, amid the chaos, that I could see a glimmer of hope— a flicker of understanding that perhaps, there was another way. But those moments were fleeting, you see. It was often overshadowed by the relentless darkness that beckoned me to retaliate.

Violence had always lurked in the corners of my life, a spectre that threatened to consume me whole. I can vividly recall a time when anger surged through my veins like wildfire. When I finally had the power to return the pain this world had given me. I had spiralled out of control, where words turned to fists and blades, and the line between right and wrong blurred into oblivion. In that moment, I felt powerful and invincible, as if I could erase the pain of the past with every strike. But it was the delusion that this could be possible is what really consumed me. It didn't bring my sister back. It only tainted her memory, and in those moments, I was simultaneously enveloped in a profound sense of helplessness.

Each act of violence was a cry for help, a desperate attempt to assert control over a life that felt chaotic and unjust. I was fighting not just against the invaders, but against the demons within me that took control long ago. The shadows that whispered lied about my worth and my purpose. Each kill was a misguided attempt to silence those demons, but instead, they grew louder, feeding on the pain I inflicted, making *them* stronger, feeding off my anger and despair.

The fog that drifted over my consciousness transformed my perception of reality. It was as if I were watching my life unfold through a thick glass pane— everything distorted, my actions unrecognisable. I struggled to comprehend the consequences of my actions, blinded by the haze that clouded my judgment. It was in the aftermath of violence that I felt the fog most acutely, as if a veil had been lifted, revealing the wreckage left in my wake, and I was standing atop the blood in the midst of it all.

I remember all of us surrounding the last man we captured. This was the chaos that I had created. We had become demons amongst the demons, feeding on the same evil we swore we'd put an end to. The shouts of pain and fear echoed in my ears, in my dreams, in every waking moment of my life, and I wanted more of it. But all I could feel was this unsettling emptiness. It was then that I really had to question who I was becoming. Was this the legacy I wished to leave behind? Am I really doing this for our freedom? For Christendom? The fog thickened once more, and for the first time, I felt glimpses of clarity. Maybe a monster is who I was meant to be? A monster for all monsters. Would this be justified?

It took me back to when we murdered Abdul. As I stood there, Abdul was trembling in his chains, his ragged breath breaking the heavy silence that hung over us like a dark cloud. The stench of sweat and fear clung to the air, mingling with the acrid scent of ashes from our charred world. Elia, standing to my left, gripped her blade tightly, her knuckles white against the dark metal. Her eyes bore into the man, a mixture of rage and pain swirling within them, and for a brief moment, I caught a flicker of regret in her eyes, dancing across her features, illuminating the chaos around her.

You could tell she was asking herself, "Are we really supposed to do this?" Her eyes flickered around, looking for answers. Her whispers barely carried over the shouts and cries echoing in the background. The uncertainty in her look struck me like a knife, piercing through the haze of adrenaline that had clouded my judgment. Annabeth, ever the fierce warrior with a heart hardened by loss, stepped closer, her voice as sharp as a blade.

"HE'S one of them! They started all of this! They deserve this!" Her words dripped with anger, snapping Elia out of her uncertainty, but I couldn't shake the feeling that we were losing something far more precious than our enemy that day. Isabelle, with her gentle heart that seemed to shine even in these dark times, stepped forward, her small frame shaking.

"We can't become like them… we're better than this…" she said.

Her voice, soft yet resolute, hung in the air like a fragile thread of hope, a reminder of the innocence we were desperately trying to preserve amidst the encroaching shadows. Catherine and Nasreen exchanged glances, their wide, innocent eyes reflecting the turmoil that twirled around us. They had never witnessed such brutality as the evil we committed. Yet here we are, dragging them into our world… our twisted reality. I felt a surge of protectiveness mixed with guilt, a heavy weight pressing down on my heart. Were we truly fighting for freedom, or had we simply traded one set of human morality and chains for another?

I took a step back, the fog of my thoughts swirling. The emptiness within me echoed louder than the screams around us, as Elia began cutting pieces through his flesh, and Annabeth was screaming at her to keep going. As the chaos of violence raged within, I felt like a puppet, strings pulled by anger and loss, but where would that lead us? Suddenly, Abdul looked up at me, eyes wide open, not with hate, but with a pleasing desperation that cut through.

"Please, I have a family. I didn't choose this fight. I just want to go home." He said.

Elia scoffed at him, "You wanted to fuck a 16-year-old, remember?" His words completely reverted her to the darker Elia, whom she was so close to getting rid of.

Abdul's voice cracked, raw and vulnerable, and in that moment, I saw a reflection of my own fears and doubts— what if one day, it was these girls begging for mercy from someone like us? Was this the monster I was destined to become? A monster of my own making, fighting fire with fire? Blood for blood? I needed clarity amongst the chaos. I needed to confront the darkness festering within me. I took a deep breath, the weight of my choices crashing down upon me like a tidal wave. I had to make a decision, one that could alter the course of our lives forever.

The tension thickened as my words hung in the air… "Wait," I said, drawing the attention of my comrades. Would they listen? Or had we all crossed too far into the abyss? As their eyes searched my face for answers, I felt the weight of the world on my shoulders, teetering between the monster I feared and the hero I wished to be. The choice between mercy and vengeance loomed before us, a crossroads that could define our legacy in the war-torn world.

That's when Annabeth handed Isabelle that knife. That's when Elia snatched it off her. That's when Elia and I broke her.

I could see the fire in her eyes, a blaze fuelled by the pain we'd all suffered, but held back by demons preventing her from harnessing that power. Was this the best way to get her into the fight? I may have been wrong. It had been days since Isabelle left her room. The shadows of her once-bright spirit felt heavy, suffocating her in her cold embrace. The memories replayed in her mind like a relentless loop; the fear that gripped her heart and refused to let go.

Outside, the world continued to spin, but for Isabelle, time had come to a standstill. The laughter she heard from us echoed through the walls. A reminder of camaraderie that was waiting for her. Annabeth's voice rang out, sharp and determined, as she strategised with Elia about their next move. But Isabelle couldn't join them. Each word felt like a dagger, piercing the fragile bubble of safety she had created for herself. She was afraid of the darkness that lurked within her, and most of all, the thought that she didn't want to face, that we let it happen to her. It wasn't until the fifth day that she heard a faint knock at her door.

It was Catherine, the younger of the twins, her voice a gentle whisper, "Issy, can I come in?

For a moment, Isabelle hesitated, the walls of her fortress trembling at the thought of letting someone inside, but Catherine's warmth seeped through the cracks of her defences, and she found herself nodding, unable to voice her consent. Catherine entered, her big, innocent eyes scanning the dim room.

"You've been in here for quite some time. We miss you, you know?" She said.

Her utter sincerity wrapped around Isabelle like a comforting blanket. Isabelle tried to muster a smile, but it faltered, leaving her feeling more vulnerable.

"I just… I can't right now, Catherine. I don't think I'll ever be okay again." Isabelle said.

"You, me and Nasreen went through the same thing together… We can get through this together. I promise." Catherine said as she stepped closer, her small hands reaching out to Isabelle's. "You don't have to be okay right now. Just being with us is enough. We're all scared, but you don't have to face it all by yourself. We're your friends, and we love you."

The weight of those words cracked the dam holding back Isabelle's emotions. Tears streamed down her cheeks, and she felt a rush of relief mingled with sorrow. In that moment, surrounded by Catherine's unwavering kindness, she realised that isolation wasn't her refuge, but a prison of her own making.

"I don't want to be a burden, Catherine. I don't want to drag anyone down with me, especially when I'm feeling like this," she confessed, her voice trembling.

"You could never be a burden. We're all in this together. If one of us falls, we all fall. But if we lift each other up, we can get through anything. We were trapped in that room, God knows how long. You taught us that we could get through it," Catherine insisted, her grip tightening.

Isabelle took a shaky breath, the warmth of Catherine's words slowly igniting a flicker of hope within her. Maybe facing the darkness didn't have to mean doing it alone. Maybe it was okay to lean on her friends. With a deep inhale, Isabelle pushed herself off the bed, the weight of her fears still heavy, but a little lighter with Catherine by her side. Catherine beamed, her eyes sparkling with joy.

"I knew you could do it," she said.

As Isabelle stepped out of her room, the weight of her fears still pressing down upon her, she felt a flicker of determination igniting within her. Catherine's presence was like a lifeline, a reminder that she was not alone in this chaotic world. Together, they walked into our arms, where laughter and camaraderie hung in the air like a distant melody, calling her back to life.

But with each step, the echoes of her past haunted her. The screams of Abdul, the chaos of violence— these were not just memories, they were ghosts that clung to her, demanding recognition. She had witnessed the darkness that had seeped into their lives, transforming her new friends into warriors of vengeance. Yet with Catherine beside her, she felt a glimmer of hope that perhaps they could forge a different path. A path of healing rather than hatred.

Isabelle's thoughts swirled as they joined Annabeth and Elia, who were deep in conversation about their next move. Her heart raced, torn between the desire to fight and the yearning for peace. She wanted to scream, to voice her fears, but the words caught in her throat, tangled with the fear of rejection. What if they don't understand?

"Isabelle!" Annabeth's voice broke through her reverie, bringing her back to the present. "We need you. This isn't just about us anymore. It's about everyone who's suffered."

The weight of those words settled heavily on Isabelle's shoulders. She understood the implications of their fight, but the image of Abdul's pleading eyes haunted her. She didn't want to become the monster they were battling.

"I know what we're fighting against," she finally said, her voice trembling but resolute. "But what if we're becoming just like them? What if our thirst for vengeance is all we leave behind?"

Elia's expression hardened, her fists clenching. "They don't deserve mercy! They took everything from us!"

"But at what cost?" Isabelle pressed, her heart racing. "IF we lose our humanity, then what are we fighting for?"

For a moment, silence enveloped the group, and Isabelle could see the flicker of doubt in their eyes. A reflection of her own inner turmoil. It was a moment of vulnerability that none of them had expected, and it felt like a fragile thread connecting them amidst the chaos.

Catherine squeezed Isabelle's hand, a silent show of support. "We can fight, but we can also choose how we fight."

As the sun dipped low on the horizon, casting long shadows around them, Isabelle felt a sense of clarity emerge from the fog of uncertainty. Perhaps they could wield their pain as a weapon of change instead of destruction.

"Let's channel our anger into something constructive," Isabelle suggested. Her voice gaining strength. "Let's help those who have suffered like us. Let's be their voice. Let's be their sword."

The group exchanged glances, the weight of Isabelle's words sinking in.

I wouldn't have expected it, but Annabeth's eyes softened.

With newfound resolve, Isabelle felt the last vestiges of the fog lift, replaced by a sense of purpose. She would not allow herself to become a monster, and neither would her friends. Together, they could forge a different destiny, one where healing and compassion triumphed over vengeance. As they strategised a new plan, Isabelle felt the warmth of hope enveloping her like a protective cloak, shielding her from the darkness that once threatened to swallow her whole.

In that moment, we knew that the journey ahead would be fraught with challenges, but we were ready to face them head-on, not just as fighters, but as a beacon of hope for those who had suffered the same. Together, I feel we would rise, united by love and fuelled by the belief that we could create a better world.

They promised to be better… but Elia and I didn't think we were capable of keeping such a promise.

CHAPTER NINE

Submit or Destroy

There was a church in Vancouver, Canada, that hit global news. This would have been the first time that it's ever happened. During a live stream of the church service, the microphones cut out for approximately 33 seconds. In that time, a low-frequency hum bled through that sounded too even to be feedback, and too structured to be active noise. The subtitles on the projected screen sent back a single word over and over again, "SUBMIT, SUBMIT, SUBMIT, SUBMIT, SUBMIT, SUBMIT, SUBMIT." Hours later, the same thing happened at a mosque in Istanbul during an evening prayer, a similar disruption, a different tone, high-pitched, almost unbearable, the same duration, but a different word, "TADMIR, TADMIR, TADMIR, TADMIR, TADMIR, TADMIR, TADMIR, TADMIR, TADMIR."

Nobody on earth was capable of tracing the source. There was no satellite anomaly, concluding that it could not have come from alien origins. There were no hacked signals and no acoustic weapon. The recordings degraded when attempts were made to analyse them, but remained intact when they were replayed. News outlets argued its source; some believed it to be some advanced technology that was used to trick the world into mass hysteria, and others believed it be a power that could only come from God. It took to the people on social media, and social media decided. People did not ask *what happened*; they simply asked *who it belonged to.*

The world, fractured by this inexplicable event, found itself living between narratives. Many believed it to be a divine imperative, a call to spiritual awakening and a rejection of secular materialism. As the news spread like wildfire, the world found itself engulfed in a whirlwind of speculation and fear. The church in Vancouver and the mosque in Istanbul became symbols of something larger— an awakening or a warning, depending on whom you asked.

In the days of the following incidents, social media exploded. Hashtags like #Submit and #Tadmir flooded feeds, sparking debates that ranged from the rational to the absurd. Some interpreted the messages as a divine command, a call to surrender to a higher power that transcended human understanding. Others saw it as a sinister manipulation tactic, a tool designed to induce mass hysteria and control. Within the fractured narratives, communities divided further. In Vancouver, parishioners of the church held vigils, praying fervently for guidance, convinced that the disruption was a sign of divine urgency.

We heard of this happening, we didn't buy it, but we wanted to make sure for ourselves. We took the next flight out to Vancouver, leaving the farm in the care of our trusted neighbours. The world had shifted overnight. The hum of uncertainty now the backdrop of daily life. When we arrived, the church where the disruption occurred became a gathering place. Hundreds, if not thousands, gathered, hoping for a seat inside. We stood at the back. Pastor Vadim, a charismatic leader known for his compelling sermons, declared it a moment of reckoning.

"Brothers and sisters! We must open our hearts to the message!" He urged, his voice echoing through the pews as the faithful murmured their agreement. "WE are here today because we have been chosen to receive a divine message! What we experienced was not a mere technical failure but a call to awaken our spirits!" His eyes sparkled with fervour, and I could see how his words stirred the crowd, igniting a fire within them.

"Submit!" they echoed back, their voices rising in unison, creating a haunting harmony that sent chills down my spine. As the service progressed, the fervent prayers turned into chants. "Submit! Submit! Submit!" The words reverberated through the walls, and I could see tears streaming down the faces of those around me.

What did it mean to submit? To what? Or to whom were they surrendering?

Suddenly, there was a hush as Pastor Vadim raised his hands, urging silence. "Let us pray for clarity, for peace, and for strength to embrace the unknown!" The congregation bowed their heads as I watched. I felt this overwhelming urge to join them, to surrender my scepticism, even just for a moment. But as I closed my eyes, the weight of uncertainty pressed down on me. What was I surrendering to? A divine power? A collective hysteria? As the prayer unfolded, I felt both liberated and trapped in a web of conflicting emotions. The line between faith and doubt blurred together, and I found myself caught in the middle of it.

Elia shrugged, her expression a mix of intrigue and scepticism. "Maybe it's just another way to control the masses…" She said, unsure of her own thoughts.

Isabelle remained silent, her gaze fixed on the congregation as if searching for an answer within the sea of faces. I could feel the weight of her past pressing down on her, a reminder of the darkness she had faced and the new strength she was beginning to find. Yet, as I listened to the growing noise, I felt a gnawing doubt. Was this really a moment of divine awakening, or merely a reflection of our own fears and desires projected onto the unknown? I couldn't help but wonder how many in the crowd were genuinely seeking truth and how many were merely caught up in the fervour of the moment.

As the service came to a close, the congregation prepared to leave, their spirits lifted, yet their minds clouded with uncertainty. Outside, the atmosphere shifted. The once-bustling streets now felt charged with a tension that lingered in the air. People moved quickly, eyes darting, whispers exchanged like secrets. I turned to Elia and Isabelle, my heart racing.

"We need to be careful. There's a fine line between faith and fanaticism, and I fear we might be crossing it," I warned.

Ella nodded, her eyes scanning the crowd. "We can't let our guard down. Not now, not ever. They won't hesitate to turn on us if they think we're a threat," she said.

As we made our way through the crowd, I couldn't shake the feeling that something monumental was about to unfold. The ripples of the church service had begun to spread far beyond the walls of the building, and the world outside was on the brink of a reckoning. In that moment, I realised that the struggle between light and darkness wasn't just a battle waged in the shadows; It was unfolding right before our eyes, challenging us to confront the fears, doubts and beliefs that had shaped our lives. The journey from this point on wasn't going to be easy, but it was one we had to embark on together.

With each step, I felt the weight of our shared history. The secrets we knew could never come to light. The pain and the hope intertwining, forging a path forward. We may have been caught within the chaos, but perhaps we could emerge from it stronger than before. As we left the church behind, I whispered a silent prayer… one for guidance, for strength, and for clarity to navigate the storm that lay ahead.

As the sun began to set, casting long shadows over the streets of Vancouver, we found ourselves standing at the crossroads of belief and scepticism. The energy from the church service still hung in the air, but now it felt charged with tension and uncertainty.

We decided to venture towards a nearby café, a place that had become a refuge for those who sought a quieter space to process the chaos. The atmosphere was thick with conversation, as patrons whispered about the events of the day. Each table held a different narrative, some praising the church's message, while others cast doubt on its legitimacy. Elia, ever the pragmatist, leaned in closer. "Look at them. They're so lost in their fervour, they can't see how quickly they could be manipulated. This isn't faith; it's fear dressed up in a holy garb," she said, her brow furrowing as she observed a group of young people passionately discussing the service.

Isabelle, still entranced by the emotional display at the church, countered, "But what if it *is* a true awakening? Maybe they're finally finding the strength to confront their fears. Isn't that a powerful thing?"

Their debate was interrupted by a sudden commotion outside. We rushed to the window to see a small group of protesters gathering, holding signs that read, "Stop the Submission!" and "Awakening or Manipulation?" Their chants echoed through the streets, a stark contrast to the devout voices we had just left behind.

Just as we stepped outside, the protest escalated. The crowd from the church had spilled into the streets, drawn to the voices challenging their beliefs. A palpable tension rose as the two groups faced off, each side shouting their convictions, the air thick with uncertainty.

"This isn't good," Isabelle muttered, her eyes darting between the escalating chaos. "We need to get out of here before something bad happens."

But something inside of me urged me to stay. I felt it was crucial to witness this clash of ideologies, to understand the depths of the divide that had formed in just a few short days. As the chants grew louder, I noticed a woman in the crowd, her face painted with anguish. Her sign reads, 'We are not sheep!'

I approached her, curiosity piquing. "Why do you feel this way? What's at stake for you?"

She turned, her eyes fierce. "They're blindly following a message that could lead us all to destruction. It's one thing to seek faith, but it's another to surrender your will. I won't let them take my voice!"

She's one of the early few that people would think was crazy, but then realise down the line that they were right the whole time. Her words resonated with me, echoing the doubts I had felt during the service. The lines between faith and fanaticism were blurring, and I realised we were witnessing the birth of a new narrative— a battle not just for belief, but for plain survival.

As the confrontation continued, I felt a deeper understanding of the power that lay in both surrender and defiance. In this moment, I knew this wasn't just about navigating through a new version of chaos. With Elia, Annabeth, Isabelle, Nasreen and Catherine by my side, we would stand witness to this unfolding calamity, not as mere observers but as participants in the dialogue that could shape the future.

As the chants grew louder, I could feel the ground beneath my feet vibrating with the weight of opposing beliefs. The woman I spoke to earlier, her fierce gaze unwavering, caught the attention of those around her. Her voice rose above the din, rallying others to her cause. "We will not be silenced! This is not about faith; it's about power!"

On the other side, Pastor Vadim stepped forward, his expression a mix of determination and bewilderment.

"Brothers and sisters! We must not let fear divide us! We are united in purpose, called to surrender to a higher truth!" The crowd responded, their fervour igniting once more, chanting, "Submit! Submit!" In that moment, the air cracked with energy, and I could sense the collision of ideals about to erupt.

Elia stood at my side, her fists clenched, ready to intervene if things took a violent turn. "Yo, this is fucking crazy. They're manipulating each other."

Isabelle was mesmerised, caught between her desire to believe and the reality unfolding before her eyes. "What if they're right, though?"

Nasreen, the voice of reason, chimed in, "There's a difference between awakening and blind obedience!"

Catherine was filming the chaos, her eyes wide open with a mix of fear and excitement. A sudden clash erupted as a protester threw a sign into the air, hitting a church member. Gasps echoed from both sides as chaos descended. The fervour turned to fury, and I found myself pushed to the forefront, caught between two sides, adrenaline coursing through my veins. As tensions peaked, a silence fell momentarily, and all eyes turned towards me. I could feel the weight of their expectations.

"We're all here seeking something, whether it's faith, truth, or even a sense of belonging. But surrendering doesn't mean losing ourselves; it means finding common ground!" In that moment, I saw nods from both sides, a flicker of recognition that perhaps we were more alike than we realised.

CHAPTER TEN

They Weaponised Scripture

As the tension simmered, two figures emerged from the crowd, one wearing a cross around his neck and the other a hijab framing her determined face. Elia and I couldn't help but gaze intensely at her as if she were going to be our next plaything.

The man, Thomas, stepped forward, his voice steady despite the chaos. "Faith should lead us to love and understanding, not division! This is a time for unity, not just within Christianity but with our Muslim brothers and sisters. We are all searching for the same light, aren't we?"

The woman, Aisha, raised her voice, resonating with both conviction and fierce resolve. "You speak of unity, but your faith has a history of subjugation! How can we trust those who have used their beliefs to silence ours? Submission is not an act of love; it is a betrayal of our own identities!"

Her words ignited a ripple of tension through the crowd. Some Christians recoiled, while others agreed with her stance. I, on the other hand, called her out for her bullshit. It was their ideologies that led to the deaths and massacres of Christians all over the planet, and she wants to talk about our history of subjugation? Isabelle, still caught in the emotional fervour, whispered, "But maybe she has a point. Some grievances run deep!"

Thomas, unfazed, pressed on. "But we are not here to repeat history! We can choose to rise above it! Let's pray for unity and understanding and not division! There has been too much death already."

Aisha stepped closer, her voice cutting through the air like a blade. "You talk about unity, but your community has often marginalised mine. This is not about forgetting our past; it's about acknowledging it. We cannot submit to a narrative that erases our truth!—"

I interrupted her then and there, "Yeah, acknowledge it! Your people massacred us and are still doing it as we speak! You love to play the victim, but you forget that it's YOUR kind doing all the erasing!"

Her defiance and my words resonated with many in the crowd, sparking murmurs of agreement. Some echoed her sentiments, recalling their own struggles against a perceived dominance of Christian narratives. Elia looked at all of us and smirked. A mix of concern and intrigue in her eyes. This may be the confrontation that we need, but where would it lead?

As we all stood firm, the crowd began to split, some gravitating towards Thomas' call for unity, some gathering for my call for truth, and some who rallied behind Aisha's fierce insistence on justice and recognition. I could feel the weight of the moment; the clash was more than just a battle of beliefs, but a confrontation of identities and histories, each demanding to be acknowledged and respected.

As the tension in the air thickened, the atmosphere crackled with a sense of impending violence. The words exchanged were no longer mere arguments; they were declarations of war. I could see Elia's jaw tighten; it almost felt like she was about to swing at a bitch.

"Stop acting like you're the victims!" I shouted, my voice cutting through the chaos. "You think your pain gives you the right to silence others? To murder us because your good book tells you so?! You're more interested in forcing Islam onto others than in facing the truth!"

Aisha's eyes blazed with fury, and she stepped closer, her voice dripping with contempt. "You think your history justifies your arrogance? You're too blind to see that it's not just about you! Your religion has been a weapon of oppression for centuries!" She says as if her religion isn't still active in the slave trade.

The crowd roared in response, their emotions boiling over like a pot about to spill. People surged forward, fists raised, and I felt the surge of adrenaline coursing through my veins. This was no longer a discussion; it was a battle, and we were all soldiers in a war of ideologies. Thomas, attempting to calm the storm, stepped forward again, but his voice was drowned by the cacophony. "We don't have to fight! We need to heal!" He pleaded, but the crowd had spiralled too far into their righteous indignation before being struck in the face.

"Your healing is a façade!" Aisha fired back, her voice strong and unwavering. Then it happened. A protester, fuelled by the frenzy, threw a heavy object towards the churchgoers. Chaos erupted as people ducked, and the air filled with screams. Elia, in a rage, swings her arm and strikes Aisha in the face, and rips her hijab off, calling her a terrorist dog before grabbing my arm and taking us away from the conflict.

Fists blew, and bodies collided. I felt the rage slip back inside me just as I was trying to let it go once and for all. The chaos was intoxicating, a raw expression of all our suppressed rage and desires for violence. This was the reckoning we had all feared but longed for, a collision of truth and deception, faith and doubt, all laid bare in the streets of Vancouver. People were no longer just screaming; they were howling, primal and untamed, shedding their civilised facades. The air cracked with tension, each shout a bullet into the heart of belief, each punch thrown, a desperate plea for validation. Who is most true?

This confrontation hit the news, you see, and the whole world was watching. The confrontation woke many people who were sleeping with their eyes open. Pastor Vadim, once a beacon of hope, now stood wide-eyed and helpless, watching as his congregation transformed from dutiful followers to a mob, consumed by a fervent rage. The chants of "Submit!" twisted into something darker, a call to arms rather than a call to faith. The line between devotion and fanaticism had been obliterated, and I watched as the very foundations of their beliefs trembled under the weight of reality.

Aisha, still seething from Elia's assault, rallied her followers with a voice that pierced through the din. "Allahu Akbar! Islam will stand above all. All infidels will be eliminated!" Her words ignited a fire in the hearts of the many, their anger morphing into a collective roar that shook the ground beneath us.

Elia, now in full battle mode, turned to me, her eyes wild with fury. "I'm going to kill them all! They think they can take everything from us?! They're dead wrong!" Her passion was infectious, and I felt the rage bubbling up inside me, an anger I had tried to suppress. Amidst the chaos, I locked eyes with Aisha, and there it was— an unyielding challenge.

"You want to claim this ground? You'd better fight for your life!" I shouted at her, my heart racing. The world had become a greater battlefield, and there was no turning back.

As the chaos escalated, I glanced at Isabelle, but there was no time for hesitation. The air was thick with the smell of sweat and blood, and the cries of the wounded filled my ears. The crowd surged forward, a tide of bodies crashing against each other, both sides unwilling to back down, each fighting for their own version of the truth, and so we fought for every voice that had been silenced and for every belief that had been demonised.

As the chaos subsided, the streets bore witness to the aftermath of our confrontation, a visceral reminder of the violence that had erupted just moments before. But while the physical battle seemed to wane, a far more dangerous war had ignited within the minds of billions across the globe. The echoes of our shouts, our cries for truth and justice, reverberated through the fabric of society, transforming the landscape of belief and scepticism into a battlefield of its own.

In the days that followed, the world divided into factions, each one more unpredictable than the last, each one convinced of its righteous path. The fervour of the churchgoers had morphed into a zealous crusade, the Islamists on the same quest for the past 1400 years, while the protesters, fuelled by anger and a thirst for validation, rallied under the banner of defiance.

The air was thick with the promise of conflict, and I could sense the tide turning. The drive for certainty was intoxicating, like a drug coursing through the veins of humanity. Those who sought answers found themselves drawn into the whirlpool of conviction. The belief that they had finally found the truth offered them a sense of power and purpose that had long been absent. It was a heady mix, a potent cocktail that blurred the lines between right and wrong, between faith and fanaticism.

Thousands of theologians, thousands of scholars, scientists, advanced AI technicians, and click baiters took to the internet, to labs, to libraries, to group meetings to interpret that recording, and many interpretations came faster than uncovering the evidence and the true answers themselves.

Christian leaders framed the incident as repentance. This *was* the second coming, and our Lord and Saviour *was* returning to us. Some Christians refused to shed blood, even in defence of themselves, because they believed that their deaths would return them to Christ as the 144,000. Muslim leaders framed this incident as purification. They believed that the earth was theirs, and it confirmed the mission that they were supposed to cleanse the earth of all Christians, all Jews and all infidels. There would be no more converts, just blood.

Commentators from all over the globe framed it as psychological warfare, and even I thought so myself. Some of the atheists believed the word "submit" was broadcast to imply that the Christians used this as a tactic to draw people away from Islam and towards Christianity. In contrast, others believed the Muslims sent this broadcast as a way to show superiority and dominance. Tech companies from all over the globe denied their involvement, while governments urged calm.

Between these two burgeoning global movements, a third, more cynical group coalesced. The sceptics. These were the rationalists, the scientists, the tech enthusiasts, and the conspiracy theorists who refused to accept either divine intervention or simple technological explanations. They meticulously dissected every available piece of data, searching for anomalies, patterns, and hidden agendas. They believed the events were a sophisticated hoax, a grand psychological experiment, but certainly not a message from God or a simple technical glitch. Their online communities were hubs of intense debate, where theories were proposed, scrutinised, and often debunked with rigorous, if sometimes speculative, analysis.

They were the ones who kept asking, "Who?" and "How?" but refused to accept the easy answers offered by the Christians and the Muslims. They pointed to the precise timing, the distinct, yet equally impactful nature of the disruptions, and the seemingly tailored messages as evidence of an intelligent, deliberate, and terrestrial origin. They theorised about advanced AI, clandestine government projects, or even a coordinated effort by a shadowy global organisation aiming to manipulate humanity on an unprecedented level.

The world's governments, caught flat-footed by the speed and intensity of these global reactions, struggled to maintain control. Official statements were issued, attempting to downplay the incidents as isolated technical malfunctions or even elaborate hoaxes perpetrated by unknown actors. However, these pronouncements often fell on deaf ears, drowned out by the cacophony of social media and the passionate convictions of the Christians and Muslims. The sheer scale of the online movements, the fervent belief systems they fostered, and the growing real-world implications, from peaceful protests to isolated acts of civil disobedience, forced authorities to acknowledge the profound impact of the disruptions.

Intelligence agencies across the globe launched unprecedented investigations, pooling resources and sharing data in a desperate attempt to uncover the source. Satellites were re-tasked, surveillance networks intensified, and acoustic experts worked around the clock, but the origin remained elusive, a ghost in the machine of global communication.

None of it mattered, you see. People came up with their own conclusions, and they forced themselves to believe it. People lived inside a lie for so long that they just wanted to find meaning in all of it, and to hell with the truth. Bible verses flooded Western social media, and Quran ayahs flooded social media in Muslim-dominated areas.

Language that reflected end-times returned to the world by force. A Christian cable network even broadcast end-of-time countdown charts for those who believed their time was near. Spiritualists came together and convinced people that the signs and messages they heard fit too neatly to be accidental, and some believers even felt quite relieved. To them, something finally made sense.

I watched it all unfold right before my eyes and felt the familiar dread, the fear I felt just like in the beginning of their war, and the relief the people must've felt when that uncertainty died. It's quite addictive though, isn't it? Certainty. Once it sets in, violence all of a sudden feels justified. My violence felt justified.

CHAPTER ELEVEN

Coded

The truth is, it had always been a war between Christians and Muslims, and now even the naysayers, I believe, are warming up to its truth. A hellscape of fire and blood where Christians are fighting to defend their Christian lands, and Muslim invaders who are willing to do anything to take them.

"What happens when God stays silent, and humans refuse to?" I raged, my fists clenched as I addressed the group, the remnants of our faith. Wake up! They see our hesitation as weakness. If we don't fight back, they will force us into submission, and we'll be nothing but ghosts in this war. We had witnessed horrors unfold — Christians branded as martyrs, ready to die for their faith, and the Muslims who were convinced of their divine duty to cleanse the earth of infidels. Each side justified its violence with its powerful beliefs, and in the eye of the storm, we found ourselves torn between ideologies that demanded blood.

Isabelle and the twins stood resolute, their faces set like stone. "We are not going to be their slaves!"

The world around us had devolved into brutal sectarian warfare, and the false leaders on both sides thrived on the bloodshed. Governments struggled to maintain order, issuing half-hearted decrees that only served to fuel the flames of dissent. The streets echoed with the cries of the faithful and the anguished wails of the fallen. Law enforcement, overwhelmed and outmatched, often stood by the belief that divine retribution was upon them. They were no longer mere citizens; they were warriors, crusaders and martyrs in a holy war.

From the shadows, dark figures emerged, promising salvation through violence, painting bloodshed as a necessary sacrifice. "Fight for your faith, or be consumed by the infidels," they preached, their voices a hypnotic rhythm that entranced the desperate and the lost. The rhetoric was intoxicating, and soon, even the most peaceful souls found their hearts hardened, their minds twisted by the relentless tide of propaganda.

As the night fell, the city transformed into a battleground illuminated by flickering fires and the glow of rage. Christians, Atheists, and Muslims claimed their territory with brutal displays of strength, and the air was thick with the acrid scent of smoke and blood. This was a hellscape, where our humanity was stripped away, and only survival instincts remained.

I stood at the forefront of our makeshift battalion. We were warriors, and the world was our crucible. Each skirmish grew more brutal, each clash more desperate. We were no longer fighting just for a belief; we were fighting for our very souls, our right to exist in a world that had turned its back on us. The streets ran red with the blood of the fallen, and the cries of the wounded reverberated through the night like a haunting symphony of despair.

In the moments of quiet, as we regrouped and tended to our wounds, I realised that the silence of God was not an absence but a challenge— a call to arms in a world that demanded we choose sides. The fight was not just against an enemy but against the very darkness that threatened to consume us. It was simple, really. Become what appears to be a hero, or die a victim.

As the violence escalated, it became painfully clear that the governments— those who swore to protect us, were crumbling beneath the weight of their own corruption. Politicians, once held in high regard, now danced on the strings of power-hungry factions, their loyalties swayed by money and fear. In the chaos, they found a perverse opportunity to consolidate their influence, manipulating the unrest to justify their authoritarian grip on society.

Behind closed doors, deals were struck with extremist leaders, allowing them to operate with impunity in exchange for political support. The promise of votes and power overshadowed the cries for justice. I could feel the betrayal in my bones as we faced not just an enemy in the streets, but the very institutions meant to uphold our rights.

Muslim factions, emboldened by this corruption, began to force conversions, wielding their faith like a weapon. They roamed the neighbourhoods under the guise of salvation, but their true intentions were far more sinister. "Join us or perish." They proclaimed, their voices a chilling reminder of the stakes involved. Those who resisted faced brutal retribution, a swift and merciless punishment that left the streets stained with blood and fear.

Elia, ever the fierce advocate for our cause, confronted one of these groups, her voice unwavering. "You can't force faith! It isn't a weapon for you to wield!" But her words fell on deaf ears, drowned out by those who believed they were doing their Allah's work. So, we killed them. The scene was chaotic. Shouts of anger and cries for help echoed in the air as we subjected ourselves to the force we inflicted upon them and twisted their beliefs into something more grotesque.

Meanwhile, in the heart of Christian factions, leaders began to weaponise scriptures just as the Muslims did, twisting biblical verses to justify their own agendas, branding anyone who questioned their authority as enemies of God. Each sermon became a rallying cry for violence, urging the faithful to take up arms and defend Christendom. Annabeth recognised the danger of this rhetoric. "They're using our beliefs against us!" She rallied us to take action, to expose the corruption and the manipulation that turned our sacred texts into tools of war. We could not allow our faith to be a weapon of oppression, like the Quran. It had to be a shield of love and unity.

How could we fight back against both the external enemy and the corruption festering within our religious and government leaders? The struggle was as crucial as the fight for survival, and I realised our greatest weapon was not violence, but truth— a truth that could shatter the chains of manipulation binding our communities.

Together, we forged a plan to confront the corrupt officials and extremist leaders who had taken our faith and twisted it into an instrument of war. We would expose their lies, dismantling the narrative that had ensnared so many. We would be the voice of reason in a world gone mad, even if it meant standing against those who claimed to be our leaders.

The battle lines were drawn, not just between Christians and Muslims, but against the very forces that sought to control us through fear and division. The question loomed large… how could we reclaim our faith AND our freedom in a world that seemed hellbent on tearing us apart?

Crowds began to form without coordination. Christians circled together in prayer. Muslims began to massacre all of them. Prayer rallies, counter-rallies. Faith demonstrations disguised as worship, worship disguised as threat. People filmed themselves crying, thanking the Lord for choosing them, believing the lie they told themselves and sold it as truth. Others filmed themselves denouncing neighbours who hesitated to give themselves to God. Muslims filmed themselves beheading Christians and Jews and giving their glory to their Allah while they did it.

While many doubted that this message came from God, those who believed became suspicious of those who doubted. Those who stood between the bridge of belief and disbelief were shunned and forced to choose. Their neutrality was considered a betrayal. Choose Christianity, and you *might* have eternal life. Choose Islam, and they may *still* kill you.

Annabeth asked me, "Why not just say that this came from God?"

And I said to her, "Do you sincerely believe that God would tell us to rush? He doesn't need us to rush."

I felt a surge of frustration. She looked conflicted. I shook my head vigorously, anger rising within me. She even considered converting to Islam… They always said to "Submit," and that was the message that was broadcast. I told her off for it. We hunted them the way they hunted us. Why be misled? That night, anonymous hackers streamed the same message across every mobile phone, every laptop and every television screen, "WAKE UP." A message that was meant to startle the masses.

Isabelle looked around. "What does this mean?"

"It means the fight is escalating," I replied. A sense of urgency is creeping into my voice. "People are being forced to choose sides. Those who stand in the middle are seen as traitors. There's no room for neutrality anymore."

The tension was electric as we realised the stakes. As the echoes of the broadcast faded, I looked at my friends, determination igniting in my chest. We will remind everyone that faith can be a force for good, not a weapon of destruction. The world was aflame, and we were at its centre, ready to carve our names in the annals of history, whether as saviours or as the damned. The choice was ours, and the battle was just beginning.

"What's our next move? Annabeth asked, her voice steady, despite the fear growing in her eyes.

As we huddled in the dim light of our makeshift refuge in Vancouver, the weight of our circumstances hung heavily in the air. The chaos outside was a constant reminder of the reality we were living in, a world spiralling into violence and madness. I broke the silence.

"Well, flights are grounded, we're stuck in Vancouver, we have no firearms, and we're squatting in some busted hotel. Top it off, Muslims are blowing up makeshift IEDs all over the place; They're literally taking that broadcast to heart. So, our plan?" I glance at Isabelle, "I know you want to be a pacifist, but these people aren't gonna stop, and you know it's just gonna get worse from here. We can't let them force Islam on us, so we're gonna make it impossible for them to live as Muslims. That's the plan."

Elia spoke plainly. "That's not much of a plan… might wanna go into more detail there."

I gave Elia the dirtiest side-eye. "I don't have a plan, but if I had to make a plan, then the new plan is the old plan, where we snatch 'em and then kill 'em, cause right now, all we're doing here is defending ourselves when they attack first. We just have to be creative because we don't know this city."

Elia had a grin on her face. Crazy bitch.

Nasreen looks at me softly. "What are you thinking about?"

"My mother. I just hope she's alright." I replied.

"She'll be alright, won't she? Don't you have a way to contact her?" Nasreen asked.

"No, I'm pretty sure she got herself a new number. For all I know, she could be dead by now. My mother isn't a violent person. Not like me." I said.

If my father and Amara were still alive, maybe she'd put up more of a fight. I wouldn't be surprised if *you* ended up like my mother if you had nothing left to fight for. At some point in our lives, we wake up to fight for something. People would fight to keep their relationships going, some to keep their jobs, some to keep their families from breaking apart, and some fight just to wake up the next day. Would our efforts be inconsequential if we fought just to end up with nothing? To be nothing? To mean nothing? To be like the snowflakes, all moving in unison for a single mission. To fall. To melt away. To be forgotten.

The time we spent in a militia in New York was nothing compared to our time in Vancouver. Vancouver was a lot more primal. We didn't fight at a distance. We fought so close that you could feel their breath on your skin. The Muslims were winning in this regard because they'd always gang up on one person at a time, leaving them outnumbered. When that man or woman fell, they'd move onto the next target, then the next, then the next. It worked for days, and we'd retreat every time.

It wasn't until Elia had the brilliant idea of siphoning gas out of cars and putting the liquid into glass containers with a firework and a few nails wrapped around it inside, which made for an improvised Molotov pipe bomb. Not only would the gas splatter all over the place and burn them, but their flesh would also be shredded. It wouldn't kill them, but at least there'd be permanent damage.

We had a few new additions to our group, whom we met at that church. Derek and Natalia— a young married couple, some guys, Elijah and Dale, and this girl, Tamara. This Dale guys a little bit of a weirdo, socially awkward, but he really switches up when it comes to a fight. Like us, these people didn't believe in the message, believing it to be another hoax. They also shared the same beliefs *we* had about the Muslim population, but they weren't as violent or cutthroat as we were.

While many believed in Islam's divine providence, and Vancouver being what it was, Christians were the minority here. Don't get me wrong, there were still 2.7 million Christians in British Columbia, and the rest being Muslim, but it explained why, with all the hate speech laws and religious persecutions, they didn't target the Muslims as much. So, whenever a Muslim would terrorise a Christian or a church, the cops would turn a blind eye. You would only see them intervene if they were at the scene, not out of duty, but because of the people recording them not doing anything.

We OGs shared what life was like for us before we met our new friends. Not everyone knew about me as much as I thought. They were really glad they didn't have to experience life as we did, I mean, who could blame them? They were still able to maintain a semblance of innocence.

While we, the OGs, did the killing, Isabelle and the newbies burned down stores that sold Halal foods at night. The whole province of British Columbia was melting away its own foundations; a few fires at local grocery stores weren't much for the authorities to care about. It did piss the Muslim community off, though, that's for sure. But the anger we were about to make them feel was nothing compared to this.

There was a mosque in White Rock that we took a fancy to. Two floors, a lot of guests, not a lot of exits. When their service started, we had the exits blocked with cars, doused them with gasoline and left the gas caps open and the car running. Half of us were at the front, the rest were at the back. When we gave the signal, we threw Elia's makeshift Molotov pipe bombs through the windows and bolted. We watched at a distance as the colourful explosions of the bombs went off. We could hear dozens of them screaming, using all their strength to get the doors open. When they finally did, women in niqabs set up in flames ran out, bumping into the car, igniting the gas that was beneath them.

It was quite the spectacle. You couldn't see the flames, but you could see the heat radiating off the ground, and then boom! The car explodes. It hit the news later that afternoon, marking it as a terrorist attack. Something to keep in mind because, when they massacred another church, killing 83 people just a few days before that, they presented it as an "attack," not a "terrorist attack." Just an "attack." But it's whatever. We left them a nice "You are the infidels" message graffiti outside their mosque. This prompted them to march in the thousands the next day with their jihadist terrorist flags, their children walking beside them, with the same bullshit chant you always hear them screaming atop their lungs.

It was really good for us, you see, because we needed them to gather in masses if our next attack was going to work. We teamed up with Christian extremists who wanted nothing more than to eliminate an army of Muslims. One of these guys was a truck driver who transports oil from point A to point B.

He didn't have much left to live for after they murdered his wife. This guy was pretty smart; he fashioned the pumps to act like hoses that would expel and redirect the gas in the direction he controlled from inside the truck. When we found out where the march would take place, he took the oil truck there. He ran through hundreds of them on the streets while dousing the rest of them in oil, and when he covered the lot, he fired a few flare gun rounds into the crowd. You should have seen it; it was like setting off a stack of dominoes, from one end to the other, everything in its wake just burst into flames. Then he started running down the stragglers before the truck itself blew up.

When *he* hit the news, they forgot to mention how his wife died. They labelled him as a deranged individual who had no sense of morality when it came to murdering hundreds. Little did we know that this guy would become the catalyst for turning the world's millions of religious fighters into billions. The entire Muslim population revolted. In Africa, the ISIS fighters massacred over 200,000 Christians, and the numbers are still climbing.

In the Philippines, Sulu, the birthplace of Muslim terrorism in Southeast Asia, the Abu Sayyaf Group conducted multiple coordinated attacks in Davao, Cagayan, Cotabato and Pagadian city, responsible for the deaths of almost 20,000 Philippine nationals. The greatest terrorist attack known to occur in the Philippines.

A friend that I had known since I was an infant died in that attack. The ones you could combat were the gunners, though they had suicide vests on, drugged to their teeth with methamphetamines. They'd go into large crowds and shopping centres, and if they got shot, then they'd blow themselves up if the bullet didn't do it for them. The ones who boarded buses and trains would start at the end and work their way up front. Once the doors were closed and they got moving, they'd start shooting. When the buses were filled with corpses, they'd kill the bus driver, take control of the bus, and drive on the footpaths, running anyone over.

The ones on the train would jump from one carriage to the next til he got to the front. Everyone would be dead by the time they got to the next station. After that, they'd kill everyone at the station until *they* got blown up. Muslims all over the world celebrated. Nations that funded these terrorist organisations gave them a big tip for each life they took. When I got the call from my friend's younger sister, I was devastated. When she asked about *my* sister, I hadn't realised I hadn't told them about her. Goes to show how many years went by without speaking to each other. Now I'll never get to speak to them again and tell them how much I loved them.

Her younger sister, Christine, was distraught. If you saw them, you'd think they were the closest of sisters, and they were, but now she has to walk the earth for the rest of her life without her other half. If things weren't so dangerous, I'd have Christine on the next flight out of there, so that Cheaster would rest easy knowing her sister would be okay. Maybe when this is all over.

I had lost so many friends and family along the way that it had only strengthened my resolve to kill every single one of them. But I was so fucking conflicted. I knew in my heart that it wasn't right, I knew it wasn't, but that anger is so hard to shake off.

There were times when I thought to myself, "Just put a bullet in your head and be done with it," and I'd have that gun in my hand ready to pull the trigger. Then I'd get this voice in my head telling me to stop. My body wants me to pull the trigger, my heart wants me to pull the trigger, but it's always my mind that doesn't want to give up just yet. It would be so easy.

But then, what happens if they win? What if they take control and force those to live under their rule? No freedom of religion, no morality, no safety, but millions, if not billions of Muslims forcing you to believe and live in their ways. I don't think that's fair at all. There are nations out there living just like that, and they are suffering, but those in power call it success.

Back in the UK, people really started to fight back after the Philippine attack. They were already living as dead men anyway, so what did it matter to them if they died a little sooner? From Bristol down to Bournemouth and all the way west to St Ives, Brits were able to take back. It spurred the rest of the nation when they heard they'd taken it back. It was really good for the UK, until the terrorist run governments dropped nukes on those areas. Yeah. The Brits fought for it, they took it back, they held it and then lost it to some nukes because the invaders couldn't take it back. 895,000 lives lost just like that. Don't forget the fallout; that shit's about to kill some more people.

I had an inkling this would spread. Not only did it affect the temperatures around the UK, but the quarantine zones that the native Brits had to make only made it worse for them because of the exposure, because why would invaders provide *them* with protective gear? What's worse is that imports into the country were suspended due to the contamination risk. Many people were starving. Good and evil.

That's what most leaders around the world feared. Them using those nukes. It begs the question: Would they risk the planet because of a few losses? I'll tell you this much. The United States couldn't risk sending their troops to the UK to take it back because it didn't want to risk them dropping bombs on its own lands. Not yet, anyway. The President knows that these Muslims don't fight fair. They know they won't win if the US decides to take it back.

If I had it my way, assuming they had no access to the British navy, the submarines and ships would still be under British control; therefore, if anything, they would assist the US in retaking the country. If they were smart, they would have sailed all their ships and subs to the United States and had them dock there, so enemy ships wouldn't have the opportunity to sink them.

I would probably feign military training around Greenland, while the rest of my subs, along with the British subs, make their way around the island. I'd expect the British Navy to hand over intel about the locations of every nuclear and surface-to-air missile in the country so that the subs could destroy them. Then I'd send US troops in by ship and plane. If it was executed quickly enough, those invaders would lose the country as soon as they got it. You'd have to be a crazy enough leader to take that risk. I know I would be.

If I could return to your time, I'd have fought harder; I would have warned you all before any of this started. If I had, you'd be walking in much safer streets, but instead, you're walking past buildings with broken glass, blown-up cars, Muslim gangs wanting to stick themselves inside you, and Christians hanging off light posts.

CHAPTER TWELVE

Holier Than Thou

I would be remiss if I neglected to tell you the actions that some Christians and Atheists took, which have been instrumental to Islam's success. You see, Christianity is one of the most, if not the most, hated religions in the world, and I cannot understand why. Was it because of the crusades? Which failed, by the way. Maybe because of the belief that nobody can find salvation other than through Christ himself. Maybe the perceived hypocrisy of love and acceptance? Perhaps the social and political stances on LGBTQ+ rights? Or maybe it's the holier-than-thou attitude some carry.

What really stood out to me was the rejection of authority. During the Roman Empire, it was deemed a threat to state authority, and that seems to be a recurring issue in today's society. This has led some to believe that Christians are attempting to legislate their beliefs upon others, but that in itself only reminds me of what Islam is trying to do whenever they march the streets calling for Sharia Law. If I rejected God for any reason, it would have been because of all the suffering in the world, because why would an all-powerful God allow such suffering to occur?

Then I realised. Free will. Imagine if there were no evil. You'd have no reason to reject God, and you'll love him always, right? Now put some evil into the mix.

Have everything that gives you security be taken away from you, everything that makes you happy, everything you think fulfils you be stripped away, and then loving God anyway despite all of it. You still have faith in spite of your pain.

When they killed my sister, I screamed at God, I turned my back on him, I cursed him, I shunned him. The anger became my new God; despite all the hope he was trying to send my way. I had no reason to have any faith in him because he took someone so innocent, someone so pure, away from me, and I wondered. If she were still here, would we still be living in the UK? If we had, would we have been affected by nuclear radiation? Would I be as violent as I am today? Would I have killed that many people because of this vengeful rage? Would I be happy? Had I not gained all this strength, would I still be weak, had this catalyst not occurred? Would my sister suffer if she were still alive? I know this, though. Had she still been alive, I wouldn't have broken my promises this much. I promised many times, never to spill blood again, knowing I couldn't keep it.

But what does Christianity have to do with any of this? Because of Christianity, those who carry this "white guilt" have corrupted the meaning of inclusivity to sacrifice their neighbours' mothers, sisters and daughters to preserve the myth of multiculturalism by allowing so many fake asylum seekers into the country to run rampant, spreading fear however they wish. Christianity brings out the worst parts of you and holds a mirror that forces you to see the parts you hide so well. Your fakeness, your hypocrisy, your anger, your misguided passions, your lust, your character.

The darkest parts of yourself. Forced to rise to the surface so that *you* can expel them. But some people embrace that darkness, and use it for their own gains. You understand how evil people can be, how manipulative they can be. How cunning, like serpents. I've said this before, but politicians are the best liars. There will never be a politician who won't promise you something they know cannot be achieved. They always have to sell it. But then, they'll never be able to deliver. You will never hear a politician tell you the truth or sell you unfiltered honesty to win office.

I promise you right now, had any of this happened to you, your stance on these issues would change immediately. You act like you are there for your neighbours, your friends or your family, but then, when it comes to keeping them safe, you magically turn a blind eye, because when they're in danger, it's not happening to you, so you're fine, right? Your friend was just raped, but it didn't happen to you, so you're fine, right? Pakistani grooming gangs just murdered your friend, but it's not happening to you, so you're fine, right? Your sister was just abducted by the same asylum seekers you spent the last hour buying groceries with, and they're going to rape her and then dump her body in the river, but it's not happening to you, so you're fine, right? But when it finally happens to you, and it *will* happen to you, what then?

How could I say something like that? It's quite simple, really. Please look into the eyes of every person you walk by. Do it, and I can assure you, you'll be able to identify which of the men are undressing you with their eyes, which men, if not many bystanders were around, would be bold enough to snatch you and take you behind a bush, and which people would be too afraid to come and rescue you. But I want you to pay special attention to the eyes that sink straight into darkness, because those are the eyes that want to kill you simply for being who you are, and you know what? The more you allow into the country, the more dangers you'll have walking around, especially at night when you are not safe.

Christians may have been taught to show kindness to all, friends and enemies, but we are all judged by the actions we take when someone is in need. Christians are taught to show mercy, but how much mercy are you willing to show your enemies when they're murdering somebody right in front of you? If it were a child, would you step in then? Or would you continue on your day?

It reminds me of that day. You just stood by and watched, and *you* did nothing. My cries for help fell on deaf ears, and those who watched fell asleep with their eyes wide open. What pissed me off? You'd rather pull your phones out and record it for posterity so you can upload it on the internet for the world to see, and when they call you out for not helping, your excuse would be, "I was recording, I figured someone was going to help," when thirty other people were recording with you.

If Jesus were walking this earth like you and I, what do you think He would do if He saw somebody getting hurt? Do you think He'd just walk away? Just let it happen to you? I think He'd stop them, then forgive them, and then show them the true way of doing things. That's what I think he'd do. If it were Muhammad, he'd probably rape you with them, but then he'd force the rapist to marry you and call it divine justice. Christians have also fought for Christian lands for centuries. Why is it now that they choose to fight when it's already too late? Or if anything, near impossible to return things to the way they were.

Christians can be so kind and welcoming that it's almost off-putting. You know that radar you got going off in your head that it takes you back and makes you think, "hmm, something ain't right here," and then you realise just how fake that person is once the mask kind of falls off? Muslim's don't hide the fact that they want to kill you and are very open about it, but a Christian who doesn't like you, the fake nice energy is pretty disgusting. That's why so many of them do "such good things" in the name of God, but really they're just out for themselves. The good Christians are doing good even when people aren't looking; they do good without the need for recognition, without the praise.

Atheists believe in fact rather than "fiction," so when they hear of Muslims and their need to invade a new nation and enforce Sharia Law, and kill all the infidels, they won't believe it. When a Muslim openly tells them that it is their divine mission to kill those who refuse to follow their Allah, they won't believe it. Most Atheists I've met are generally happy people, you know, they don't need religion to feel fulfilled, and that's great, but I just know they feel empty inside. They don't want to believe in a God that could be watching down on them because Atheists are generally extremely logical. They always seem to be the ones that I've noticed who lack the moral compass that the respective Christians and Muslims have.

Muslims will always defend another Muslim, unless they leave Islam, then they'll kill them. A handful of Christians will always do what's right, even if nobody is watching. For instance, maybe an old lady is struggling to cross the street, and you see a few men walk right past her, but when you decide to help that woman, all of a sudden, those men will come back, stop the cars, take her other arm, just so they can be seen doing good. That kind of kindness is disgusting. Atheists will fend for themselves at the end of the day, because as long as it doesn't happen to them, they're okay. Muslims are doing something right in that regard; they don't lack the community, but I could be wrong, because they always turn on each other whenever necessary.

Derek, Natalia, Elijah, Dale, and Tamara— the newbies we met at the church. They had similar points of view to us; they knew the growing threat of the

Muslim population, but didn't know how to speak up or fight against it. They were there at the bloody brawl that happened a few weeks ago, and we've been fighting against the horde ever since. Even now, we've all become a really close family these long years, if not for a few losses along the way.

While they didn't lose anyone that they loved, they were terrified of the idea that they could. Neighbours they knew but barely spoke to were attacked by the same religious group, and a pattern was established for them. They chose to act accordingly. They didn't terrorise the Muslims back at first, but defended against them.

The newbies were positively radicalised when they were at the scene of an active terrorist attack at a shopping centre, where 32 lives were taken. Elia, Annabeth and the rest of us became the newbies way forward. When they saw us fighting during that brawl, I guess it inspired them to do the same, but on a much greater scale. I look back at them now, and I realise some of us wouldn't be alive today if it weren't for them. Dale, despite his weirdness, has saved my life on multiple occasions. Tamara saved Annabeth a few times, too.

It gets a bit heavy, this war. If you stood where I'm standing right now, looking down at the rest of the world, you'd blame yourself for what happened. You'd even second-guess whether you made the right choices leading up to now. Now you're wondering, "Well, how do I fix this then?"

I would tell you that you already know how to fix it, that the answer to your question is that burning need in your stomach to do something. When you get that feeling where you know something isn't right, fucking act on it and fix it. This woke mind bullshit is cancerous, and you know it. It twisted the minds of so many people who just wanted to be included, and it turned them into belly-up namby-pambies.

The weight of personal choices cannot be overstated, because every individual faces crossroads that challenge their character and shape the collective fabric of our society. Many cling to this false sense of security that comes from distancing themselves from the violence and suffering that plague this world. But because of this, it fosters this stupid behaviour to ignore the plight of others under the pretence that it doesn't affect them directly.

When news of violence fills our screens, a phenomenon of desensitisation emerges, and so our emotional responses to such tragedies dull over time, which leads to a chilling acceptance of brutality as a norm rather than a call to action. It's why so many of us are numb, where we lack empathy for others, and why we have this innate need for self-preservation like demons, doing whatever it takes to survive. Even if it means doing nothing.

This is where psychology takes effect. Bystanders. When you stand around doing nothing but recording the whole thing, people like you will assume that someone else will intervene, which results in a collective paralysis that allows injustices to thrive. It's quite ironic, actually. How passivity brews cycles of violence.

At the heart of it all lies a moral responsibility. We grapple with the weight of our choices, I get that, but when fear dictates behaviour, it transforms us into complicit observers of the very injustices we claim to abhor.

But you know what? Nobody seems to want to reflect on these things. It starts and ends with you, after all.

CHAPTER THIRTEEN

Name Your Price

I had this thought. I wonder if the Left is that easily brainwashed, or if they're just that stupid. Muslims vote for the left because they *can* be easily manipulated, and that seems to be the only conclusion that makes the most sense. Nothing will ever justify committing treason under the assumption that it will make your country better. Why vote for someone, knowing they will ruin a great nation? Why sit there and expect something to change when *you are that change*? If you hate your home so much, then leave. Don't ruin it for everyone else.

When you leave the house in your ridiculously coloured hair and preaching to whoever will listen, "Yes, I'm the fucking queen, and you're a low-level incel," and then abusing anyone who rejects you, you're part of the problem. When you have white coloured skin, and you feel guilty for all the slavery and colonisation your ancestors committed, and now you're trying to make up for it because you don't want to "repeat the cycle," out of the expense of everyone else, you're part of the problem.

When you continue to vote for the same side for 20+ years, even though you can see how much your party has fucked up your country, you are part of the problem. If you sincerely believe that importing 3rd world immigrants into the country will bolster the economy, and think a few more rapes, murders, thefts and petty crimes are worth absorbing, you are part of the problem.

Gay, Lesbian, Transgender? I almost feel bad for you all, because you're supporting the very people who will kill you the moment they get what they want. Don't believe me? That's fine. Watch what happens when they take over the world. Look at every Arab/Middle Eastern nation in the world, do you really think they allow people like you to live? They want to bring those laws to your backyard. I have nothing against you or your community, but this is a tough truth to swallow.

Lower your pride and do your research. If kids weren't brainwashed into believing they were different genders, maybe there wouldn't be any misgendered school shooters. Yeah. Males aren't built to handle the high levels of estrogen that women do, because they aren't used to handling a highly intense level of emotions; only real women can do that. Women cannot handle high levels of testosterone either, which is why so many of them are depressed.

If you want to be gay, then be gay. If you want to be a lesbian, then be a lesbian. If you want to be bisexual, then be bisexual. If you want to be a transgender woman, go ahead, chop your dick and balls off and get yourself a freshly made lab pussy, prop on some fake tits and pump your body full of estrogen for the rest of your life. If you want to be a transgender man, go ahead, give yourself a full hysterectomy, chop your tits off, get yourself freshly made lab dick and pump your body full of testosterone for the rest of your life.

Just understand that the hate you think you're getting right now will be nothing compared to the hate you *will* get when Sharia Law is in place. It doesn't matter if you're a lesbian or a transgender male; they'll rape you and then kill you. Gay men, transgender women, they'll just kill you and deep down, you know it.

Don't fight for a lie because you're afraid of what people might think of you. People will hate you no matter what you do. They'll resent you simply for having opposing beliefs. The need to be included shouldn't be a driving force for you, because those motivations are what led to this burning world in the first place. Every piece of culture was destroyed because they believed Islamic culture was the only thing that mattered. They killed all the dogs on the planet. If you didn't attend prayer, they'd kill you. Every street corner, women were chained up and put on sale, and guess what? It was the same woman who said, "Inclusion is our strength."

Those with common sense fled to the mountains or went underground. They were the ones fighting to win *your* freedom back. These were the same men and women you called fascists, the same men and women you called white supremacists, the same men and women you called racists, the same men and women you called traitors. We tried to warn you for years, and you hated us for telling you the truth. We warned you that our government was going to betray us, and you wouldn't believe it. Because you let your pride get in the way, you lost everything. Your governments fell, your children brainwashed, the lives of your friends and family taken, and you, barely struggling to survive.

I wonder why.

Muslims may have taken control of this world, radicals or otherwise, but you are as much to blame for allowing this to happen. I know the government is reading this, too. They know damn well this is their fault. They allowed it to happen, too, but we all know they don't care.

The terrorists say, "I want to terrorise your country and bring Islam to every house."

The governments ask, "How much?"

It's what happens when you choose selfishness and lack of morality over the promise you made to your people. You're easily manipulated when you think you have all the cards. You don't have the upper hand when you aren't tethered to anything that holds no value. Muslims always believe that Islam will be the only religion on this planet, and they believe their actions, no matter how cruel, are sanctioned by their Allah. When your God is money, you're useless and inconsequential, because you only have power so long as money has value. At the end of the day, it's just a piece of paper, and when it loses value or purpose, so do you.

There was a man the whole world knew. A God-loving man by the name of Charlie. Many people hated him for his beliefs, but he was really the only man who made any sense in this generation, and people hated him for it. He also spoke many truths that got him killed. He spoke about fraud, about God, about Islam, about Christianity, about transgenderism, about Israel, about the woke mind virus, and about your rights. For years, he tweeted about what those in power were doing, about what those in religious sects were doing, and after his death, years of tweets have begun to resurface, aligning directly with all the dangers happening at this very moment, about all the lies our governments have tried to bury. They killed Charlie, but the truth cannot be buried forever. His death only fuelled the rage many of us had buried. His death created a million more Charlies.

When the second wave of this war began, Minnesota was like Michigan. No other state was as dangerous as Minnesota and Michigan. Minnesota's governor Dick False committed treason and fraud for years, selling government secrets and military intelligence to China, and had his hand in the Minnesota daycare fraud scheme along with Walaal Fukar, siphoning billions of federal funds amongst them and their colleagues. False even had one of his constituents killed for attempting to expose this.

When he and Fukar were finally arrested, the terror cells in Minnesota were activated, and because the people's distrust of these people was proven right, the government itself began to topple completely. This forced standing governments to forfeit their power to religious leaders across Christianity and Islam. It wasn't forfeited willingly. They created radicals on both sides, and that power was taken by force.

The world burns down to complete dog shit. Do you know who profits from it? Billionaires and large-scale corporations. At its peak, thirteen of the richest, most powerful families this world has ever known. Some live directly under the spotlight, but the rest of them choose to live in the shadows, like puppet masters moving the world, its money, its resources, its people, its pawns, however they wish. You think the monarchs rule this world; you're mistaken. They're merely figureheads.

They are known as the Crown Council. Beneath them, the Committee of 300. The richest and most powerful subfamilies. Billionaires and top millionaires you know today. Some you even admire for their intellect or good looks, and even the services their corporations provide you. This tier will consist of influential individuals and families who hold the most significant power over global affairs. Political leaders, business magnates, and key figures in spook organisations. They are your masters.

Then you have The Round Table. The think tank of this great pyramid. The Trilateral Commission, the

Council on Foreign Relations, The Royal Institute of International Affairs, The United Nations, The Club of Rome and The Bilderberg Group. These groups meet in secret. Meeting kept away from prying eyes, closed to the press, and no public meeting taken. These men and women are all a part of the shadow world government; an elite group determined on imposing a one-world government. These groups alone control the consensus around the free market and their leaders' interests around the globe. They influence markets like nobody else. They can steal your wealth and make it look like a market crash.

You thought you were free? Guess again. Beneath the Round Table, you have World Financial Control. The IMF, WB, Bank of International Settlements, Central Banks, Tax Revenue, and Interest Revenue. Your world simply stops without it. You want true freedom? Live in the wild, build a cabin on an island, and even then, it's just a taste; they'll find you eventually. Choose to live amongst your kin? You have the corporations that control you. Control the food, control the product, you control the people. Control the money, you control the world.

How do they keep you in check? Media. Education. Governments. Religion. The media controls the elite's message to the masses, and many of you believe the bullshit they tell you. Academia is where you're brainwashed. They make you believe that birth, school, labour, taxes, and death are the meaning of life. Guess what, it's not. They turn you into debt slaves and call it progress. Those who rebel, the class clowns, the C-graders? Yeah, they're the ones who end up in charge, because whether they know it or not, they are the ones who cannot be controlled. The governments that continue to fail us? They're the ones tasked with silencing you and people like me from telling the truth. You will disappear like you never stepped foot on this earth. Finally. Religion. The truth they have corrupted the most. Follow your faith, and listen to its teachings, and in doing so, will be rewarded in heaven for obeying the rules. And we're at the bottom, you see. The foundation for keeping them all up. And at its highest point, atop the peak, is the Great Eye that sees all.

What gave them that right, do you think? You'd be lucky if you were born into those families; you wouldn't have to worry about a thing. People like us, we have to fight for the things we want. A lot of these billionaires are living in their own private bunkers that can stretch the size of a football field, and maybe even more. A built-in underground palace just for them and their family to wait out the storm they brought upon all of us. The movies don't lie to you. They tell you the truth that is so bold that you think it's a lie, but it's not. The only reason why they've gotten this far is that you've allowed them to. There are billions of us, and hundreds of them, and yet they have the power to control every step we take like a video game.

The celebrities you love are the pawns they use to distract you from the real problems. Christians massacred in Africa, here's a new concert! Millions facing homelessness, here's a new scandal! The cost of living is rising too high; here's a new movie! You love them, so you *can* be distracted. If darkness surrounds you, it's because you let it. There can be more to your life had you just spoken up. They wouldn't have been in control had you fought. The world wouldn't have ended had you a little courage.

CHAPTER FOURTEEN

Gone The Gemini

They didn't call themselves prophets; that would have been too obvious. No. They called themselves the anointed ones. One spoke for Jesus, and one spoke for Muhammad. Neither of them claimed divinity, but many marked them as divine. Both of them claimed they were necessary, and many contributed to their flock. The Christian speaker had a clean record and a long background in humanitarian work. He thought himself sinless. Dressed in an immaculate white suit that gleamed in the fading light, the Christian man looked almost ethereal. His hair, dark and slicked back, framed a face that radiated confidence, though a hint of something darker flickered in his eyes. He smiled broadly, revealing perfect teeth that sparkled like pearls, a façade that belied the complexities of his character. There was an unsettling charm about him, a magnetism that drew people in, yet left an unshakeable feeling of unease in the air. For me, anyway. As he spoke, his popularity grew greater than that of the Pope.

His voice was smooth and resonant. "Thank you for your ears, for they have been blessed to receive the truth from God. Unity is the very essence of our existence, as it is the key to unlocking divine purpose with us all!"

The man's rhetoric flowed like a river, each word carefully chosen to resonate with the crowd's deepest desires for belonging and purpose. He spoke of love and compassion, painting a picture of a world united under a single truth. But within his truth lay an insidious expectation that true unity could only be achieved by following *his* teachings, by submitting to his vision of righteousness. Even he himself believed it was a crucial foundation that would allow them to return to God.

The Muslim was a reformed criminal in his 60s. A devout Muslim. An intellectual. Measured, charismatic, and obsessed with order. He spoke of restoring dignity through order and cleansing the world of infidels before the return of the Messiah. The glow of screens illuminated in a darkened room, dressed in a black thobe that conveyed authority and strength, the Muslim's presence was commanding. His beard, once a symbol of his devotion, now seemed to bristle with the intensity of his convictions. He leaned closer to the camera for his growing viewer count, his voice low and measured, yet laced with an underlying threat.

"Brothers and sisters, we are at war! A war for our dignity, our faith and our future!"

As the chat exploded with emojis and comments, his charisma was undeniable, but it was entwined with a violent obsession for order. "Order must be restored! We cannot allow the infidels to turn these lands into sinful abominations that our Allah has already made beautiful! We cannot let them corrupt us!" He exclaimed as each word dripped with conviction, resonating with those who hungered for direction in a chaotic world.

His hands gestured empathically, slicing through the air as he spoke of cleansing the world of impurity, of taking action against those who opposed his vision, and of standing against those who threaten the existence of Muslims. His eyes burned with intensity, his demeanour shifting from measured to menacing.

"We will not wait for the Messiah to save us; we will take matters into our own hands!" His rhetoric took on a darker tone as he painted a picture of violence as a means to an end. "Join me, and we will cleanse these lands, drive out the impure, slay them wherever we find them, and restore the honour that is rightfully ours!"

The chat erupted with frenzied support, hearts and fire emojis flooding the screen, a testament to the intoxicating power of his message. Yet, a few voices questioned his path forward, though their comments were drowned out by the overwhelming tide of agreement. The Muslim savoured the adoration, feeding off their energy, unaware, perhaps even uncaring of the looming danger in his call to arms. As the livestream continued, the Muslim leaned back, a satisfied smile creeping across his face. He was no longer just a man broadcasting from a dimly lit room; he had become a figure of strength, a self-proclaimed leader rallying his followers for a cause that blurred the lines of right and wrong.

You would think that their followers grew because of their signs and wonders, and miracles and divine authority given by their respective Gods, but no, they could not produce miracles. Their following grew because of clarity; the eureka we're all addicted to. They both offered rules, they both drew red lines, they both marked their enemies, and they both gave their followers purpose.

Of course, anyone who would be given structure would follow it, especially in uncertain times, and structure was a religion that people followed during uncertainty. What I had noticed was that violence spread rapidly in regions where their speeches took place. No matter where they went, they were emboldened by the idea that their words carried significant weight, that their lives had more meaning compared to those of others. The people didn't need miracles to believe in them; they just needed the permission to act on their primal natures.

Because of the anointed ones, governments acted rapidly to stop the spread of violence that their teachings set forth, and reestablish government. Emergency laws began to pass very quickly. Religious councils began to assume new legal authority, a development that hasn't occurred in centuries. While we didn't agree with their methods, it allowed us to act freely without worrying about the repercussions. Governments tried so hard to win their power back, but the repercussions *they* had to face against religious factions were diabolical.

Governments under Islamic rule were executed for standing against the caliphate. Government employees under Christian rule were imprisoned for trying to return to the corruption that once eclipsed over their great nations.

The same things kind of happened here in British Columbia. The government here was toppled, unable to control the wave of Islam. The deals the government made with them backfired, effectively losing their power in a matter of months since the broadcast, but what I found strange was how they were able to amass such an occult following. Two distinct factions that were at war with each other for over a thousand years, their tension bubbling to the surface once again.

"Here we go again," Elia exclaimed.

"Nothing has changed. It's still hell, just with new management." I replied.

The anointed ones claimed to be Godly men, but they both had a hand in drawing the people away from God. Let's be real, I only liked them because I could inflict violence without repercussion. But millions, drawing near billions, died in the war of two fronts. At home, many houses of worship began coordinating with police, where some sided with Christians and others with Muslims. The apocalypse didn't arrive with fire, or beaming rays of light from the sky… it arrived with paperwork.

I can understand now why this war had to take place. When the fate of the world is uncertain, and security concerns are at an all-time high, advanced surveillance systems began to spread rapidly, "For protection." The whole world really did follow in the footsteps of China. Every street, public space, and private residences, were riddled with facial recognition cameras. Every neighbourhood had entry and exit blocks where you had to identify yourself to leave. Tracking you was their priority; if you turn your location services off, guess what? You can't because it is now mandatory to be tracked with every step you take.

Social platforms even adjusted their algorithms to reduce the spread of spiritual misinformation. To push this further, governments have compelled these social media platforms to require their users to disclose their religious affiliations for safety, unity, and clarity. Depending on which religious affiliation their government was leaning toward, the opposition seemed to be the ones affected most.

This greatly affected wartime efforts, too, because Christians and Muslims were already fighting against each other, and yet were forced to fight together, and against each other. Some let their comrades die over spiritual beliefs, and some spared the lives of their enemies because they looked like them. Muslim's disobeyed orders because their officer in charge was a Christian and vice versa.

Those who weren't conscripted, and were fighting the war within, employers from all over the globe began filtering their applications, only hiring Christians, or only hiring Muslims, or only hiring Atheists. They even refrained from sharing their religious beliefs among their coworkers because the idea that they might catch a bullet to the back of the head was a possibility. Mixed-faith families began to fracture, and some even to the point of spilling blood.

You see, honour killings were at an all-time high when the anointed ones came into power. Muslim families murdered their wives, sons, or daughters when they converted to Christianity. The apostates had it in their right mind when they left Islam; it was clear there was no violence in their hearts. But the Muslim anointed one, he encouraged the immediate killings of any apostate in the family, as doing so would secure the family's place in heaven, and prevent the apostate from eternal damnation, per their beliefs anyway.

Annabeth and I stopped speaking for a while because of this. All of us were strongly opposed to Islam, whether we believed in Christianity or not. Annabeth seemed to be the only one who was swayed by Islam, because the things we did directly aligned with the teachings of Islam, but the only difference was that we were using those teachings against them. But for some reason, when you use the same teachings against them, you're vilified for it. Annabeth couldn't see the difference between Christianity and Islam at that point; they were all the same to her. Killing was killing, and death was death. Our beliefs were so divided that we almost killed each other, and I don't think either of us had gotten over it.

When it comes to "work," we still have good synergy when it matters most. But once we've moved on to the next, we go back to not speaking to each other. It was kind of sad. I mean, we were there for each other since the beginning, but because of opposing beliefs, we drifted apart, and neither of us seems to want to push our pride to the side and resolve things. Quite poetic, actually.

Isabelle refrained from involving herself in our affairs entirely. She preferred to be a pacifist, doing good to heal instead of torture, which was fine. Ever since we met her, she'd always been the red line between right and wrong. She never agreed to us hurting people, although we tried to make her, but it didn't pan out. Having her around does help us from going too far, so I appreciate her for that.

Elia, who I'm pretty sure is the devil incarnate, was bringing home a new guy every couple of days and torturing the life out of them. But this is British Columbia, you see. Couldn't stay in one place for too long if she was going to be doing that kind of stuff. At some point, we did decide it was best to return to New York, as our home there was better suited for our activities. The journey home was rather horrid.

When things began to escalate too much that they could handle, Derek and Natalia jumped ship. It was just getting too hot and too dangerous. We all got into the habit of looking over our shoulders because we didn't know who had an itch in their brains to kill us. Antifa, annoying little shits, thought it was wise to work alongside Muslims, and while they seemed dangerous in a group, when we singled them out, they seemed to cower in their own piss when we threatened to take their life. You could tell some were incels, Elijah and I stripped who we could naked, Elia would then slice their fun bits off and crush them with her boot. I can't even repeat the words she'd say every time she did it, but you can imagine.

Dale and Tamara were like Isabelle, often refraining from violence, but would only step in if any of us were in immediate danger. They believed violence should only be necessary if one was in immediate danger and nothing more. Yeah, they knew about the shit we did, and while they were against it, saying we were acting just like them, they did admire the idea that we were simply returning the favour.

As for the twins. Well, let's just say they didn't make it. We uh, ran into some trouble and bit off more than we could chew. We thought we were good enough to take on an entire terrorist cell. The twins, Elia, and I were captured. We tried locking them in a trap house they were meeting up in, but what we hadn't considered were stragglers outside. They have been following us ever since we came into the neighbourhood. If it hadn't been for Annabeth, who stayed back to keep watch, I'm pretty sure we'd all be dead.

They tortured us, raped the twins, beheaded them slowly right in front of us, and some guy still decided to face fuck their corpses. Like, I've heard of necrophilia, but to see it happen firsthand was something else entirely. I don't know how Annabeth did it, but she took out most of every guard outside and made her way in through the back before setting us free. This is where she was swayed. What they did to us, we did to them, but she couldn't see that we were the good guys; rather, we were just the same as them.

There isn't a day that I don't regret taking the twins with us. Honestly, if we told them to stay in New York instead of coming out with us to British Columbia, I'm pretty sure they'd still be alive. But instead, I let this vendetta get ahead of me, and now two good people are dead, and they both died in extremely tragic ways. This really broke Isabelle. Those three were each other's rock, you know? She still has us, but to lose people you shared a traumatic bond with for over a year is incomprehensible. It completely shattered her.

How could I ever make up for that?

CHAPTER FIFTEEN

Breathe, Child.

The guy in charge of, I suppose, killing us, we took him alive when Annabeth saved us. We took the twins' bodies with us to have them buried somewhere nice. As for this guy, we felt no joy in hurting him, no anger, no fear. Just empty. Isabelle couldn't bring herself to take vengeance, while we did out of necessity. We cut out his tongue cause he really wouldn't shut up. We had him bound and his limbs spread. I took a sanding machine and scraped off every bit of skin he had on his body, including his scalp, in his crack, even his ball sack, until his body was covered in a jelly-like substance. An enemy screaming, writhing in pain, usually makes me feel good, but these guys really fucked me up.

I even sanded off his face, cut out his eyelids, his ears, and his nose, leaving the cartilage exposed. When he stopped screaming, I doused his body with salt. I stuck needles under each of his fingers and toenails, and then heated them with a blowtorch, searing the flesh from within, until the nails melted from under themselves. When he calmed down, I carved the soles of his feet until the bones within exposed themselves. Then I tore the bones out of his feet, leaving the meat dangling, unable to control it. He kept begging me to just kill him, but I wouldn't have it.

I said to him coldly. "You took people we loved dearly."

I grabbed the blowtorch and cooked his feet until it smelt like cooked pork. When I sliced a piece off of him, he barely felt it. I forced him to eat his own flesh. When he started to throw up, I took the sex machine back out and popped a dildo onto it. This one was covered in blood and shit; he knew that, too, because he could smell it. He fought for a while, and I was having trouble putting it in his mouth, so the muscles in his jaw, I sliced them up so he couldn't control it. He couldn't fight after that. That guy was getting deepthroated by a fuck machine for a good twenty minutes before he passed out. Then I turned it off. When he woke up, I started it back up again.

He started crying, so I asked him why.

"Kill me," he said.

I replied plainly. "No."

I left him to rot for a few days. When I came back, his wounds had festered, stinking up the place. I figured he had died, but he was still alive. Extreme will to live that one. I used some spreaders to keep his mouth open, and I put a deep enough cut in the back of his throat that would keep bleeding, choking him slowly if he didn't keep swallowing. Even after an hour, he wanted to die, but he refused to let go. I used that sex machine on his asshole afterwards, didn't even use lube. He didn't even scream. He sounded like what a Down syndrome kid would if you socked him in the stomach. He refused to eat, so I forced food down his throat. When he had the runs, I forced that shit down his throat too. That infected the wound in the back of his throat. The guy was literally turning a pale green, and his eyes were bloodshot red; I'm pretty sure he was going blind.

When he apologised for what he did, it almost upset me. He kept begging me to kill him, to end his suffering. I said to him that I *was* killing him. Just as slowly as possible. The shit he ingested killed him about 4 days later. Funnily enough, he was the last man I killed until many years later.

I heard a voice that entered my mind, a thought that didn't seem like my own, calling out to me. It kept saying my name over and over again like a chant. I kept fighting that voice until that figure showed up in my dreams. A man bearded and cloaked. He was a figure in the distance at first, just saying my name once, or maybe a few times and then I'd wake up. It was like he was coming closer every single time I fell asleep. Then, in one dream, he was as close to my face as my hands were. Blood dripping from his eyes, and his eye sockets on fire. He didn't speak to me, but his presence did. It jolted me awake. I sprang up as if lightning travelled through every cell in my body, and then he spoke to me in a language I couldn't understand, but the message was clear enough.

I had officially come face-to-face with my actions. The guilt had finally made its way to me. It was at this point that I stopped killing and fighting altogether. Deep down, I knew it was a losing battle. I haven't heard from my mother since she left, so I can only assume that she's dead, which means that I am the only one left in my bloodline, which is a depressing set of affairs because my sister was the good one. The farm was beautiful.

There was a little pond nearby that had super clear water and little fish, some frogs, and some ducks. I'd sit by the deck just contemplating every decision I made leading up to this point. And one day I thought, "This is it." I walked to the barn, grabbed some rope, and walked back to the pond. Tied it into a noose, wrapped it around a tree, and around my neck. I sat up on the tree branch, deciding whether I should do it. Then I said, "Fuck it," and jumped. I swung for a little bit. Felt like my eyes were about to burst out of my eye sockets until I finally blacked out. When I opened my eyes again, I was in my bedroom. Figured it was heaven.

I looked in the mirror, and the rope burn marks were around my neck. Elia and the rest of the group walked into the room and slapped the shit out of me.

Isabelle was pretty mad. "What the fuck did you think you were doing?"

"Ending it," I said.

She said I was being selfish. They already had to deal with the twins' death, and they weren't ready to deal with mine. It turns out that Annabeth actually saw me carrying the rope down to the pond. She was the one who saved me.

"We still need you." She said.

The girls were more than capable of taking care of themselves. They didn't need me.

I exhaled quickly, "Guys, I'm tired. I don't want to fight anymore; I don't want to be here anymore. Look around you, yeah? They've won. This world has gone to shit. Everyone is too fucking delusional to see through their own bullshit, or they refuse to. Clearly, people want to watch their world burn, and then ask how it all went wrong, so what's the point of being here?"

"We're here to fight so we can drive them away," said Dale.

I laughed. "Be for real, guys. There are six of us. What the fuck are six people going to do? I'm sorry for even making you believe that we could make a difference, because the reality is, we can't. This is all a waste of time. We're all gonna die, and this was all for naught"

Elia said in defeat, "Wow, you really lost it, huh?"

I told Elia how I felt, and she said I was going crazy. I wasn't going to tell her to stop killing. I doubt she had it in her, even if she wanted to. After the twins' deaths, she really went on a killing spree around the state of New York. She put on a prosthetic of a black woman and put on a fat suit.

She had no reservations or any care about where she was at the time; if she saw a Muslim, or someone who even looked Muslim, she would walk up to them and kill them right there. It was unfortunate because she took the lives of a few Coptic Christians during her killing streak.

Whenever she had time, she'd throw her victim in the trunk of her car, and she'd drive over to some bridge. While they were still unconscious, she'd tie a rope around their necks and have them seated at the edge of the bridge. Then she'd wake them up, and once they felt the startle in their stomach, she'd push them off. She'd leave once they stopped struggling. One of her victims hung quite low; once they hit the end of the rope, their necks snapped instantly, but then they'd feel the weight of a full-size truck going 80mph splatter their bodies like flies on a windshield.

Elia, to this day, hasn't been caught. There'd always be a description of a black, semi-obese woman in her mid 30s as the person of interest, but they'd never find a woman in the fat suit.

There was no point in fighting anymore, not for me anyway. "You all do what you want, just leave me out of it from this point. I want nothing to do with it."

"All of a sudden, you grew a conscience?" Annabeth asked.

"No. I couldn't care less what you do, or who you kill. I am just done." I replied.

The room fell silent for a while, and so I told everyone to leave. To vent out her frustrations, Elia went out to go hunting. Dale and Tamara, the sweethearts, brought me up some food later that night. I spent almost two years isolating myself in that bedroom. While the rest of the world burned, and while the group went out to fight, I was just here.

Whenever they tried to make me feel better, they'd receive the darker side of me speaking to them. Angry, murderous. I'd scream at them to get out. I wanted to be left alone, so I pushed them away. It's easier for them if they had a reason to hate me, you know? So, if I ever tried again, they wouldn't stop me. I had completely given up on life by this point. If I died today, it wouldn't bother me. If anything, I'd be grateful.

I watched the sun rise and set from my window. I watched the moon rise and set from my window. I watched the group leave the farm for days and come back bruised from my window. Elia, in her off time, is always bringing somebody home. The pigs have gotten real fat.

By the time I stepped out, the sun burned my skin like thin bacon. I even got used to only taking showers once a week, so I hadn't realised how badly my room smelt. It was weird timing, though, because once I found the courage to reestablish my strength, I suffered a stroke. Elijah found me and thought I'd tried killing myself again, so he rushed me to the hospital. When he found out I had a stroke, he updated the group. I was in a coma for 8 months, and when I woke up, half my body was paralysed, I had trouble speaking, and I was practically blind in one eye.

It took me months of rehab, learning how to use my limbs again, and it took me much longer to relearn how to speak. I never recovered my vision in my left eye. All the while, New Years celebrations started off with a bang. I'm talking like a big bang. The war in Ukraine was a cluster fuck, and everybody knew it. The USA handed billions of dollars of military aid to Ukraine, and high-ranking officials, including their President, funnelled that money into their own bank accounts.

What topped it off was the new leadership in Britain. Savages without a brain decided it was a good idea to bomb the Russian President's home with explosive drones in an attempt to assassinate him. This inevitably kicked off World War 3.

There's a timeframe, you see. January. The beginning of the end. Venezuela has one of the largest oil reserves and a wealth of natural resources, including gold, iron ore, nickel, diamonds, rare earths, coltan, thorium, and bauxite, making it a highly resource-rich nation. The President of the United States just bombed it. While I don't condemn his actions because he captured a narco-dictator who has relentlessly violated human rights, broken international law, and disguised his narco business as sovereignty, it does set a dangerous precedent.

You see, China purchases most of Venezuela's oil and then distributing them to North Korea. This challenges their energy and economic interests. However, after the attack, China strengthened its anti-U.S. rhetoric regarding Taiwan, stating that if the President can authorise the capture of Venezuela's President, then China can do the same with invading Taiwan, and capturing their President. While China and North Korea are allies, it sets alarm bells regarding regime change as it exposes the limits of China's material power to protect its allies, thus reinforcing North Korea's beliefs that its nuclear deterrents are justified.

When the dust settled from the bombing, the international community stirred with uncertainty, as European nations, which were once hesitant to intervene in Latin American affairs, were now forced to reconsider their stance. They feared that this aggressive U.S strategy could destabilise not just Venezuela, but the entire region. Brazil, with its own political tensions, begins to fortify its borders, wary of the ripple effects that might spill over into its territory.

Meanwhile, in Russia, the President sees this as an opportunity. With historical alliances with Venezuela, Moscow steps in, offering military support and economic aid, framing itself as a protector of sovereign nations against U.S. aggression. The Kremlin's rhetoric intensifies, warning of severe repercussions should the U.S continue its unilateral actions. In the markets, oil prices spike as uncertainty grips global investors. Speculation about future supply disruptions leads to heightened volatility, and energy stocks roar. Countries dependent on Venezuelan oil scramble to secure alternative sources, accelerating the shift towards renewable energy and energy independence.

But what of the Venezuelan people? They're celebrating. Yeah, their country just got bombed, but they're now free from a tyrant. As the international community grapples with the fallout, diplomatic channels begin to fray. The United Nations convenes an emergency session, but divisions emerge. In Venezuela, the humanitarian crisis deepens. NGOs scramble to provide aid, but the chaos makes it difficult to reach those in need. But the rest of the world, a bunch of paid-off dumb cunts who are protesting against the capture of a tyrant, because the person who orchestrated his capture was somebody they hated with a passion. A bounty was put on the tyrant's head for fifty million by the democrats elected president, so why be outraged when it was a republican that captured him? TDS?

Though as tensions escalate, military manoeuvres begin in the region. The U.S. deploys naval forces to the Caribbean as a show of strength, while China conducts military drills in the South China Sea, signalling to the U.S. that it will not back down from defending its interests. North Korea, emboldened by the perceived weakness of the U.S, conducts missile tests around Japanese waters, further escalating tensions. That's when the UK dropped explosive drones on the Russian President's home, and now we're here. Ta-da. War had always been the plan. An excuse was just needed to redraw borders and win new resources.

Russia, China, North Korea, Iran, and their allies, against Western Europe, the United States, Australia, and their allies, forced to fight each other because some dumbass with a limp dick decided they wanted to drop bombs on one of the most powerful leaders in the world. January 22nd, if I remember correctly, is when the world officially lost it. Not only were we already involved in a religious war that decides one's eternal life in heaven or hell, but now young men and women are condemned to fight a war that *nobody* signed up for, while the politicians who started it get to hide in the little underground bunkers.

Many died and are still dying in this war. Yeah, 23 years later, and we're still going at it. I didn't enlist. I tried to, but with my history of attempted suicide, it wasn't wise to let someone like me near a gun. If only they knew what I got myself into in the middle of the night.

Many may not share the same sentiments, but Russia was never the enemy. They're communists, yes, but they were never the enemy. Russia has the greatest land mass compared to every other nation in the world, and parts of Russia are still untouched, leaving one to question the amount of resources their land has in stock. Should the West win and take control of Russian lands, you can already tell how they're going to divide Russia into multiple new nations controlled tightly by the West. China will most likely take the closest piece of Russian land before the West gets its hands on it. Eastern Russia most likely has the greatest oil repositories and other rare earth materials, so China will want to snatch that for itself before anyone else can.

By the end of it, the chances are Western Russia will be given to the West and its leaders, primarily the United States, and the Rest will be split between China and North Korea. But to be frank, China will only be able to obtain this if they invade Mongolia. It wouldn't be much of a struggle for them, and they would win; however, it would also raise tensions between China and North Korea. Having access to a vast potential of resources, anyone would fight over that.

While they were both evil, it was kind of a saving grace, these self-proclaimed anointed ones. Imagine two separate governments that want absolute control. You have the anointed ones who have rallied two of the largest religions together, following the laws made by their respective Gods, and then you have the world's one unified government that seeks absolute control amongst the people, in which they have no right to.

One side of the coin demands you follow the Laws of Moses, and the other side of the coin, where you are being watched 24/7, your finances controlled 24/7, where everything you say can and will be used against you. Everything you do must be to benefit those who do not care about you, those who are willing to throw you into the depths of war for *their* benefit. Which side would you throw your support for? The will to do what you want, when you want, without the control of others, is something I'd want.

CHAPTER SIXTEEN

The Final Declaration

In a few years, the Christians' first public execution was livestreamed. An anointed one's own follower was accused of deliberate spiritual destabilisation. He questioned his teacher's sermon in front of thousands and was ordered to be executed. He did not deny his Lord's teachings, but had doubts about the anointed one himself. He began to realise that God had not sent him, and when he was asked to recant his statement, he refused. The blade that removed his head was sufficient, and the crowd was calm like a river wading through the wind.

Later that night, people posted up prayers, and I... I felt disgusted. Not because a man had died, but because the people who believed in that false prophet felt righteous. It was here that I felt regret for expressing gratitude towards that man. To order the execution of a devout Christian who didn't agree with your teachings like that? It wasn't right. Reminds me of Islam. Did they not see the hypocrisy in their beliefs? I felt betrayed towards the entire Christian community, and maybe I was blinded to the manipulation.

As I sat there watching the livestream unfold before my eyes, I couldn't shake the uneasy feeling that settled in my stomach. The execution was not merely an act of punishment; it was a spectacle and completely unnecessary. It was a twisted display of power masked as divine justice. I had once looked up to him, convinced that maybe his mission was pure, and maybe his teachings were guiding us through the darkness, yet I saw the truth for what it was in that very moment.

It was a manipulation of faith to silence dissent. The parallels to other religions, particularly Islam, flooded my mind. I remembered the stories of persecution and the way belief could become a justification for violence. It was a cycle that seemed unbreakable, and I felt trapped in it.

Christianity, in all my many flaws, was still something I held sacred. As the days turned into weeks, the weight of that execution and the many that followed lingered in my mind like a storm cloud. I was looking for answers in places the darkness couldn't follow. I spoke to anyone who left the path of violence I had been treading. As I lay awake at night, thoughts swirling in my mind like autumn leaves caught in a tempest. I felt the deep-seated anger rising within me. I'm so stupid. How could I be so naïve?

The very essence of faith is supposed to be rooted in love and understanding, yet here I was, with firsthand experience betraying those very ideals. I felt like a fool, a mere pawn in a game I *knew* I was playing. What did it mean to believe, anyway? Was it simply a matter of following a leader? Or was it about seeking a personal connection with the divine? Regret washed over me in waves as I reflected on my past convictions. It's like playing a game of Monopoly, but you don't ever win.

These anointed ones… they really knew how to get a crowd going. The Christian always spoke about doing things peacefully, but the masses always left with anger in their hearts. The Muslim spoke about war, but the people were happy about it. It was kind of funny. Both of the self-proclaimed anointed ones issued statements within days of each other. The language was the same.

"The world will be bathed in blood, but do not be frightened. This is a necessary cleansing, for this is the age for alignment. Peace must follow obedience."

It was official. They did *not* declare war. They sanctioned it, and what they shared soon came to pass.

Maybe Annabeth was right, killing is killing, no matter who the target is. I was so set in my beliefs that Muslims were the only evil in this world, but they're not. There's evil everywhere, even in the mirror. Once you let the psychopath in, you don't really want to stop.

I can still feel love, but killing turns me on now. Ah, it's such a pull between chaos and control. I want to feel guilty, but why? I really turned into a serial killer, didn't I?

Why am I telling you this? Picture yourself in a world where war is the norm, missiles flying overhead, bodies blown to pieces, strangers trying to kill you for your clothes, food, for following a different God, or maybe they haven't had sex in a while, and you happen to be very attractive. I hope you never have to experience it, but if you already are by the time you read my story, then I hope you don't walk the same road that I do. I hope this violence doesn't swallow you whole, because hatred is a very corrosive thing, and sometimes it can never be sated. I'm still waiting for the day that God punishes me. Maybe he'll throw my ass in hell, and I'll spend eternity there. Taking the life of a terrorist isn't that bad, right? It shouldn't constitute eternal damnation if you're making the world safer by expelling a few evils now and then... right?

But you know what? The decision is yours at the end of the day. Sometimes the road you take can't be helped. I was a coward before my sister died, but after I lost her, I let go of that fear and fed it to those who deserved it. When Elia lost her brother, she promised herself she'd never be helpless again. Annabeth? She was stripped of her identity and broken down like leftover meat; you can understand if she has a lot of hatred in her heart. Isabelle? She's still an angel in spite of it all. I do wonder what *you* decide to do, though. I'm excited to see which road you take.

Strangely, you'd think a place like Iran wouldn't be so opposed to Islam taking over the world, but its citizens had differing beliefs with its Islamic Caliphate. Many of Iran's citizens have called for the end of the Islamic revolution and free the nation from its oppression. Many have even called for the return of the Crown Prince to lead a new, free Iran. Citizens are fighting their police, their military, and their government directly, knowing that they may not be alive the next day.

I admire the bravery of the Iranian people because they fight with their voice, as well as their fists, knowing they may be silenced. They're fighting in a specific part of the world where your rights as a human have no value, where you would be shot dead for things we Westerners do every day.

Are you capable of finding the strength these Iranians have for fighting back against their oppressors? To put it in perspective for you, these are millions of men, women and children risking their lives against people who have no compunctions about putting a bullet in their heads, yet they're willing to risk everything for *their* people, in the hopes that they may have a better future. That is the most Christian thing I have ever witnessed, besides Christ, if I had to pick one. The Persians have awoken.

This is no longer the time to stay quiet. After WW2, the generations that followed cosmically fucked things up for us. Honestly, why was inflation a thing anyway? Did you know that you can fit the entire world population in Texas? Or Alaska? You can even fit the whole world's population in Australia, and you'd still have space left over. They act like resources are limited, but it isn't; they act like global warming is a thing, but it isn't. Those in charge of you have a habit of lying straight to your face when it comes to getting what they want, and I don't know what it'll take for you to believe that.

I wouldn't be surprised if you haven't quite yet grasped the consequences of your actions. You still have that "It hasn't happened to me, so I don't care," mindset, and it's really doing you numbers. Your selfishness is really the icing on the cake.

Oh, to see the look on your face once you finally come to terms with the bullshit you've been feeding yourself. I want you to remember this and consider that it isn't that bad yet, as compared to how bad it will be, but it's still bad as of right now, you get me?

At this point, to alleviate the fear, many children were taught to believe that dying young was an honourable thing for God. Many parents filmed their sons and daughters reciting holy prayers for both Christians and Muslims before joining militias to kill each other. Many parents smiled through the tears because grief had become a sinful thing in this world. Death was no longer considered tragic, but something productive; something to look forward to.

Against their will, the children were taken from their parents, forced to fight a war for their Gods. Hundreds of thousands of kids died at each other's hands in a brutal battle with rifles and blades. While many Muslim children lie dead on the streets, many Christian children were crucified atop makeshift crosses. Some were attached by their hands, their wrists, through their eye sockets, some upside down. Children are pure, forced to stain their souls with the blood of other innocents just like them.

Would you like to know what it feels like to be one of the few left in your generation? And knowing that only 12% of the generation that followed you remains? Adult Muslims killed all the Christian children, and all the Christian men killed all the Muslim children, and all the Christian children and Muslim children killed each other. All for faith. Don't even think to yourself that you can have kids in this life, because you'd only be condemning them to a life not worth living. You'd be selfish to do so.

Go get a time machine and fast-forward to my time, and I wish I could say it got better. A lot of the cities around the globe have been turned into ruins, and the war is still as strong as ever, with no intention of slowing down. It's safe to say that it's gotten really quiet. Missiles flying overhead have become the new normal, and those who thrive in chaos are roaming freely out on the streets, preying on the weak. Religion doesn't seem to matter at this point, but there are cases of different factions fighting for whatever resources are left, because a lot of it, you see, is divided amongst the wealthy first, then the rest is sprinkled down, but nobody really buys anything when it gets down to us; it just gets stolen, more so by store employees. I don't blame them.

There aren't really any police officers anymore, either. Not ones you can trust, anyway. It's basically every man for themselves these days, but at least I still have the group. Now, unless you know your way around fixing a car, you're on foot. Power is out for most places, too. Home is basically whatever roof you can find. Because many of the big cities, like New York, are… how should I say this… blown to bits? Radioactive?

Landlocked states were the best places to go. Colorado and whatnot were safe enough, all things considered. We found ourselves this nice warehouse that was converted into a residence, most likely for some bachelor on the outskirts of the city, borderline country town. Now and then, we'd run into some desperate people, and we look like we have a lot of gear, so they always have the dumb idea of coming back. They become a significant source of income over time. People get hungry, you see.

When they sanctioned the war between religions, it made every single person in the world a target for "salvation." Crucified men, women and children were the new norm as they refused to convert to Islam. There was no place you would look where you couldn't see somebody hanging from their limbs, and many couldn't help these people, as they would be crucified too if they were caught. If you had to take a pick, Muslims had won the war because they were killing hundreds of thousands of Christians, Atheists and minority religions, many converted out of fear, while many more were born into it. Cousin marriages and shit like that.

This was the worst case scenario of what would happen because of weak leadership and indecision. Even the ones who think they are almighty are puppets to the same terrorist groups. They laugh now, but next thing you know, they'll be chopping your balls off and feeding them to you.

CHAPTER SEVENTEEN

Mirrors Reveal Truth

You. How many times have you and I walked past each other, I wonder. I wonder what life was like for you. Do you often find yourself reflecting on your choices? More often, the ones you regret? Do you regret not doing anything? Or doing too much perhaps? At what point in your life did you say to yourself, "I'm never getting involved again"? If somebody were getting hurt, would you be there to rescue them? Would you expect someone to rescue you if you needed rescuing? There are quite a few instances where questions like these flow through the minds of people just like you, and while you may call yourself a man/woman of action, you still won't act on it. Are you afraid? You must be.

Even when you want to do the right thing, those who may see your actions otherwise might think differently, right? And then what, you'll be arrested for doing the right thing? You most likely would because that is what you've allowed to happen. You see, when more and more people get arrested for doing the right thing, wouldn't you think the system is at fault here? And if the system was at fault, don't you think you had a responsibility to fix it? And if you had a responsibility to fix it, don't you think others would feel the same way? And if others felt the same way, don't you think you'd grow in numbers too great to ignore? If you grew in numbers too great to ignore, don't you think you'd be able to change things in ways you thought weren't possible? And if you could achieve that, don't you think life would be a lot safer, not just for you, but for your children? And if that were the case, won't it mean you won't have to worry about them getting snatched on the streets and sold on the black market? But wouldn't it all be avoidable if you stepped up? What do you think would happen if you didn't step up? Say, just let things happen because you're not a powerful enough voice to make a change… oh wait.

It must hurt.

Whatever dissatisfaction you have with your life, it isn't fair that you force that dissatisfaction on everyone else. If you don't like the rules and regulations of your home country, then move somewhere else; don't be part of the problem by seeing it destroyed.

If you support illegal immigration, understand this. Not all who enter your country are good. Some may have criminal records that have been swept under the rug because their home country does not want them there, so then you will have no choice but to let a potential murderer into the country. If you support illegal immigration, then house them yourself, let them take your bedroom, let them eat your food, use the money *you* earn through hard work and give it to them instead, and bear the consequences on your own if they turn to a life of crime and rape you or your daughter. If you don't accept these terms, then you're a hypocrite, and you're a fake.

If you're so passionate about being a human rights activist, don't protest in places where you know you'll be safe. Go to the source. If you're a homosexual in support of Islam, go to a Muslim country, and be your authentic self there and find out for yourself. I hear Afghanistan is nice this time of year. Stay in those countries for a week or two and show them how happy you can be. If you sincerely believe you'll be fine, then you have nothing to worry about! You know what? The Iranians are fighting back against the Islamic regime, but all of a sudden, y'all are quiet about it. They've been oppressed since the 70s, why haven't you said anything then? Oh, wait… it didn't fit the agenda, right? Y'all fight for the act, you don't actually give a shit.

If you're somebody who wants communism, then move to a communist state. It's not that hard! If you're a politician who wants communism, or what you call socialism, which is the same thing, quit your job as a politician and move to a communist state, because you know damn well how much money you can steal for yourself as someone who works in politics in a communist state. You can't do that as a normie. You can try do that right now, but you'll get caught eventually. You think communism is good until you realise the wealthiest house their money anywhere but their home country because money that is housed inside a communist state belongs to the communist state. Even if you're poor, none of that money belongs to you.

Spreading discord for the sake of it, you must be retarded. There is absolutely no reason for you wanting to see your country in ruins unless you're being paid off to do so. You're an embarrassment for two reasons: either you've been made so many promises in high school that you'd be this big shot once you graduate, but haven't been able to accomplish a single thing, or you had nobody in high school to be friends with you or protect you, and since you couldn't shoot your classmates down, you instead want to burn the entire country down because some Jihadis said you were the only one they could trust. Either way, you hate your life and dislike seeing others enjoy theirs.

I wish you could see how pathetic you are to turn your back on your country. There are those out there fighting to keep your freedom alive, so you can go out there and protest about how your country failed you, and how you're all alone, and so you find other incels to be powerful together, but deep down, you know you're still weak because you know you could never compare to the strength of real men and women who fight for you every day. You talk and talk and talk a big game, but when it finally comes down to it, you cower like the incel you are. More often than not, all cowards look the same. If you're wondering what they look like, it's whoever has no love for country.

I can respect all the men and women who fight for the truth, who fight for their families, who fight for their country and who fight for themselves. I can respect all the men and women who have not been brainwashed and have the capacity to see things for what they are. I can respect all the men and women who defend the weak instead of preying on their weakness.

I know there are still many of you who aren't blind to the truth and who refuse to live in a lie. Don't silence your voice for approval. The enemy will scream lies to whoever will hear, but your whispered truths are enough to shatter their reality.

Perhaps one day, politicians will have to submit themselves to a live polygraph test so that the people can see their true intentions. I think we're all done listening to politicians lie to us every day and turn their backs on their people for their own gain. There will come a time when the Western world, as you know it, will fall. I've lived it. It's not pretty. Those who were against the country quickly regretted their actions, but they'll never take accountability because that's what cowards do. This is a promise, because it has happened, and it will happen again, and again, and again until there is nothing left. Don't be part of the problem. Be part of the solution.

Prevent this. Do your research. Your high schools teach you to be complacent. Your universities brainwash you. Your pride is what poisons you. If you're a man or woman of faith, you know that it starts and ends with Christ. Those who do not believe will be forced to live with Islam, and believe me when I say this: Death is much more forgiving.

Don't believe me? Just wait and see. You're probably thinking it doesn't matter, because you'll be dead by the time they take over, right? But what if I told you that it was going to happen sooner than you think? For you, it could be happening right now, or maybe it kicks off a year from now. But one of these days, it will happen for you.

White liberals will be the death of you. Their white guilt fuels their virtue signalling.

Man, it's so hard not to tell you off right now. I guess some of you still got their screws twisted on tightly, but the rest of you are so batshit stupid. I'm so unbelievably mad at 80% of this world's population's stupidity. What calms me down is that I realised just how damaged they really are. Some people who are broken inside often externalise their kind of trauma, and so they create this external conflict so that it gives them temporary relief from their own bullshit because they can't sit with it internally.

You know what else, if it applies to you, you're an attention-seeking brat so much to the point that even negative reactions make you feel powerful, even though you're an insignificant little twat who's angry at the world because you've been unseen and ignored your whole life. Instead of meaningful change that does good for the world, you thrive in conflict because it's proof to you that you think you can affect the world. This is why you hate us. Contrarians, truth tellers, provocateurs, you hate us because, without anyone to conflict with, you don't know who you are. You're an individual without identity.

You have so much envy, so much shame, so much fear, and so much anger that you project your weaknesses onto the rest of the world. You want to destabilise others like a terrorist, because doing so in that moment, you can avoid looking inward, which is a pathetically weak thing to do.

Cowards march together every single day, particularly in groups like you, stupid antifa fucks. Peace can feel threatening for you, I get it, because when you're left with nothing but silence, it leaves room for self-examination. You do whatever it takes to avoid self-reflection. I bet you go home to a mind that doesn't shut up. I can bet the guilt eats you up, huh?

Hang on! I get it! You aren't evolved! You see, our brains scan for threats and disagreements, but some people, like you, potentially, are stuck in that mode, treating every difference of opinion as danger instead of truth. People who are fulfilled, people who are grounded and self-aware rarely seek to destabilise others, but retards that do, like you... Well, that kind of behaviour usually stems from pain, insecurity and emptiness, rarely strength, which you probably have none of. Protests, man. I'm all for it if there's value to it. But people who get paid to protest? Bet y'all cry like pussies once you're forced to face accountability, huh?

CHAPTER EIGHTEEN

A Family Divided

The group planned an outing without me, but I guess it's nice they haven't forgotten me. They wanted to go to this new diner that was in town. Apparently, everybody was talking about it.

"Hey, we're gonna go into town, you wanna come hang out?" Tamara asked.

"Yeah… Sure." I replied.

When we pulled up, there was a lot of foot traffic, something we haven't seen in a while. It was as if there was a festival going on that we didn't know about.

"There's a parking spot over there!" Tamara said, also noting that the diner was nearby.

We saw a lot of Arabs once stepping out of the car; it's like they were scouting the whole place out. I locked eyes with one of them. Soulless eyes, just empty. Then he looked at the girls, nudging the elbows of his comrades to grab their attention. I already felt this sinking feeling in my stomach.

We walked into the diner and asked for a table for six.

Concerned, I said, "I think we should leave."

"Why? We just got here." Elia asked.

"Those guys I saw outside. Something didn't sit right." I replied.

Elia laughed at me, said I was being paranoid. Like, who wouldn't be? We've been through some shit, and she's just gonna act like nothing's wrong? Come on. I shrugged it off for the moment and at least tried to have a good time, but it just kept bugging me. Every time I looked at the window, one of them would be looking inside. Unless you're looking for somebody or scoping the place out, you don't do that shit.

We were in there for about thirty minutes until I suggested leaving. I could tell they were getting annoyed. Before Tamara could say anything, the Arabs I told them about came barging in and started to shoot up the place.

"I fucking told you dumb cunts," I said.

They left roughly thirty guests alive and instructed us to go to the back of the diner. The Muslims singled us out after that. They snatched Isabelle from us, and when she tried to fight back, they struck her. When we tried to fight back, they shot me just below my collarbone. Elia was seething. So was Annabeth. Tamara was keeping pressure on my wound; almost forgot she was a nurse. Dale was ready to lunge, but the gun was pointed right at him.

Those men ganged up on her. They threw her to the ground, reciting verses from the Quran, stopping on her face and her ribs, kicking her in the stomach, while we all watched helplessly. Someone tried to intervene, but the Arab shot them instantly. They stripped her naked and bent her over our table. They took turns raping her while we were forced to watch. All I could do was tell her I was sorry, cause Lord knows I was getting dizzy because of that blood loss.

A strong girl, that one. One of the Arabs tried to force a blowjob, but Isabelle, she, um, hahaha, she bit his cock clean off. She laughed as they put a bullet in her skull. That guy would not stop screaming after that.

They tried to do the same thing to Elia, but that's when the police came barging in. A whole 15 minutes. The quality of the American police force was quite… remarkable. Not. There was a massive shootout that happened after. Some of the Arabs used the hostages as human shields, but cops nowadays didn't care much for friendly fire, so a few innocent lives, along with Isabelle was taken that day.

Isabelle was our embodiment of hope, and we lost her. As if we didn't suffer enough, right? I miss her so much. I thought I'd get used to losing a loved one by now, but that's just not possible. I felt no anger, though I knew in my gut that something was wrong. I listened to it, but I didn't act on it. Safe to say, this was partly my fault. I went soft.

When it was over, an ambulance rushed me straight to the hospital. Turns out the bullet rebounded from my shoulder blade and down to my lung. That shit was supposed to keep me in the hospital for a good 6 months, but I opted to check myself out early. I wasn't going to miss Isabelle's funeral. It was just the five of us for the service. She didn't really know anybody else. Everybody said really nice things during the ceremony.

After God called Isabelle home, I thought to myself. "God takes home the pure first, so that way they needn't suffer any longer." It was the only way I could keep myself from breaking down completely. She was younger than all of us, but deep down, I looked up to her the most. She never fully gave in. She knew deep down that she was not like anyone of us. As much as I tried to release the demon from her, she wouldn't take the bait. She lived like Christ. She refused to live with anger in her heart.

This whole journey has been fraught with so much danger, death, and destruction. I, for such a long time, had control of my life before any of this happened. The only thing I could control now was which memories I chose to remember. Your brain shuts its memory cortex and emotional responses down if an event or response is too much for you to handle. Only until you have the capacity to handle these extremely stressful situations will your brain allow you to feel what it has chosen to delay. That's why it comes during times you're wondering why you're crying, but don't have a reason other than just for the sake of it.

I chose to forget. I chose not to feel. I'm what you'd have called… numb.

After Isabelle's funeral, Tamara and Dale said they wanted to leave. They figured it was best to get away from all the painful memories. None of us objected because we all had the same idea. Annabeth flew to Hawaii, free of any Muslims, while Elia thought to see how South Korea fared for her. South Korea's stance on immigration was rather strict, with a no-Muslim policy since the whole religious war broke out. Not to mention the rising tensions between North and South Korea. I left the farm in the care of Elijah and our neighbours and flew to Australia. The tensions there seemed to be dying down, so I thought I'd give it a shot. It wasn't our final goodbyes for each other, as we did reconnect again after a few years.

When I landed in Melbourne, Australia, it goes to show how much the media lies to you. You find out that all mainstream media report on the same things; however, the media presented by ordinary citizens is when the real truth comes out. Riots have been happening in the city every single day since I got there, and without a doubt, someone's always leaving in an ambulance.

Australian citizens, particularly Gen Z, aren't particularly happy about being conscripted into the war front, and this resulted in a lot of negative blowback from the left because that's the only time they'll actually acknowledge how fucked up the country has gotten. This is what I mean about people just supporting a cause that they don't even believe in, because when it finally comes down to it, they don't have the gumption to back it up.

Melbourne's streets were riddled with African gangs, who excelled at stealing vehicles, breaking into homes and stabbing men, women and children with their machetes, even though the Prime Minister spent twenty million dollars on machete amnesty boxes around the country. It's funny, actually. They banned ordinary citizens from arming themselves, but they can't do anything about the criminals breaking the law.

Bono, the Prime Minister, is really a communist at heart. He gave himself and his administration a 40% raise, bumping his already inflated salary close to one million dollars a year, plus remuneration totalling over one million dollars. There had also been reports that he had instructed police officers to arrest anyone with tattoos that were deemed offensive, mainly targeting the white community or anyone he labelled as far-right. All public schools are now required to learn about Islam from kindergarten, brainwashing them right from the start. But why? Islam already took over the major cities in Australia; Bono's just doing it to get on his knees and suck up to the new caliphate. If he only knew, right? He imported millions of unvetted Islamists throughout the years until they replicated what they did in the UK.

He came to his senses eventually, and he even tried to get the assistance of China to help expel the issue, but once the caliphate found out, they had him castrated and forced him to walk the Harbour Bridge as he bled. Whenever he fell to the ground, they kept whipping him until he stood back on his feet. I actually got to watch this unfold on live television.

The bastard kept yelling, "Someone help me!" It was rather laughable; the Aussies were actually on the Muslims' side for that moment. When they were done with him, they attached hook chains through his palms and had him hang atop the bridge. The man starved to death, and the Muslims left his body up there to rot; now and then, pieces of him would fall to the ground, while the crows fed on him.

Leaders who just want power, without a doubt, have the capacity to ruin their country. They call out true leaders and brand them as dictators, while they themselves put themselves above their own people. So long as the power is in their hands, and nobody else's, they couldn't care less if their people starved.

I was walking through Flinders Street, and I witnessed a handful of African youths beat the living shit out of a white kid no more than eleven years old, and they ended up snatching all of that kid's belongings. Cops just stood there, bystanders just stood there, and I just stood there too. I couldn't bring myself to do anything. I was still recovering from that bullet.

I sat by the state library, watching all the people go by. You couldn't tell who voted for whom for the most part; greasy individuals with coloured hair and black piercings were the outliers. Religiously or politically, they're completely divided, but when they're just living life as best they can, given the circumstances, you wouldn't have even guessed that there was conflict. There's no judgment, no murderous intent, they're just surviving.

Sitting there in that moment was the only time I'd ever feel a sense of peace in such a chaotic world. I could hear police sirens, people yelling, and gangs of African youth dressed in black, and clearly, they have not assimilated, because why are they fighting people? Do I hate them, or do I just hate what they stand for? I guess I've always been racist, but they've always proven me right. Don't you hate that, though? When they live up to the stereotype?

You know, a lot of the Muslims that I've seen walk by have so far… encouraged people to convert. They'd surround somebody and force them to say the words, and if they refused, they'd get jumped. If they said the words, they'd show them some love and walk off. I don't know what came over me. When they walked up to me to pull the same thing, I zoned out elsewhere. It wasn't until one of the guys slapped me in the face because I wasn't paying attention to him that I locked in. I reached for a knife that was in my jacket pocket and stabbed him in the throat, leaving the blade in as I stood up.

I looked at the other two men, and they looked at me with quite some shock. They didn't completely react until after I pulled the knife out of his neck.

"You dogs are all the same," I said.

Then they ran off, presumably to get some backup, but I was long gone by then. Nobody is going to report a dead Muslim in Australia, and I know this because a group of Australians ran up to his body and stomped on him til he stopped breathing. I guess people still want to fight, but they've been conditioned to fear the consequences.

The guy's death was reported on the news, and they claimed it was a racially motivated, Islamophobic attack, but left out the fact that the same group of men had beaten ordinary civilians senseless because they refused to convert to Islam. I don't understand. They're evil, yet they defend them. From what I remember, a lot of the terrorist attacks that have happened, a Muslim was always behind them. You'd think they'd have learnt their lesson by then.

A lot of these Australians are angry. They just don't know how to voice that anger outside of protests. They don't want to hide their faces like antifa either, because doing so incriminates them, so, either way, their free speech has been threatened, just like the UK, because they haven't properly established free speech laws. Commonwealth countries are full of shit.

You know what I want? I want to go to a concert, and not have it blown up because some Muslim wanted to commit jihad. I don't want to pick my phone up, jump on X and see another news headline about a 12-year-old gang raped by Muslim men. I don't want to hear politicians and news journalists calling terrorism anything other than what it is, because all it does is spread more division.

I want governments toppled and rebuilt for something better. I want these politicians to face accountability for their actions. I want their power to be conditional. I want the true power to lie with us when it comes to our sovereignty. Let them handle the defence, we can handle the welfare, and if the government isn't living up to our expectations, we can have them replaced. Governments are working for us as they always should have been.

I watched what the world had turned into. It was like everything around me was moving in slow motion, and I was moving so fast that it took many years for the world to catch up. It was once a beautiful planet, but we have destroyed it through greed, corruption and violence.

I miss my mother; I miss my friends. I miss the person I used to be. I miss when people used to be normal. I miss the days when men weren't in women's sports. I miss not having to see tucked-in ball sacks in women's swimsuits. I miss the old peaceful days.

I hope God take my life soon, because to live in a world so broken is torture within itself. Muslims are uncompromising in conquered lands, following the traditions of human cruelty. I hope you know that I speak to you many years into the future, and what I see, really, is a fate worse than death.

The United States was a really good place for me to vent out my anger and unleash vengeance on my enemies. It turned me into something less than human and borderline demonic, but it helped me send a clear message to the Muslims: that not everybody can be threatened.

Australia really helped me calm myself down. It was a good place to recover, despite the Islamic takeover here. I met some new friends, non-violent ones, and they've helped me find some peace. They reminded me that things can still be okay, even if the world is ending all around you, so long as you have the right people to surround yourself with.

It made me miss the group.

When Elia took the time to spend her days alone, I think she finally came to terms with the darkness she's had to face. I think the time we all spent together helped her bury those emotions until she was forced to face them. Spending some time in South Korea really helped her reflect on the things she's done. As did my trip to Australia.

She started to get a lot of nightmares about the people she's killed, hearing their voices in quiet rooms, or flashbacks to their dismembered bodies, haunting her during the night. I think it was a sign that she was moving on from that part of her life, because she began to feel an insurmountable feeling of guilt. I never thought I'd imagine the day that *she* would find a semblance of peace.

Annabeth, too, came to terms with things, but she wasn't as affected as Elia was when it came to her trauma. She slept with a lot of island boys and went surfing practically every day. She wasn't happy, she wasn't sad, but she was content with her life, and she wasn't particularly interested in anything. Violence? She avoids it at all costs. I think she grew apart from us, which I completely understand.

As for Dale and Tamara, well, I haven't heard from them since they left. I still keep in touch with Elijah, but between you and me, I couldn't see myself returning to the States. I figured I'd just hand the farm over to him so I could figure out what to do with the rest of my life.

After a few years, I did reunite with Elia in South Korea, and that's when we moved back to the States together, but we couldn't bring ourselves to go back to New York, so we headed to Denver. Good thing we did cause we'd have died had we returned there.

CHAPTER NINETEEN

It's Time To Wake Up.

I woke up today, and I thought I was going crazy. Britain held another trial for the rape and murder of an innocent Muslim woman in Central London. The suspects with the same MO were the same men who murdered my sister. Flights to Britain were grounded, so I came in through France, the same way I left. I'd have suspected they'd be held in a federal prison, but they kept them locked up at a police station. The benefits of Sharia Law are that you can rape any woman you want, so long as they aren't Muslim. These men fucked up by raping a Muslim woman, and it was Muslim women who had them reported with video proof.

I broke into the station where they were kept and murdered all the police officers who were on duty that night. I had my sisters' killers tranquilised, had them hogtied and thrown into a police van, and took them to a secluded property I found on Google Maps. I killed the occupants. I didn't care who they were. This was *the* rage I could not keep contained. These men were knocked out cold, and no matter what I did to them, they would not wake up.

I stripped them all naked. I stitched two of those men's mouths together and added super glue just to be safe. As for the man who had his arm impaled inside my sister, I made sure to place his friend's cock inside his mouth and stitched the two together. I waited for them to wake up, and when they came to, they tried their best to get out of their stitches, but they weren't going anywhere; they were still bound in cuffs.

I look at those men. "Do you remember me?"

Their leaders' spine crawled up his back. "Yeah, you remember me," I said calmly.

I wasn't sure if it was going to work, but the man whose dick the leader had his mouth around, I shoved a funnel up his asshole and poured gasoline inside him. Apparently, the gasoline burns the skin, so I can only imagine what was happening to his organs. I set his asshole ablaze when I lit the match. It took a few seconds until his friend was spitting fire out of his ass. The pain forced him to piss right into the leader's mouth. Turns out you can kill a man pretty quickly that way. I wanted him to die slowly.

I stitched the leader's mouth closed before I cut his friend's dick off; I didn't want him spitting it out. He kept shaking his head as if to protest. It was then that I had the most genuine smile on my face. If he didn't want that dick in his mouth, he'd have to swallow it.

The home had a wood chipper, so I took the remaining two outside, and with his other friend, I put him in the wood chipper, feet first, and I made sure that the leader was watching the whole thing. When he knew he was next, I could see him pissing himself.

"You laughed when you raped and murdered my sister. I guess I'm the one laughing now." I said to him.

I sliced the tendons in his arms and legs so he couldn't move them, then I cut out the bones from his hands and feet, leaving the flesh behind. I ripped the stitches from his mouth and pulled every tooth, while he begged and apologised. He had nice hair, so I pulled it out, bundle by bundle, until there was nothing left. I made an incision in his scrotum and popped his testicles out, exposing them. Apparently, dry hands touching them hurts quite a lot, so I yanked it out of him, pulling the nerves out along with it. When he was done screaming, I fed it to him.

I carved his feet off and then burned his ankles afterwards to stop the bleeding, then I forced both his feet up his ass; it took some work, but I got it done. Olive oil helps.

He sounded like an old man. "Please leave me alone."

I replied coldly. "No."

I cut his hands off and burned his wrists afterwards too. I carved rapist and murderer on his chest. Then I cut up his dick like silly string cheese, but I didn't cut it off. I left it like that.

I stopped for a moment and thought about what I was doing. I laughed. "You know what? Maybe I shouldn't kill you. Maybe I should let you live instead. You're a devout Muslim. If you killed yourself, there is no paradise for you, and you would be forced to live like this for the rest of your days. That's what I call divine justice."

He looked at me with his eyes wide open. "Ah, that reminds me. I should gouge your eyes out. I wouldn't want you describing me." I said.

So, I took a spoon from the kitchen and cut his eyes out with a blunt edge. I felt complete. I felt free. When I was done with him, I threw him back in the van and drove up to the coast. Once I was close to France, I called the police using his phone to go and rescue him. Ah, if only I could see the look in their faces. He could describe what I looked like from memory, but they'd never be able to confirm it. He has no hands, no feet, and no more dick. They left his scrotum with no balls inside it. They tore his ass open to pull his feet out. They could risk infection by reattaching it. He was found guilty of his crimes, and his face was plastered over every news board.

I walked around the rescued city of Paris with no Muslims in sight. There was graffiti plastered everywhere saying, "I was never asleep. You were." It was a truth that many of you refused to accept.

By the end of it all, the world had maybe 11% of Christians left? It's as if we were saying goodbye to a religion we thought would be here for an eternity. We thought we'd pass it on to our children, and they'd pass it on to theirs, but now, it's a crime to be a Christian. Now, there are still normal governments running the place, but a Muslim shadow government heavily controls them, and the faces of government are often threatened by these Muslims. The world survived, but it was smaller, much quieter, a lot less certain. Religion didn't retreat back into churches or mosques, but into private spaces. God himself became a question again. The world had to ask itself once more.

"Who are we?"

Christians finally faced defeat, and the Muslims finally tasted the sweetness of victory. They don't know how to manage political affairs properly, and they don't know how to manage production control. When the nation they've conquered runs out of food and clean water, they don't know how to resolve that. They simply aren't smart enough. When they need someone to fix it, who better than the Chinese to seize control of this opportunity?

So, I guess it's the Chinese that wins the throne at the end of it all, and the Muslims will bow to them, because if they act out of line, the Chinese will simply put them back in their place. Perhaps the Chinese will restore Christianity, under the condition that they pledge their loyalty to the CCP.

The ironic part is that every Muslim nation in the world turned Christian, but every Christian nation in the world turned Muslim. The Muslims traded in their third-world cities for ours, and so the Christians rebuilt their new lands themselves, surprisingly at a much faster rate, building great walls around all borders, and many who feared the Islamic regime fled to those Christian nations. These Christian nations finally did what they were supposed to do and turned every

Muslim away, and more often than not, were shot on sight. They learned too late.

The world's population reduced by almost half, and you can still see corpses decaying out on the streets, with nobody bothered enough to dispose of them properly. You don't see many dogs around either. Anything considered haram was destroyed, and when the Muslims finally got what they wanted, they started fighting each other for territory or more power. That's why a lot of the cities became radioactive. They couldn't win them, so they made sure nobody could have them.

Many fell to their knees, but prayer changed nothing. The violence continued to massacre thousands without restraint. People waited for confirmation, but nothing came. When they expected him to, after all this time, God didn't intervene, and so for the first time, people felt abandoned by the very certainty they'd worshipped.

When news agencies began to report the numbers of how many Christians were dying by the day, they began to turn on their anointed one. He tried to do damage control, but nothing was working. Then one night, he was kidnapped by his closest followers, and they flayed him alive and crucified him. They all had enough of his lies, but it was already too late by then. They fell for it as they always have. Upon hearing the news of his death, many Muslims around the world celebrated his death and their victory, giving glory to their Allah.

Many Christians turned their backs on God, believing that He failed them, and they all started living in this limbo. They weren't alive, but they weren't dead either. They were just waiting for it all to end. There was no life in them whatsoever. The world had understood this truth too late. Faith had never been a channel, but a force multiplier. For the faithful, they knew that God never commanded this. Human certainty commanded this.

A quiet resistance formed. Not atheists, but believers who refused violence. They were the true believers, and I found myself falling short of it. They lost their protection from us, they lost their platforms, and they lost their status, and it didn't matter how much influence they had. But for what they lost, they regained their consciences, and they were called traitors... the damned ones because of it, but you know what? They woke up because of it.

Without absolute belief, the system failed. Compliance dropped, enforcement fractured, the moral narrative dissolved. The war itself lost its momentum. Not through peace but from confusion. It was at this point that people started asking the forbidden question.

"Why were we so sure?"

I wonder what kind of life I'd be having right now if it weren't for all of this. Maybe find an incredible person whom I could call the love of my life and spend the rest of every waking moment with them forever. Maybe we'd go explore the city and find a niche café that has old, worn-out books you can take and return once you've finished with them. Maybe we wouldn't have to worry about hiding our tattoos in fear of being beheaded for them, and maybe our friends could love who they wanted and be who they wanted without the fear of true persecution.

If everybody had common sense, if they were moderate, politically, I think everyone would truly feel included without having to sacrifice oneself because of the fear of judgment. If they were well informed from the beginning, without all that censorship bullshit, I think people would make more informed decisions about who they vote for, despite how many lies their politicians feed them. If politicians truly loved their country, the thought of allowing third-world militants wouldn't even be part of the agenda. Screening would be extra cautious, and any minor offences would be deemed deportable or citizenship revoked, which is even better. Fraud would be deemed as treason, and no president would be safe from persecution.

The final lesson was brutal and simple. The end of the world wasn't divine providence. It was human certainty left unchecked. Awakening was not salvation. It was a responsibility. We had the opportunity to act before things got out of control, but we didn't. Fear is what held us back. Yet, as we stood on the precipice of our own making, we realised that fear was not an insurmountable wall; it was a choice. A choice to retreat into complacency or to forge a path of courage amidst uncertainty. Each moment we hesitated, the consequences of our inaction loomed larger, like shadows creeping over a sunlit landscape.

The awakening demanded clarity, a collective recognition that we were the architects of our fate. We began to understand that our voices mattered, our actions mattered, and each small decision could ripple outwards, creating waves of change. The final lesson was not just a warning; it was a clarion call to engage and to resist the inertia that had defined our past. We all die eventually, but let it not be in vain.

It was time to dismantle the illusion of certainty, to embrace the chaos that comes with change. We had to harness our fear, transforming it into a driving force for innovation, compassion, and resilience. The end of the world as we knew it did not need to be an endpoint, but rather a turning point. In the end, the responsibility was ours to shoulder; to move forward with intention, to challenge the status quo, and to unite in our shared humanity. The final lesson echoed through our hearts; the power to shape tomorrow lies not in the hands of fate, but in the collective resolve of *those who dare* to act today. Of those like you. I've told you everything.
Save us.

Wake up.

I want you to know that when they call for Sharia Law, this is what they mean.

- Theft is punishable by amputation of the hands.
- Criticising or denying any part of the Quran is punishable by death.
- Criticising their prophet Muhammad or denying that he is a prophet is punishable by death.
- Criticising or denying their Allah is punishable by death.
- A Muslim who leaves Islam is punishable by death.
- A non-Muslim who leads a Muslim away from Islam is punishable by death.
- A non-Muslim man who marries a Muslim woman is punishable by death.
- Homosexuality is punishable by death, but sodomizing boys is fine.
- Girls' clitoris should be cut.
- Girls can be sodomised until and vaginally raped after 8 years of age.
- A woman or girl who has been raped cannot testify against their rapists, unless with the testimonies of 4 male witnesses to prove rape,

and failure to provide these witnesses, the woman is guilty of adultery and is put to death.

- A male convicted of rape can have his conviction dismissed by marrying his victim.
- Muslim men have sexual rights to any woman/girl not wearing the Hijab.
- A woman can only have one husband, while a man can have up to four wives.
- A man can beat his wife for insubordination.
- A man can divorce his wife, but the woman needs her husband's permission to divorce.
- A divorced wife loses custody of all her children, and her testimony in court is worth half that of a man's.
- A woman cannot speak alone to a man who is not her husband or a relative.
- Meat to eat must be halal.
- Muslims should engage in Taqiyya and lie to non-Muslims to advance Islam.

So please be careful when considering your support for them. They forced these laws on my home, advocating for Muslim-only territories, and when they wanted more, they took it. It's okay to be wrong because you still have time. I was wrong, and I didn't pay attention until it was too late. Don't make the same mistake that we did and stay complacent. You need to do something, and you need to do something now. I need you to wake up.

End.

Jesus Christ Prevails.

✝